Tales of Aurduin

volume 1

OROBAI'S

VISION

by

Martin W. Ball

Orobai's Vision
Tales of Aurduin, Volume I
By
Martin W. Ball

All contents

© 2006
Martin W. Ball

Kyandara Publishing

ISBN: 978-0-6151-3674-5

TALES OF AURDUIN

by
Martin W Ball

Volume I – *Orobai's Vision*
Volume II – *The Fate of Miraanni*
Volume III – *The Alchemist and the Eagle*
Volume IV – *The Fifth Temple*

Music of Aurduin, audio CD

For more information visit:

WWW.MARTINBALL.NET

For Miranda

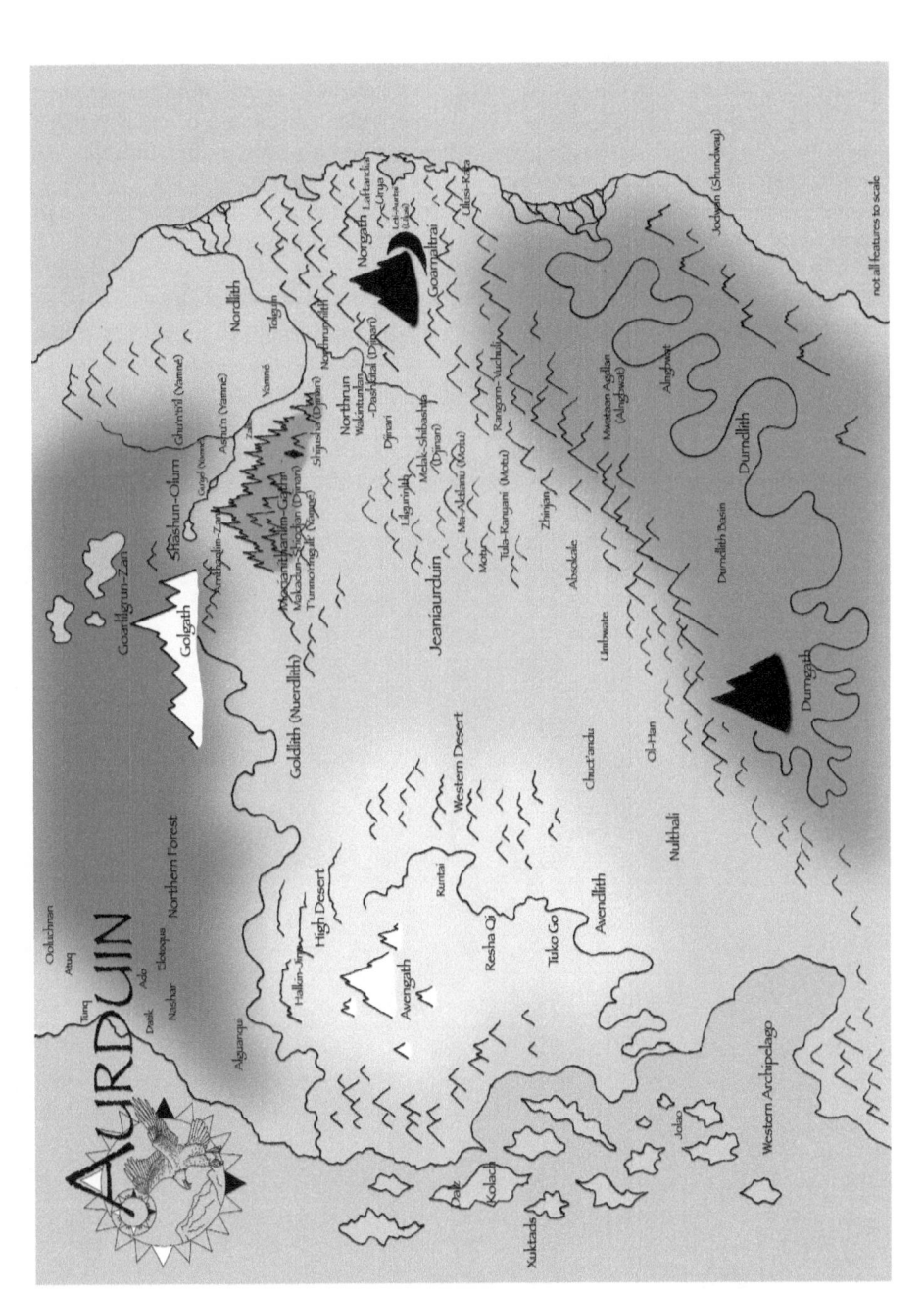

In the years since the rising of the Fifth Temple, many legends and myths have flourished across Aurduin among those who survived, all attempting to explain how the world changed, and why. Consumed by an apocalypse of unimaginable proportion, Aurduin as it was died and a new world was born as the Temple rose from the depths of the turquoise waters. How did this happen, and why? Who, if anyone, was responsible? And how did the world that we now live in come to be as it is, a world rent asunder in fiery destruction, and miraculously made anew?

Many have tried to answer these questions, grappling with the terrible fate that befell our world of Aurduin. In the face of awesome change, the mind struggles for answers. In the midst of unimaginable suffering and bittersweet hope, we cling to our stories, our myths, our legends. We search them for answers, for reasons, for the ultimate causes of things and for a sense of balance, purpose, and meaning.

But none have yet answered these questions fully, or with complete knowledge of those involved, who they were, what drove them on, and why they did what they did, for good or ill.

The true cause of things has not been known . . . until now.

These are the Tales of Aurduin.

Nataali-Wantalth of Hyanchalth-Murira

Raven
Here he comes
Watch him
Shimmering, shimmering
Black feathers
Rain around him
Dance to the ground
Hear him
Singing, singing
Pure tones
Sounds of Creation
All around
All around
See how he moves
Feathers lightly
Dancing, dancing
Hear him
Hear him
Raven
White light follows behind
Follows behind
See it coming
Hear it
Hear it
The One Sound
The crystal sound
Mystery
Mystery
All is change
All is change

- From a Song of the Raven Spirit Society of the Yamné

Prologue:

The Illan and the Altfein-Aryat

At the foot of the Great Mountain Golgath lived the Grundin. The ancient Gem Seeker was many things to many people. He possessed many names, wore many identities, and was the fabric of more stories than there are feathers on a bird. He was the Raven, the Black Sorcerer, the Singer, the Dark Mystery, and the last practitioner of the ancient art of creation, the Altfein-Aryat. He was Orobai, the Preserver of the Four Ways of the Illan, the final repository of the knowledge and symbols of Creation. A solitary being, Orobai had no family, no community, and no people to call his own. He was a creature of the forest and sought out the wild and lonely places and the council of the great eagles, the mighty Arnyar. Orobai was unique.

Long had Orobai studied the lore of nature and the ways of the wild through the courses of many lifetimes, always returning to his home by the White Mountain, Golgath, in the north of Aurduin. He roamed to the east, to Norgath, the Black Mountain, and to the south, to Durngath, the Green Mountain, and even to the west, to Avengath, the Yellow Mountain. In these distant and remote places he sought jewels and gems of all kinds. He took great delight in the precious stones of Aurduin and to obtain them he traveled into the far reaches of the deepest and darkest caves and caverns of the Great Mountains.

Though Orobai loved all gemstones and valued them all equally, the true focus of his passion was the sacred Sarnfein and Alkeinfein stones, the Stones of Creation. For these Orobai would pray to the mountains in wordless song and coax them to share the sacred stones. These were neither gems nor jewels of an ordinary sort, but the Altfein. These were the Sarnfein and the Alkeinfein, unique in all the Ever-changing World for their powers of creation.

But the knowledge of how to use the Sarnfein and Alkeinfein was neither Orobai's discovery nor his invention. The lore of the sacred Altfein stones, the

Altfein-Aryat, was the original knowledge of the Illan, the First Beings. Far more ancient than even Orobai himself, this ancient philosophy had long been lost and forgotten by all but Orobai and the Arnyar. It was the Illan, the First Beings, the Awakened Ones, who were the first and only masters of this mystical science, for they were the Creators of Aurduin and lords of this world.

Yet even the story of the Illan is not the First Tale of Aurduin. The first Tale of Aurduin is that of the Stayor. It is the beginning of all that came to pass in this world and it is the First Myth.

* * * *

The Stayor

In ages past, when Aurduin was still new and unformed, long before the rising of the Orgathen, the Four Mountains, there were the Stayor. The Stayor were the original spirits of wind and light and it was they who transformed their spiritual essence into the sacred stones. The power of the Stayor passed from formlessness into form and entered deep into the body of Eyar, and their spirit became embodied in matter. This was the first transformation of Aurduin. It was the origin of the Altfein, the sacred stones of creation, and was the origin of all later transformations of Aurduin.

It was with great selflessness that these primordial spirits undertook this transformation, for the Stayor saw that in the ages to come the minds of others would fill with the desire to create and shape Aurduin and bring forth physical life in the world. They freely gave of their own power for this purpose, so that others could create life through their sacrifice. Thus the power of the Stayor passed from the wind and light and forevermore remained in the mystical Altfein stones.

There the spirits of wind and light waited, sleeping within the body of Eyar, awaiting the time when others would learn how to unlock their potential and sing life and creation into being.

* * * *

The second Tale of Aurduin is the story of the Illan. The story of the Illan is the story of the shaping of this world of Aurduin, from the mountains and rivers to the beasts, birds, trees, and people, and all that lives and moves in this Sacred Land. This is the Second Myth. This is the story of the origins of the great change. It is the story of why the terrible transformation came to be. It is the story of why Orobai came to be.

The Illan and the Altfein-Aryat

* * * *

The Awakening of the Illan

Many ages passed on Aurduin after the original transformation of the Stayor. For eons the Altfein slept within the body of Eyar. But a change was at work upon the face of the world. Slowly the Illan, the First Beings, awoke to self-consciousness and knew themselves and the world. They perceived and knew that they were, that they existed.

It being before the time of the great eagles and the birth of language, the Illan communicated only with musical sound. In tone, shape, color, and rhythm all knowledge and intent passed between them in a great musical harmony. Their melodies were beautiful and expressive and they joined together in choruses and lifted their voices to the sky with beauty and harmony in their hearts, celebrating their being and giving thanks for all that was.

In time, the Illan learned that their beautiful sounds stirred the spirits dwelling within the Altfein. Not just any sounds, but certain and precise tones awakened the Altfein and manifested their inherent power. The Illan learned that with the Altfein they could sing the world into being. They had discovered the knowledge of true creation. Through the voices of co-creating pairs, one of a high tone and the other low, they could shape and transform the world about them and they could give life to what they sang into being.

With the Altfein and their sacred songs, the Illan shaped the land that had been empty and formless and sang into being the mountains, rivers, hills, and plains. They sang grasses and plants and trees into being. Forests, jungles, and deserts they sang into being. Creatures great and small they sang into being. They sang the creatures of the land, the air, and waters into being and gave them life through the power of change and transformation. In this way, all of Aurduin came to be. It was the birth of the world, and the world was defined by constant change and transformation and this law governed all things within it and was the great music of Creation. Every being, every life, had its own rhythm, song, and music, each to play out in Aurduin in its own way in its own time.

The Arnyar

The songs of the Illan echoed about the world of Aurduin and carried on in the voices of their creations, especially the birds. Chief among the birds were the Arnyar, who took flight and soared to the farthest reaches of the sky and the Sacred Land of Aurduin. They were the special creations of the Illan; the guardians of the mountains and all of Aurduin, for all the world fell under their protective gaze.

In great awe the Illan sang to the Arnyar and the Arnyar sang with them. In time this became language and the birth of all tongues of Aurduin, for all languages came from Illanii, the First Language, the language of the Illan and the Eagles, the language of the First Knowledge.

The Eagles spoke to the Illan of all they saw. They spoke of the mountains, the rivers, the forests and deserts, and all the beings that lived within Aurduin. They named all things and through these names all things became known, and through this beauty was increased, for knowledge was beauty.

With this new knowledge the Illan began the Altfein-Aryat, the telling of the Gift-Givers, and this became their sacred lore. This was the knowledge of all things of Aurduin and how they came to be through the power of song and the sacred stones. It was the knowledge of the Power of Creation.

The Four Temples

For many countless ages the Altfein-Aryat was preserved only in the hearts and minds of the Illan. Desiring to make the glory and power of the Altfein visible to all, they sat in great council and debated in their musical language what should be done to give the most beautiful shape and form to preserve and honor the Altfein-Aryat and the knowledge of creation.

To this end they decided to sing into being the Orthirnen, the Four Temples, and they were to be a living symbol of the Altfein-Aryat embodied within the world itself. They would be a symbol upon the face of Aurduin.

They began their great work in the east where the sun rose over Aurduin. There they sang into being Northirn, the Black Temple. From there they followed the sun to the south, and there sang forth Durnthirn, the Green Temple. Next they moved across the great realm of Aurduin and went to the land of the setting sun, the west, and there sang forth Aventhirn, the Yellow Temple. Lastly they moved north to the realm of the night sky, and there sang forth Golthirn, the White Temple.

These temples they made great and resplendent. Each they made of crystal light, and the sound of wind and music was everlasting in them, though ever changing in shape and form, constantly singing the sacred tones of creation as embodied in the four directions.

Each temple had the dominant color that the Illan gave in its naming, symbolizing a fundamental pillar of their esoteric philosophy. Black was for the deep Abyss of Chaos from which all things came and was the indefinable origin of existence. Green was for the great symphony of all life and all individual things manifested from the Great Void that lived and moved in Aurduin. Yellow was the symbol for introspective reflection and the power of awakening to the dream of life and awareness of the subtle currents that exist beneath the appearances of all things. And lastly White was the color for the eventual return of death and dissolution, the return to the original source with full awareness and enlightenment. Taken together, these were the four symbols, the four notes, the four great songs in the ever-manifesting symphony of creation. This was the foundation of the Four Temples.

At first, the Illan shared all the temples equally, but as time passed the hearts of the Illan grew fond of particular temples according to their spirits and temperaments. The Four Orders of the Illan then came into being, the Norin, Durnin, Avenin, and the Golin. Each order sang into being great works of beauty, each according to their kind, and each became masters of their own wisdom.

In time, their music began to diverge and the sounds of their tongues grew apart from each other. Though the remnant of their original tongue remained, as time passed, the Altfein-Aryat of each order became somewhat unique unto itself. When great council was held among the four orders, only their common music remained and their communication again took on the form of a great music, though now it was more diverse and more complex than ever before as the different strains and themes became intermingled from the Four Temples of the Four Directions.

Yet the Arnyar traveled freely among all the Orthirnen and became messengers and translators of the Illan and knew all their music and the Four Tongues. In this way the Eagles too became the masters of the Altfein-Aryat of the four realms, and indeed, they knew the lore more fully than any of the individual Orinen, for each of the Four Orders now knew primarily their own lore and the teachings and knowledge of the others became as mysteries to them in the greater passing of time.

Karinduin, the Other World

Despite their separation in different orders, the Illan all came to know of Karinduin, like a great simultaneous awakening that swept across the world of Aurduin. Karinduin is the Other World, the subtle world that lies behind the shifting forms of the visible world. It is subtle, yet eternally present. It called to the Illan as a beautiful music, one that was more ethereal and transcendent than even their own songs. In hearing this music, the Illan knew that passing into Karinduin was their destiny. It was the next stage in their process of transformation and awakening.

It was then that the Four Orders of the Four Temples came together in great council. With a unitary will the Illan entered deep into a collective trance and there sought a revelation of how they could achieve their aim of passing into Karinduin. Doing so, their music and collective song gave birth to a great vision of the transformation of Eyar that would have to take place in order to obtain their goal. They knew that all transformation of the mind was coupled with transformation of the body. Karinduin and Aurduin were like mind and body, spirit and heart. Their passing into Karinduin would transform Aurduin. It was the way of change and transformation.

It was also in the depths of their vision that the Illan finally understood the source and origin of the Sarnfein and the Alkeinfein. They came to know the nature of the Stayor who had first transmuted themselves into the precious gems. They saw that all transformation meant the death of one form and the birth of another. Transmutation of spirit into matter and back into spirit was the cycle of birth and death. In this way Karinduin and Aurduin were locked into a cosmic dance of creation, destruction, and creation anew. Cycles of change and transformation ruled all. Just as the Stayor had been spirit transmuted into matter, the Illan would be matter transmuted back into spirit. It was the great distillation of essences, the great music of change, and the eternal permutation of spirit and matter in the endless dance of creation.

Thus for the Illan to return to Karinduin a further transformation must come to pass. The Illan had to relinquish their individual selves and collectively join the subtle body of Eyar. It would be a change that would profoundly affect the shape and form of Aurduin, just as it would change the essence of Karinduin.

The Gem Seeker

Emerging from their great trance, the Arnyar gave counsel. Knowing what the Illan intended, the Eagles desired that there might be at least one who would remain to preserve the Altfein-Aryat and practice its art. With prescient vision they saw that in the ages to come a terrible apocalypse would sweep across the face of Aurduin, destroying all in its path, though they could not discern its cause or reason. This destruction would wound Aurduin to its very heart and all that the Illan had created would be in danger of complete obliteration. All their great works would be undone. The great eagles knew that the only way to regain some of the beauty that would be lost would be through the Altfein-Aryat. The knowledge and ability to use it had to be preserved.

Their hearts filled with fear, the Eagles asked the Illan not to forsake Aurduin. They pleaded that the Illan think of their creations and not give up their place in Aurduin without leaving some hope for the future. It was they, the Arnyar, who urged the Illan to preserve their ancient wisdom in one who could practice the esoteric art. Only one with the voice of the Illan could master the sacred tones to bring the Altfein to life, and the Arnyar, as powerful as they were, did not have this ability. For this, the Illan would have to choose another.

Hearing the Eagles, the Illan consented to create the Grundin, the Gem Seeker. The essence of the Grundin would be the love of jewels and gems of all kinds. He would be drawn to the Altfein as part of himself. He would be the charge of the Arnyar and they would pour their knowledge of the Altfein-Aryat into him like an empty vessel ready to receive the riches of their wisdom. Through the Gem Seeker the teachings of the Four Orders of the Four Temples would be preserved and thus the Illan also called this being Orobai, the Preserver of the Four Ways.

Again the Arnyar counseled the Illan that the true need of the Altfein would not come to pass for many ages hence. They cautioned that any creation that the Illan might conceive would be subject to the law of change, as he too would pass away in death in the depths of time. To this the Illan answered that Orobai would also be Rundi, the Returner, who, upon death, would return again to Aurduin and live life anew.

Yet no creation could be permanent in this world, not even a returner, who would eventually pass into the realm of Karinduin. The Illan thus decreed that in ages unforeseen Orobai too would leave the world of changing forms. Even this special creation would be subject to this governing law of change and transformation, though this would not come to pass for many thousands of years.

Lastly, Orobai would also be unique in this world, for of all the living creations of the Illan, he would not be born of a mother, but would be born of the earth, Eyar. Each lifetime would begin and end within the body of Eyar and thus his fourth name, Eyarlum, Earth-Born. Upon his death his body would return to the earth, only to be remade and be born anew. The body of Eyar would preserve his memory and identity, so that each life would build upon the one previous and death would be to him as a dreamless sleep. From the earth itself he would awaken to new life, refreshed and remade, fully aware of himself and who he was.

The Arnyar took all this into consideration. They sought deep in their prescience, yet they could still not see the end of this plan. They saw that there was no foretelling whether Orobai's passing into Karinduin would come before or after the terrible apocalypse that haunted their visions of the future. Yet they also saw that there was no other choice, for the Illan's desire to pass into Karinduin had now become too great to challenge. Thus the choice was the Grundin, the Gem Seeker, or nothing at all.

The Arnyar accepted.

Orobai was therefore the Arnyar's choice. Though a creation of the Illan, it was the counsel of the Arnyar that gave reason for his being. It was from the Arnyar's fear of a future disaster and terror that would sweep across the face of Aurduin that they gave this counsel. Knowing the great eagles' hearts, and the consequences for this fateful choice, the Illan agreed to one final creation made in the full light of wisdom.

The Rising of the Four Mountains of Aurduin

Thus began the Illan's final song of transformation. In unity they joined their minds and voices in a symphony that was so complete and overwhelming that each of the Illan merged in unity and oneness. Through their collective song, they merged into the body of Eyar, and passed from coarse matter into subtle spirit and they crossed the barrier between worlds.

In so doing, their greatest works until that time, the Orthirnen, transformed as well. They turned from luminescent temples into the Goargathr, the Great Mountains. Each mountain grew in kind to its origin and retained the color and name of the Four Temples, being Black, Green, Yellow, and White. As it had been with the Temples, the Orgathen came into being first in the east, then south, then west, and finally north. Each mountain embodied the knowledge of its temple of origin and symbolized all the wisdom of the Illan and the Altfein-Aryat.

The Great Mountains lifted to the sky, towering over Aurduin, becoming the pillars of the world and the foundation of Heaven.

When all was complete and all Four Mountains stood tall over the land, at the foot of Norgath, the Black Mountain of the east, Grundin Orobai Rundi Eyarlum came to be, emerging from the waters of the Great Abyss. Taken into the fold of the Arnyar, only one practitioner of the Altfein-Aryat now remained, and with his creation, the Illan had passed forever from the realm of Aurduin, leaving behind the Black One as the hope of the future world.

This is Orobai's story. Orobai's tale is the Tale of Aurduin. To know how and why the great change came to be, one must begin with the Raven.

The day that everything changed for the Raven was the day Orobai found the Jewel.

The Jewel

Tired. So very tired. Even here in Jeaniaurduin Orobai could feel his strength and vitality leaving him. *It won't be long now.* Not yet, but soon he would lay himself down to sleep his dreamless sleep of death, only to be reborn from the body of the world, Eyar. For over 23,000 years it had been the same. Every one hundred and thirty years or so Orobai would "die" and be reborn again. He could feel it now. Soon the process would happen again, but he still had a little strength left in him.

Orobai pushed the weariness back from his mind and tried to cast it from his body. Closing his eyes, he struggled to recall the dreams. They had started coming to him not long ago. Images he couldn't recognize. Strange shapes and machines that he had never seen before filled his mind with visions of metal and suffering. Digging, tearing at the earth, odd metal bodies stirred up death and destruction, poisoning Aurduin.

People were suffering. They seemed to be from many cultures of far and distant lands in Aurduin. They were forced to work against their will. *Slaves.* There was so much he didn't understand in the dreams. *What can they mean?* Never before had his dreams been filled with so much darkness.

Orobai had come here to Jeaniaurduin, the Heart of the Sacred Land, to rest through the cold winter. Even now, in late winter, the lush and verdant lands of Jeaniaurduin seemed to teem with the life and energy of perpetual spring. Clear, life-giving waters bubbled up from deep underground springs, fed by the far away abyss of the Goarnaltrai near Norgath. Orobai always felt perfectly at home here, lost among the twisted branches of oaks and the soft murmuring of leaves in the characteristically pleasant breeze, accompanied by the songs of birds and babble of brooks with water lapping on stones.

But none of this comforted Orobai now. The dreams had only become more frequent. The rest he so badly needed only seemed to drift further away from his reach. Instead, he was filled with dark visions and an anxious heart.

Something was changing in the world. Orobai could feel it. He knew it. The dreams were only the beginning. Something profound was happening.

Orobai had long been one to dream. The Arnyar had always emphasized the significance of dreams to him and he had learned that much of value was revealed to the sleeping mind. Sometimes the meaning was immediate and obvious. Other times meanings were hidden deep within esoteric and cryptic symbolism and vague and shadowy images. There were techniques that would help to reveal such hidden meanings through meditation, even while sleeping. These recent dreams, however, had impressed Orobai with a firm sense of reality, as though the surface of the dream was reflecting actual events in the world. Something terribly disturbing, something that had never happened before, was now taking place somewhere in Jeaniaurduin. He knew he had to see for himself. Perhaps then the dreams would lose their anxious power. He was apprehensive about what he might find.

Orobai waited until Urya was a quarter of the way through the sky before starting out to the southwest, where Jeaniaurduin met the great plains of Nulthali. Orobai had been camped at one of his favorite spots on Lilgurinlth, Clear Water Creek. Here the oaks were ancient and wise and all the land, air, and water were clean and pure. Orobai had come here often through his many lives simply to meditate and be with the creatures of the oak forest – the foxes, wildcats, raccoons, squirrels, and all the many birds who made their homes here. He would sit by the clear running water and listen to the songs of the birds in the early morning and late evening, watching the rising and setting of the sun and moon. It was peaceful here and was a place of eternal spring, for even in the dead of winter the grass was still green and many plants continually gave flowers. It was as though a perfect balance of natural elements existed here so that life could eternally flourish. But now something was changing and its effects reached even here, into this sanctuary. The peace and tranquility was threatened, but by what?

The sun was high enough now to break through the twisting canopy of the towering oak trees. Orobai climbed to the top of a small outlook above Lilgurinlth and "sang" the rest of his belongings home to Golgath. Long ago, really as far back as he could remember, Orobai had learned how to use the Altfein to temporarily collapse spatial distances. He was never exactly sure how he was able to accomplish this, but he knew that when producing the proper combination of tones while blowing on an object he could direct it to far away locations. It did not matter much to Orobai how this happened, only that it did, and that it was exceedingly convenient. In this manner he could quickly deliver whatever he wanted to his home in the north and all would be waiting for him, just as he had prepared it, when he returned. Now he sent back a final collection of stones, clays, and dried herbs and plants he had collected in Jeaniaurduin. Once everything was gone, he quickly performed one of his many shape shifting transformations and in an instant was circling up on the warming morning air as a jet-black raven.

In his natural form Orobai was a rather unusual looking creature. His most distinguishing characteristic was his pure black color that rivaled the darkness of the night sky or even Norgath, the Black Mountain. Upon his face was an inordinately large nose that protruded like a large beak and contrasted sharply with his dark, penetrating eyes. Stooped over by a severely hunched back, he carried himself about with a staff. From his head fell long strands of matted and tangled black hair, giving him a wild and untamed appearance. Though he did his best to hide his unusual form under a heavy black cloak, Orobai was clearly unique. There was no other like him.

Though Orobai had the ability to transform himself into any kind of being, albeit temporarily, he found the form of the raven to be most suiting to his "natural" form. Like himself, the raven was black, had a large "nose," and had the ability to produce impressive vocalizations from the common squawk to intricate gurgles and trills, which Orobai likened to his own singing ability of being able to produce rich vocalizations of multiple tones simultaneously from a deep drone to high-pitched soaring whistles. What was perhaps even more fitting was that Orobai had learned long ago that like him, ravens had a proclivity for finding and collecting bright and beautiful objects. They too found shimmering jewels nearly irresistible.

If he wanted, he could be a majestic eagle, but then he'd have to worry about someone trying to get his feathers. Or he could be a graceful waterfowl, but then someone might try and eat him. These other forms just did not feel right anyway. The raven simply fit.

Dressed in black feathers, Orobai took to the wind. Urya was warm and bright, the land below was green. If it weren't for his dreams, Orobai would have thought all was well in Aurduin. To the north Orobai could see distant clouds that threatened snow, and on the mountains to the west he could see the white tips of far-off peaks. To the southwest the land sloped away to the great plain of Nulthali where many of the waters of Jeaniaurduin that bubbled up from its natural springs ran and the great herds of grazing animals roamed. From there the waters flowed into the sea among the many islands and reefs beyond the horizon in the western archipelago.

Looking out to the west and imagining the flowing of the water to the ocean in his mind, Orobai thought of how long it had been since he had traveled to the far west. Aurduin was a vast place, and though Orobai traveled about it regularly, he gravitated more towards some areas and peoples than others. Recently, which for Orobai meant the past several hundred years, he had passed much of his time with the Yamné in the north and the Ulusi-Rata in the east. He had found a place among these peoples and was happy to have their company and share in their joys and tragedies.

From the lands of the Yamné and the Ulusi-Rata the west coast seemed far indeed and it had been many generations since Orobai had spent any time among the peoples of the west. In fact, it had been so long now that Orobai supposed there had probably been great changes in their cultures, languages, and customs. Perhaps he would have to learn them all anew. Maybe in his next life he could concentrate some time and energy on getting to know these peoples again, Orobai thought to himself. Perhaps in his "old age" he had gotten too sedentary, too accustomed to old friends and old habits.

After a couple days of flying, Orobai finally arrived where he felt his dreams had been pointing him. Circling about in the air, Orobai's attention was called back from his mental wandering to the view below him. Something seemed amiss in Nulthali. Usually he could see some of the grazing animals on the great plain, but even from his vantage point high in the air, he could see none. As he looked closer he saw that even the small birds seemed to be absent and all below him was quiet.

Yet there was something far more disturbing. Just as in his dream, in some areas it seemed as if some great beast had dug at the earth with enormous claws and raked the land clear of all living things, leaving barren, gaping holes in the landscape with dark tunnels leading deep into the ground. Indeed, it had been many years now since he had come to the edge of Nulthali, but he could never remember seeing this before. There was no doubt in his mind that this was not a natural phenomenon, and certainly was not the result of any creature that he had ever encountered.

Almost fearful of what he might find, the raven flew down for a closer look, settling into a circular pattern drifting over the damaged terrain on gentle currents of air. It was clear that the waters that flowed through and around these damaged areas were not pure and clean as they once had been. There was an odd color to the water and nothing living remained on the banks of the creeks and streams. All was dead and desolate. And in the dust and dirt left over from the excavations were strange tracks that were not of any animal. Mixed in with these odd tracks were the footprints of many people, all leading off to the west on distant roads that passed beyond the horizon. *What could all this be?* Orobaï wondered to himself.

Orobaï began to think of his home. Though it would be very cold to the north, he longed to sit by the fire and rest his weary body. Besides, the Yamné would be coming soon, looking for their sacrament, and no doubt wanting him to join them in their annual winter ceremony. Yes, he could go home, despite the unusual marks on the land below. He would continue to sort through the strange images of his dreams. The answer would come, in time. There was always more time, and as curious as he was, this was a mystery that could wait.

Just at the moment when the old one circled to the north, about to make a direct line toward his home, something caught his eye. Down below in one of the excavated areas something flashed in the now-waning sunlight. Orobaï knew the glint and flash of all of the gems of the world and could easily identify them in an instant, even with his raven eyes. But this was new. Something different. Something he had not seen before. And that got his attention.

Quickly he swooped down. Still in the form of a raven, he hopped close to where he had seen the glittering jewel. He kept his raven form as he felt very ill at ease here in this desolate area and thought it best to be prepared for a quick flight, if necessary. Though he told himself that he had not seen anyone, he could not shake the feeling that something here just was not right and thought it best to be on his guard. A nervous raven, he hopped about cautiously, turning his head from side to side and pausing every few moments as he sought out the shimmering object he had seen from above.

The Jewel

Hopping up on a small mound of dirt, Orobai could see that the jewel that had caught his raven eye was in the center of a small lake that had been drained in the course of the strange excavation that had gone on in the area. Why no one else had seen such a radiant gem seemed puzzling, but for whatever reason, it had been completely overlooked.

But how could anyone miss this? What a jewel!

It was large, for one, easily requiring two hands to simply hold it. *And its light!* It shimmered in pure and translucent white light that seemed not only to reflect the light around it, but seemed to actually emanate from its own depths, from somewhere deep within its core.

It certainly was not one of the Altfein. Those were not nearly so large, and they came in pairs with the Sarnfein being sharp and angular and the Alkeinfein being rounded and smooth. This was neither, however, and it was alone. This jewel was rounded, oblong and somewhat egg-shaped, but cut at clear and precise angles, much like a large, expertly cut diamond. It was unlike a diamond, however, for the pure white radiance that emanated from within it was unlike any ordinary stone. And what was more, as he came closer to it, hopping cautiously across the bed of the now dry lake, it seemed to hum and resonate in a soft and beautiful tone. Never had Orobai encountered such a singing stone as this.

What, in all of Aurduin, could this possibly be?

Orobai hopped all around the gem, inspecting it from all angles, cocking his head this way and that, listening intently to its soft song. It was utterly magnificent. No imperfections or blemishes of any kind were apparent. And its sound! *How enchanting!* It would be just the thing to give him something beautiful and mysterious to ponder through the long winter nights that lay ahead as he awaited the spring. Something this attractive might even help him forget the disturbing images of his dreams.

He decided to take the mysterious gem.

Orobai quickly transformed himself into his natural form, after having taken one last brief look around to make sure he was still alone. The gem came easily from the dry lakebed with the dirt quickly falling away, revealing a perfectly formed and unblemished stone. It was heavy, yet sat comfortably in his hands. It had a good solid feeling to it, though it also felt paradoxically light, almost buoyant in his hands. He turned it over several times, getting a good look at it and assessing it with his lifetimes of experience with gems. "Truly unique!" he pronounced to himself with satisfaction. This would be the find of a lifetime, or even many. Finding something new and yet unseen was always a great, and now exceedingly rare, occurrence for Orobai, and this was rare indeed. *Perhaps the Arnyar might have something to say about this,* he thought to himself. He took one more loving glance at the mysterious gem and quickly sang it back to his home where he would find it waiting for him among all the other things he had already sent back from this journey to Jeaniaurduin. "The trip to Nulthali has certainly been worth it," he concluded, speaking to himself.

Turning back into his raven form, Orobai began the long journey north to his home at the foot of Golgath as Urya sank beneath the western horizon and

5

Ranya began to peak over the hills to the east. His wings felt propelled by his growing fascination and wonder for the strange gem. Now if only the weight of the disturbing dreams could be left behind, then he'd truly feel young again.

Miraanni

The journey home was long and tiring. Orobai did not have the strength to fly as he once did. He was getting old, and with age came the weariness, as it always did. The thought of the wondrous jewel spurred him on, however, and he was eager to study it more closely. Anticipation gave his tired wings strength and he pushed onward.

After what seemed an interminable time, Golgath finally loomed on the far northern horizon. Orobai had crossed over many mountains, hills, and valleys to reach this point and he flew down for one final rest before making the last leg of the journey. Perched on a rocky outcropping before the valley of Nuerdlith, Orobai surveyed the area. The Strong River was flowing with a great torrent as it often did. Nuerdlith flowed from the northeast to the west around the base of Golgath. In the far west it cut into a labyrinthine maze of canyons and deep gullies as other streams and rivers flowed into it out of the high desert. Generations ago a joint effort of desert people on either side of the divide had created the only bridge that spanned the great river. Other than this crossing, one had to travel far to the western edge and pass around the far side of Avengath or come this way to the south side of Golgath and ford the river at its rare low points.

The valley immediately below Orobai was open with many grasses, small trees, and plants and herbs of many kinds. It was a common wintering ground for the herds of elk and deer from the north that would frequent this area at this time of year and then move back north in the summer. Their migrations were often shadowed by the wolf packs as well as the nomadic peoples of the north who relied on the elk and deer for meat, hides, and ceremonial artifacts such as hooves, skulls, and antlers. In the warmer months bear made their homes here too and might even spend some time in the grasslands in a mild winter such as this. Orobai had many lifetimes to study this place and he knew its rhythms and patterns well.

Life was passing through its normal courses. The flow of seasons and the movement of time were as music to Orobai. Now was the slow and quiet time, when families of animals gathered for strength and security. It was a time for reflection and silence, and for awaiting the burst of music and song that was spring. The renewal of Aurduin would not be far off now. Already Urya was creeping back from the southern skies and bringing with it light, warmth, and new life for all of Aurduin.

There upon the ledge overlooking the valley below, Orobai found a suitable cave, one he had visited many times before, and bedded down for the night. He would rest this final night before making the last stretch toward home, which he should reach by midday tomorrow. For now he was content to sit by a fire, letting himself feel the pull of anticipation as images of the wondrous jewel filled his mind.

* * * *

That night Orobai was troubled by strange dreams once again. When he awoke, he struggled to recall the quickly fading details of the dreams as he searched through fleeting images behind closed eyes.

Where was I just now?

Shadowy images of serpents coming up from the earth filled Orobai's inner vision. More images surged forward. There were many people toiling, working the earth, and suffering. *So much suffering, anger, and bitterness.* Some were sick and dying, others did not seem to have the strength to go on, falling where they stood, never to rise again. But others compelled them to continually bend down and take the serpents in their hands. The serpents would bite them, putting their poison deep within. Others would come and take the serpents in strange metal creatures, always leaving to the west, abandoning those who could not follow who had already succumbed to the poison working its way through their systems.

In the midst of all this darkness Orobai saw the jewel. Just as when he had found it, the jewel radiated a brilliant light in the dream that seemed to fill the world. The serpents shrank and crawled back deep within the earth, trying to get away from the jewel's radiance. In the light Orobai thought he could see some form, some being. Yet he could not make out who or what it was. He only knew that it was there. Something immeasurably powerful and profound was there, just beneath the surface, a mystery to be unraveled. The remaining images passed from Orobai's mind quickly as the light of day filled the world and chased away the shadows of night and the omens that had come with the darkness.

Perplexed, Orobai opened his eyes. He rolled over to see the darkness being pushed from the morning sky. At his back the fire he had made the night before smoldered slowly as the remaining coals turned to ash and gave out a little warmth. The world looked as it always had, but something was unmistakably different. Something was wrong.

These dreams portend something, but what?

Orobai couldn't remember ever having felt this way. Dreams had never left him with such a definite sense of the uncanny, as though some deep current had barely breached the surface, hinting at something unimaginable just below. Mulling the images over in his mind as he sat silently in his cave, slowly stirring the ashes and coals, Orobai knew that there was some relation between the digging, the serpents, the jewel, and the light, but exactly what he could not say. Only one thing seemed clear to Orobai – something that had been sleeping, perhaps for millennia, was now awake. Some course of events had been set in motion. The appearance of the jewel was just the beginning.

Why now, and when I'm so tired?

If he were younger, he could go about quickly to learn what was happening in the west, where he had spent precious little time in his past few lifetimes. It had been even longer since he had been out to the western archipelago. Though much was unclear, Orobai felt certain that these people were connected to the disturbing aspects of his dreams. Surely they had something to do with this, or why else would all the signs point in their direction? *What have they been doing to bring about these strange and fearful dreams?* All this left Orobai feeling uneasy and more disturbed than he would have imagined.

Brushing the dreams aside, Orobai once again set his mind to getting home. He waited until Urya was high enough to heat the earth and create the warm updrafts that helped him to rise easily into the sky. Moving up to the precipice above his cave, he changed his shape into a raven and took to wing once more.

As soon as he was aloft he began to feel better. It was another clear and beautiful day. The warm air rising from the earth caressed him and made him feel light, like he was a feather floating on a sea of wind, leaving behind the dark remnants of his dreams in the cave. Below him he saw elk and deer grazing on the dew-dripped meadows. In anticipation of spring, the bucks and bulls were beginning to grow their antlers and the urge to reproduce was slowly building within them. Soon there would be a new generation and the elders would pass on. The rhythm continued, the music of life flowed ever on.

Maybe they were just dreams.

But Orobai didn't believe that wishful thought.

With Golgath looming large before him, Orobai decided that he would make one more stop before returning to his house. A short ways to the northwest of his home, in the foothills of the great mountain, there were some hot springs, and the thought of a good hot soak felt just right to the weary traveler. He swooped to his left and climbed a little higher. Soon he could see the steam rising from the hot pools and it soothed him just thinking of the rejuvenating waters and their healing warmth.

Landing beside his favorite pool, Orobai assumed his natural shape. He removed his clothes and sank deep into the warm waters. *What relief! What comfort!* How fortunate Orobai was to have these private pools of hot, bubbling water in which to soothe his tired body. Here he could relax in private. No one else ever came here. Most humans gave Orobai a wide berth and would not trespass within the forest about his home. Even those who knew and respected Orobai were generally wary of him, given his unusual nature, and thus he could pass his days in the forest and streams about his home without much worry of unexpected visitors or the wayward stranger. Here he could pass his time in quiet solitude and let his reflections wander where they might.

As Orobai floated in the water he began to sing, as he often did. At first he hummed quietly to himself, but as he began to feel more relaxed his singing grew in strength and soon the hillsides were resonating with his vibrant tones. As always, the Altfein responded to his beautiful singing and the space about him filled with light made of complex undulating geometric patterns and arabesques that flowed to the rhythm and texture of his voice. Enraptured with his own work, Orobai floated in the water, a smile breaking across his face. Indeed, moments such as these were some of Orobai's favorites and he could float, sing, and watch the play of lights for hours on end.

But such was not to be the case, not today. Orobai's singing had caught the attention of an unexpected visitor. It took Orobai a few minutes to notice that there, patiently waiting next to the pool of water, was Faen, a she-wolf of the northern pack. She got Orobai's attention with a quick snort as Orobai's song came to a fading conclusion.

"Greetings, my old friend," said Orobai, coming to the edge of the pool, smiling broadly as he feigned formality with this old familiar. "To what do I owe the honor of your fine company on this beautiful winter day?"

"Forgive me for disturbing your relaxation, Orobai," said Faen, sitting directly in front of the old being at the edge of the steaming pool of water. "I heard you singing and have just come from your home where I have made a den."

"A den?" asked Orobai, surprised.

"Yes," answered Faen. "I was traveling with the pack to the south to our winter hunting grounds when I found myself pregnant. I had to stop here to birth my two pups, Elkil and Fenruk."

Orobai furrowed his brow. "Where are they?" he asked, looking about.

"There are down the hillside, by your home. I have made a small place for myself there and have been keeping them warm and caring for them," answered the wolf.

"And pray tell, where is Kru, your mate and companion, Faen?" asked Orobai, looking about for the weathered old wolf that had been the she-wolf's lifelong mate.

"He has passed from this world, Orobai," answered Faen, lowering her head in sorrow. "He was taken by an avalanche. There was no hope for him."

"I am sorry to hear of this sad news," said Orobai regretfully. "But the young are healthy?"

"Yes, they are doing well," said Faen, glancing down the hill in their direction.

"Strange that they should be born now," said Orobai as his expression went momentarily blank, his thoughts having recessed deeper into his mind. *It means something . . .*

Orobai looked back at the old wolf. He could tell there was something she wanted to tell him, and it was not the sorrowful news of the death of her mate, or the unusual birth of cubs in winter.

"What is on your mind, Faen?" the old being asked. "There's something you want to tell me, but you're puzzled by it."

Faen didn't keep Orobai waiting.

"There's something inside your house," she said.

"Something?" asked Orobai, intrigued.

Faen began to explain. "Having nowhere else to go, I made a den just outside your house. My pups were born and we were fine. During this time, no one came and no one left. But then, not too many days ago, a burst of light came out of your home. It wasn't the light of fire or any other light I have seen. It was strange and beautiful. And when the light receded, I could hear something. Orobai, though this is strange indeed, I heard crying. There is something crying in your home, and it sounds like a child."

Orobai could not hide the look of astonishment on his face as his mouth fell partly open, briefly holding his breath as though caught in mid-thought, not sure how to react. How could there possibly be an infant in his home? Where did this being come from and who would have thought to leave a helpless infant in *his* care, of all beings? Orobai knew nothing of children. Indeed, he could not have children himself and in all his many years he had never had the responsibility of a child. He had never even had a mate, let alone attempted to reproduce, which he knew he was incapable of doing. It didn't make sense. *It must be some animal. Faen cannot possibly be correct.*

Without speaking his doubts or concerns, Orobai pulled himself anxiously from the warm waters. He quickly turned into his raven form, gave his black feathers a good shake, sending droplets of water all about. Satisfied, Orobai changed back into his usual form, now nicely dry, replaced his clothes, and began the descent down to his home with Faen tagging along a pace behind him on the narrow trail.

Faen had been correct. Upon drawing near to his home, Orobai could hear the unmistakable cry of a young infant coming from within. Though he had never raised children of his own, he knew well enough what a young one sounded like. Faen's two pups crawled out to greet them from the den she had made, making plaintive cries of their own for their mother. Faen quickly identified the dark black one as Elkil and the lighter grey pup as Fenruk. They both cried out as only pups do upon the return of their mother, but her attention was more focused on the sounds from inside Orobai's home. Given this obvious contrast between the sound of the pups and the sound from within, the cries sounded far more like a human child than an animal. Orobai and Faen exchanged puzzled looks and Orobai opened the door.

Like the wandering black one himself, Orobai's home was old. Before it was a house proper it had been a cave, cut out of the hillside here near the foot of Golgath. Many thousands of years ago Orobai had selected this cave as his own and had gradually transformed it into a comfortable, yet modest, home out of the hillside. Using the skills he had learned among the peoples of Aurduin, he had furnished it with windows, a door, and small and inviting rooms with a fireplace, a place to cook, room to sleep, and deep within the cave, more than enough room to store the many rocks, gems, and other odds and ends he regularly collected as he went about Aurduin.

Now his home was dark and cold from his extended absence. Opening the front door, the sounds of crying grew louder. Orobai glanced down the long dark corridor that led into the hillside. It was back there, whatever it was. He walked about, opening the curtains on his windows to let some light in and lit a few candles. He invited Faen and her two cubs to come inside. For Faen this was a familiar act, having spent many nights by Orobai's warm fire, listening to his tales of ages long past. She carefully guided the still fragile cubs inside and sniffed cautiously at the air as she perked her ears, listening.

From somewhere deep in the back of his home they could all hear the unmistakable sound of crying. It was desperate and sorrowful, like a baby in great need, though still vibrant and surprisingly resonant. Taking a lantern in hand, Orobai and Faen made their way down a dark winding passage to Orobai's storage room. Here is where he would sing home all that he collected in his travels. He would find everything neatly arranged upon his return, almost as though everything knew just where it should go. As they walked down the corridor, Orobai thought of how all that he had recently collected in Jeaniaurduin should be waiting for him, along with the wondrous gem, which he had nearly forgotten about with the puzzle of the crying child.

The sounds of crying grew louder as they approached. Orobai was anxious, but he was not afraid, for surely, as strange and unlikely as it seemed, it was only a small child – nothing to fear. Slowly opening the door to the room, he and Faen cautiously looked in as Orobai held up the lantern, chasing away the dark shadows of the musty chamber.

And there it was. Orobai stood astounded in the doorway of his storeroom, almost letting the lantern fall from his hand, his mind hardly accepting what his eyes told him. There, in the middle of all his recent collections, was a baby girl, crying and wriggling from side to side. She seemed cold and hungry, but otherwise healthy, and truly beautiful.

More than beautiful, she was absolutely stunning. Never had Orobai seen a child such as this. Her skin was a pure milky white, as were her soft wisps of hair. She appeared human, but not like any human Orobai had ever seen, for though the skin pigments of the peoples of Aurduin varied from very light to very dark, there were none that were as stark and as pure white as this. Not even albinos were this pure of a color. And her eyes! A brilliant silver, they were alive with a bright intelligence that was far beyond the age of a newborn child. And stranger still, a light was about her that was subtle, yet radiant, and Orobai got the impression that from somewhere deep within her being a great music was taking shape. She was truly a marvel to behold.

But from where did she come? And why was she here, among the trappings of Orobai's collections of jewels, gems, stones, clays, herbs, and miscellaneous wonders? Who could have brought her and why? What would Orobai do with a child? He didn't know how to raise a child, and certainly he could not nourish it himself. He was at a loss. "Amazing," he said, as much to himself as to his wolf companion. How could this be?

Orobai suddenly noticed that something was missing. Among all the objects of the room, Orobai could not find that which he had most anticipated seeing. The great jewel was gone. He should have seen it right away. Yet it was simply not there. Had someone come and taken the jewel and left the girl-child in its place? Was this a trade of some kind?

Orobai did not have time to ponder these questions now. His first concern was for the child. She needed care and she was no doubt cold and hungry. "Get a blanket," he said to Faen as he approached the girl. Faen ran off and quickly returned with a warm robe. Taking it from her, Orobai gently picked up the infant and wrapped her snugly. Upon touching her he felt a surge of power unlike he had ever felt before. Truly this child was something special. Her power moved through Orobai viscerally. There was a music that worked its way into his mind, yet he could not fully make it out or follow its rhythm and melody. It all seemed very auspicious. She seemed so familiar, yet so totally other, so unique. She was something radically new.

Taking her to the front room, Orobai hurriedly built a warm fire and set some water to boil to make tea for himself and a cleansing bath for the child. Lifting her up in the firelight and turning her about in his hands, he found the girl-child faultless, entirely without imperfection of any kind and perfectly uniform in her stunning white color. Curiously, despite that fact that she seemed a newborn, she had no umbilical cord and had no navel whatsoever. Orobai knew of only one other warm-blooded creature without some wound from its connection to its mother, and that was himself. The only one of his kind, Orobai had no mother as he was born of Eyar, the very earth itself. Yet here was another that seemed as he, though exceedingly more beautiful and radiant in every way.

The child needed food. Though seeming to take comfort in Orobai's attention and presence, her continued cries made it clear that something more was needed, and quickly. At first, Orobai did not know what to do until he noticed that Faen was nursing her two young cubs by the fire.

Orobai caught the wolf's eye and a knowing glance passed between them. Faen did not need to think this silent proposition over, for indeed, her motherly instincts were already drawing her to the child. She gladly and willingly took the desperate child to her, who, nestling in between Fenruk and Elkil, nursed happily until she fell asleep.

The night drew on and Orobai sat in his chair before the fire deep in thought. At long last Orobai spoke, saying, "Faen, these are strange events indeed. This mysterious child has come to me, though I cannot fathom why. Because of this, I shall call her Miraanni, the 'Mysterious Child.'"

Faen said nothing and only looked quizzically at the tiny girl.

As Orobai's eyelids grew heavy and his breaths deepened, he gazed ponderously through bleary eyes at the radiantly white infant nestled warmly in the old wolf's fur. One burning question passed through his mind that threatened to unbalance his entire world – *Who are you, Mysterious Child?* Orobai didn't know it then, but the true answer to his question would be a long time coming, and it was far more complex than he could imagine.

Elder Brother

That night Orobai again dreamt a provocative dream. The dream began in the familiar surroundings of his home. All appeared normal and all things were in their places. In the dream Orobai was just coming in from doing something outside. Upon opening the door, a great light came out of his living room. Looking around he saw that the light was coming from neither the lamps nor the candles or the fire that he usually kept going. At first, the light did not seem to come from anywhere in particular. It was simply there. It was clear and had a sense of utter purity about it. Though it was bright, it was neither blinding nor harsh. As it grew in intensity it became almost overwhelming, though it never hurt Orobai's dream-body eyes. At its peak, the light enveloped everything in Orobai's sight and all that remained was the light itself. With it came a profound sense of peace, compassion, and fulfillment.

Yet there was something else there in the light, something unseen. Behind its brilliance lay something dark, something secret and hidden. It was as though there was a purpose to the light that was not yet fully revealed. It must serve some end, but what this was remained dim and unclear. Orobai only knew that it was there, somewhere, and that it held a terrible darkness. Yet even in this darkness, there was still a strange sense of completion and fulfillment.

Gradually the light began to recede and Orobai could once more recognize the familiar objects of his home. There was his chair, his handmade string instrument, his andrim, his flutes, and his many other odds and ends. Everything looked normal enough.

With the passing of the dark purpose Orobai felt comfort return to him as the light took on a more pleasing and soothing tone. But now he noticed that the light indeed did have a source, and it was coming from his storeroom down the corridor in the rear of his home. Slowly Orobai stepped forward and began to pass down the dark hallway. Each step felt significant as though he were on the verge of some great and profound discovery.

He finally reached the storeroom. Just as he had originally expected when he had first arrived home that day, he found the wondrous white jewel he had sent from Jeaniaurduin. It was just as he had seen it before with his waking eyes. As in the waking world, it seemed to emanate a music within the dream that he could not yet understand or catch on to, which for Orobai was a rare event, for he was far excelled in the art of music.

Looking at the jewel he could plainly see that it was the source of the white light that cascaded all about him in a warm and comforting glow. Moving closer to the jewel, Orobai suddenly realized there was something different about it that he had not noticed before. Deep in its core, something was there. There was something moving. As Orobai focused on this image, the clearer and more distinct it became. It grew larger and the sight of this form now overshadowed his vision of the jewel, which had receded from view. Slowly the form solidified before him and he saw that it was a child. Indeed, it was *the child*.

It was Miraanni.

The child matured quickly as he watched. Almost before he realized it, she had transformed into the shape of an exquisitely beautiful young woman, absolutely without comparison or equal in all of Aurduin. Still the white light radiated from her pure white complexion. Just as Orobai himself was immeasurably blacker than any other living thing in Aurduin, this young woman before him was likewise whiter than any being he had ever seen. And just as Orobai was strange and unpleasant to look upon, this young woman was unparalleled in beauty. It seemed impossible not to look upon her without wonder and awe, such was her power. And in all this, Orobai somehow felt that they were part of each other in a way he could not explain or fully understand. Somehow they were bound together, he could feel this unmistakably. *What could it mean?*

Orobai was about to ask her who she was, but his thoughts were cut short and in one quick statement, much was revealed. Miraanni opened her mouth, and in a great effluence of musical sound, clearly stated in the most eloquent Illanii accent, "Dalnae-urn."

Orobai suddenly awoke. He quickly glanced around and saw that dawn was just breaking outside. There with him were Faen, Fenruk, and Elkil, the three wolves, and nestled between the two cubs was Miraanni. In a flood, the revealing dream poured over Orobai with a cascade of meaning.

"Why did she call me that?" he demanded out loud. "Dalnae-urn! Dalnae-urn! Why would she use that term?"

Orobai's forceful questions caused Faen to stir, who, until then, had been sleeping peacefully by the glowing embers of last night's fire with the young ones curled between her legs. "What is the matter, Orobai?" she asked, forcing her eyes open. "Why are you talking so loud this early in the morning? There's no one here, is there?" she asked, taking a quick look around the room with her now alert eyes.

"No, there's no one here. Forgive me, Faen. I didn't mean to disturb you, but I've just had the most amazing dream," answered Orobai, telling Faen all he could of his nightly vision.

After hearing Orobai's tale, which he now augmented with the account of how he had initially found the jewel, Faen asked, "But what does 'Dalnae-urn' mean, Orobai? It has been long that the tongue of the northern wolves has diverted from Illanii and we no longer understand all the meanings of the old words, save a few, such as your names. What is the meaning of this word and why does it startle you so?"

"'Dalnae-urn' means 'elder brother' in Illanii," answered Orobai flatly, as though the significance of the word would be as immediately obvious to Faen as it was to himself.

"'Elder brother,' is that so?" responded Faen with a quizzical look that only canines can achieve with a perk of the ears, raised eyebrows, and gentle tilt of the head. "So you think that this little one here, what did you call her – Miraanni – is your younger sister?"

"I did not say that," responded Orobai in haste. "I said that *she* called *me* elder brother in the dream. I did not call her 'sulsar-urn,' 'younger sister,' mind you."

"What do you think it means?" asked Faen. "Do you think that she really could be your sister? Everyone knows that you have no other family, but could it be possible?"

"I don't know," replied Orobai honestly. "Dreams can tell much, but they can also deceive. Often what a dream communicates should not be taken too literally. The language of dreams is symbols, not Illanii. Surely this must mean something, but I don't know what, as of yet."

"Well, she certainly is unique, Orobai, as are you. I wouldn't be surprised if there were some connection between you. And she does seem to have come to you. Whether she is actually the jewel or not, your mind has connected them together. You sent the gem here, only to find this little one. I would say that there is some purpose at work here even if you cannot yet see it," advised Faen.

"You are of course correct, Faen," said Orobai, stroking his chin thoughtfully as he gazed at the beautiful young girl. "This will require greater contemplation. I must seek the counsel of the Arnyar. Perhaps they will know something more of this than I can determine from just this dream. If anyone could know more about this child, it will certainly be the great eagles."

The Council of the Arnyar

With some breakfast in his belly and some good tea to set his mind at work, Orobai was ready to seek some answers. Before he could leave, however, he wanted to get something for Faen to eat so that she could care for Miraanni without interruption. They decided that fish from a nearby stream would do fine.

Orobai gathered up his net and spear and headed down the hillside to his fishing hole. As was usual for Orobai, soon he was fully absorbed in the meditative task. Orobai loved fishing, even if he did not always love eating fish, as the act of fishing itself was for him a kind of contemplation. He would sing quietly to himself, losing himself in the rhythms of the water and the sounds of nearby birds, letting his mind wander. At such times he didn't care whether he caught anything, for the time spent by the water was pleasant enough. He had always had more than enough time and Orobai was in the habit of not rushing things.

It was while in a peaceful and meditative state as this that Orobai noticed a dark shadow passing overhead. Startling him out of his reverie, he could clearly see the image of one of the lesser eagles reflected in the pool of water below him.

Looking up, Orobai gave a signaling cry to the eagle overhead. The eagle banked and its golden crown of feathers flashed in the light of the early morning sun. It opened its wings wide, circled around, and glided down quickly to a perch close to where Orobai was fishing, pulling up at the last minute and extending its talons out before it, firmly grasping the tree branch as it came to rest.

It was Sto'orn, messenger for the Arnyar. Whenever the great eagles had something important to communicate they would send Sto'orn, or one like him, to bid Orobai to come to them, or simply to pass on some message.

Sto'orn was not one of the true Arnyar. He was what Orobai knew as a lesser eagle, not having the dramatic size and stature of the great eagles. This significant difference in size was the only real physical difference between the lesser and greater eagles as they tended to have similar plumages and characteristics. Despite their similarity, however, only the true Arnyar were the keepers of the Altfein-Aryat. The lesser eagles might know bits and pieces of the sacred lore, but the keeping of the Aryat was the responsibility and privilege of the True Arnyar alone. The majority of the lesser eagles in fact had very little to do with the Arnyar and went about their business and their own lives with little to no contact with the great eagles of the Goargathr. However, a few trusted lesser eagles were the servants of the Arnyar and carried out their bidding.

Such was Sto'orn's place in life. He was a servant of the Arnyar and had come to Orobai before at their command. Taking his duty seriously with a fierce pride that only eagles could express, he had always maintained a terse and formal relationship with Orobai. He was not one for casual conversation or for visiting. He came and went as he was directed and no more. In contrast to Orobai's relationship with other beings and creatures of the forest, Orobai knew virtually nothing about Sto'orn personally, other than his place in the hierarchy of power within the ranks of the Arnyar and their servants.

"Atluin," said Sto'orn, greeting Orobai with the standard Illanii hello.

"And atluin to you as well, Sto'orn," responded Orobai. "I see you have come just in time and have saved me the trouble of having to go looking for one of your kind. I have news that the Arnyar will want to learn of."

"Your news is already known, Grundin Orobai Rundi Eyarlum. Council was called several days ago," said Sto'orn formally. "I and three others were sent out to find you. This morning, when I saw the smoke from your fire, I knew you must have returned and thus I have come. I have been instructed to bring you to the Council as soon as you are able. The Arnyar say that it is urgent," Sto'orn said somewhat cynically, knowing of Orobai's tendency for lingering and taking his time. It was, after all, notoriously difficult to motivate a being that had lived for thousands of years into acting on the spur of the moment.

Orobai was pleased to hear that the Arnyar did have some idea of what was happening and would be able to help sort through these curious circumstances. Knowing that the Arnyar were far-seeing in both eye and mind, he considered that perhaps these events had been foretold. Maybe some key might be hidden away in the Aryat itself. Though if so, Orobai wondered why he had never been told before, for surely the Arnyar had revealed all of the Altfein-Aryat to him long ago. However, Orobai also admitted to himself that the Arnyar were often reticent to freely give information of any kind. They only gave bits and pieces of knowledge when they deemed it appropriate and he had often wondered in the past what they might be withholding from him. *Perhaps this time it will be different.*

"I'm more than happy to leave immediately," said Orobai, "but first I do need to catch some fish."

Sto'orn saw no point in delaying and with a few quick passes over the water he soon had a suitable collection of fresh fish for Orobai. Orobai thanked him and asked him to wait a few minutes for him to take the fish back to his house.

Entering the house Orobai saw that Miraanni was nursing once more, along with the two pups. Faen was glad for the fish, some of which she ate right away. The rest Orobai placed in a cold, wet sack for Faen to have later. He pointed out that he also had some bread and dried meats and fruits about the house in case he was going to be gone longer than the fish would hold out.

Orobai was about ready to leave when Faen called him back with some urgency and a tone that indicated that Orobai had neglected something terribly significant. "Orobai, surely you must know that the child needs to be cleaned! What goes in one end must eventually come out the other!" chided the old wolf.

Orobai had not thought of that. He went over to Miraanni, unwrapped her, and sure enough, she certainly did need cleaning. He took out a washbasin, poured out some warm water from the kettle, and cleaned her quickly. In doing so he noticed that she looked slightly larger than she had even the day before. She also seemed somewhat more aware, especially in the way that she looked up at him and smiled. *What a strange child*, he thought to himself, a now familiar refrain in his mind. He then wrapped her back up in a new blanket to which he added lichen and moss, which he hoped would absorb whatever came out, at least for a little while. *Truly this child needs a mother!* he thought to himself. He added some fuel to the fire, and said good-bye.

Sto'orn was waiting for him perched in a large pine tree just outside. "Are you ready now?" he asked, impatiently.

"Yes, yes. Let's be off," Orobai answered as he transformed into a raven and took to the air, struggling to catch up to the eagle who had already set off at a fast pace, not wanting to keep the Arnyar waiting any longer than they already had.

* * * *

Being a lesser eagle, Sto'orn was about three meters across at full wingspan, whereas even a smaller great eagle could be ten or more meters from wingtip to wingtip. The true Arnyar tended to range mostly on the Orgathen where they kept their aeries at the peaks of the Four Mountains. Only once, many ages ago, Orobai had seen an Arnyar when he was far to the north beyond the Northern Forest, far outside the normal range of the Arnyar. He had only seen this great eagle from a good distance and had never seen one of its kind represented in council. Curiously, this Arnyar was all white, unlike any Orobai had ever seen, before or since. Judging by the look of it, it was perhaps the largest and most magnificent of all Arnyar. It was only this once that Orobai had seen a white Arnyar such as this and he had never heard the other Arnyar make any mention of its kind. That had been some seven thousand years ago now, but Orobai still thought of the unique encounter from time to time.

The lesser eagles, on the other hand, tended to roam throughout Aurduin and generally could be found most anywhere, if one had an eye to look to the skies and mountain ridges. These lesser eagles varied in overall size and color depending on range and habitat. Sto'orn was a golden eagle of the Northern Forest. These eagles were relatively large and strong for their kind and preyed on fish, small mammals, other birds, and even the young and sickly of the larger animals such as elk and deer. They also carried the prized feathers of the peoples of the north who would often ritually take an eagle and remove the feathers for religious and cultural purposes as they were emblems of spiritual power. No one would dare to attempt to approach a great eagle in this way, though they were widely revered above all other beings.

Despite the relatively large size of a raven, the lesser eagle dwarfed Orobai and he felt small. He had considered taking the form of an eagle of equal size, but even Sto'orn might take offense with his characteristic eagle pride were Orobai to do so. The Arnyar did not take eagle-imitation lightly, even if it was Orobai, and the lesser eagles were similar in this regard. But Orobai never felt comfortable, despite all his many years, in taking on the form of an eagle with another eagle present. They were sensitive and watchful and Orobai had no desire to bring upon their scorn or disapproval.

Thus Orobai flew along in his jet-black raven feathers with the wind whistling around him. It was not long before some true ravens caught sight of Orobai trailing behind the messenger eagle. A group of young males launched into the air to follow after the two and have some fun. The gang of ravens climbed high and began to take turns diving at Sto'orn, crying aloud as they did so. For the ravens this was both sport and practice. At times it was necessary for them to chase off hunting eagles that might be coming around to pick off one of their kind for a tasty meal. But other times "eagle diving," as they called it, could be a fun and exhilarating game that tested skill and strength of nerve. Each raven would seek to come the closest to an eagle without getting caught in the eagle's razor-sharp talons with their bone-crushing power. Any raven that managed to actually get a feather from an eagle would be greatly honored by the others.

Though Orobai knew that his escort must have been greatly irritated by this playful game, he took some pleasure at watching the ravens have their fun. They were probably wondering why he too was not joining in on the game. Sto'orn was clearly having a difficult time of it, however. Occasionally he would flip at the final moment and present his menacing talons to the sky and give a piercing cry, which would put pause and caution into even the most brazen raven. But there were just too many of them, however, and Sto'orn was beginning to tire. The onslaught of the ravens was simply too overwhelming and the game threatened their progress on the long journey to Arnthanlim-Zan.

Thinking that Sto'orn had had enough of the ravens' torment, Orobai decided to do something about it. He began singing, setting his plan in action. The Altfein responded to his thoughts and melody by creating an image of hundreds of quick swallows, sweeping up from a canyon below. Instantly the ravens were set upon on all sides. Everywhere they turned they found another purple and green blur of a swallow diving and grabbing at them. They quickly forgot their own game with Sto'orn and dove down into the cover of the forest to avoid the smaller birds, which preferred open skies to closed places.

Orobai, being quite pleased with himself, stopped singing, causing the swallows to dissolve just as quickly as he had conjured them up, and flew a little harder to catch up with Sto'orn who was busy recomposing himself as he flew along.

"Those lousy Salusir. Don't they have anything better to do?" complained Sto'orn. "I don't know why you choose to use their form when you fly, Orobai. Certainly you can find a more dignified bird for yourself?"

"No, I don't suppose I can," responded Orobai. "After all this time, why would I go changing now, and just to please you?"

"I just don't like them," said Sto'orn gruffly. "They don't know how to mind their own business and they always make so much noise. Unlike the Arnyar, the ravens have no dignity."

"But they are curious and creative. You have to give them that. And besides, if it were not for the ravens, who would there be to remind the Arnyar of their place! Even the dignified must suffer a little humility, Sto'orn. Surely you must agree," lectured Orobai playfully.

Avoiding answering Orobai's remark, Sto'orn suggested that they concentrate on their flight and continue on for they still had a great distance to go before they would arrive at the council. The two birds flew on with only the sound of the wind in their feathers.

* * * *

Orobai kept to himself and mulled over recent events as he watched the land pass by beneath him. They were flying well around to the east of Golgath towards Norgath. On the horizon the Morianithanlim-Gathr were beginning to rise up out of the mists below in the afternoon light. The Elk Horn Mountains were so named after the many jagged and rough peaks that were virtually impassable from the regions below. Only the most sure-footed, such as the mountain goats, dagger-toothed cats, or the strong-winged, such the Arnyar, could reach the peaks of these rugged mountains. Here is where Orobai and Sto'orn would meet the Council of the Arnyar.

Running below the Morianithanlim-Gathr on its northern side was the Nordlith, the Black River. This river passed from Shashun-Olurn, Salmon Lake, to the eastern seas. Nordlith was named for its slow, dark waters and Shashun-Olurn for the countless salmon that would swim up the Nordlith to spawn in the many creeks that fed into the lake at the headwaters of the river. From the lake, the river meandered east, eventually heading out into the eastern oceans, beyond the northeastern plains at the edge of the Northern Forest, which was still far on the horizon from the Elk Horn Mountains. To the north was the land of the nomadic peoples of the Nordlith, the Yamné, as they called themselves in their tongue, "The People of the River." Orobai knew much of their ways and had spent a great deal of time among them throughout his more recent lives. He had seen them grow and change as a people, as he had with many of the peoples of Aurduin. As he and Sto'orn flew over their lands he thought of their upcoming Winter Feast. An ancient and intricate ritual, Orobai was a regular attendee and he was no doubt expected to attend this year just as he had for many generations now. With the arrival of Miraanni, Orobai wondered if he would have to miss this year's Iryuah'eeh'né, the Yamné's annual "World Renewal Ceremony."

After a long and tiring flight Orobai and Sto'orn were circling about Arnthanlim-Zan, Bull Elk Peak. It would have taken Orobai several days to make this flight on his own, but Sto'orn had pushed him on without rest. Here the great eagles met to discuss matters of importance for all the beings of Aurduin. It was here, many ages ago, that Orobai had first been instructed in the ways of the Altfein-Aryat, before the Arnyar took him to the Orgathen.

On the very pinnacle of the peak was an open space with sharp rocks jutting up to the four directions, only to fall away to sheer cliff faces on all four sides. It was utterly unapproachable save from their air. Here the winds could be vicious as they swept westwards from the open seas and rushed over the ridges of the Morianithanlim-Gathr. This was where the great eagles met, upon one of the highest peaks in Aurduin.

Fortunately for Orobai, the winds from the east were not strong today and the world seemed to breathe with a warm breeze of the coming spring. As they circled, Orobai could see that the council was already gathered, no doubt having been notified by sentinel falcons of their immanent arrival. Orobai and Sto'orn circled twice about the peak in a sunwise manner before descending to the gathering of great eagles below.

The Arnyar had assembled according to direction, as they always did. From each of the Goargathr a wise pair of eagles had come. From Norgath Orobai could see To'wern and Sals'u'un; from Durngath Stal'ru'ki and Woten'i'ir'a; from Avengath Utra'a'ki and So'math; and from Golgath there were Sem'antu and Rowah't. Thus an elder couple of each of the Four Mountains represented their region in the great Council of the Arnyar. For all of Orobai's many lives, this was how the Arnyar always kept council, two eagles from each mountain, a male and a female, aged in wisdom and experience, and fully learned in the Altfein-Aryat. In this manner they had kept the sacred lore alive and the wellbeing of all of Aurduin was their charge. With each generation, the elder eagles selected new representatives among the true Arnyar at the Four Mountains in a mysterious process held secret even from Orobai.

In appearance the Arnyar were not much different from the lesser eagles of the same lands. While there were many kinds of eagles in Aurduin, the Arnyar tended to be most similar to the largest eagles in their regions. From Norgath the Arnyar were almost always the large black-bodied and white-headed and tailed fishing eagles. From Durngath the Arnyar looked closest to the crested grey-and-black-banded eagles of the tropical forests that fed upon large mammals such as sloth and monkey. The most common look of the Avengath Arnyar was very similar to Sto'orn himself with dark banded black and grey wings with brown bodies and a golden crest about the head and upper neck and along the front edges of the wings. And from Golgath the Arnyar tended to be somewhat similar to the Norgath Arnyar except they were substantially larger with more white on their shoulders and enormous beaks that tended to take on a dark orange color with age, as opposed to the bright yellow beaks of the Norgath Arnyar. Regardless of their origin, however, all the Arnyar were impeccable in appearance and had a majesty and grace about them that no other beings could achieve or even hope for.

All of these Arnyar present now, save Utra'a'ki and So'math, had served on the council for many years, crossing several human generations. Unlike lesser eagles, the true Arnyar lived extraordinary long lives by any standard other than Orobai himself. The newest representatives, Utra'a'ki and So'math, had only served at council for a relatively short time, in comparison to the others. There had been trouble in the west many years ago now. The previous representatives had been lost to some accident that Orobai still did not know all the details of, and had needed to be replaced rather abruptly. It had been an unusual transition for the Arnyar that had never been fully explained to Orobai.

Orobai had seen many members of the council come and go in his many lives. He was always impressed at the council's ability to maintain the Altfein-Aryat over so many countless generations of Arnyar. Of all the beings of Aurduin, certainly the Arnyar were the most knowledgeable and subtle, having preserved this most important sacred lore through their bloodlines and their teachings to Orobai. He was always honored to be in their presence.

Sto'orn directed Orobai to fly down to the council. Sto'orn would have to wait elsewhere as only the representatives could take a place at council and lesser eagles were rarely among their audience. Thus Sto'orn and Orobai parted, and Orobai flew to the center of the circle of great birds. Returning to his natural form, Orobai turned and faced all the Arnyar, starting in the east with To'wern and Sals'u'un. He bowed low to each couple, palms pressed together, held at his chest, saying, "Atluin," and addressing each eagle by name. In return each eagle responded by greeting Orobai and using each of his four names as given to him by the Illan. They too bowed low, showing Orobai the respect they held for him.

As with all things with the Arnyar, there was a precise and measured ceremonial rigidity to their actions. All things had their time and place and the proper order must be followed. Thus it was Sals'u'un, the large female eagle from Norgath, who spoke first.

"Grundin Orobai Rundi Eyarlum, we have called you here because there has been a change in the body of Eyar. Two things have come to be on the surface of the earth that have never before been. One has been taken, and continues to be taken, from Jeaniaurduin by the people of the west. More of this Utra'a'ki and So'math will have to speak of later. Also in Jeaniaurduin, you found a great gem, Orobai. This is the second new thing to come forth from the body of Eyar. Never before have we Arnyar encountered such a gem. Not even within our great foresight did we see this. Its manifestation now means that some change has occurred, though we do not yet fully understand it. We also believe that your destiny, Orobai, is approaching, if indeed it is not already upon us."

"The Arnyar first learned of the strange gem some time ago," joined in To'wern where Sals'u'un had left off. "It was the lesser eagles who first spotted it and soon news of this strange gem spread to all the aeries of the Goargathr. We decided that the gem was to be left for you, the Gem Seeker, the Grundin. We have long known that some part of your destiny awaited you in Jeaniaurduin as we have foreseen it in our prescient dreams for many generations. Upon learning of it, we knew that you would eventually find this gem and that through you its meaning would be revealed. We have now heard that you have indeed found the gem and that you have it in your possession at Golgath. We thus wish to learn what you make of it, being greatly learned in all things that come from the body of Eyar, most of all the precious jewels and gems and the sacred Altfein. Speak now, Grundin Orobai Rundi Eyarlum, and tell of this gem and what you know."

Orobai began his tale of how he had found the strange jewel. He told of how he sent it to his home, only upon returning to discover that the gem was not to be found and that a young girl was there in its place. He also told of his recent disturbing dreams in Jeaniaurduin and how they had led him to the jewel. Furthermore he told of the previous night's dream of the jewel changing into the girl.

The Arnyar marveled at Orobai's fascinating story as they listened with rapt attention. Clearly the mysterious appearance of this child was not what they had anticipated hearing from Orobai and the news startled them, though none yet spoke and only listened quietly as the old being spoke. At last, one of the great eagles asked where this strange child was now. Upon hearing that Orobai had left her with wolves, the Arnyar were visibly upset.

"How could you have left her with wolves! Of all beings in Aurduin, why wolves?" thundered Stal'ru'ki from Durngath. "Wolves are not to be trusted. They are far too clever in looking out for their own interests to be left with a young girl. That's like giving them a gift of a choice meal, Orobai! What kind of judgment is this?"

"It was my best judgment," answered Orobai cautiously. "Faen has been a friend and sometimes companion for many years – for her entire life, in fact – and I have long kept a friendship with the wolves of the Northern Forest. Though they are clever and seek out their own needs and desires, as you say, Stal'ru'ki, I have known them to be true to their word and of good judgment. The girl, Miraanni, as I call her, is safe in Faen's keeping until I return. Faen would do nothing to raise my anger and is filled with her own motherly love at this time as she is nursing two cubs. She has taken to the girl as if she were one of her own. I could do no less than enlist her aid as I myself cannot nourish and care for a child such as this. Faen is the girl's very link to life at the moment, and without her I would have no hope of the girl living more than a few days. The girl was already in my home crying for several days before I arrived, according to Faen, and very possibly she was there longer than that, given the time it took me to return from Nulthali."

"This may be as you say, Orobai," commented Woten'i'ir'a, the great she-eagle from Durngath, "but this is not suitable as a permanent solution to this problem. What will happen when the wolf needs to return to her pack, which surely will come sooner or later? And what about her two cubs? They will soon grow large and curious! You do not know these two and therefore cannot trust them as you would their mother."

The council all agreed with Woten'i'ir'a. Wolves were not to be trusted with this young girl who was obviously of some as-yet-unknown significance. Some better arrangements would have to be made, and quickly. To this all agreed and they set about discussing the matter.

Orobai had his own idea and decided to propose it. "I think I should take the girl to live with some of the people of Aurduin," he said. "I myself cannot raise her. When she is older, I will happily take charge of the girl and watch after her according to your wishes and foresight. For now, she needs a home and a mother. I can set about this as soon as I return to my home and the girl." Orobai already felt better at the thought of being relieved of this strange burden.

The council was pleased at this thought but were unsure to whom Orobai should take the girl. It was then that Utra'a'ki and So'math spoke openly. "Before we decide where the girl should go, we should discuss the matter of the people of the west. It is because of them that these events have perhaps come to pass and thus they are crucial in our decision-making. It was their doing that brought the two of us to this council in the first place. Orobai does not know of this and he should now."

The others agreed. Orobai looked about at the great eagles and they all shifted almost imperceptibly, but Orobai could see their discomfort. This was heavy news he was about to receive.

So'math continued, "The two who came before us, Tur'orn and Ya'lan were not lost in an accident, as you have been led to believe. The truth is that the people of the west killed them. Never in all the history of Aurduin have the peoples of this land dared, or even been able, to kill one of the great Arnyar. Lesser eagles may be taken by people, but never a true Arnyar . . . not until now."

Orobai could hardly believe his ears. It seemed impossible, but the Arnyar would not deceive him. It had to be true.

"For many years, the people of the west have taken to devices of their own making," said So'math. "We do not understand these things that are made of metal, and seem to move about on their own, without people or beasts to power them, and they shoot lightning at will. I tell you, great and strange changes have taken place within their society. At first these new creations were limited to the farthest islands of the western archipelago, but they have consistently moved further east and have now come to the mainland with their strange devices. With these things they murdered Ya'lan and Tur'orn, even taking what remained of their burnt and tortured bodies. These people have committed a great offense not only against the Arnyar, but against all the beings who are under the protection and sight of the Arnyar."

"But there is more to this than even this great offense," added Utra'a'ki, staring down hard at Orobai. "For the people of the west are the ones who have been digging on the edge of Jeaniaurduin in Nulthali. Using other peoples to do their deadly work, the westerners are digging in Eyar and bringing up some mineral, some kind of stone, which they use as a source of power. But the stone is deadly and everywhere they bring it to the surface, death and disease follows. This could be the 'serpents' you have reported seeing in your dreams. This is why they do not dig it themselves, but rather use others to do their bidding and take the punishment of the earth for their actions. As they move east, more free peoples fall under their power. Already many cultures have been affected and we fear that there will be no stop to this ruthless expansion. While Aurduin has seen its share of the violence that can be wrought by humankind, what happens now is unprecedented. Thus, wherever you take the child, it must not be to the west or to the nomadic peoples where she may be captured and forced to work as a slave. I fear that such a mistake could mean disaster, perhaps for us all," concluded Utra'a'ki.

"Though we do not know what all of this means, we feel that there is a connection between the digging, the stones they use for power, and this jewel-girl you have found, Orobai," spoke Sem'antu, hardly giving Orobai a moment to take in all he had already been told. "In some manner all these are tied together, and are intimate to your destiny. This is the unfinished teaching of the Altfein-Aryat, the end for which you yourself were created as the Preserver of the Four Ways. There is a terrible sickness growing in Jeaniaurduin. You yourself have seen it. Now there is the appearance of this special girl. But we do not yet understand what role she has to play in this or her relationship to you. It very well may be that you two are Elder Brother and Younger Sister to each other, as you recounted from your dream. It would indeed explain much, and if so, then you two together are of the utmost importance, though your destinies may lie along different paths. This we are not able to see."

Orobai was amazed by these revelations. Indeed, he had already felt and guessed as much, but the words of the council brought the conclusion home forcefully. They were taking these developments with the utmost seriousness, which meant that Orobai must as well. He knew that according to the Altfein-Aryat, it was not known whether he would exist long enough to fulfill his mysterious destiny. All that was known was that at some point, the "Preserver of the Four Ways" would be needed, as would his ability to work with the Altfein. Nowhere was the role of a girl prophesized, but it was also true that the test to which Orobai would eventually be put was unknown, as were the circumstances of the foreseen cataclysm.

"I will take the child to Laftandiar-Urya," proposed Orobai at last. "There she will be protected in the City of the Rising Sun by their wise women. They will appreciate and care for her like none other, of that I am certain. This is far from the west and there she will be safe."

"Are you sure you can trust those people?" asked To'wern. "They are distantly related to the aggressive westerners. They may share something of their ways."

"The Ulusi-Rata of Laftandiar-Urya parted ways with the people of the west many thousands of years ago," countered Orobai. "They are ethical and wise. I can think of no better place for the child." *And besides*, thought Orobai, *given their distant relation, perhaps they will be able to shed some light on these westerners and their motives . . .*

The Arnyar pondered this for a time and discussed what other possibilities might resolve the issue before them. At last they agreed that Laftandiar-Urya seemed the best choice and that this should be Orobai's destination with the child. They also decided that Orobai was not to go without a watchful escort. They chose Sto'orn to travel with him and report back to the council of any important tidings.

"One final matter awaits us, Orobai," spoke Rowah't at long last. "There is something of the greatest significance that you must do."

"Tell me and I will do as you bid," said Orobai, respectfully.

"You must perform a vision quest and ritual, the likes of which has never before taken place in Aurduin. For this you must travel to each of the Orgathen. At each Mountain you will find one Sarnfein and one Alkeinfein. You will know them by their unique and individual natures. Finding them will be different for each Mountain and thus you must follow your insight and intuition carefully. Trust what your heart tells you. You must find the right ones! To choose incorrectly in this could be disastrous. More than this we cannot say, for we cannot make the decision for you. It is your burden and yours alone.

"You will also need to collect many other stones from the Great Mountains, as we will show you. These stones you will need to crush into fine-grained sands. You will need to take with you water from each of the Four Mountains, enough to keep the Altfein in. Your quest will begin with Norgath in the east and conclude with Golgath in the north. During this time you must not deviate or become distracted, for your concentration and meditation will be all-important to the success of your quest. We cannot stress this enough, Orobai. You must concentrate! Set your mind firmly to what you need to do. Fix your intentions and do not wander from the path of completion!

"Once you have done these things you will need to perform a vision ritual. You are to use the stones, sands, and waters precisely as we show you. Any mistake will render the process ineffectual and you will have to begin again. As you can surely understand, there is not time to suffer such a careless mistake. When done correctly, this will give you direct contact with the spirit of the Illan. Perhaps they may reveal your destiny to you at that time. We do not know what they will show you or what will happen. Indeed, it may very well be your undoing and end, for perhaps they may take you with them. We cannot say.

"We have known for generations that this time would come and that it would be our last teaching of the Altfein-Aryat to you, Grundin Orobai Rundi Eyarlum, but we do not know to what end it will come. The future is uncertain, and not just in this, mind you. Before our inner eyes there is a darkness that cannot be penetrated. The future shifts and ebbs in currents we can no longer follow. The future, which once presented itself to us in streams of possibilities and rivers of manifestation, has sunk beneath the surface, like the water that flows from the Goarnaltrai into Jeaniaurduin. We know not where it goes or where it may emerge, if it emerges at all.

"Unlike us, Orobai, you have not had the gift of prescience. Nor have you ever communed directly with the Illan. Always you have had to rely on our own memory of the Illan and our preservation of the Altfein-Aryat. This ritual, this vision, will change these limitations that have been placed upon you. In this ritual that you will perform, we believe that the Illan will make a final revelation directly to you. They will show you the future, Orobai. We believe they will show you what must be done, and what your part is. It will be the fulfillment of the Altfein-Aryat."

Having made this fateful pronouncement, the Arnyar began a direct mind-to-mind teaching, pouring their knowledge of the ritual and quest that Orobai must perform directly from their collective mind into his, which was how they always shared the more esoteric aspects of the Altfein-Aryat. The teaching hit Orobai with a direct and palpable force as it worked its way into his consciousness. He could see and feel an image or diagram that he was to make with the crushed gems. It was rich with symbolism and seemed to overflow with meaning. Each grain of sand, each shade, each shape, each color, all of it had meaning and its own logic. He reveled in its profound newness, yet also felt deeply at home within this teaching and it felt right to him, as if it were something he had always known but somehow forgotten. The meaning was rushing through him like a torrent and the exact sequence of events and images was firmly impressed upon his mind. Without words and in complete silence, all was made known to Orobai and he knew precisely what he must do.

An Invitation

Orobai and Sto'orn returned to Orobai's home by Golgath in the early morning before the rising of Urya and the setting of the full face of Ranya. Sarnrhobi, the Morning Star, was just showing itself in the eastern horizon and the air was brisk and heavy with nighttime moisture.

Even at a distance Orobai and Sto'orn could see that they were not returning to Orobai's home unaccompanied. There in a glade, near Orobai's home, they saw a kughain of the Yamné, the spherical lodge of willow tree and elk-hide that the People of the River used as their portable shelters as they ranged about the river and the Northern Forest. The visitors were still asleep and no one had yet come out to greet the new day. Orobai looked carefully at the kughain but did not recognize any distinguishing marks about it. He'd be surprised if it weren't his friend T'lan, or at least one of his relatives, come to invite him to their winter ceremony. Regardless, they'd wait in the grove for Orobai to come to them and would not encroach on his home, for certainly the great Mu'shué would know when they had arrived. Though tired, Orobai was looking forward to speaking with them.

Sto'orn could only see this development as an inconvenience. His impatient looks at Orobai indicated that he thought they would complicate the task of taking Miraanni to the east as the Arnyar desired. "What are you going to do about these travelers at your door?" Sto'orn demanded of Orobai forcefully. "We can't be bothered by them now when we have to move quickly with the child."

"They won't be a problem," said Orobai. "In fact, they may be just what we are looking for – a way to travel with the girl down the Nordlith to the east. And besides, in a hurry or not, I am tired and need to rest. I had just returned from a long journey and then you have me set off for council and make me fly all through the day and night. Now I need some time to rest and regain my strength before I go anywhere or do anything. My limbs are weary and I long for a good sit by the fire with some nice tea and a little music for but a while before we go. I will need two days, I think, before I will be rested enough to carry on."

A week would be even better, Orobai thought to himself.

"All right, Old Feather," resigned Sto'orn, seeing the weariness in Orobai. He had pushed him hard and he knew it, making him fly non-stop like that. "I'll be nearby for a few days, keeping a watch on you from a distance. I don't want to get too close or those river people might try and take my feathers. Four mornings from now I will return and you will be ready to set out to the east without delay, I trust."

"Most reasonable of you, Master Eagle," said Orobai, thankful for more days than he had asked for. "In the meantime, I'll take care of the Yamné. You'll see – they're just what we would have had to go looking for if they hadn't had the foresight to show up here first," said Orobai reassuringly.

Sto'orn flew off into the nearby forest, but not too far, where he could keep an eye on Orobai. The old raven flew to his door, changed his form, and quietly entered the house. There, by the dying fire, were Faen, Elkil, Fenruk and little Miraanni – beautiful little Miraanni, his little sister. Orobai's heart warmed to look upon her, curled up between the two wolf pups. Even in the darkness she shone with a light that was all her own. Orobai quietly went and placed a little more wood on the coals to rekindle the fire. At this Faen stirred and looked up at Orobai. Seeing the weariness on his face she simply acknowledged his presence and went back to sleep. Orobai slowly eased himself down into his chair and felt himself drift off to a quiet and peaceful sleep. His urgent mission would have to wait just a little longer.

* * * *

Orobai awoke sometime in the afternoon to find Faen lying at his feet with Miraanni resting quietly at her stomach. The two cubs were clumsily playing and tumbling over each other some distance away. After preparing himself some tea, he sat back down to speak with the old wolf.

"Faen," he began, "much has been revealed and there is now something very important for me to do. Though it is much to ask, I would have you help me, if you are willing. I must take the child to Laftandiar-Urya to live amongst the Ulusi-Rata for some time. This is by decree of the Council of the Arnyar and I must follow their wishes in this. As you well know, I cannot take care of the girl, Miraanni. If you would travel with us to the east, then she would have someone to care for her on our journey, someone to give her the sustenance that she needs and that I cannot provide. I know that it is a long journey and that you and your children will be separated from your family. The decision is yours. But I do not know how else to care for her. She needs a mother, and you are the only mother she has, at the moment."

Faen considered Orobai's plea. Having known Orobai all her life, since she was a new-born pup, she knew that Orobai never asked things of others lightly and preferred to do things on his own. To travel so far from the wolf pack, and having two young cubs besides, was much to ask. But she knew that she had come by Orobai's at this time for a reason and perhaps even her own cubs were bound to this purpose, having come early into the world themselves.

30

At last she answered. "I will need to think on this, Orobai," said the old wolf. "How long is it before you must begin this journey that I may consider your request?"

"We have three nights before you must decide," said Orobai, and that was the last that was spoken of it between them for the time.

* * * *

When the next morning arrived Orobai decided it was time to visit with the Yamné, who would surely be anxious to meet with Mu'shué, the "One Who Sings with Images," as they often called him. Being well rested, Orobai strode out into the glade in an almost youthful fashion with renewed energy in his mind, body, heart, and spirit. A small Yamné girl was the first to see him coming and called out to a group of men who were behind the kughain. One came forward to await Orobai's arrival as two others went into the kughain. They quickly came out again with two women and a few children, along with a pile of different pelts and stores of dried meat and salmon. They had clearly come with Orobai's invitation to the Iryuah'eeh'né, the Winter Feast or "World Renewal" ceremony, which the Yamné held late each winter. With this ceremony the Yamné did their ritual part of ensuring the coming of spring and a bountiful new year.

For more years than Orobai could count, he had been a participant in this sacred ceremony, joining his voice with their holy people to sing the new year into being in beauty and harmony. The Yamné had long marveled at his singing ability and the way that the light of Altfein danced about him as his voice flowed out of his inner being like liquid sound. It was the perfect complement to their ceremonies and they treasured the years when he could be present.

And there was another reason they would come to Orobai as well. Orobai had a habit of collecting many things in Aurduin, including the Ul'mult'ah, the sacred mushrooms of Jeaniaurduin. The Yamné ate these visionary mushrooms in their ceremony and they were a regular feature of their spiritual life, especially for their holy people. But Jeaniaurduin was far from their lands and they had learned long ago that they could rely on Orobai to have enough for their ceremonies ready for them when they came to visit him. Even on Orobai's recent stay in Jeaniaurduin he had gathered a significant collection of the "Giver of Exalted Visions" in anticipation of this meeting.

Orobai knew the man who awaited him by the kughain. It was Gen'shu'n, son of an elder Want'é, a Holy One, a seer and healer of the Yamné named T'lan. Gen'shu'n had no doubt been sent by his father to ask Mu'shué about attending the Winter Feast and for the trade of Ul'mult'ah for the skins and dried meats that they had brought with them.

Orobai was the first to extend a greeting. "Atluin, Gen'shu'n," he said in Illan, walking directly up to the young man with a warm and inviting smile.

"Atluin Mu'shué," responded the handsome and proud Gen'shu'n, showing Orobai respect by answering in his own tongue.

31

"It is good to see you, son of my old friend, T'lan." Knowing full well the answer to his question, Orobai asked, "What is it that brings you to this glade by my home this winter?"

"We have come as the Winter Feast is upon us when the moon turns her face away from the earth in two weeks time. We would have the great honor of your company for the feast and my father has also instructed me to bring a trade for the Ul'mult'ah," answered Gen'shu'n. "For this we have brought you many pelts of fine quality and a store of dried meats and salmon. We are sure that it will all be to your liking."

At that Orobai was invited to come and inspect the items for trade with a gesture by Gen'shu'n. The others who were standing about by the goods moved aside to let Orobai have a look. The quality of the skins was indeed fine. There was worked buckskin, doeskin, elk hide, and even a wrap of bear fur. As for meat, there was dried and spiced deer and elk meat along with strips of smoked salmon. Gen'shu'n came over and offered a sample of the salmon to Orobai who gladly took the proffered fish. Orobai found its taste exquisite and did not hesitate a moment to accept the trade, wiping the fish grease off his fingers. Really, the trade was largely a kind gesture. Orobai would gladly provide the sacramental mushrooms regardless of what he was offered. He was simply happy to be able to do some small service for the Yamné and to have the pleasure of attending their ceremony. Orobai was admittedly fascinated by human cultures, and the Yamné had provided much for Orobai to ponder over the years. And in many respects, the Yamné were the closest Orobai had to family, until the appearance of Miraanni, that is.

The trade agreed upon, Gen'shu'n asked the two other men to carry the gifts up to Orobai's home. Orobai followed after them and after showing them where to leave the items, shuffled back into his storeroom. There he found a generous bag of the mushrooms, which he had dried while at Lilgurinlth and sent back before him. "What wonders will you reveal this year?" Orobai asked the mushrooms as he peered into the bag, looking over their dried and shriveled forms. How strange it was that something so small and ordinary could be so profound, he thought. He caught a waft of their earthy scent and his memory drifted through the many times he had eaten them with the Yamné. How many times had it been now, he wondered. It seemed as if he had always known the Yamné and shared in their ceremonies.

Orobai walked back over to the glade where Gen'shu'n was waiting, playing with the children. Seeing Orobai approach, the young man stood up rigidly and prepared to receive Orobai's gift in the proper way. Orobai first offered the mushrooms to the four directions, starting in the east, and then raising them to the sky, the earth, and finally gesturing to Gen'shu'n four times. At the fourth gesture Gen'shu'n accepted the sacrament and followed the same procedure as Orobai, offering them to the four directions and the above and below while saying the proper set of ritual prayers.

"I happily accept your offer to be a guest at this year's Feast," said Orobai at the completion of the brief ritual. "I will arrive within two weeks time before the moon fully turns her face from us. I will have travelers with me. While they will not be what you might expect, they will need to be shown the proper respect and deference. When I come you will understand," said Orobai.

"Anyone whom Mu'shué would bring with him will be given all the respect of an honored guest, for we know that you would not bring strangers among us who would themselves be disrespectful of our ways," assured Gen'shu'n. "We will show them all the respect that we would show you."

"Very good," said Orobai. "Then you may look for Mu'shué when Ranya turns her face."

"Good," said Gen'shu'n. "My father will be happy to hear this news. We will look for you when Ranya turns her face. Together, we will all sing in the new year in beauty."

* * * *

The next few days were relaxing and Orobai felt even more invigorated and began to look forward to their journey together. The more time he spent with Miraanni, the more comfortable he became and he grew to like the thought of her as his little sister. Indeed, it almost seemed natural and he began to take pleasure in the thought of having a true family, and the thought of showing her off to the Yamné was a new kind of excitement for him. What would they think of her, he wondered. There was no doubt in his mind that they would accept her just as they had accepted him. Yes, he was looking forward to this Winter Feast. This was going to be something special.

On the last evening before they were to depart, Orobai sat by his fire and took out his andrim, his homemade stringed instrument. It had been a while since he had played it. He tuned it up and strummed a few chords. Its strings needed replacing before too long, but the tone was still good and its soft sound resonated about the room. Miraanni perked up instantly upon hearing it, staring intently at the instrument in Orobai's hands. Orobai suddenly realized that he had not yet made any music nor sung any songs in Miraanni's presence. He thought that he should play something that might be soothing and pleasurable for the child. It was, after all, a human custom to sing sweet songs for babies, and Orobai saw no reason that he should not do so for his own little sister. Why it took him this long to think of it seemed silly to Orobai now, but then again, he was new at this, so better late than never.

Orobai began to play. At first he quietly plucked at the strings, regaining his feel for them. He began to hum along with a beautiful little melody, which brought out the power of the Altfein, though only subtly. Miraanni noticed this change immediately and gazed intently at Orobai and the subtle movements of lights about him and the slight distortions of the objects in front of her. Seeing her reaction, Orobai began to sing more strongly now, letting his voice come out in full with its many layered and rich overtones. At this the Altfein jumped to life and soon the room was filled with their brilliant show of light and geometric forms. Miraanni was delighted and stared before her with eyes opened wide.

Closing his eyes, Orobai concentrated on his song, thinking of how he wanted to make it beautiful for his little sister. But then he noticed something strange. Mixed in with his own voice, Orobai could hear something that reminded him of the sound that the gem had made when he first came upon it. It was soft and as yet still immature, but it was there. Looking at Miraanni, Orobai saw that her mouth was open and was imitating the shape of his mouth and lips. She was trying to sing with him! Making his own voice softer, he could hear her little voice clearly now, and just like him, she was singing with multiple tones. How beautiful it was! What joy it brought to Orobai to be joined in song by this child, this strange little being. She could follow his melody perfectly, adding in complex harmonies of her own, giving it a richness and depth that he could never have achieved individually.

It was then that Orobai noticed that the work of the Altfein was affected by Miraanni's singing as well. He was no longer the sole director of their shape and image for Miraanni was directing them as well. The interplay of light and form took on a quality that Orobai had never before experienced. There was more power, energy, and purpose behind the ever-changing play of geometric light. At first the patterns were indistinct and Orobai could not clearly make out what was there. But as it grew clearer and became more defined, Orobai could see a perfect image of Golgath, down to every last detail. Orobai could even see his home and all the places on the Mountain. He then noticed, in looking at the image of his home, that there was something different. There, directly by his home, he could distinctly see a spring of fresh mountain water where none had been before. Around the spring were many beautiful flowers and plants of all kinds. It was like a small piece of Lilgurinlth right by his home. It was as if the child could look into his heart and had sung forth a little bit of that place he so loved.

The image then changed from looking at Orobai's home to looking out across the landscape to the east. Orobai could see Shashun-Olurn with the waters of the Nordlith flowing from it. Along the bank of the lake and river he could see the Yamné in their preparations for the Iryuah'eeh'né. Beyond this were the Morianithanlim-Gathr and farther still, he could see the mountains of Laftandiar-Urya. It was the course of their journey! It suddenly occurred to Orobai that Miraanni seemed to know where they were going and what they were doing. She was somehow aware of the events surrounding her and was expressing this in the music that they were creating together.

Shocked at the revelation, Orobai abruptly broke off his singing. Miraanni seemed somewhat dismayed by this sudden end, looking at Orobai quizzically. "How do you know these things?" asked Orobai aloud. "You are but a small child yet you are aware! Truly you are a marvel in all of Aurduin, little sister!"

Miraanni simply smiled up at Orobai as he took her into his arms. He held her to his chest and gently rocked her in his chair before the fire. He thought that this was enough singing for the night, for who knows what this strange child could do with the power of the Altfein clearly at her command. A strange and wonderful child indeed!

"Soon we will travel across Aurduin, and then I will show you to all the people who mean something to me," Orobai cooed softly to his little sister as her eyes began to close. In a short while they were both asleep before the glowing fire, with anticipation for their journey in their hearts and images of their passage floating through their minds. In the morning, the long trip to the east would begin.

To Shashun-Olurn

When morning came everything was ready. Orobai had packed the meat from the Yamné along with various dried fruits and nuts that he had stored away. He also packed some of the clays and pollens that he had collected in Jeaniaurduin for the Yamné and others he might meet along the way, along with some semi-precious stones such as turquoise and quartz. For Miraanni, Orobai had created a comfortable sling that he could wear across his chest to keep her safe and warm. For the cubs, he had also fashioned a backpack where they could curl up together as they were still too young to walk very far on their own.

The night before Faen had reached her decision regarding Orobai's request. As Orobai knew she would, she agreed to accompany them and serve as a mother for Miraanni. She was quite fond of little Miraanni by this point, having nursed her for nearly a week now, and did not want to abandon her to fate. Faen thus told Orobai that she would journey as far as need be to ensure that Miraanni found a safe home in the east. By that time the cubs should be big enough to make their way with her back to the Northern Forest and eventually rejoin the wolf pack. Until then, she would keep Orobai and Miraanni company and help in any way she could.

Together they all set foot outdoors into the brightening world, ready for their journey. Orobai had slung Miraanni across his chest, and readied the bag to carry the two cubs. Orobai also fitted Faen with some bags slung over her back to carry their supplies. It was an awkward arrangement for the proud wolf, but she understood the greater need and thus suffered the indignity of being used as a domestic animal, but only for Orobai.

Immediately, something peculiar caught Orobai's eye. There, in a small glade in front of Orobai's home was a beautiful spring with many plants, flowers, and herbs growing about it as though it had been there for generations. The clear water bubbled up and ran in a small trickle down to the creek below where Orobai did his fishing.

"What strange magic is this?" proclaimed Faen, fully aware that the spring had not been there before. Cautiously she crept up to the spring, sniffing the air, and then finally tested the water. "The water is good, and by the looks of it, I would say that this spring has always been here, what with all these good herbs growing about it. Is this your doing, Orobai?"

"I suppose in a sense it was, Faen," answered Orobai, unsure of his own answer. "Last night Miraanni and I were singing together and in a vision I saw this very spring. I wondered why it was in the vision for there has never been a spring at my door, yet here it is!"

"So you made this? How?" asked Faen.

"I cannot say exactly," said Orobai, "only that Miraanni had some doing in this."

More than that he would not say, but Orobai knew the greater significance of this development. In all his many years of working with the Altfein, he had never created anything in the manner of the Illan, something with an independent existence. As his name among the Yamné described, he had the ability to create images of things through song and could also distort and alter his own appearance and physical form, but he had never truly made something independent of himself in this manner. His creations were only temporary, and though seemingly very real, real enough to drive the ravens away from Sto'orn, for example, they lasted only as long as he directed his mind towards them. He did not, by himself, have the power of true creation to sing beings into existence or actually alter the shape of Eyar, as did the Illan. According to the Altfein-Aryat, the Illan accomplished such feats in a minimum of co-creating pairs, one using the Sarnfein and the other using the Alkeinfein. Only in combination could such true creation take place, and as Orobai was always an individual, he had never had this power, despite his knowledge. With Miraanni here, the possibilities were obviously different. Between the two of them, they wielded the power of true creation. Miraanni, like Orobai before her, was now an able practitioner of the Altfein-Aryat. It was a profound revelation and had deep implications.

This was not knowledge that Orobai wanted known. The Illan had purposefully created the beings of Aurduin to be ignorant of the use of the Altfein. They had to rely on the powers of their own minds and the works of their bodies to engage in acts of creation. As Orobai understood it, the Illan had never intended humans or other beings to know the Aryat. They deemed this power far too dangerous, at least in potential. Humans, for all their intelligence, could not be trusted, or so the Arnyar were fond of saying.

It was this same sense of caution that guided Orobai now, knowing that the awareness of the combined power of Miraanni and himself could be a very dangerous thing. Who knows what plans might be devised to use or coerce them for others' intentions and designs. He had seen humans exploit power before and knew that they would do so again, if given the chance. This was a secret he must guard carefully.

Happily, Faen did not inquire further, knowing that Orobai would tell more if he desired or deemed it necessary. It was not her place to press him so she simply enjoyed the refreshing drink that the new spring provided. It did raise her curiosity, however, as to what might develop on this journey of theirs, for certainly strange forces were at work.

It was then that Faen noticed Sto'orn sitting in a nearby tree. Immediately she went on the defensive and bristled up her hackles, bared her teeth, and gave a menacing snarl. While lesser eagles would not bother a full grown wolf, they were known to take cubs unawares, and Elkil and Fenruk were carelessly tumbling over each other, simply excited to be outside and exploring the world, Orobai not yet having tucked them into the pack he had fashioned for them.

Noticing Faen's quick change in demeanor, Orobai looked up at Sto'orn in the tree. "Have no fear, Faen," said Orobai calmly. "This is Sto'orn, servant of the Council of the Arnyar. You have nothing to fear from him. He will be our companion and will do nothing to bother your cubs. You have my word," Orobai assured her.

At that Sto'orn flew down to them and perched on a nearby rock, just out of reach of Faen, who still looked distrustfully at the golden eagle, letting her fangs show as her bristled hackles slowly lowered.

"So what is this?" asked Sto'orn. "I presume that this is the she-wolf you spoke of before. Surely she will not be going with us to the east?"

"Yes, she will, Sto'orn," answered Orobai. "I have need of her yet, for Miraanni is still dependent upon her milk. Without her we would have no hope of succeeding in this quest. If you two can get along, which I certainly hope you can, then we will have no problems." Orobai smiled at the two, the wolf and eagle, showing that he would not tolerate anything less than full cooperation by the hint of firmness in his dark eyes.

"Very well," replied Sto'orn grudgingly. "I will trust your judgment in this. But what of the River People? You had mentioned before that they might be of help. You sent them away four days ago. How is that of help to us?"

"Oh, they are still very much of help. It is my hope that they will provide us with a boat to journey down the Nordlith to the east. Surely you don't think that someone my age would be able to walk all that distance?" asked Orobai. "They have invited me to their Winter Feast, and I have accepted. We will all attend together, and by gaining their favor, make use of one of their fine boats. We'll have a pleasant ride down the river, all the way to the east."

"This is becoming ever more complicated," said Sto'orn with an edge of irritation in his voice.

"We'll see," was Orobai's easy response.

All disagreements aside, the companions set out together. Glancing back over his shoulder at the spring one last time, still marveling at its creation but not wanting to give his thoughts away, Orobai was happy that Sto'orn either did not notice or perhaps did not care about the strange appearance of the spring. Sto'orn had no idea how complicated this really could be.

* * * *

Despite Orobai's age, the journey went well. He truly felt buoyed up by Miraanni's presence and his mind was busy contemplating the latest revelation of their intimate relationship. The cubs were happy to snuggle together in their pack and Miraanni was peaceful. She occasionally cried out of hunger, at which times the company would stop and each have something to eat and some rest. Sto'orn flew above them, always keeping them in sight, and when they rested he would go off on his own to hunt for something to eat, not wanting to partake of the dried meats the Yamné had supplied. At night Orobai built a fire to keep them warm and they all curled up together, while Sto'orn roosted in a nearby tree.

Their journey carried them around the south side of Golgath. Here there was a path that the Yamné took to Orobai's when they came to trade or to get to the Goldlith on Orobai's side of the Great Mountain. The path was relatively well used so they had no trouble following it. Though Orobai usually liked to sing as he walked along, as was his custom, he forsook this comfort on this journey, not wanting to arouse Miraanni and have another strange event to explain as had happened with the spring at his home.

As the days passed the face of Ranya became smaller and smaller until it was a thin sliver in the night sky. It would soon be time for the Ceremony. They would have to make good time. Orobai urged his companions on, telling them that he wanted to make the western shores of Shashun-Olurn before nightfall. Only a day or two remained before the ceremony would begin. They quickened their pace and kept going with only minimal rests.

At twilight they came upon a ridge where they could look down on the lake. There on the far northern shore they could see many Yamné dwellings. It was clear that this was to be a grand ceremony and that many bands of the River People had come together to commemorate this important annual event. There were perhaps several hundred families in all, by Orobai's count, given the number of structures and burning fires. In the center of their temporary village was a series of large ceremonial structures made of pine and oak trees, each with a large central fire. There were seven such structures, the Yamné's ceremonial Shan'i'ruh, all stretching in a line from west to east, gradually increasing in size with the largest in the east. Orobai had seen this architecture many times and his heart was glad upon seeing it again.

"What do we do now?" asked Sto'orn. "It is too late for us to travel all the way around to the other side tonight. Perhaps we should rest here."

"No, I don't think so," said Orobai. "It's best that we reach the village. We won't have to walk, however," he said as his gaze followed the line of Faen's attention.

Faen had noticed some movement below them at the bottom of the ridge and was focused intently with ears perked and nose raised in the air to catch any peculiar scents that might be drifting her way. There, below the ridge, emerging from the brush into the fading light, were two young men.

"Umyu'á!" called out Orobai in the Yamné greeting to the two figures below. "T'anli Mu'shué. It's the One Who Sings with Images. T'lan is expecting me and my company. Will you take us to him?"

"Umyu'á," answered the two men together. "We have been told to look for you. Wait there and we will show you the way down. The Want'é is expecting you. We were afraid you might not arrive before the ceremony begins, but you are in time, for the ceremony is not until tomorrow night."

It took a few moments for the two young men to reach Orobai and his companions. They were visibly startled to find Orobai with a wolf and eagle by his side, hesitating a moment to assess the situation. The Yamné knew Orobai was a friend of the beasts, but this was quite unexpected. He had never before brought such company with him.

Seeing their perplexed looks, Orobai stated, "The wolf and eagle are my companions. They will not cause you any trouble. The eagle will need for nothing other than to be left alone, and it goes without question that his feathers are his own. As for the wolf, she is a vital part of my company and will stay with me. Though you may fear her, there is no cause for worry."

The two young men accepted this and did not ask any questions. By the fading light they led Orobai and Faen, unaware of the child under Orobai's cloak and the cubs at his back, down the ridge to the lake's edge where several boats were pulled up on the shore. They all climbed into one of the larger boats and the two men respectfully bore them to the far shore in silence. Not wanting to be ferried across, Sto'orn flew in gentle circles above them, patiently waiting for them to reach the shore.

The lake was beautiful, Orobai thought. On a calm evening such as this the colors of the sky reflected in its smooth waters and the gentle shimmering of stars danced on its surface. To the west loomed the eastern peak of Golgath, which appeared now as a dark monolith in the night sky beyond the foothills and low valleys, watching over all that took place below it, catching even this small boat in its ever watchful gaze.

Upon reaching the far shore, the young men asked Orobai and his company to wait while they went to find T'lan. A short while later, T'lan and a small company of elders came to greet them at the lakeside, bearing torches so that they might see in the waning twilight.

Despite his advancing age, T'lan was still a striking figure, as were his other elderly companions. The Yamné took great pride in personal dignity and strove for impeccability in appearance, demeanor, and behavior. Such mores were amplified at such a time as this and the Yamné tended to look and act their best at ceremonial occasions, and there was no more important ceremony than the Iryuah'eeh'né.

The group of elders came forward in full ceremonial regalia. Their clothes were filled with emblems and symbols of their positions within Yamné society. They wore their finest deer-hide clothing of intricately worked leather embossed with esoteric symbols and designs that served as a visual grammar of Yamné spiritual power. Finely polished shells that glimmered and danced in the firelight decorated their clothing which was accented by carefully placed colorful stones and highly polished beads made from the seeds of various plants. Upon their heads each wore further symbols of their ceremonial roles indicating which society they belonged to or what their personal spiritual power was. Having obviously come from a prayer meeting, their faces were covered with dried white clay, which made them look almost ghostly in the twilight and flicker of the flames.

T'lan stood somewhat taller than the rest. He had been very handsome as a youth, and even in his old age the sharp lines of his weathered face gave one the impression of strength and wisdom. One only need look into his dark eyes to know that he had endured much in his life and had sought out the deeper meanings of things. One could also see his patience that had come with age. As a young man T'lan had been quick to act, as many young men are, and had been eager for results. Now, in his elder days, there was a peace and quiet about him that could only come from years of careful contemplation and learning the ways of spirit. T'lan had become the archetypal Yamné Want'é, or Holy Person. As the Yamné would say, he had reached his "point of completion," for he no longer "walked the path," but had "become the path." It was high praise and it was well deserved.

"Atluin, Mu'shué," said T'lan, greeting Orobai. "It is good to see that you have arrived safely."

"Atluin T'lan," said Orobai in response. "It is also good to see you and so many of your people gathered for the Feast. I can see that it will be a grand ceremony."

"That indeed!" said T'lan joyfully, clasping Orobai's weathered black hand in his own and extending his other to Orobai's shoulder with a firm grip that communicated his subtle but deep joy upon seeing his old friend.

The others stood back, respectfully, and also clearly wary of Faen and Sto'orn. Orobai could see their apprehension and said so that they all might hear, "These are my companions. They will cause you no trouble. I ask only that they be shown the proper respect."

"Of course," said T'lan quickly. "We would not do otherwise for companions of Mu'shué. Gen'shu'n had told me that you would bring unexpected companions with you, but I must say that this is not what we imagined. As I am sure that you know, while we respect the wolves, we have never taken one into our company before and thus you can understand our wariness. Never before has one come to us with such a companion and requested lodging."

"I hope you understand that it is of my own need that the beasts travel with me," said Orobai. "The wolf, Faen, is crucial to my journey, and she herself is with pups, which I carry upon my back. At my breast I carry my own infant sister, whom Faen has been gracious enough to nurse. The lesser eagle, Sto'orn, is here as a sentinel for our company and is not at leave to part from us."

Hearing this, T'lan and the group of elders were greatly astounded. Learning that Orobai had a sister was like hearing something beyond all imagination. After all, Orobai had been coming around the Yamné for hundreds of years now, if not longer, and never had anything such as this taken place.

"Very well," said T'lan after considering the situation for a few moments in silence. "I trust you in this and will leave the beasts in your care. I ask only that the wolf not roam about the village, as she will only scare the people. One of our young hunters might mistakenly try to kill her. I therefore request that she remain in the kughain that we have set up for you. The eagle may do as he pleases. As for the child, we will have some of our women look after her during your stay.

"Now you must all be tired and hungry," said T'lan in a warm and welcoming tone, resisting the temptation to inquire about Miraanni and her mysterious entry into Orobai's life. "Your kughain is close by. It has all that you might need for food and comfort. We will show you to it and leave you for the night to rest and renew yourselves. I will send a wet nurse to you shortly to care for the girl. She will set up camp directly next to you so that you and your young sister need not be parted."

"Excellent," said Orobai, pleased with T'lan's response to what he knew was somewhat of an awkward and unexpected situation. "I knew we could rely on you and your gracious hospitality."

T'lan then led the company to their kughain where they passed a restful night in the comfort of soft skins and a warm fire. As Orobai drifted off to sleep he thought of how much coming to Shashun-Olurn was like coming home and hardly noticed the whispered rumors of his arrival with strange guests that passed about the encampment as news of Mu'shué's sister quickly spread, a deep wonder and mystery for all who had gathered for this great ceremony of renewal. Already consensus was forming in the camp. This would be a very special ceremony, full of unexpected mystery. Miraanni's appearance, the people whispered, was only the beginning.

The Iryuah'eeh'né Begins

Excitement filled the air when Orobai awoke the next morning. He could feel the collective anticipation even before he stepped outside. Orobai pushed open the door to his kughain and let the warm light of Urya flood over him as he emerged from his lodge. Many children were already playing about the village and the adults were busy preparing for the ceremony. Seeing that Orobai was up, a young woman who was camped next to him came out to greet him.

"Umyu'á, Mu'shué," said the young woman, standing at a respectful distance. The tightly coiled braids at the back of her head showed that she was married and the small white markings on her forehead and the yellow dot between her eyes indicated she was the mother of a young boy. At times of big ceremonial gatherings, it was always important for young women to indicate their marital and child bearing status so that others might know of their availability, or lack thereof. This young woman here was obviously spoken for and would not be taking part in any of the marriage arrangements that would occur later in the ceremony. Though she looked familiar, Orobai couldn't think of her name or recall whose family she was part of.

"It is good that you have come and that you have brought many blessings for our people," said the young woman rather formally. Her body language matched the stiffness of her words, holding herself rigidly and awkwardly holding her hands. "The young girl whom you have entrusted to us is in good care and you need have no worries for her while you are among us. We are honored that you would trust us with her wellbeing. If there is ever anything that you need for her, please ask for me. My name is Lilt'a. I will nurse the girl and take care of her needs," she said as she bowed her head and looked away.

"Thank you, Lilt'a," said Orobai warmly, remembering the young mother now as T'lan and Mayé's niece. When last he saw her, she was a teenager. She had clearly blossomed since that last encounter. "I am happy to know that she is in your hands for you come from a noble family. And I can tell right away that you are an excellent mother," Orobai added with a smile. "Please, let me introduce you to Miraanni."

Orobai went inside and took the just-stirring child from the warmth of Faen's underbelly and gently handed her to Lilt'a. The young woman took to the child right away, almost instinctively signing a soft Yamné lullaby as Miraanni snuggled into her bosom, rubbing her small fists in her eyes.

"My uncle, T'lan, wishes to see you," said Lilt'a after breaking off her lullaby. She seemed warmer now and somewhat relaxed. "His camp is at the northern side of the village on the other side of the arbors," she said with a smile, pointing with a tilt of her head. "There you will find a fine morning meal for you, if you would join them."

"Very good," said Orobai, reaching out to stroke Miraanni's hair and return Lilta's smile. "I trust that everything will be fine for my sister."

The encampment was busy with morning life. Young women were going to the lake, fetching water in dried gourds and tightly woven baskets with intricate and elegant designs, while young men were gathering supplies for the night's ceremony, going out into the forest to collect wood and various plants that the Want'né would use in the evening or playing games of skill and strength. Other Yamné were preparing ceremonial paints and decorations along with readying their ceremonial attire for the dances that were an integral part of the ceremony. As Orobai walked through the village the adults kept a respectful distance while small children ran up behind him or peaked out from behind lodges and quickly scattered when their parents chided them not to bother Mu'shué.

Orobai walked past the ceremonial arbors, the Shan'i'ruh or the "Seven Stations," as they were called in Yamné, glancing inside to see how things were coming along inside. This is where most of the activity would take place over the coming days of the feast. On this night, the first, there would be ceremonial dances, storytelling, and consumption of the Ul'mult'ah by the adults. The following day, all the children that had been born within the last year would be honored and welcomed into the world by their extended community. On the third day, the elders would initiate the young men and women who had come of age into the secretive spirit societies. Then, on the forth and last day, there would be the "releasing of the spirits" of those who had passed away the previous year. At this time those in mourning would dedicate themselves to carry their relatives' spirits for the coming year in the form of their "spirit stones," while those who were completing their acts of dedication from the year previous would give the sacred stones back to the lake, officially bringing their mourning to a conclusion as the flow of life moved on. On the final morning there would be healings, blessings, and a feast. Afterwards, the camp would break and the various bands of Yamné would go their respective ways.

Moving north past the ceremonial arbors, T'lan's camp was not difficult to find. As with other Want'né, T'lan had decorated his lodge with symbols of his spiritual power and authority, clearly identifying his home. Reflecting Yamné cosmology and their ecology of power, at the base of his kughain were abstract images of water and salmon. Above the water and salmon were images of deer. At mid-section were painted eagles, and above these were images of the moon and morning star. T'lan was conversant with these powers in spirit and used them in his healing and divinatory practices and their emblems here served as T'lan's sign, letting all know of his powers and abilities.

T'lan had learned the ways of the spirits through many years of study with his grandfather, who had taught him how to use the Ul'mult'ah to contact the world of the spirits and learn the mysteries of nature. T'lan, as a ritual leader and healer, had worked hard his whole life to both preserve the ancient traditions of his people as well as continually breathe new life and meaning into Yamné culture.

Maye, T'lan's wife, greeted Orobai outside their kughain. Like T'lan, she too was aged and weathered with time, though a little less so than T'lan, for as was usual among the Yamné, she was somewhat younger than her husband. Though not a Want'é herself, she shared T'lan's presence of spiritual authority and maturity. Her strong dark eyes gave the impression of seeing beneath the surface of things. In her youth she wore her hair in the manner of Lilt'a and the other young married women, but now, in her later years, she let her long silvery hair flow with the wind, wearing it down, letting it frame her still beautiful, though aged, face.

"Atluin, Mu'shué, you honor us with your presence," she said with a deep smile crackling the edges of her mouth. "We have food and drink for you. Please come in and join us."

"Thank you," responded Orobai, giving Maye a grateful embrace. "It is good to see you again and it is a pleasure to be among your people. When your niece told me that you were expecting me, I came right away."

"Very good. You will find that my young niece is a fine woman and your younger sister, whom I am very anxious to meet, will be well cared for. Now come inside. T'lan is waiting."

Maye held open the door and Orobai entered the old couple's kughain. He found T'lan inside, quietly preparing some paints and clays for the ceremony. Hanging up along the side of the kughain was his ceremonial outfit of a buckskin shirt decorated with symbols similar to the outer surface of his kughain along with feathers, stones, and other symbolic elements. He also had an intricate headdress of deer horns and eagle feathers with the image of a crescent moon and evening star beaded on the front with small metal rivets around the bottom edge. T'lan's spirit bundle, in which he kept the sacred objects of his craft, his krin, hung upon a small tripod by the inside of the door in the east. In the center of the kughain a warm fire was burning, sending its smoke up through the smoke hole in the center of the ceiling. Along the sides of the kughain were various skins for T'lan and Maye's bed along with other items of Yamné culture and everyday life such as storage baskets, utensils, and whatnot.

"Atluin and good morning to you, Mu'shué," said T'lan cheerfully, looking up from his work. "You are just in time. Maye has just finished making some strong tea. Come in and drink with us."

Orobai gladly accepted the invitation and entered the kughain with Maye following behind him.

Maye walked around the kughain sunwise, in typical Yamné fashion, and went to the far side of the fire where she took out three small cups made from dried gourds. These she filled with the tea that had been brewing over the fire. It was a common drink, called nur'ual, or "black water," that the Yamné made from an herb that only grew along the banks of the Nordlith. The particular herb used for this drink was known for its restorative and energizing powers and the River People would often drink it in the morning or during the late nights of ceremonial activities to help sustain them through the night. For Orobaï, it was a welcome refreshment and he gratefully took the cup proffered by Mayé, who held it before her, cupped gently in her hands.

The three sat and drank their tea in silence, as was Yamné custom. Orobaï could feel the tea at work, giving strength and vitality to his tired body and enlivening his mind. When they were finished, T'lan indicated with a glance to Mayé that she should give some of the dried herbs to Orobaï for his own. She quickly went into her supplies and handed over a generous portion of the herb to Orobaï.

"This is for the mornings when you are not so fortunate to have my wife prepare you tea," said T'lan with a smile.

Orobaï thanked Mayé and T'lan and then brought out small gifts of his own. For T'lan he had a small collection of turquoise and quartz, both of which T'lan used in his practice as a Want'é. To Mayé he gave some shells that he had traded for in the south some time ago, knowing that she could use them to make jewelry. He also gave them some clays and pigments that he knew they would find useful. The couple thanked him for the gifts.

The three then turned to more personal conversation, discussing events that had come to pass since they had last shared each other's company. Mayé and T'lan recounted the various births, deaths, and marriages of their relatives and close associates. T'lan told of some of the healing work he had been hired to perform over the past year and of their various journeys on the river and through the forest.

Sadly, Mayé's mother had passed away the previous year and her memory had been honored at the last Iryuah'eeh'né. She had lived to a ripe old age and had passed peacefully, so Mayé was thankful. Over the course of the past year she had carried on the memory of her mother by pledging to carry her spirit, in the form of a turquoise stone, and performing the required mourning rituals. At this year's Feast she would take the stone to the center of the lake, where she would send it to the bottom, returning her mother's spirit to the wellspring of new life. Mayé was looking forward to completing her ceremonial obligations and moving forward with her life. All three reminisced freely about her mother now that Mayé was far from the grief of the previous year and the mourning was now coming to an end for her. "That is part of the power of this ritual," Mayé commented reflectively. "We learn how to let go and accept what comes."

Though it was clear that T'lan and Mayé were naturally curious about the appearance of Miraanni in the Ancient One's life, they did not question him directly. Orobaï remained largely silent about the strange young girl as he was filled with more questions than answers himself, merely informing them that he was taking her to the east and that for the time, Faen would serve as her surrogate mother and Sto'orn as her guardian. T'lan and Mayé were satisfied by this and pressed no further.

"It is good that you brought her to us now," said Mayé. "Our ceremony teaches us about more than just death and mourning, as you know. It is also about new life, and new beginnings. Just as we must leave this world with ritual, so should we enter it."

T'lan nodded in emphatic agreement with his wife's wisdom. "Yes, it is truly a good thing that you are here with the child. It will be a good blessing for her."

After a good breakfast of bread, dried fruits, smoked salmon, and more talk of the ceremony, Orobai left T'lan and Mayé to their business. Before taking his leave, T'lan had informed Orobai that later in the day he would be conducting a sweat bath ceremony with other leading members of the Salmon Spirit Society and that Orobai should be sure to join them in a pre-Feast cleansing. He would send Gen'shu'n after him at midday.

Orobai took the opportunity to wander about the encampment, visiting with families he knew, greeting old acquaintances, and meeting the newest members of Yamné families. After some time Gen'shu'n appeared, as promised, to take Orobai to the sweat bath and ceremonial cleansing. Following Gen'shu'n, Orobai walked along the edge of the lake to the eastern end. There, representatives of the different spirit societies had constructed numerous sweat lodges where many of the Yamné would come to cleanse themselves in body, heart, mind, and spirit, preparing themselves for the deep spiritual work that was to come.

T'lan's sweat lodge was among the cluster of Salmon Spirit Society lodges. Both T'lan and his son Gen'shu'n were members of this society that was dedicated to the sacred fish, having received visions of the salmon in their initiations with the Ul'mult'ah. The other lodges of Deer, Moon, Sun, Eagle, Morning Star, and Raven Spirit Societies were similarly grouped together.

The group was just getting ready to enter the sweat lodge. It was mostly older men with a couple younger ones around Gen'shu'n's age. As Gen'shu'n and Orobai came up, the men were beginning to disrobe and were rubbing down their bodies with fragrant sage. Orobai was greeted by all and followed the example of the other men, disrobing and crawling into the low sweat lodge.

T'lan called the water maiden to the entrance where she passed in a gourd filled with lake water. The door was then shut, leaving the men in darkness, save for the red glow of the heated stones. Taking a small cup, T'lan, while saying a prayer that was echoed by the other men, poured the water over the rocks to the four directions. The water hissed as it hit the heated stones and instantly turned into pungent steam mixed with the smell of sage. The men breathed deeply and wafted the steam towards themselves as they drew it deep into their lungs as T'lan pushed the fragrant air towards each man with a raven-feather fan while saying a prayer.

As the hot steam permeated every pore, each man was left alone in silence, deep in his own meditation. Orobai took the searing vapor deep into his lungs. He shut his eyes, blocking out even the faint glow of the hot rocks at the center of the small enclosure.

47

T'lan began to sing the sacred songs of the Salmon Spirit Society as he accompanied himself with a small ceremonial rattle made of a gourd filled with salmon teeth. Orobai let the rhythm and melody of the song carry him, letting the meaning of the words pass by him unnoticed. He went deep into his mind, and there, in his inner vision, he saw a star. Orobai knew right away that it was Sarnrhobi, the Morning Star, as it was called in Illanii. For the Yamné it was called Yu'rin, or more affectionately, Sará'é, the Heavenly One. It blazed brilliantly in a field of pure black. It was so clear that Orobai felt that the star was actually there, present before him in the darkness of the small lodge. It was strange, this vision, as it carried no meaning for Orobai, just a puzzle. Why was he seeing this?

T'lan finished singing and the vision faded from Orobai's awareness. The rattle was passed and many songs were sung by all present, with T'lan periodically calling for the door to be opened, fresh air let in, or for new water, and new rocks, but no more images came before Orobai's inner eye.

After what seemed an eternity, the men filed out of the sweat lodge and quickly made their way along the path that led to a series of small waterfalls at the eastern end of the lake. There they all rushed into the falling waters that rained over them like ice as they rubbed it all over their bodies, washing away the past. It was something of a competition among the younger men to see who could withstand the icy waters the longest. Not needing to prove themselves, neither Orobai nor T'lan lingered long in the waters and had soon wrapped themselves in warm furs and gathered around a nearby fire. All felt refreshed and renewed.

A short while later, when Orobai returned to his own camp, he found Lilt'a out front, cradling Miraanni in her arms.

"Everyone agrees that your little sister is truly beautiful," said Lilt'a as Orobai approached. "They find her pure white skin strange, but they see a light and beauty within her that they have never seen before. All wonder where she came from, as it is strange for you to have a sister, they say. Some say that she is the Morning Star and they have given her the name Sará'é, the 'One of the Heavens'."

"Is that so?" asked Orobai, surprised by the coincidence, his vision in the sweat lodge floating through his thoughts once more. "And why is this?"

"She has the sign," said Lilt'a, matter-of-factly, as though Orobai himself should have known.

"What do you mean?" asked Orobai.

"See, it is here," said Lilt'a pulling back the covers of Miraanni's wrap, exposing her small chest. There on her breast above her heart was an image that resembled a silvery four-pointed star, the traditional Yamné symbol for the Morning Star. "As you can see," said Lilt'a, "it is the Star."

Orobai knew for certain that there had been no such mark there before. He had examined Miraanni's body thoroughly and there had been no marks of any kind anywhere on her small, white form. Yet here it was, undeniably. It was unmistakably the Yamné symbol for the Morning Star.

What could this mean, both for Miraanni and for the Yamné, for whom this would clearly be taken as a highly significant omen, Orobai wondered. He bent down to Miraanni and reached out to touch the strange mark, wanting to get a feel for it. When his hand came in contact with the star there was a sudden shift in Orobai's awareness. Looking at the image he saw Miraanni and Lilt'a fade away to a vast expanse of sky. What was left was a vision of a star burning brightly in the heavens with a warm light.

It is the same vision. It is Sarnrhobi.

Then the blackness of night faded but the star remained. Together with the star were Ranya and Urya, the moon and sun. In the vision Ranya was passing before the face of Urya and in a few moments had blotted out the sun completely in a full solar eclipse. The star remained, however, and grew ever brighter. The light of the star then seemed to drive Ranya from the face of Urya and the sun shone again, and it seemed the birth of a new day, a new beginning. And then the vision faded, bringing Orobai's sight back to the young woman and the girl in her arms.

"Indeed, that is a good name for her," said Orobai, keeping his vision to himself.

* * * *

With evening soon to arrive it was time to begin final preparations for the commencement of the Iryuah'eeh'né. Everyone was busy putting on his or her finest clothes, the ceremonial leaders were donning their regalia, and the ceremonial dancers and singers were retreating to their private camps to prepare. It was Gen'shu'n who came to retrieve Orobai and bring him to the Shan'i'ruh.

Gen'shu'n took Orobai to the east side of the arbors where T'lan was busy blessing the people with the other Want'né. There, the old Holy Man said a prayer and blessing for Orobai, who then went and got his supper with the others and took a seat inside the Shan'i'ruh to await the dancing.

Orobai could hear the soft rustling of the costumed dancers and singers as they shuffled to the ceremonial arbor from their camps. They gathered into groups on the eastern side and were already beginning to dance to the beat of the drums of the singers. Excitement was in the air.

The order of the groups never changed. Following the progression of the Yamné creation story, the first group was the Raven Spirit Society. Their dancers wore large wooden masks shaped like the heads of ravens and wore black robes decorated with countless raven feathers (something Orobai always kept in mind when he was in Yamné territory in his raven form). Following them was the Morning Star Spirit Society. The Yamné associated the Morning Star with the kite, an elegant bird of prey with delicate white and black feathers with long pointed wings and a forked tail. The dancers for this society wore white doeskin shirts with a silver image of a four-pointed star on front and back and a crown of white and black kite feathers that hung down over their faces, keeping their identities hidden.

After them was the Sun Spirit Society. As with the Raven Society, they wore elaborate masks fashioned after a sun disk and decorated with the yellow feathers of golden flickers. Behind them came the Moon Spirit Society. They wore plain masks made of whitened elk hide to which they had attached pronghorn antlers.

After these four came the three principal animal societies of Salmon, Deer, and Eagle. The Salmon Spirit Society had large and elaborate masks shaped like salmon heads in the spawning season, which trailed over the dancers' backs into a large hump and then extended down into a tail. Their bodies were painted with mud from the river bottom. The Deer Spirit Society wore the skins of bucks and does with the head of each animal riding atop the painted faces of the dancers. Lastly the Eagle Spirit Society wore large masks shaped like stylized eagle heads and on their arms they carried a full complement of eagle wing feathers with a bustle made of the tail.

Orobai loved watching the dances and listening to the songs. Together they told the story of how the world came to be and how the Yamné people came into existence, according to their own beliefs and understanding. The dances were rich in symbolic and often esoteric elements, whose exact meaning was only known to devotees of those societies who had received a vision from the various spirits in their initiation into adulthood, as would happen again this year in later portions of the Ceremony.

One by one the different societies danced their way through the tree arbors, extending their blessings and prayers for everyone and dramatically bringing the Yamné creation story to life. After several hours of dances and songs the procession was finally finished. Following the last of the dancers who trailed out to the east, all the people moved into the seventh, and largest, of the tree arbors. Now was the time for telling of creation story, the story of the Yamné. It was the time to remember who they were, and why they were there.

As in many years past, T'lan had the honor of being the official storyteller. He was gifted in this art and knew much of the Yamné sacred lore. Orobai truly enjoyed listening to T'lan, an appreciation shared by others. He spoke of the authority that only an advanced Want'é could command and his words were rich with meaning and power. When everyone was settled and all ears and eyes were directed towards him, taking center stage among the assembled Yamné, T'lan began in his most dramatic voice, gesturing with the sweeping motions and fluid body movement of a great storyteller.

"I am Yamné and this is my story. This is your story. This is the story of our beginning. This is the story of our origin. This is the story of the Yamné. It is the story of who we are.

"I learned this story at the knee of my grandfather and he learned from the knee of his grandfather. So it has been for countless generations since the beginning of time. You all know this story but it is good to hear it. To hear this story brings blessings to our people. It reminds us of who we are and where we have come from. And not only us does it bless, it brings blessings for the whole world, for that is why we are gathered here.

"We do this great ceremony, the Iryuah'eeh'né, not only for us, for our own sake, but for all the beings of this world. It is to remind ourselves of our sacred relationship with the Waters, the Air, the Mountains, the beings of the forests and rivers, the deserts and plains, of those that are seen and those that are unseen. It is a gift to all the world.

"Thus I was told and thus I tell you now, for I have the authority and knowledge to do so. I am T'lan, Want'é of the Mo'rinldah, keeper of the sacred lore. What I tell you now is what has been said and will continue to be said as long as Yamné people walk this earth. When the story is no longer told, there will no longer be Yamné and the world will have changed."

T'lan then began to weave his enchanting tale of creation, the story of who the Yamné were and how they had come to be. He told of the Spirit that rested in the Void that created the Waters, the Wind, the Light, the Four Mountains, and the Brother, the Raven, and the Sister, the Kite. Through the magic of storytelling, T'lan brought these ancient, guiding stories to life once more, just as the Holy People had done for generations upon generations. It was the sacred story that wove together the fabric of the lives of the Yamné, binding them in the master narrative of their people and their connection to this place and all of Aurduin. It gave the Yamné purpose and perspective. Through the sacred story, they could peer back to their mythical beginnings, reminded of where they came from, their sacred origins. But it was more than this, for it told them of their present, and showed them the way into the future. It was their story.

How many times had Orobai heard this story? How many Want'né had paraded before him across the depths of time? Orobai closed his eyes, listening to T'lan's textured voice, the depth of his sincerity resonating about the large arbor. He heard other voices in his mind. Want'né from long ago were there, all telling the same story. It was a moment that transcended the present, yet was thoroughly embedded within it. Orobai opened his eyes and thought he could almost see the echoing figures of other Want'né from other times, standing just where T'lan was standing now, telling this story with the same passion and dramatic urgency. For a moment, Orobai felt as though they were all telling the story directly to him, right then and there.

Orobai listened with new ears. On this night, he heard the story in a way he had never heard before. There was something much deeper than Orobai's familiarity from having been among the Yamné for so long. This time, the story was not just speaking to the Yamné. This time, it was speaking to him.

There is truth in this. This is much more than I ever thought it was. I have underestimated the depth of this wisdom.

As soon as T'lan was finished and Orobai could break free from the mesmerizing spell of the all those voices of the ancient Want'né in his mind, he called Lilt'a over to him.

"It is late," he said to the young mother, "and I am sure that my sister could use some rest from all of this. I think it would be best if you took her back to your kughain so that she can get some sleep."

"She's slept some," assured Lilt'a, seeming to mean that Miraanni would be fine where she was.

"I know," said Orobai, "but I think once the singing starts again that she might be disturbed, and I want to do the right thing for her."

"Of course, Mu'shué," Lilt'a said quickly, as though a little embarrassed that she hadn't agreed to Orobai's request outright.

Orobai watched as Lilt'a took Miraanni from the ceremonial arbor. He knew that she would be fine, but that wasn't why he asked Lilt'a to take her away. After that experience of T'lan telling the creation story, Orobai had a feeling that there was something going on here that he didn't quite understand. Recalling what had happened when he last sang with Miraanni present, he didn't want any such incidents here. There was no telling what might happen in this spiritually charged atmosphere. Orobai could see that Miraanni was already quite a fascination for the Yamné, and listening to the creation story now, with its imagery of the raven with a sacred sister, and the star that had appeared on Miraanni's chest, not to mention the two visions, it was all too much. No, there was no need to impress the Yamné further. If Miraanni showed any more of her ability, Orobai might have a fervent religious movement on his hands. He had seen such movements grow around charismatic and powerful people before. What would he do then?

The Ul'mult'ah

With the conclusion of T'lan's retelling of the Yamné creation story, it was now time to take the sacrament, the Ul'mult'ah. The elders required all the children to leave, along with the young people who were to have their initiations on the third day of the ceremony. Young children never consumed the Ul'mult'ah, a sacred mystery of adulthood. The neophytes would have their first experience with the sacrament during their initiations later.

Once the transition was complete, with various people having come and gone, all was ready to bring in the Ul'mult'ah. The Guardians of the Sacrament had boiled large pots of the mushrooms into an earthy tea. To each person they gave a gourd cup as they circulated about in a sunwise manner, pouring the steaming brew from larger serving gourds.

The Want'né, T'lan included, were seated on the east side near the fire. They began chanting prayers, accompanied with various kinds of rattles and small water drums. The music filled the Shan'i'ruh with the peculiar feeling of the Ul'mult'ah. A skilled Want'é could make a person feel the effects of the Ul'mult'ah even without having consumed any of the sacrament, and a roomful of singing Want'né produced an even stronger effect with their rattles, drums, and haunting voices. As an especially honored singer, Orobai was invited to sit with T'lan and the other Want'né, though his time to sing would come later.

The Want'né, both men and women, received their own pot of the sacramental tea from the circulating guardians. Before the ceremony had begun, the Want'né had set aside what they deemed the strongest and most potent mushrooms for themselves, as they were the most skilled in managing the sometimes-difficult ordeal that the Ul'mult'ah imparted to those who consumed them. These were then used for the tea that the guardians set before the holy people now. T'lan and Orobai filled their small gourd cups, carefully dipping them into the larger pot of dark liquid. It had a strong earthy smell and a distinctive taste to it that most new initiates found unpleasant, but for the Yamné it was an acquired taste that they greatly appreciated, for it was the taste of enlightenment and spiritual ecstasy.

Orobai brought his cup to his mouth, pausing only a moment. He had participated in this ritual many times. Still, he was always a little apprehensive of the Ul'mult'ah. Despite their nature as a religious sacrament, they were ultimately unpredictable and those who consumed them had to be ready and willing to take whatever they presented, pleasant or not. *Be open to the lesson and the wisdom they will bring*, Orobai told himself, repeating the words T'lan and generations of Want'né had told him many times before.

He drank.

The tea tasted like ancient earth. It was a deep brown with bits of the ground sacrament making it a cloudy, watery brew. Orobai could feel the sacrament begin to work almost immediately as the warm liquid slid down this throat. Radiating from his center, the Ul'mult'ah coursed through his body and psyche, uniting his being in body, heart, mind, and spirit. Waves built up in his being, slowly at first, and then gained momentum, pushed on by the hypnotic singing of the Holy Ones.

Orobai felt the songs of the Want'né wash over him. The rhythms and textures were rich with meaning. Messages hid within the sounds and revelations secreted themselves in the rattles and water drums.

Surrender . . . become the Witness . . . let the revelations unfold . . .

Orobai let the visionary waves pass over and through him. He breathed with the flow and felt the sacrament work its way through his body. Boundaries between self and other, self and world, self and cosmos melted away and there was a complete union where all was One in the great undulating flux of organic existence. For the Yamné, this was the highest state of knowledge and being and it provided an unmediated experience of the pure spiritual nature of reality.

The utter beauty of unity . . .

Orobai felt himself on the verge of some realization. The experience consumed his entire being and his mind flowed over with visions of himself, Miraanni, and the tasks before him. His feeling of connection to the small child became overwhelming. For a time he seemed to lose all distinction between himself and his younger sister. Never before had Orobai felt a similar connection to any individual in all his many years. He had always felt a strong bond with the Arnyar, given their relationship to the Altfein-Aryat and the Illan, but it was nothing like this. Orobai now knew that in all his time, his own being had been fundamentally incomplete. Something he had never realized was missing was now present in his being like a gaping hole in his existence. He felt as though he were only half-formed, only half a being. And as Miraanni filled his mind and vision he saw that through her there was an unexpected fulfillment, an utterly profound completion. He was overwhelmed by the desire to be with her and for them to remain in each other's presence. And most of all, he felt the powerful desire to sing with her, to create as they had done back at his home with the formation of the spring. The urge to sing with her was almost more than Orobai could bear and the desire filled him like a burning fire, consuming everything else before it.

Our purpose is to sing, to bring forth the Sounds of Creation. The sacred tones of the Illan. The sacred tones of the Four Temples. The sacred tones of the Four Mountains. This is the desire of the Illan, the desire of True Creation.

Was this what the Illan felt when they created Aurduin? Was it the desire of the Altfein themselves – the original desire that caused the spirits of Wind and Light to transmute themselves into the body of Eyar, becoming the Altfein, the original act from which all later creation proceeded?

The questions and their profound implications poured through Orobai. He began to understand something of his essential nature that he had never even questioned before. At root was this profound desire, only to be fulfilled through Miraanni. And in this desire, there was no thought of himself, or of Miraanni, as two separate beings. They were as one with each other, and not only one with each other, but also one with all other things, with all of creation. All boundaries were removed, all isolating thoughts of self and other were obliterated, and what was left was absolute unity. In their combined being, Orobai could embrace and love all of creation as one great Self, one unified organic being which Orobai could only describe as "suchness," and it was complete and without distinction.

This is who we are. This is who we are meant to be. Our fates are one. Our fate is the fate of all of Aurduin.

Time ebbed and flowed as Orobai drifted through his deep meditation. Gradually, he returned to where he was and was once more present in the unfolding ritual. When T'lan saw that Orobai was again in their shared world, he invited him to sing with a subtle gesture. Noticing the transition, the other Want'né began to fall silent, save for a few who were still helping people through the difficult stages of the Ul'mult'ah. Everyone now looked upon Orobai expectantly, as though revelations and spiritual power would pour forth directly from his open mouth like water on parched land.

Orobai began to sing.

He felt the music emerge from a place deep and hidden within his being. It came slowly from the imperceptible depths of his existence and passed out from there in patterned waves of musical revelation. His voice began to take form and slowly the sound escaped from his throat. Orobai felt as though he were a hollow conduit from which this great expression of life and being could flow and manifest in the world. It was not himself singing, but rather it was the Song of Creation passing through his body and being, revealing itself to all. As such a conduit, Orobai could perceive the minds and hearts of all those around him and their prayers and the concentration of their thoughts broke through into his own awareness. He could see into the inner being of all present. He felt the history of their hearts and the living vibrancy of their bodies and physical beings. Beyond this was the endless pulsing of spirit and life force that took shape in each individual being.

The music was beautiful and exalted. In rapturous song the sound poured forth from Orobai's body, taking him over completely along with all present. Reacting to Orobai's song, the Altfein began to resonate and vibrate with their own spiritual energy and filled the Shan'i'ruh with a pure and healing light. The spirits of all present cried out to greet the light and many began to cry uncontrollably, not from fear or pain, but for sheer joy and love of the warmth of the beauty of the light. And as each person added their thoughts to Orobai's, the light began to take shape and form into all that was held to be beautiful and sacred to the Yamné.

Sensing their hearts and desires, Orobai, through shaping the tone and structure of his singing, let each individual perceive his song in his or her own way. Orobai would never let his own thought dominate the music and images produced, but would instead let the minds of those around him help to shape what they experienced, each according to his or her own understanding and spiritual sensitivities. This was very similar to the singing and working of the Want'né, yet it was profoundly more effective and direct, given Orobai's unique relationship to the Altfein. It compounded and greatly enhanced the revelatory effects of the Ul'mult'ah in ways that could not be achieved without him. It was no wonder that Yamné considered the Ceremonies that Orobai attended to be the most powerful.

Though rapturous and beautiful, without breaking his song, Orobai began to feel as though his singing were incomplete. Despite all the minds and hearts that he could perceive in his visionary state, he was consumed with the feeling that there was still an absence, still something missing. He did not feel whole or complete the way he usually did when he sang for the Yamné with the Ul'mult'ah. It was then that the image of Miraanni again arose in his awareness. In his mind he could see Miraanni respond to his singing and he felt her desire to join him. In his mind's eye he saw her awareness take shape as the star emblem above her heart began to glow with a penetrating silver light. He could see that she was drawn to him, that her being felt just as incomplete without him as he did without her. The desire emanating from her to join him in singing, and creating, became overwhelming, almost unbearable. It was like nothing Orobai had ever experienced and it threatened to consume him like a fire that could not be controlled by any strength of will or intention.

It was then that Orobai noticed another sound, almost imperceptible at first, but distinct and clearly growing louder and stronger. As it began to resonate with his own voice, Orobai noticed that the images from the Altfein were beginning to change and respond to the new sound. There grew in the images of the Altfein a new light, a light which had not been there before, and it was as the starry heavens, soft and twinkling with silver and white.

As all focused on the starlight, images of stars emerged and then began to change into images of kites with the silver light flowing around them and radiating from their feathers. In a great flock, the delicate forms of the slender birds of prey swirled about. The faster they flew, the more solid they seemed to become with the rushing sound of feathers in the wind filling the large enclosure. In this transformation the ethereal birds had passed from visions to living beings right there above the sacred central fire.

Suddenly, the birds all simultaneously rushed to the eastern door and circled in a flurry of feathers. And there, standing just inside the threshold behind Orobai and the Want'né was Lilt'a, holding Miraanni in her arms.

Lilt'a stood as though in a trance, gazing absently before her. In her arms little Miraanni sang with the voice of one far beyond her years in maturity and ability. Her wrap of bear fur that had been covering her had fallen away and there her breast shone in the silver light hat radiated from the star design above her heart. The elegant birds of prey all rushed about Lilt'a and her little charge, circling round them and enveloping them in a blur of white and black feathers. Everyone stared in utter rapture for it was as if part of Yamné sacred lore had suddenly come to life. Here before them was the one they called Sará'é, the Morning Star, and just as in Yamné creation stories, she was accompanied by the star's alternate form of the white Kite.

The people were transfixed upon this sight before them. T'lan and the other Want'é were both mesmerized and concerned, for Lilt'a had brought a child to the sharing of the sacrament, something that was strictly forbidden. But it was clear that Lilt'a had little control over herself and that it was Miraanni who had somehow caused Lilt'a to bring her here. Several Want'né, confused as to what to do, stood up quickly and looked to T'lan for direction. They clearly did not want to interfere, as it seemed that this was a sacred sign and should not be disrupted. But Yamné culture explicitly dictated that children, and infants especially, should not be present at the sharing of the sacrament.

T'lan looked to Orobai for direction. Orobai felt torn. He knew the Yamné injunction against children at this ceremony, and had the thought that if he stopped his singing, Lilt'a would be able to take Miraanni away. But he could not stop. No matter what his rational thought was, he felt utterly compelled to continue. Singing this way with Miraanni, Orobai felt completely fulfilled. He knew that through their combined singing and Miraanni's will, the kites had become real – they, like the spring they sang into being by his home, were true creations. The hearts of the people were filled with spiritual excitement. T'lan and the other Want'né had little choice but to let Lilt'a enter the Shan'i'ruh with the small child in her arms.

In a swirl of feathers the kites then rushed out of the eastern door as the light from Miraanni's breast burst forth in radiant beauty. Lilt'a unconsciously brought the girl farther into the enclosure and the Want'né parted before her as Lilt'a made her way towards Orobai. Reaching out her arms, Miraanni clearly wanted to be taken up by Orobai. As Orobai took Miraanni from her nurse it was as though Lilt'a suddenly awoke and was astounded to find herself amidst the Want'né in the Shan'i'ruh. Looking around confusedly, others quickly eased her mind and told her what was happening.

With all looking on, Orobai and Miraanni were caught up in each other's presence. Orobai felt their minds and intentions merging and becoming one. All boundaries between them fell away to reveal a complete unity of thought and being. Their song now soared to new heights and the Altfein responded with a flurry of activity. All present were completely held in sway by the music and later many reported having intense spiritual experiences. For many it was the greatest experience of their lives.

For each person present, gifts began to manifest. A relic or object appeared before each person according to his or her own spiritual understanding or role within Yamné culture. Feathers, stones, shells, and numerous other krin began to appear, each with its own spiritual power and significance according to the nature for whom they manifested. Forever after this night was known as the "Night of the Krin" and lived on in Yamné memory as a night of revelation and profoundly spiritual consequences, not just for the Yamné, but for all of Aurduin.

It seemed an eternity that Orobai held Miraanni in his arms as the people swayed in heightened exaltation with the song of the brother and sister flowing through their very beings. Word quickly spread outside of the Shan'i'ruh of what was occurring and all the Yamné gathered, completely filling the enclosure, with those who could not fit inside waiting patiently outside to witness and experience the miracle. To the Yamné, it seemed that prophecy and the spiritual teachings of their elders had come to life before them, for here was the Morning Star and through this wondrous little being, all the people received spiritual gifts. Many were praying and weeping for joy. Others stood in awe and amazement at what was unfolding. It was a night they would never forget.

As time passed, the effects of the Ul'mult'ah began to fade. Orobai was weary and his song grew ever softer as the sacrament began to leave his being. Miraanni also began to grow quiet and peaceful as well, and as the light of dawn began to fill the sky, their song died down and all the people fell into a state of quiet and introspective contemplation. When the Morning Star breached the eastern horizon Miraanni fell completely silent at last and quickly passed into a deep and profound sleep as the light from her own star slowly faded.

In procession with the Want'né and other participants following behind, Orobai carried Miraanni out the eastern door to greet the rising of the Morning Star. All stood around them in awed silence as Orobai lifted the little girl four times to each of the four directions, starting in the east and directed towards the Morning Star. The people then spontaneously lined up to approach and touch the mysterious child. They all brought forth the relics and gifts that had manifested for them, clutching them to their breasts as they came forward to gently touch the star on Miraanni's chest and say a prayer. Never before had they been able to directly touch the sacred in this very tangible way.

At long last Urya broke forth from the eastern horizon and the world filled with radiant yellow light. The birds sang and announced the dawn as the darkness and the stars faded from view. Exhausted and weak, Orobai finally handed Miraanni back to Lilt'a, who had patiently and reverently stood at the ready. Though the experience had been positive, Orobai felt drained, as though every ounce of energy had been sucked from his being and passed into the work that he and Miraanni had accomplished. All he wanted was to pass into sleep and join Miraanni in her peaceful rest. He felt as though he could sleep for days. He could carry on no longer.

It took Orobai's last remaining strength to hand Miraanni over to Lilt'a. Seeing his overwhelming fatigue, Mayé directed two young men to come to his aid. They came forward and each took Orobai by an arm and supported him with their shoulders. Mayé and T'lan told them to take Orobai to his camp. They helped Orobai in, cautiously stepping around the resting wolf and her two cubs, and laid the Ancient One down on his soft bed where he quickly slipped into a long and silent sleep, but not before the sober thought passed through his mind – *What have we done?*

Revelations

Orobai finally awoke sometime in the late afternoon after a long and dreamless sleep. It was the sound of the playing cubs that eventually brought him back to consciousness. They grunted, growled, and barked, rolling over each other taking turns being hunter and prey.

"Good morning – or should I say 'Good afternoon?'" said Faen, seeing that Orobai was up. "They've brought you some tea that just needs warming up. From what I'm able to gather, there seems to be a good deal of talk about you and the girl going around the village today. They're saying that the girl is the Morning Star and that she is the same one as in their ancient stories. They say that she is sacred."

"I'm not surprised . . . after last night," commented Orobai somewhat grimly, with images of last night's performance swimming through his mind. Possibilities of what might come to be overwhelmed him. *What did we do? What will it mean for these people?* "I imagine that it might be difficult for us to leave with her now, after what she did for them. They won't be eager to see her go." Orobai could only frown.

Orobai filled Faen in, leaving out certain aspects that he deemed she did not really need to know. Faen took it all in and was relatively unfazed, saying that she had already decided for herself that the girl was special and had an important destiny. "I don't think that she is meant just for the River People, though," said the old wolf. "I think it is clear that her destiny lies elsewhere and that she is of more significance than for just these people and their stories. I have a feeling that they will realize this and will not try to keep her here. They seem like they are reasonable, even if they have a religious devotion to the girl."

"You are probably right," said Orobai, considering her words. "I too feel that her destiny is perhaps more than any of the people of Aurduin can imagine. I see great beauty in her but I also sense darkness. There's something there that I have not yet been able to see that holds dire consequences for us all, I'm afraid. I think it will only be when I have completed the task set out for me by the Arnyar that I will truly understand this. Perhaps only then will the darkness that awaits us show itself openly."

Orobai decided to keep his remaining thoughts to himself and began to prepare the tea that had graciously been brought for him. Once heated, it was good and refreshing and breathed more life into his tired body than he had expected it would. Despite his long sleep, Orobai still felt drained from the night before and took heart in the knowledge that last night's performance would not need to be repeated any time soon.

After having his tea and breaking his fast with the food that had accompanied the strong drink, Orobai stepped outside to find that Sto'orn was standing watch at his door.

"What has the girl done?" demanded Sto'orn abruptly, obviously upset. "Word has already spread about the forest of her strange abilities. Soon everyone in Aurduin will know of her and we will no longer be able to move in anonymity. Even the Arnyar already know and they want to know how you could have let this happen."

"I really had no control over it," explained Orobai with a shrug and his hands open before him, hoping that a relaxed demeanor might help defuse Sto'orn's righteous-eagle indignation. "I was participating in the ceremony as I have done countless times before. I had the girl removed as is dictated by Yamné custom when they take their sacrament, but the girl has a strong will of her own. She was drawn by my singing, and by the Altfein, I believe, and she somehow caused her nurse to bring her to the Shan'i'ruh against my instructions. There was nothing I could have done to stop it, except not to sing, but by then it was already too late. And besides, I do not think that I could have stopped then even if I had wished it, for the bond between us is as strong as it is strange, and I felt compelled to continue – perhaps just as compelled as she felt to come and join me. Regardless, it could not be helped, and what's done is done." Though he knew this to be true, Orobai had to admit that this was not the best situation.

"Well the Arnyar are not happy with this turn of events," chastised Sto'orn, accentuating his superior tone with a brisk ruffling of feathers.

"That is to be expected," said Orobai with a sigh of resignation. "Perhaps it is a good thing yet, however," offered Orobai, hoping to salvage some positive thoughts about the incident, perhaps trying to convince himself. "Indeed, we may need the Yamné sometime later, and we still need their help in getting down the river, as I had originally planned. I would say it is also a good thing that we learn something of her abilities now, when she is young. I can only presume that she will become stronger and more powerful with age and I would not want what she is truly capable of to catch us unawares. I feel the pull of her destiny growing stronger every day. It is calling us to some pivotal moment in time. I have not seen it, but I sense it. Perhaps you do too."

"I don't know of these things," answered Sto'orn quickly, dismissing Orobai's attempt to draw him into his speculation. "I do what I am told. If the

Arnyar know more than I, they have said nothing. Such is my lot and I do not question their wisdom. And neither should you, Orobai."

"Agreed," said Orobai. "I regret that Miraanni has created such a public display of her abilities and I mean no disrespect for the Arnyar or their wishes. I will do what I can to control the girl, but she will do what she will do. When the time comes, I feel she will be far beyond anyone's ability to control, and any sense we may have of that now, I think, is but illusion. But let us not judge what has passed. It may serve greater ends than we can yet see."

"Very well," said Sto'orn, somewhat relaxed by Orobai's rationalization. "Just try not to let this happen again, whatever it was exactly that she did. We do not need more publicity than we already have. The last thing we need is to be swamped by devotees seeking the child who works miracles, or worse, those who might seek to use her for their own purposes. She is a strange being indeed, and the Arnyar are adamant that she reach the east in all due haste."

"Yes, I know, but we have at least three more days here before we can move on," said Orobai. "The Feast has only yet begun and to leave now would greatly upset the Yamné, and I am sure that even you can see this."

"I'll be watching," said Sto'orn as he leapt into the sky and flew away.

* * * *

Orobai had expected as much of a reaction from the Arnyar. He was a bit surprised that they already knew something of what had come to pass, but then again, they could see far and had many who did their bidding in the forests, continually bringing them news from all across Aurduin. Did they see something that he did not? Was there a concern that they had not expressed? Had they seen the darkness that Orobai could clearly perceive yet not comprehend? Orobai wondered if perhaps the darkness was something that might be averted, or perhaps it would be something of Miraanni's and his own doing. Maybe even the previous night would somehow play into it. It was a veiled future, however, and Orobai could not pierce it, nor, he suspected, could the Arnyar. If they could, then why send him on a grand circumlocution of the Goargathr and give him the instructions to perform this new ritual? Orobai concluded that only time would tell and that for now he would just have to proceed as they had planned. Though he felt the urgency of his task, he still had time among the Yamné to sort things out with them. *Perhaps it will all turn out for the best*, he thought to himself.

After Sto'orn left, Lilt'a, along with a group of other women who eagerly doted on Miraanni, came forward to speak with Orobai. Seeing his little sister, Orobai's heart was glad. Miraanni appeared supremely aware and looked up at him with knowing eyes, as if they two shared some secret that was sealed off from everyone else in the world. Looking at her, he once again thought to himself that she was yet bigger than even the day before, or even the night before. Truly she was a child beyond compare. Being in her presence, it was as if he could feel her in his mind, as though he was no longer alone in his uniqueness in Aurduin.

"Mu'shué," said Lilt'a tentatively as she cast her gaze down towards Orobai's feet, "I beg your forgiveness for what I have done. I meant no offense by bringing the child to the sharing of the sacrament, but I was not myself. It was not until it ended that I was aware of what I had done. My mind was not my own. I think that it was the girl herself who had me bring her to you and I pray that you will not be angry with me or my people for this mistake."

"Do not worry, Lilt'a," said Orobai in his friendliest tone, drawing her face upwards with a gentle lift of his hand beneath her chin. "I know that you could not have prevented what has happened. Not even I could have stopped it if I had wanted to. I suspect that you are correct in judging that your mind was not your own. The child has many abilities and this would seem to be one of them. I am quite sure that she would do nothing to bring you or your people to harm. Perhaps she had her own reasons for what she made you do and only time may reveal what these are. Know that I hold no ill will towards you, and besides, I believe that your people are most likely grateful beyond all expectations for this seemingly chance event."

"Thank you, Mu'shué," said Lilt'a happily, a broad smile breaking over her face. "You are truly wise." She seemed relieved that Orobai was not angry with her.

Having noticed the activity at Orobai's camp, Gen'shu'n had alerted his father, who now approached the group gathered outside of Orobai's kughain. "Good, I see that you are up, Mu'shué, and that the women of the Yu'rindah are looking after Sará'é," said T'lan as he approached. "I have been waiting for you to awaken. Many of the Want'né would like to speak with you about the girl and they are eager for your presence. If you would come with me, it would be best not to make them wait any longer, if you are ready."

Orobai went with T'lan without hesitation, for he was curious about what the Want'né would have to say. T'lan seemed in a good enough mood, so he expected that the others would probably be likewise. As they walked to the gathering place, T'lan commented to Orobai that most of the Want'né were very pleased, as were all of the people. However, he cautioned that there were a few who had expressed doubts about the girl. They thought that perhaps Orobai was manipulating them for reasons they could not comprehend, and they did not trust the girl. This was only the feeling of a small minority though, so T'lan urged Orobai not to worry.

Evidently the rapture of the Ul'mult'ah had faded away to rational doubt for a few individuals. Orobai was not surprised. He was well familiar with the profound sense of meaning and significance of even the smallest detail when feeling the influence of the sacrament that often led to questioning and uncertainty when reflected upon at a later time. Perhaps some of the Yamné were feeling this now.

The Want'né had gathered in the center of the village close to the Shan'i'ruh in a tree arbor. Both men and women were present. They were mostly elderly, but there were a few younger people who were newly started on the path of the Want'né. They were all seated in a circle and made way for T'lan and Orobai, whom they directed to sit in the front in the east. As he situated himself, Orobai scanned the crowed of people. He saw most people looking upon him with reverence and gladness in their hearts. However, as T'lan had cautioned, he could sense that this was not so for all present. Looking into their hearts, he saw that there were two in particular who were not pleased. They were both younger Want'né and Orobai was not familiar with them. There were also some who had not yet passed judgment and were perhaps waiting to see what would be said here before coming to a decision about Miraanni.

It was T'lan who began, standing before the crowd and speaking with a clear and authoritative voice.

"All of us witnessed what took place in the Iryuah'eeh'né last night. With our own eyes we saw a great wonder come before us and give blessings for all our people. For this we owe thanks to our friend, Mu'shué, for it was he who brought Sará'é among us.

"Our people have known Mu'shué for longer than any in our memory, this you all know. He is ancient and wise and knows much of the doings of Aurduin. We have always trusted him and he has never sought to deceive or abuse us in any way. Though his ways are strange and he is not one of us, he has brought us a great gift. The girl, Sará'é, is truly a blessing. She is the Morning Star incarnate here among us. I have no doubt that she is the same as the one spoken of for generations in our sacred stories. The mark is upon her. We all saw the kites when she entered the Shan'i'ruh when we were sharing the sacrament and many of you received spiritual gifts from the child. Of this there can be no argument. We owe the girl our thanks and our prayers, as many of you have already expressed. I would thus ask that tonight we show her the honor that she is due. This is my mind and I have spoken."

The gathering received T'lan's introductory comments well with many nodding in agreement, accompanied by general murmurs of approval. The next to speak was Alu'inir, the matriarch of the Yu'rindah, the Morning Star Spirit Society. Given her status, Orobai was keen to hear what she had to say, knowing that her judgment would carry a great deal of weight among the other holy people. Orobai could easily see that he was not alone in this, with many looking to the older woman expectantly.

"I agree with the words of T'lan," said Alu'inir, standing up and looking out over the others. "We of the Yu'rindah have long known that one day the Morning Star would return to remake the world. For many generations we have passed on this teaching within our society, though we have not shared it openly until now. In dreams and visions the brothers and sisters of our society have seen the return of the Star, though we have not known when or in what form She might take until now, for the spirits do not reveal all and some things are not known until they occur. We have discussed this together and have agreed that this is the truth and we believe that through this girl great blessings will come. These blessing will not just be for the Yu'rindah or the Yamné, though. Long we have taught that the Morning Star is for all the beings of Aurduin and though we, the Yamné, are created through her, she is not our possession. She belongs to no one but Herself.

"I know that some of you feel that the girl is to stay with us, but this is not our decision to make. She is the younger sister of Mu'shué and we cannot make a claim over kin, nor could we make a claim over one so great even if she had not come with kin. Only her brother can make decisions such as this now, and in time, she will make her own decisions and follow her own path, whatever it may be. For now, in agreement with T'lan, I too feel that we should honor her, for truly she is sacred and through her countless blessings will come to be. This is my mind and I have spoken."

Again sounds of general agreement passed around the gathering. Looking about, Orobai could see that many thought Alu'inir reasonable. He was especially pleased that she had explicitly reserved the decision of Miraanni's fate to him. Perhaps this would all work out well after all.

Next spoke Ushun'ah, patriarch of the Kagdah, the Raven Spirit Society, taking his turn standing before the gathered crowd. "We of the Kagdah have also met in council and we agree with much of what has been said here. We all witnessed the power of Sará'é and we feel that there can be little doubt of her authenticity. However, we would caution that we, too, have had our own secret lore within our society. In this lore we have preserved the knowledge that, one day, the Raven would return as well. With the return of the Raven, as our ancestors have taught us, comes the destruction of the world, as well as a destruction of the Raven Himself. In these teachings we have known that this destruction will be followed by a great renewal and it will be a passing from the time of the Raven to the time of the Morning Star. We thus caution that these are great events indeed. That the girl is among us now would indicate that the Raven also walks among the beings of Aurduin. Through these two we can expect a great cataclysm, if we trust in the wisdom of our ancestors, which surely we must. Yes, the girl should be honored, but beware, for grave times may be upon us. She has given us many gifts, and it is perhaps these that will help our people to overcome the dark times that lie before us all. We must be ready for what is to come. This Feast might be the last that we know before the Great Change. What we do now will ripple through time for many generations to come. Therefore we must walk with wisdom and must see with our hearts. Those who walk in beauty with a clean heart may do great deeds. This is my mind and I have spoken."

These revelations from the Raven and Morning Star Spirit Societies surprised many who were present, for the other societies had no such prophecies of their own. Even Orobai was somewhat surprised by how these revelations and prophecies seemed to coincide with his own perceptions of Miraanni and the fate that awaited them both. Could it be that the Yamné had even more foresight in this than the Arnyar?

Before anyone else addressed the crowd there were private conversations among the different spirit societies concerning all that the elders had said. Many just sat in silence and took their own time to consider the three speeches carefully before speaking. At last, one of the two younger Want'né in whom Orobai had sensed disagreement spoke up. He took a posture of defiance before the crowd, clearly intent on challenging the prevailing wisdom. He glanced coldly in Orobai's direction, only catching his eye for a moment, and then spoke, having turned back to the crowd.

"Why have we not heard from Mu'shué himself?" he began rhetorically with an icy coolness in his voice. "It was he who brought this girl to us, but he has told us nothing. He has given us no explanation of how it is that after all these generations he has a younger sister. Though it is not our custom to pry into the lives of others, he should speak now, for are we not due some explanation if we are to take this girl to be a fulfillment of our own sacred prophecies? Our ancestors accepted Mu'shué as one from outside our families and they let him into our lives. But what of this young girl? Perhaps, knowing our traditions well through participating in our sacred ceremonials for generations, Mu'shué has decided to deceive us and take advantage of us for his own purposes.

"We all know that Mu'shué has many strange powers, many of which we have long suspected are unknown to us. He speaks with the beasts, has no family, save for now his 'younger sister,' and is strange in appearance, unlike all other beings in Aurduin. He is not one of us, nor is this child. Why should we trust him, or her? They are not like us. They work strange powers and follow their own paths. We must awaken to this fact and know that their intentions are not necessarily good for us. This one here may be a great deceiver. Think on this well before you heap praises and prayers upon this strange girl.

"Who is she? What does she want of us? And why are you all so willing to accept her? Has your faith and hope made you blind?

"This is my mind. I, T'urk'nan, have spoken."

The forcefulness of T'urk'nan's speech caught many off guard. The elders were especially concerned for, as T'urk'nan himself stated, it was not Yamné custom to be so direct and confrontational with others, especially honored guests, regardless of what kinds of mysterious events might accompany them. Several of the others murmured their agreement, however. Looking about, Orobai could see that the young man's words had had more impact than he would have expected. Clearly several were on the verge of being swayed and were ready to speak up in support of this minority view. Seeing what was happening, T'lan seized the moment and stood once more.

"T'urk'nan," he said authoritatively with a scowl of disapproval, "you are young and rash and you bring dishonor on us all by your behavior. You have only started on the path of a Want'é and still have much to learn. Many of us have known Mu'shué all our lives, and he has been a close friend of my own family for generations beyond number. Never has Mu'shué sought to deceive or manipulate any of us in any way. I challenge any of you here to speak otherwise."

To this no one responded, not even T'urk'nan, who sat staring at T'lan indignantly. After a few moments of silence, sounds of agreement with T'lan's words could again be heard in the room. Not wanting the friction to continue, Orobai thought that he should speak now and take advantage of the momentum of T'lan's counsel.

"I have known many of you your entire lives," Orobai said as he rose to his feet, "and I have been a friend of your people since the time of your distant ancestors. I have never sought to deceive you before and I do not seek to deceive you now. Young T'urk'nan is correct in reminding you that I do have many strange powers and abilities. But I have never used these abilities to harm or hurt others in any of my days and I will not begin to do so now. My task in life is unique and I carry a burden that none other in all of Aurduin has ever borne. T'urk'nan is again correct in saying that I am like no other, for my life is different from all others. Should it thus be strange to you that my sister is also unique, and her life one of strange and mysterious power?

"She is almost as new to me as she is to all of you," Orobai continued. "This you should plainly be able to see by her youth. I fear that I cannot answer many questions about her as some of you might wish. As for what part she may have to play in your own lore and sacred knowledge, I would say that that is for all of you to decide. It is not my choice and it is not my doing. The girl has a mind and will of her own and I cannot say to what end she may direct her abilities or what ultimate purpose she may serve. All I can tell you is that her purpose is great, and as many of you have felt or learned through your traditions, her purpose is beyond the scope of any here now. This I feel with certainty. She is a special being and she has a special destiny. Even the beasts of the forest know this. Why else do you think I come with wolf and eagle as part of my company? There are concerns here far beyond your own.

"You may make of all this what you will. That is your choice, though perhaps your people have already made the choice for you, and even this may be beyond the control of the Want'né. The people already speak of her as the Morning Star. They have named her Sará'é. Even if any of you wanted, could you stop the people from thinking of her thusly? She has given you gifts. This cannot be denied. What you make of them is neither my choice nor my doing. This is my mind and I have spoken."

Orobai looked about as he returned to his seat next to T'lan. Again there was silence and quiet, private conversations as the Want'né considered Orobai's words. Eventually others began to speak up in support of Orobai and Miraanni. Before long, it seemed that all except T'urk'nan and his companion, who never spoke, were in agreement. They did not hold Orobai accountable for Miraanni, nor did they feel that they were owed any kind of explanation about her, as T'urk'nan had demanded. They decided that for now, Miraanni would be accepted as Sará'é, the Heavenly One, the Morning Star. For many of the Want'né present, there were just too many signs pointing to that conclusion and they could not bring themselves to think otherwise. They then agreed that there would be a special portion of the child blessings that night to honor and bless Miraanni, accepting her as a holy person.

With this issue settled for the time being, T'lan escorted Orobai from the meeting arbor. "I am sorry for the way T'urk'nan treated you, my friend," said T'lan with a tone of regret and embarrassment in his voice. "T'urk'nan is young and wants to make a name for himself among the people and thus has acted rashly. As a Want'é he is very inexperienced. It is not proper for one such as yourself to have to endure such treatment and I am ashamed."

"There is no need for such feelings," said Orobai, patting his friend's shoulder. "I too think the girl to be something strange and perplexing, so why should your own people think otherwise? Not even I know the answers to the questions that are in the hearts of so many of you. But your prophecies and stories are compelling, for they fit with many of my own thoughts. As to how they may apply specifically to Miraanni, I cannot yet say. But perhaps in time we will understand more."

"So now that she has been accepted, what will you do with her?" asked T'lan. "What is to become of Sará'é? I think that many would like to see her stay with us, for she is sacred to our people now and they will not want to see her go, even if they are persuaded that her destiny lies elsewhere as Alu'inir and Ushun'ah indicated," said T'lan.

"I knew that this would be the case after what happened at the Ceremony last night," answered Orobai. "All I can tell you is this – reasons that are beyond my control compel me to take the girl to the east. I know that you trust me, and you must accept this fact. It is not something that I can change and it is certainly not something that your people can change either. To attempt to do so could only bring the wrath of the Arnyar upon you all. There are greater forces at work than you might imagine or even your spirit societies might imagine.

"Furthermore, I am worried that word of the girl is already spreading about Aurduin and I am concerned that those who might attempt to misuse her and her abilities could soon learn about her. This would not be good for your people, for if it were known that she was with you, it might bring unwanted visitors into your lives. I would not want to be responsible for allowing that to happen."

"But why east? Why must you go there, or is there nothing you can say?" asked T'lan, both puzzled and concerned.

Seeing that he had to tell T'lan something, Orobai made the decision to speak openly. He stopped and turned, looking T'lan directly in the eye.

"I will tell you this, and only you, for this is grave news," he said, followed by a long and dramatic pause. "The people of the far-west have killed two of the Arnyar. These were not the lesser eagles, mind you, but the true Arnyar. As I am sure you can imagine, there are forces and events at work that do not bode well for Aurduin and this is but a sign. The Arnyar themselves are very concerned for the child's safety. This journey that I am undertaking now is according to their instructions. In a word, I believe that they are afraid."

T'lan was stunned into near shock to hear this news. Never had he heard of anyone killing an Arnyar. Not even the most powerful peoples of Aurduin had ever had such an ability. And the blow of this news was doubly hard for T'lan, not just for its foreboding implications, but also for the fact that the true Arnyar were among the most revered of all beings by the Yamné. It pierced his heart to the core to hear such news and he could only respond with silence.

"So you see," continued Orobai, "there is much to be concerned about. Your people are far from the west, but perhaps not far enough to protect Sará'é from these dark designs. It is the Arnyar themselves who bid me remove the girl as far to the east as I can take her, and for that reason our destination is Laftandiar-Urya.

You can help us in this and I only pray that none of your people try to hinder us – for your own good, not my own – for my task will be completed by the will of the Arnyar."

These revelations impressed T'lan more fully than any that had yet come over the past two days. He could see clearly now that Orobai spoke the truth when he said that there were greater forces at work and, despite Miraanni's significance to his people, much more than their own tradition and culture might be at stake.

"You have my word," said the old Want'é, "that we Yamné will do all we can to help you and will do nothing to stop you from what you must do."

"Thank you, T'lan," said Orobai, reaching out and clasping his friend's shoulder firmly in his black hand. "I have always known you to be a most reasonable man. Your people are lucky to have you and you are a good leader. You are able to think of the greatest good and see beyond your own horizon. But I will not ask much of you – only a boat to travel the river and some supplies. If you wish to provide anything more, it will be welcome, but this is all that I will ask of you and your people."

"You ask too little of us, Mu'shué," replied T'lan, "for you know that we will do anything for Sará'é."

"No, I do not ask too little. In time, you may find that your own destinies are bound with hers in ways that you cannot even yet imagine, and perhaps at that time your service will be required in ways that will leave much to sorrow. Your own stories would seem to say as much, and I have felt this too. I thus ask as little as possible of you, for you may yet have much to pay."

T'lan looked carefully at Orobai, sensing something more.

"The Ul'mult'ah have opened the way for you, haven't they?" asked T'lan in a knowing tone. "They are showing things to you that you did not know."

"Yes," said Orobai.

"More visions will come," said T'lan, slowly nodding his head back and forth. "What you have seen thus far is only the beginning. The path to the future is opening before you. It is good that you have come to us now, for our sacrament will help to show you the way. In time, your vision will show you all you need to know. That is the way of the sacrament. The truth of Spirit will always make itself known to those who seek with an open heart."

Honoring Miraanni

E vening was near and soon it would be time for the ceremony to continue. Many individuals and groups of people were passing from camp to the sweat lodges to purify themselves. Others who would not be participating in the night's activities were busy hiring various Want'né to perform private blessings or healings for themselves or for their families. Still others, mostly women, were busy preparing the evening meal that would be served shortly.

Orobai had spent some time walking about the village with little Miraanni in his arms, making her available to the public for people to come up and show their respect, which many eagerly took advantage of. Miraanni seemed to enjoy the attention and the chance to get out and about with her elder brother. She was bright and alert and was quick to smile or give people inquisitive looks.

Most of all she was captivated by the natural world around her. Trees, birds, small animals scurrying about, and the eagle Sto'orn circling overhead keeping a watchful eye on his charge, all caught Miraanni's fascinated attention. All this gave Orobai great joy as he felt he too could see and experience the world anew, just as did the small child in his arms. He was again overcome with feelings of a deep connection to the little girl and a profound sense of completeness. Never had he imagined that one such as Miraanni would enter his life and change his thoughts and feelings so compellingly.

Gen'shu'n eventually came after Orobai once more to bring him to dinner. Lilt'a was with her cousin and gladly accepted Miraanni back into her arms to nurse her and let her rest before the ceremonial activities that would take place later in the evening. Many people were already gathering for the meal, lining up in the west, ready for the food that servers were setting out in rows to the east. Several of the Want'né came forward to bless the food. It only took a few moments for them to say their prayers and make the necessary ritual gestures, sprinkling the food with sacred pollen.

Orobai sat with T'lan, Mayé, and their large extended family. There were young parents, cousins, brothers, sisters, grandchildren, aunts, uncles, and relatives of every kind. It was one of the few times where the families would all gather together in this way during the Iryuah'eeh'né as there were many restrictions about who should be with whom at various times in the larger ceremonial procedure. This was family time, however, when all gathered to eat together and share in the blessing of the children who had been born over the previous year.

This year T'lan and Mayé's family were paying special attention to Miraanni as they would honor her as one of their own in the ceremony, given their family's longstanding relationship to Orobai. As they ate their dinner they decided that T'lan and Mayé themselves would serve as adopted grandparents for Miraanni and that Orobai and Lilt'a would serve as the "parents" of the child. This was perhaps not ideal, but it would do to satisfy the ceremonial requirements of having proper family representatives. As Miraanni had no immediate relatives, outside of her elder brother, T'lan's family was happy to serve the surrogate role for this special child, and indeed, it was an honor for them.

Lilt'a was especially honored to be the "mother" for Miraanni in addition to her own young son, Sa'yun, who had been born to her and her husband T'inshar just that year. Sa'yun was now nine months old and was his father's pride, being their first child. It was because Lilt'a was still nursing Sa'yun that T'lan had originally asked her to be the wet nurse for Miraanni.

The sun had now set and the sliver of a crescent moon was just beginning to rise on the eastern horizon at the end of the row of tree arbors. The stars were shinning in the sky above and a cool, clear breeze flowed in from the east. It was a beautiful night and Orobai was happy to be having his little sister go through this sacred Yamné ceremony. He had always enjoyed the ceremony, but now he truly understood it in a new way with the weight of the responsibility of family. It all took on a completely new meaning and significance that he had scarcely imagined. He saw now how important it was for cultures to nurture and guide children into the complex world of adulthood, individuality, and meaning. What effect this would ultimately have on Miraanni, Orobai could only guess. He had never been a child himself and had never struggled through childhood, adolescence, and coming into a sense of personal identity. All of this was foreign and strange to him. All he knew was that he truly wanted for Miraanni what the ceremony promised – a blessed life guided by the spirits of Aurduin through all the changes of her being.

The meal finished, it was time to begin Miraanni's initiation. As with so many other ceremonies, the first step was purification. In the first Shan'i'ruh a large group of women were in charge of ensuring that there was plenty of hot water available for all the infants to be bathed in as well as fresh water for each child, for no two could share the same water in this ritual. Several of the women were constantly moving back and forth between the Shan'i'ruh and the lake where they got the water to be brought back up to be warmed with heated stones. A mild natural soap from a local plant proved ideal to wash the infants clean. Seeing

Orobai, Lilt'a, and the little one in their arms now, the women quickly brought everything they would need to bathe the pure white infant and begin her on her ritual journey of a life guided by the sacred.

Never before in his many years had Orobai washed an infant in this way. Miraanni felt slippery and vulnerable in his hands, yet vibrant and full of life. He carefully cradled her as Lilt'a's delicate fingers spread the soap over her body. Miraanni smiled and cooed receptively, staring up joyfully at her ceremonial parents. She seemed so precious to Orobai right then. He wanted to remember this moment and the significance of it all. He thought of how similar this was to his own ordeal in the sweat lodge, a ritual cleansing and purification. He could see why the Want'né used a similar procedure for patients who were too ill or infirm to withstand the sweat lodge. The infirm and infants alike were cared for and nurtured in a loving embrace, helpless and completely dependent on the compassion and gentleness of others. Orobai could hardly put into words how it made him feel. *My beautiful little sister . . .*

Miraanni smiled happily throughout her warm bath and did not cry or fuss, as did many of the other infants. When they were done, Orobai and Lilt'a, with Miraanni in their arms, moved in a sunwise circuit about the first Shan'i'ruh and passed Miraanni off to T'lan and Mayé who were waiting at the doorway to the second arbor. There the elderly couple ceremonially dried her off with sweet sage and smudged her clean. As if she were their very own grandchild, the old couple cradled her with love as they passed the sage about her soft and exposed body, letting the scented oils rub into her milky-white skin. As they did so, Mayé gently sang a Yamné lullaby, telling the story of how the Morning Star once fell to earth and transformed into a kite, which Miraanni answered with her own soft coos, bringing a tear to Mayé's dark eyes. She was now ready for the next Shan'i'ruh.

In the third arbor it was Lilt'a's job to paint Miraanni with white clay, a substance the Yamné held in the highest regard as they considered anything it touched to be blessed and healed. It was cold when it first touched her but dried quickly into a thick coat of clay. Miraanni was now marked as a sacred being, as were all the other children, sacred all.

In the next Shan'i'ruh was the dance to the four directions. Here Miraanni's entire "family" could participate together, each having done their individual parts. There the Sun Spirit Society sang for the new children and their blessed families. The sun defined the movement of sacred power and the very process of creation, bringing all lives to their fulfillment and destiny.

Up to four families could go through the dance simultaneously and the Shan'i'ruh was a constant wheel of motion and sound, catching up Orobai, Lilt'a and the others in a great solar turning of sacred energy. Moving through the process was a constant turning and spinning in sacred motion, all accompanied by pulsing songs of the sun and its power. Taking Miraanni in his arms, Orobai and the others spun into place in the west where singers and dancers guided them through the spiral dance of power. At each direction they sang and danced, honoring the power of that direction and all the symbolic associations that it held for the Yamné.

Orobai thought of what the directions meant to him, as a keeper of the Altfein-Aryat. He thought of how much the four directions defined him both through the ancient philosophy as well as through his experiences of living among the Goargathr, the Great Mountains, and the temples that they once were, the original homes of the Illan. He thought of all that he had to teach Miraanni of the directions and how they guided all life through the power of the Four Mountains. He wanted to share so much with her, and almost lamented the thought of having to wait until she was older when she could truly comprehend the deep mysteries he wanted to impart. For perhaps the first time in his life, Orobai felt that he was not entirely at peace with time.

In the two following Shan'i'ruh, the Raven and Kite Spirit Societies performed their dances, respectively. In both arbors families gathered around the central fire and dancers moved sunwise around them in their particular blessing dances of highly stylized movement, gesture, and sound.

In the second of these two Shan'i'ruh, the Kite Spirit Society held a special honoring dance for Miraanni and had her "family" dance with them when they performed their blessings for the other families that were present. They were all very happy to perform with Miraanni and the other families seemed to feel especially blessed and honored by having her in their group for that portion of the ceremony. Miraanni was completely taken up by the process and seemed to truly love every moment of it. *She is at home*, Orobai thought to himself.

In the next two Shan'i'ruh Lilt'a and Orobai received the two sacred stones of a person's spirit. In Yamné culture, as told in the creation stories, all individuals had two aspects to their spiritual being, these being embodied in turquoise stones and quartz crystals. It was the Salmon who gave the turquoise. It went first to the parents, who kept it in trust for the child until his or her initiation at puberty. Then at death a descendant, preferably one's child of the same gender, would keep the turquoise for a year. Then on the final day of the Iryuah'eeh'né, the stone-bearer would toss the stone into the lake to return it to the Salmon, who could then bestow it upon a new individual, symbolizing the cyclical nature of life.

For Miraanni, Lilt'a was to carry the quartz, and Orobai would keep the turquoise. Having gone through this ceremony together, they were now obligated to participate in the Iryuah'eeh'né together again when Miraanni reached the age of initiation, when they could pass the stones on to her as she took on the responsibilities of full adulthood. Until that time each would have the task of keeping Miraanni's stones safe for her.

For Lilt'a this was more a symbolic gesture than any real mark of responsibility, for she knew that soon Orobai and Miraanni would leave on their journey to the east, perhaps never to return. She accepted it gladly, however, and beamed with a deep pride at the great honor of having such a symbolically meaningful role in Miraanni's life. As for Orobai, he received the turquoise with the utmost seriousness, feeling the weight of all that it meant, for him, Miraanni, and the Yamné. Holding the bright turquoise stone in his rough, dark hands, Orobai pondered how something so seemingly insignificant could carry so much meaning.

In comparison to the Altfein, the turquoise was irrelevant and meaningless, but for the Yamné it was everything – a person's life-essence was embodied therein.

What would Miraanni's life be, Orobai wondered. He rolled the stone over in his hands, as though if he turned it enough it would reveal the secrets of Miraanni's fate and all the significance that it had for Aurduin. It was just a small stone, but it was heavy with meaning, and even heavier with unseen potential. He clasped the stone firmly, silently vowing to never let it go, until the time that he must. He knew that at some point, Miraanni's life would be her own. She would have to make her own decisions and face the consequences of her choices. She would have to carry her own stones, as the Yamné would say. No one would be able to do that for her, not even Orobai. Would Yamné culture serve as her guide, as it would for the other children who were passing through this ceremony with them? Could it even mean anything at all to Miraanni, not truly being a part of this culture – regardless of what the Yamné thought of her or what cultural significance they placed in her being? Only time would tell.

After several hours of passing through the seven Shan'i'ruh, Miraanni and her "family" were finished with their ceremonial duties. They had collectively brought her into the world and Yamné culture. In the eyes of the Yamné, she was now a real person, with all the hopes, potentials, and frailties as anyone else. Though not a human, she was now a person. Just like the Raven and Kite, the primal brother and sister who had brought the Yamné into the world and given them their place and their customs, the Yamné had sought to give Miraanni her place and her own identity. In this all life was bound together and tied to the sacred, giving it meaning, guidance, and purpose.

As the Yamné would say, Miraanni had been welcomed home.

Endings and New Beginnings

The following day and night were relaxing and carefree for Orobai. He was not involved with the initiation procedures for the youth who had come of age, so other than visiting with friends, eating some good food, and wandering about the village, Orobai did not have much to do. The two previous late nights had tired him out and he was happy to have the respite from any formal duties and ceremonial responsibilities.

Today, the fourth day of the ceremony, it was colder than it had been over the past few weeks and it rained some. When the sky eventually cleared in the late afternoon there was a fresh layer of snow in the mountains, though Golgath was completely obstructed from view with thick, dark clouds enveloping it. A cold wind blew from the north, which, with the rain, kept Orobai indoors most of the day, wanting to be by the fire sipping tea and softly humming to himself, mindful not to draw Miraanni's attention lest some power go to work as before.

As he sat before the fire, the break in activity allowed Orobai's mind to wander and contemplate the significance of recent events and all that had changed in his life in such a short period of time. Looking into the flames, it was almost as if he could make out images and signs, yet he could not fully understand them. So much was still a mystery. *All will be revealed in time*, Orobai told himself, knowing full well that in some fashion these events were foreordained even before he came to be. He wondered how much the Arnyar and the Illan had really known, however. Even the Arnyar admitted that not all the future could be known. *Creation works in mysterious ways. Goar Saum edi laur.* Only the Great Mystery knows, as the ancient dictum of the Illan so eloquently stated.

Time passed quickly. That night would be the concluding evening of the Iryuah'eeh'né, marking the end of the mourning period for Mayé and those like her who had dedicated themselves to carrying their deceased loved ones' spirit stones.

Though Orobai had no particular need to participate that night, he decided that he would, out of support for Mayé and her family, especially after all that they had done for him and Miraanni. It was the least that he could do.

Before everything got underway, he wanted to make arrangements for their departure, knowing that once the ceremony had come to its conclusion Sto'orn would be eager to get their journey underway. Orobai would have to find someone willing to part right away, or at least get an extra boat so they could go on their own.

Orobai sought out T'lan and Mayé. He found them, as he expected, resting in their kughain. T'lan was recuperating from the night before, as he had played an instrumental role in the initiation procedures. Both were drinking tea and eating a small meal, which they invited Orobai to join them in.

"It will be a good year," said T'lan, as much for himself as anyone else. "We had many new initiates last night, many strong and brave young people. All the spirit societies gained new members, and there was a particularly large number of young women who received visions of Yu'rin and thus joined the Morning Star Spirit Society. It would seem that Sará'é's presence has had a strong effect on our maidens. They want to be as one with her and all that she is expected to do for this world. There were many who had visions of Kag and the Raven Spirit Society grew significantly as well. Clearly great forces are at work. The times to come will be great indeed, with so many young people dedicating themselves to the spirit-paths of their ancestors. Our stories have always guided and instructed us through the voices of our grandfathers and grandmothers. They were wise, and through them we know how to live. This is how it has always been, and our stories speak to us with even greater meaning now that Sará'é herself has come among us."

"I wanted to ask you, T'lan," said Orobai, seeing an opportunity to cull more from the learned man, "if you could tell me more about the Morning Star. I know your stories from the Iryuah'eeh'né, but I would like to understand more of what Yu'rin did in the beginning times. Is there more that you can tell?"

T'lan thought for a moment before responding. He seemed to be deciding how forthright he should be. Eventually a look of acceptance passed over his face and he spoke in a tone that was reminiscent of his oration on the first night of the ceremony.

"Our ancestors say that the Morning Star is the one who taught us of our origins. Though it was the Eagles that taught us how to hunt and fish, it was the Morning Star who gave us knowledge of ourselves as a people when we failed to learn the lessons of the Eagles.

"They say that long ago, when the world was still new, she came among us. The brightest star in the heavens, she came to earth to teach us. After the creation of the Eagles, the Morning Star had gone back into the sky. She flew away as a Kite and returned to the heavens, though she was not as bright as she was before. The Raven too returned to where he came from, back to the Spirit, and the Morning Star was as a messenger or intermediary between the Raven and the world, for the Morning Star rests at the edge of night and day, between that which is seen and that which is not seen. With her she brings the day and all knowledge and enlightenment.

"They say that when the Kite and the Raven left this world below, the people became lost in their hearts and minds. We could survive, but we did not know how to live in balance with the world and we abused our knowledge. We used what we had learned from the Eagles and we hunted, but sometimes we hunted too much, and then there were not enough deer. Then they say that we fished, which we also learned from the Eagles, but we fished too much, and then there were not enough salmon. When the deer went away, the forest became overgrown with grasses, and lightning struck, lighting the grasses on fire, which burned much of the forest. And with the disappearance of the salmon, the river began to run dry, for there were no salmon to bring the waters with them from the oceans when they returned. Through our greed and carelessness, we destroyed those things we needed to survive.

"They say that the people were starving and hungry. Our knowledge failed us, for we did not listen closely to what the Eagles taught us. We abused our powers of what we had learned, bringing ruin to ourselves and others. They say that we thought only of ourselves, and not of the other beings of this world. Our knowledge, though useful and necessary, was dangerous, and it brought us too close to our own destruction.

"They say that it was then that the Morning Star returned to earth for some time. She came to earth as a great Kite, and when she touched the earth she changed into a beautiful young woman, and the people called her Sará'é, the Heavenly One. It was then that she, the Heavenly One, gave us the Iryuah'eeh'né. She taught us of our origin and gave us these sacred ceremonies by which we live our lives. She also taught us of the use of the Ul'mult'ah and taught us that the Ul'mult'ah was the power of the Raven, and that through them we would know Spirit.

"Through the ceremony and the sacrament we learned how to live in balance with the other things of this world, they say. We learned how to take only what we needed, and we learned how to honor the spirits of nature so that there would always be plenty for all. We learned how to renew the world in the cycles of life, the four seasons, and the power of the four directions. We learned how to raise our young in a sacred way, and we learned how to initiate our young people, and to honor the dead, they say. It was Sará'é who first began the Seven Spirit Societies, the Shandah, they say. She taught us all these things and brought balance to our lives.

"So you see, all these things come from her. It was through her that we learned to truly live in a sacred way that honors the earth and all our relations of land, water, and sky, and all those that are unseen as well.

"When she had taught the people, she returned to the sky, telling the people that they could always look to her for guidance and protection and that she would announce the coming of dawn, the new day, the new beginning, which brings blessings for all beings. It is through her that we have learned how to live, how to be Human Beings in this world, they say. She is sacred to us. Without her, we would not know who we are or our place in this world."

T'lan then shifted his position a bit, almost imperceptibly, and spoke once more, though now with a less-authoritative voice and was more conversational.

"As for what Alu'inir said of the return of the Morning Star, I do not know. As you know, Orobai, I am of the Salmon Spirit Society and do not share in the secret teachings of the Morning Star school – that is only for their initiates. Were you to ask them, they probably would not say more than you already know. Perhaps in time, when Sará'é is older, they will tell her what they know. If we are correct, Sará'é already knows more than any of us. They say that she brings with her a new beginning. Perhaps this is the end of our way of life as we know it now. Perhaps there is something that we have done wrong, as happened so long ago. I do not know. All I know is that she is here now. When she is older . . . we will see . . .

"Now Orobai, let us talk of your travels," said T'lan, having revealed all he felt he could of this sacred persona. "You have said that you must leave us when the Feast is completed. Tomorrow morning all will be made new and the people will go their separate ways in a few days time, after they have had enough of singing and dancing with their relatives. What can we do to help you on your own way?"

"I need to travel down river, to the east. I will need a boat that can hold me, the girl, the wolves, and some provisions," answered Orobai. "We will need to leave tomorrow, before most. Perhaps you know of someone who will be willing to make the journey a few days early, or of a boat we could take. If you could also provide some provisions to help us along, it would gladly be received."

"That we can easily do," said T'lan cheerfully, "and we would happily do more. Lilt'a herself, along with her husband, T'inshar, will be traveling a portion of the distance that you must travel, and were you to ask her, I am sure that they would go farther. They can take you all the way to the ocean if you need it."

"I am sure that you are right," said Orobai, "but I will not ask that of her or her husband. Lilt'a has a family of her own that she must raise. She has been of the greatest help here in the village, but we have Faen to look after the girl. In the future, Lilt'a will be needed again, of that I am sure, for if nothing else, there will be Sará'é's eventual initiation, to which she is now obligated. I would not have us burden Lilt'a further, though I know that she would give of herself willingly, as would many of your people."

"This is true, Mu'shué. My people are dedicated to the girl now. There is nowhere that she could go that she will not be in our hearts and minds. We will look forward with great anticipation to the time when you are able to bring her back to us. Perhaps then we will see how all our destinies are entwined.

"As for tomorrow and the days after, we will gladly give you a sturdy boat, provisions, and any supplies that you need. Lilt'a will help you as long as you like or need. Eventually your journey will take you from our lands. What lies beyond, I do not personally know, for I have never traveled far beyond where we live upon the river. Such is the life of the Yamné. At that time you will be beyond our immediate help, though you will be in our prayers, always. We will pray that you will bring Sará'é back to us soon."

Thus the arrangements were made for Orobai and his company to begin their journey down the river. Orobai was pleased at the thought of having his Yamné friends with him for the beginning and would enjoy the company. But he also looked forward to being on their own, beyond the reach of Yamné prophetic expectation.

* * * *

With his plans set, Orobai took his leave of the old couple so that they might finish their preparations for the mourning ritual in private, and walked in a meditative state about the edge of the lake. His mind kept turning back to the details of Yamné oral tradition and all that was revealed therein. He had always appreciated their culture, but now he had to reevaluate it all in light of what it seemed to reveal about both Miraanni and himself.

Orobai's meditations were disrupted when one of the young men he had seen at the council of Want'né approached him. It was the young man whose concern Orobai had sensed, yet he had said nothing of his feelings at the time, letting his outspoken and brash friend, T'urk'nan, make all the accusations. Now it seemed that he had something to say.

"Mu'shué," said the young man, walking up to Orobai. "I do not think we know each other. My name is Jinru. I am a Want'é of the Raven Spirit Society. I would speak with you for a moment."

"Very well, Jinru," said Orobai, wondering what was on the young man's mind. "Have a seat and tell me what troubles you."

Orobai sat down on an old log, facing the lake. He looked ahead of him as the young Want'é came and sat beside him. The young man looked him up and down for some minutes before speaking, as though weighing what he was about to say carefully. Orobai appreciated this difference between this young Want'é and his outspoken friend, T'urk'nan.

"You will remember what my friend said at our meeting," said the young man at last. "I too, and some others as well, still share his cautions, though many keep to themselves given the general feeling among the people now. I do not accept their unquestioning enthusiasm. I think that you know more than you are willing to share with all of us and I do not like that. It is your right, however, and I will not press you to reveal your secrets. But I know that you and the girl have them.

"I will share some of my own mind with you," continued the young Want'é, "for I saw many things when I took the sacrament the other night. When I watched you sing, I saw you as a large black bird. You were covered in feathers with a large black beak, and instead of singing, you were croaking out your song as a crow or raven. At first I was surprised, but when I saw your 'sister' it began to make sense to me and it seemed that you have not revealed your true self to us. This is what makes me think that perhaps there is some deception here.

"But then the more I looked into you, the less I could see the image of the bird. I then saw four colors radiating from around your heart. As the colors grew strong, black, green, yellow, white, they formed into four different crystals of the same colors. When this happened, it seemed as though it were the end of the world and there was a great darkness. I do not know the cause of this and the spirits have not revealed more, but I know in my heart that it had to do with you and the girl.

"As you now know, our Spirit Society, Kagdah, has foretold of a coming time when all the world will be cast into destruction and that there will be a great remaking of Aurduin. We have not known what would cause this great destruction or why, but some of us now believe that it is because of you and the girl and something that you will do, or perhaps have already done.

"There are some, like T'urk'nan, who would work to prevent this, if possible. I am not like T'urk'nan, however, and I take longer to think and to speak than he. Spirit works in mysterious ways, and who are we to presume to know what should or should not be? But T'urk'nan will want some action. He will not rest, even if you take the girl away from us. He has a love for his people, even if he acts rashly, and he would not have any harm or disillusionment come to them. He acts from a quick heart. He is passionate, and at times his passion makes him act without forethought. This you should know, for you do not have all the Yamné as friends with his influence. If T'urk'nan can stop what you and the girl are going to do, I think he will, and perhaps this is for the best. I do not know. Perhaps in time the spirits will tell more of what is to come and what we may do.

"But you are a dark secret, and the girl is still a mystery, regardless of what any of my people, or any of the Want'né, say about her. I will be watching and seeking with my spiritual eyes for the answers. I just want you to know that I have not made up my mind about you and that there are some others who feel likewise. I do not truly know who you are. I do not know what these four jewels were that I saw in my vision. You are not related to us. You have no family, no roots. You may have known us for many generations, but to me, you will always be a stranger."

Not wanting to give Orobai a chance to respond, or perhaps not wanting to hear what he had to say, Jinru quickly got up and walked off, leaving Orobai where he had found him. Orobai respected the fact that the young Want'é was troubled and was intrigued by his vision. The image of the four colored jewels was interesting. Could it be a representation of the quest he was to embark upon to the Orgathen? Or was it something else? Why all this connection to a sense of impending destruction, and at his own doing? Surely Orobai himself would not be a cause of destruction and death. Never would he wish such a fate upon the world, nor would he knowingly participate in anything that would have such disastrous effects. *But what if . . .*

Regardless, it seemed clear to Orobai that the Yamné, let alone this wary Want'é, had a great deal to say of events to come. Their insight was profound and their oral histories revealed surprising depth. He had known their stories and traditions for centuries, but never, even in his most prophetic moments, had he dreamed of how they would impinge upon his own destiny, as they seemed to do now. *Are these stories the past or the future*? They perhaps were not so much what had happened as what was to come, at least in some sense. Perhaps their greatest relevance was ultimately outside of time, outside of history, and spoke to more universal forces at work beneath the surface of time and appearances.

Is it the Ul'mult'ah that have revealed so much to the Yamné?

* * * *

The sky was getting dark. Soon it would be time for the final night of the Iryuah'eeh'né to begin. On this night, mourning families would honor death and loss and give it the respect and recognition it was due. Already there had been the celebration of life, birth, growth, and now it was time to honor the great return of death so that new life might flourish in the world, free from the lingering spirits of those who came before. A world made new and cleansed through ritual, prayer, and purification. This was what the Feast was all about. With these acts the Yamné renewed themselves, their culture, and their world. The cycle of life would continue for another year.

Taking his sister with him, Orobai found T'lan and Mayé just completing their preparations for the evening's activities. As with other mourners, Mayé was busy painting her face with red clay, the sign of mourning in Yamné culture. Mayé was also wearing her mother's ceremonial shawl, which would now become hers. All the rest of her mother's belongings had been burned the year before, as was Yamné custom.

Soon all of the immediate family had gathered at T'lan and Mayé's camp. Gen'shu'n was there with his family, Sané and her husband had arrived, and Lilt'a and her husband and son were there was well. Like her sister Mayé, Sané had her face painted as well.

The family moved out together and joined the others collected at the east end of the Shan'i'ruh to receive the blessings of the Want'né. Orobai stood among the Want'né with Miraanni in his arms so that the people could once again come and show their respects and receive a blessing from her. Many of the people went first to a Want'é and then to Miraanni and Orobai, whispering quiet prayers, asking for blessings, and extending their own blessings to the brother and sister.

Eventually, Orobai, still holding Miraanni, went with his host family to the Shan'i'ruh. Each family went to the society in which the deceased had been a member. With Mayé's mother having been a member of the Yu'rindah, Orobai followed Mayé and Sané into the second arbor, the station for the Morning Star Spirit Society.

Large fires burned brightly inside each arbor. Families that were just beginning their year of mourning were bringing items that had belonged to their deceased. There, the Want'né would remove any spiritual potency from the objects and have the families toss them into the central fire, as custom dictated.

As Sané and Mayé had performed this aspect of the mourning ritual the previous year, they had nothing to burn of their mother's. Now they extended their condolences to those who had lost a loved one over the course of the year and were just beginning their yearlong honoring of their dead. Many came with tears in their eyes and carried each other in their arms as they committed their loved one's belongings to the fire. For many this was a difficult act, and for some, it was the first real recognition of loss of a family member.

Like many, Orobai stood watching the flames as each family took its turn placing various objects and belongings into the fire. The respectful and meditative silence was broken, however, buy an argument quickly escalating on the other side of the arbor. It was T'urk'nan, marked with the mourning paint on his face and looking angrily at those about him. They were all concerned that some items meant for burning were apparently missing. The others who were with T'urk'nan were clearly not pleased and there were nervous and angry looks among them and accusatory comments began to fly. There did not seem to be anyone in particular to direct the displeasure at, however, and thus tensions remained unresolved and grew worse with each passing moment. In apparent anger, some of their company left hurriedly, while others remained with T'urk'nan.

When T'urk'nan saw that Orobai and Miraanni were in the same room he at first seemed surprised. Then, speaking loudly so that others might clearly hear, T'urk'nan said, "Perhaps those two over there know something of this!" pointing at Orobai and Miraanni. "I knew that we should not trust them!"

T'lan reacted immediately in defense of his friends. "What accusations are you making, T'urk'nan? Did you not learn before that you must show our guests some respect? Can you not see that they are here now to honor our dead in a sacred way?"

"As all of you here know, my father was a great healer of the Morning Star Society," said T'urk'nan, looking around the room as he addressed the crowd, whose attention was now fixated on the growing dispute. "He helped many people over the years and always used his power in a good way. And now that I am here to mourn him and show him the respect that he is due, I find that many of his krin are missing. Someone has taken his power objects – his stones, shells, feathers, and beads. I know in my heart that none of my family would dishonor his spirit in such a way. But I have seen how these two have sought to deceive the hearts and minds of my people, and most of all, of the people in my father's beloved Spirit Society, the Yu'rindah. I have said before that these two manipulate us for their own reasons, and now I believe that they have had some part to play in my father's missing krin!"

"This is absurd," countered T'lan. "My own mother-in-law, Malin'ur, was a member of the Morning Star Society and we honor her here tonight. Mu'shué and Sará'é have done nothing in offense to her, her spirit, or her memory. Why would they do so for your father, whom they do not even know? And what possible proof could you give as evidence for this outrageous claim?"

"You all saw what they did on the first night," proclaimed T'urk'nan, becoming even bolder, stepping closer to T'lan and staring at him defiantly. "They have power over the krin. You all saw – they made them materialize out of the air. How easily they might then also take some for their own uses. And as for you, T'lan, your mother-in-law's krin were passed to Sané, your sister-in-law, so we all know where they are. But my father died only last month when he was caught in a snowstorm. He did not have a chance to pass them down properly. They were to go to me, to strengthen my own spirit and help me along the path of a Want'é. Now many of his possessions are missing, though I saw them all only a few days ago, before these two arrived and started to deceive us with their sorcery and cloud our visions with their deceptions and cunning."

"But you have no proof," said Sané calmly. "Yes, my mother's krin were passed to me and I carry them with honor. Perhaps you too would have been able to carry your father's krin in honor if he had not passed away as he had. Yet we have neither seen nor heard anything that would indicate that Mu'shué has had anything to do with what you accuse him of. And what is more, he would have no reason to do so."

"Perhaps he did it out of spite from what I said of him and his 'sister' earlier," said T'urk'nan, clearly becoming frustrated as he paced back and forth with a furrowed brow and wild look in his eyes. "He seeks revenge on me and my family for speaking the truth to all of you. He should be cast out from our midst now lest he do us some harm and work his sorcery on us again. I will not have my father's power abused by this stranger!"

"For the loss of your father I am truly sorry," said Orobai at last. "He must have been a great man and I am sorry not to have known him. However, I assure you that I know nothing of this. Your father's life and death are a mystery to me and I have no desire for his krin or anything else that may have been his. I have no use for such objects anyway, even if I did covet them. You can be assured that I had nothing to do with this and it would be best for you to seek answers elsewhere, as the longer you accuse me, the longer the true perpetrator will remain unknown."

Sensing that the mood of the crowd was against him, T'urk'nan backed down and did not pursue his accusations further. He seemed strangely satisfied with what he had said, however, as if it did not even truly matter if Orobai had taken his father's krin or not – it was merely important that he had said so, and made a good show of it. Seeing that others were not very pleased with this outburst during this sensitive time, T'urk'nan, and those with him, left the ceremonial arbor in a dramatic flurry.

T'lan again felt it necessary to apologize to Orobai for T'urk'nan's behavior. Orobai was not so much offended as he was concerned about what T'urk'nan's true motives might have been. Perhaps he truly thought that Orobai had taken his father's krin, but why make such an accusation without any proof, or even any direct clues other than the fact that Orobai and Miraanni had some strange power over the krin – at least over those that were manifested on the first night of the Ceremony? It did not make any sense, other than to serve to discredit Orobai, which T'urk'nan clearly wanted. But if the krin truly were stolen, then T'urk'nan should be looking for the true culprit. Something was not right.

But it was time to think of other things for the ceremony was moving on. Mayé and Sané were now ready for their final act of mourning.

By the time Orobai and the others reached the water's edge, Gen'shu'n was waiting there for them with a longboat that would easily fit the family and their honored guests. No one spoke and all observed the beauty of the night in reverential silence. Above them the moon waxed and shed its silvery light about the lake. In the distance Golgath shone in the night sky with the light of the moon reflecting off its white stone and snow, the dark clouds having blown away in the cold night air. The stars glimmered above and the waters of the lake were still. There was peace within their hearts.

Knowing what must be done, the family filed into the longboat with Mayé at the very front, carrying her mother's turquoise stone at her breast. Slowly the men paddled the boat out to the center of the lake. All that could be heard was the sound of lapping water against the boat, the splash of oars, and the quiet sound of breathing accompanied by the subtle ripples of grief that occasionally passed through the family.

Before long they had passed far from the shore and were at the center of the sacred lake. There were already several other families there, performing the same acts that Mayé would now do herself.

Standing at the bow of the boat, Mayé took the stone from her breast and offered it to the four directions. In her prayers she gave thanks to the salmon for all that they gave to the people, including their lives for the lives of the Yamné. She showed them the proper respect for imparting the turquoise stone to her mother and giving her spirit and life. For each direction she said a different prayer as her mother had taught her to do when she was still only a small child. At last, after having offered the turquoise to the north, she bathed it with pollen, a symbol of the east and new life, and let it drop from her hands to sink into the dark depths below. In a flash of moonlight, the turquoise stone quickly sank beneath the surface and was gone.

Watching the stone fall from Mayé's hands and slip into the dark waters, Orobai's attention suddenly shifted. The scene he saw before him was changed. It was day. He saw a Yamné boat floating on crystal clear waters of turquoise blue. In the boat were two people whom Orobai did not recognize and in their hands they held long curved knives. Lying at the front of the boat was a beautiful young woman, all white and luminous. She was struggling. As odd as it was, it seemed to Orobai that she was attempting to give birth. *Miraanni . . ?* In the distance, surrounding the boat, Orobai sensed the presence of four colored jewels. *Four jewels – just like Jinru described.* Then the scene shifted again, and Orobai saw a large crystal egg sinking down into the turquoise waters and was gone. The vision faded. Orobai found himself in the boat once more, Miraanni looking up at him with her large silver eyes.

"Do you know what it means?" Orobai asked his sister, almost inaudibly. "What is this vision?"

Miraanni only looked up at her brother and made no sound or sign.

In silence, the company rowed back to shore. With the coming of the dawn, their long and uncertain journey to Laftandiar-Urya would begin.

Parting Gifts

With the coming of the cold dawn, it was time to begin the journey down the river. Gen'shu'n and T'inshar had risen early and moved all of Orobai's belongings to the bottom of the falls where they had a longboat waiting. Orobai had offered to help, but the two men would hear nothing of it and instead invited him to wait for them by the boat. The morning was foggy and overcast, a heavy mist floating above the surface of the black waters. Visibility was less than half the span of the river. Orobai pulled his cloak tightly about him and drew his hood over his head, watching his breath mix with the fog.

Once the two men had everything ready, T'inshar disappeared into the fog one last time, going to retrieve Lilt'a, who was busy preparing the two children for the boat ride. Gen'shu'n similarly slipped away to find his parents, knowing that they wanted to see Orobai and his sister off. Sto'orn fidgeted nearby, eager to get the journey underway.

Orobai stood by the boat with Faen and the two pups, looking over their belongings, wondering how soon he could send the over-abundance of gifts home when suddenly Faen bristled at the sound of a twig breaking behind them. Orobai turned to catch sight of a dark figure, barely visible through the shroud of fog, standing silently just a short distance off.

"Be still," said Orobai to the wolf, sensing the tension of her reaction. "It's nothing to worry about," he added, gently putting his hand on her head and smoothing down her raised hackles. Then, speaking to the dark figure, "Good morning" said Orobai, calling out in Yamné.

No answer came. The figure hesitated a moment, and then slipped away just as stealthily as it had arrived.

"That one was no good," said Faen through her snarl.

"I know," said Orobai. "Now that we're leaving, he'll be better off."

In the place of the lone figure several others now arrived, slowly coming into definition through the uniform grey of the fog. It was T'lan and Mayé, wrapped in warm furs to keep out the cold, obviously having just woken up from the looks on their faces. Gen'shu'n came up behind them, along with T'inshar, Lilt'a, and the two children.

"Everything ready, I see," said T'lan.

"Yes," said Orobai, "thanks to these two young men."

"That's quite a load you have there, Mu'shué," said Mayé, looking over the large pile of gifts that had been given to Orobai and Miraanni over the course of the four-day ceremony in the longboat.

"Yes, we've received many offerings," said Orobai, looking over the full boat. "Your people have been very gracious this year and have given us far more than they should have."

"It just shows their love," said T'lan.

"And I hope you have room for a few more," added Mayé. She had made a small beaded bag with the Yamné symbols for the Morning Star on one side and the Kite on the other. Inside the bag was a mixture of cattail pollen and white clay. "Keep the child's turquoise stone in here," she explained. "It will keep it sacred and protected. When she comes of age, you can give it to her when you bring her back for the rest of her ceremony."

Orobai gladly accepted the small gift, putting Miraanni's turquoise stone within the intricately beaded bag and then slipping it into one of his many pockets. He then watched as Mayé gave a similar bag to Lilt'a, which she explained was for the quartz crystal.

Next it was T'lan's turn to give a special offering. He came with a gift of the Ul'mult'ah. This too he had put into a small beaded bag that was tightly sealed. "This is a talisman," he said, as he handed the bag to Orobai. "It will bring you luck and good dreams that will protect you and show you any troubles that lie on the path before you. Keep it close to your heart, and your vision will always be true. With this, you will see troubles before they come. Keep it safe."

Orobai was moved by these small but highly significant tokens. As he had already dispensed the items that he had originally brought with him, he had nothing to give in return. Both Mayé and T'lan insisted that Orobai and Miraanni had already given them more than they could have ever asked for. That they had been with them for this ceremony and had officially become family through the ritual was gift enough, they said.

"Now remember," said T'lan, "now that Sará'é has started the path of a human being, she will need to complete it. This ceremony here, this initiation, has only been her first. To complete the path of a human being, she will need to return for her initiation when she comes of age. Then these two stones that you and Lilt'a carry will become hers and she will be her own person. Do not forget. What has been started must be brought to fulfillment. The ritual must continue."

Orobai did not have a chance to respond as just then the matriarch of the Morning Star society, Alu'inir, approached with a procession of leading figures in the Yu'rindah. All eyes turned in their direction in anticipation. Not bothering with formalities, Alu'inir came right to her point.

"May I see the girl?" asked the old matriarch.

Lilt'a looked to Orobai for direction and with a nod he indicated his approval. Lilt'a handed the little girl over to the old woman. The subordinates of the great matriarch instantly began a blessing chant for their journey. While the others chanted out their prayer, Alu'inir raised the child to the four directions, starting in the east. As Alu'inir lifted Miraanni her wrap fell away and all could see that the star on her breast shone in a pure silver light that was brilliantly radiant, casting aside the misty gloom of the foggy morning. Seeing this, the devotees of the Morning Star increased the intensity of their chant and some even began to weep. It seemed for a few fleeting moments that Miraanni's light might chase away the dark fog, but when the chant stopped, the light ceased along with it and Alu'inir quickly wrapped the exposed child back up to keep out the cold.

Alu'inir turned back to Orobai, handing Miraanni to him, saying, "We weep for we are saddened that this Blessed One is leaving us. We do not want to see her go and would give anything to keep her here among her people who love her dearly. However, we know that your destiny draws you on. We only pray that you will bring her back to us. Do not forget us, Sará'é. Do not forget us, Mu'shué. We will await your return with great anticipation."

"We are sorry to leave you as well," said Orobai, accepting his sister back from the old woman, "but today we must leave for the city by the sea at the urgings of the Arnyar. There, Sará'é will stay in seclusion until I am able to return for her. The journey to the east is long, but I have a far longer journey awaiting me once this first task is completed, and time is pressing upon us."

"Very well," said Alu'inir in resignation. "We would have you know that the child is welcome to stay with us where she would be much loved and well cared for. But you say that the Arnyar have something to do with your choice and thus we will leave it be. Just know that you and the girl are always welcome among us. She is sacred to us and will always carry a special place in our hearts. Return her to us safely and with many blessings."

At that Alu'inir called over one of the other members of her order who pulled an object out of a bag she was carrying. As it was wrapped in deerskin, Orobai could not initially see what it was. Before removing the wrap, Alu'inir said a quiet prayer over the bundle, one hand hovering above it, and then opened it only slightly so that she could place pollen on it. She then lifted it to the four directions as she had done with Miraanni and then passed it to Orobai four times, handing it over on the forth gesture.

It was a beautiful abalone shell, a kind Orobai had only rarely seen before. Its outer shell was a deep and impenetrable black sheen. Its inside was a luminous pearl white that glistened and shone brilliantly with an opalescent glow, even in the dim morning light.

"This is a very special shell," explained Alu'inir as Orobai turned it over in his hands, appreciating its subtle beauty. "In our tradition, it is said that this shell of black and white combines the power of both the Raven and the Kite. It comes from the ocean far to the east and has been with our society for many generations now. It is said that this shell will give its bearer blessings and protection. It contains the light and dark, the seen and the unseen. From the darkness comes all creation and all blessings. From the light comes beauty and all evil is reflected back to whence it came by its incorruptible surface, they say. Though this has been a sacred krin of our society, we give it to you now with willing hearts. It will watch over you and the girl and will protect you wherever you go. No sorcery or dark forces will be able to hold power over you as long as this is in your possession."

"I thank you for this gracious gift," exclaimed Orobai, knowing full well that it was as difficult for the Yu'rindah to part with this sacred relic as it was for them to part with Miraanni. Krin were never given out casually. Orobai wondered if the Yu'rindah wanted to make a strong statement with this gift, or if they perhaps had other reasons as well.

"You have honored me beyond compare by sharing this most sacred krin," said Orobai. "I will keep it safe for you. When our journey brings us back to you, I hope to return it to you."

"Very good," said Alu'inir with a wistful sense about her, her eyes slightly misting over. "Walk in Beauty!"

The company of the Yu'rindah turned and left in solemn procession without looking back. Seeing that the moment was upon them, Orobai gave T'lan and Mayé one last embrace and then, along with his other companions, climbed into the sturdy longboat. With a silent wave, T'lan and Gen'shu'n pushed the boat off from the shore as T'inshar took up his paddle and skillfully began to guide them down the long dark river. In only moments, there was nothing but the soft lapping of water along the boat as they drifted off into the grey veil of fog.

The Cursed Island

"We're being followed," said the eagle.

Sto'orn was always one to get right to the point.

"I know," said Orobai.

Sto'orn was too taken aback by Orobai's comment to respond right away. Finally, he said, "Then what are you going to do about it?"

Orobai thought for a moment. "For the time being, nothing."

"Nothing?" blurted Sto'orn. "What do you mean, 'nothing'? He's spying on you right now, and you will do nothing?"

It was their third day on the river. Orobai had sensed early on that they were not alone. At first he told himself that he was just being too cautious, rationalizing that there would be many Yamné traveling down the river. However, when they were never joined for a meal, or for sharing a warm fire at night, Orobai began to grow suspicious. Now they were stopped along the river for a midday break. Orobai had wandered off to pick some herbs for tea, and consider their options.

"You have to do something," said Sto'orn. "Several times now his boat has come close to yours, close enough to see, and each time he has slowed down so that he might slip back into this eternal fog. Even now he's not far behind us. He has pulled his boat to the side of the river. He's left the boat and has slipped into the trees. Right now he's out there, in the trees, watching us. You have no idea what he is thinking."

"Perhaps I do," responded Orobai, having given the situation more thought than Sto'orn gave him credit for. "Keep a close eye on this one, and inform me immediately if you see anything else that bothers you. I do not think that we need to be too worried. He might just be curious, but we should be careful, nonetheless.

For now you can go and watch over Miraanni. I will return shortly and we will continue."

"Very well. I leave it to your judgment. Be careful."

Sto'orn flew off into the misty air out of Orobai's sight. Wanting to have a look for himself, Orobai decided to see what he could find up-river before returning to his companions. Quickly changing into his raven from, he leapt into the air and followed the bank of the river, retracing where they had recently passed.

Orobai did not need to go far before he found the boat Sto'orn had spoken of run up on the bank of the river. It was a small boat, designed for only one or two passengers, not like the longboat that they were using. Orobai saw that there was some gear in the boat but there was nothing in it that was recognizable to him that would clearly identify its owner, though Orobai already had his suspicions. The owner had gone off into the forest. No doubt he was spying on Orobai and the others, just as Sto'orn had warned.

In stealth Orobai followed the tracks with short flights through the branches. They clearly led off in the direction of his companions, though he was not able to follow them very far into the underbrush before he lost clear sight them.

Orobai found nothing obvious in his search. He quickly returned to the others, uncomfortable with the apparent increased brazenness of this stranger. He changed back into his usual form before stepping forward where the others could see him. Everything seemed fine and T'inshar and Lilt'a were happily tending to the children. He looked to Faen, but the wind was blowing in the wrong direction. If the stranger were near, she wouldn't be able to smell him. Orobai watched as T'inshar was brushing his fingers through his hair, letting some loose strands fall away, catching on some plants next to where he sat. Orobai felt uneasy seeing this, thinking that they should not leave any trace behind them, even something as seemingly insignificant as hair.

"Where have you been?" asked Lilt'a, seeing that Orobai had returned.

"Looking for some tea," said Orobai, pulling out the herbs he had picked, handing them to Lilt'a. "We can brew some when we stop for the night."

"You don't want to stay here?" asked T'inshar, apparently having thought that this would be their resting place for the evening.

"If you don't mind, I'd like us to try and make a little more distance while it is still day," said Orobai.

T'inshar looked down river. Orobai knew what he was thinking of. Just the thing T'inshar was looking to avoid was what Orobai had in mind.

"Yes, a little ways," said T'inshar. "That will be fine."

* * * *

It was beginning to get dark by the time they drew upon the island of Gu'yel. The name in Yamné said volumes about what they thought of this island in the middle of the Nordlith. It was the "cursed island." Here, long ago, the Salmon Spirit Society used to hold secret rituals. When an epidemic took the lives of the majority of the society after one such ritual was prematurely interrupted by a raid by an enemy group, the interpretation was that the island had been cursed and that all who set foot upon it would fall ill. It was the one place that Orobai could think of that was taboo for the Yamné. It was the one place they would not go.

Therefore, it was the one place he wanted to go.

When Orobai directed T'inshar to steer around the south side of the river island, he knew immediately that something was wrong. According to custom, they were to pass along the northern side. Seeing that T'inshar would not continue without an explanation, Orobai had to say something.

"This is where we are going to make our camp for the night."

T'inshar's reaction to this suggestion was swift and clear. "With all due respect, Mu'shué," he said, obviously very concerned, "we cannot do as you suggest. It is bad enough to even think of passing along the southern side of Gu'yel while we travel east, but to stay there is completely beyond question. The island is cursed. Are you not familiar with our customs regarding this island?"

"Indeed I am," replied Orobai, "and thus you should realize that I do not make this suggestion lightly. I did not say so before, as I did not want to worry you or Lilt'a, but we are not alone on this river, T'inshar. There is someone following us who has been spying on us ever since we left the lake. At first I did not think much of it, but the further we go, the more I worry about this pursuer. I can feel his thoughts and intentions. They are not good and they only grow stronger with time. I fear that he will attempt to act against us soon. I doubt that any Yamné would think to look for us on Gu'yel, however. There we can be secret and kept safe from unwanted eyes, and hopefully our pursuer will simply pass beyond us."

"But how do you know that this other traveler is not just someone going to his home down the river as we are?" asked T'inshar, still unsure of the wisdom of Orobai's suggestion.

"I think you would agree that anyone with friendly intentions would simply have joined us for a meal or camped with us for the night, but this one has made every effort to keep us from being aware of his presence. He lingers in the fog, just out of sight, lets out when we do, and watches us secretly from the forest. I do not believe it is Yamné custom to sneak about in the forest to spy on the actions of their kin."

"True," said T'inshar, starting to take Orobai seriously now, "but surely we can stay elsewhere than on Gu'yel," he pleaded. "Our people have not landed on that island for generations and I would not be the first to risk the wrath of the spirits of that place. The island is cursed. You must choose otherwise."

"I will not, T'inshar," said Orobai firmly, indicating that he wanted no more debate on the matter. "I appreciate your anxiety in this, but it is the best option for us. My first concern is for my sister and her safety, and anything else must be put into perspective of this goal. I do not fear this island, but I do fear the stranger who pursues us. For all of our sakes, I urge you to consider my counsel in this. We will be safe on the island."

Reluctantly, T'inshar agreed to Orobai's wishes. Against his better judgment, he steered their longboat to their right and they were soon traveling along the southern side of Gu'yel. Watching behind them, Orobai saw no one before the river curved out of sight and they were concealed from the view of any who might have been following them.

The island seemed completely overgrown. At least, what they could see of it was. The fog still limited their view, and now with it getting dark, it was even harder to see. The trees were a thick tangle of branches, with long strands of moss and lichen hanging down, swaying hypnotically in the wind. Orobai could tell that T'inshar and Lilt'a were uneasy simply seeing the island. Orobai, however, felt only the quiet peace of undisturbed nature there, not having any of the cultural associations of his companions. For him, it seemed the perfect place to hide.

Sto'orn came up behind them as they rounded the bend and Orobai called out to him, speaking in a way that neither T'inshar nor Lilt'a could understand, and told him to go around to the north and then come back up the southern side and meet them at their camp. Though it was getting dark, it was Orobai's hope that anyone who saw the eagle would presume that they had gone the usual route along the north side of the island and would be further confused by their deception.

About midway along the island a small creek let out from the interior. At Orobai's direction, T'inshar moved their longboat up the narrow stream as they crouched low to make their way under the thick tangle of branches that reached out over the water. They only had to go a short way before they were completely out of sight of the river.

There they found a nice glade where they could make camp. T'inshar warily went about finding young saplings to build a frame for a temporary structure, trying his best not to make any noise. Lilt'a took to feeding her son, Sa'yun, who was getting fussy and starting to cry. He soon quieted down, but Orobai could tell by the look on Lilt'a's face that she feared that the boy's cries had already given them away.

Before long, Sto'orn had found their camp. If the stranger had followed Sto'orn along the northern shore, the eagle did not know it. The far side of the river had many overhanging trees along the bank and it was possible that the stranger might have slipped along the river there unnoticed, he said. Sto'orn volunteered to go look more closely, but Orobai thought that this might draw attention and he dissuaded the eagle from doing so. For now they would sit and wait and see what might come in the night, if anything. It would be up to Faen to keep a look out for them now.

As night fell T'inshar and Lilt'a became increasingly uneasy, though they did their best not to let it show. Despite the fact that the island seemed pleasant and comfortable to Orobai, they would not be able to relax as long as they were on it and would have been much happier camping on the shore of the river, even with the knowledge of being followed and spied upon. They made fitful conversation as they tried to keep themselves busy and keep their minds off of their situation.

At last it was dark enough for them to make a fire safely. It brightened their spirits just as it brightened the darkness surrounding them. The persistent fog was even thicker now and it enveloped their small temporary home in a wet cold, though it was now warm and dry inside.

T'inshar and Lilt'a eventually fell asleep, leaving Orobai awake with Miraanni. He too was tired, but he couldn't shake the feeling that gnawed at him. He thought again of how T'inshar's hair had fallen from his fingers, catching on a nearby twig. Though he had never given it much thought, he couldn't help but think now about how sorcerers were said to use anything that came from a person to work their dark craft; hair, finger nails, even feces. Orobai tried to tell himself that he was letting his imagination carry him away, but he wasn't so sure.

As Orobai cradled Miraanni in his arms, he noticed that she was staring at him intently with that beyond-her-age gaze that spoke of a great intelligence. Seeing that she had caught his attention, Miraanni then began to sing quietly. Instantly, the Altfein began to react to the tones in her voice. Orobai watched as a scene began to unfold before him. He could see a lone individual outside before a fire. It was a man, though no face or identifiable feature was visible. The man held some objects in his hands and others were laid about before him in front of the fire. These appeared to be krin and the man was conducting some ritual actions, though what he was doing was not entirely clear.

What did seem clear to Orobai was that Miraanni was showing him the person who was following them. He was not far, perhaps somewhere on the bank of the river on either side of the island. The entire vision had an undertone of darkness and ill intent. Orobai could distinctly see that the individual was moving in a counter-sunwise direction, which could only mean ill in Yamné culture, for only dark arts were performed with such movements with rare exceptions in ritual. Orobai's fears seemed confirmed. Their pursuer was a sorcerer and he was practicing his craft.

The vision faltered when Orobai heard a sound outside their small kughain. Miraanni fell silent. Cautiously peering outside, Orobai saw that it was only Faen.

"What have you seen?" Orobai asked quietly so as not to disturb those inside.

"I have seen our stranger," said the wolf. "He passed along this side of the island, though he did not stop. I first saw him when I went to the western end of the island. He wavered there for a few moments, seeming to be making up his mind, eventually deciding to pass the same way as us. I followed him, staying among the trees where I could remain concealed. Though he lingered for a short time about the mouth of the stream here, he continued on. I do not think that he knows where we are, though it would appear that he has some intuition. I followed him to the end of the island where I lost sight of his boat in the darkness. More than that, I cannot say."

"You have done well, Faen," said Orobai. "Tend to your children and rest now, but stay alert while you can. I think that our 'friend' has now stopped for the night and will not be seeking us out further this evening, at least not by foot or boat."

Orobai returned to the interior of the small structure. T'inshar appeared to be sleeping fitfully but otherwise things were calm and quiet. Miraanni was still awake, having awaited his return. Though worried, Orobai could put off sleep no longer. He took Miraanni up into his arms and together they fell into a deep sleep that Orobai badly needed by this point, hoping for the best and a better, less worrisome day tomorrow.

But their pursuer had no intention of going to sleep. In fact, the stranger was only now just getting started with his plans.

A Dark Morning

Orobai awoke in the early morning to find Lilt'a hovering over her prone husband in a state of near panic. "T'inshar is ill, Mu'shué" she said with a sharp edge of fear in her voice.

"What's the matter?" asked Orobai, quickly pushing the sleep back from his mind as he lifted himself from his bed. Given the vision from last night, he feared the worst.

Lilt'a was shaking and her eyes were wide. She could barely get her words out. "T'inshar was right," she answered quickly in a broken voice that was a mixture of fear and blame. "He will not wake up, and his body is cold. He's still breathing, but barely. I have been trying to wake him but nothing helps."

Lilt'a turned and looked coldly away from Orobai. "He was right! We should never have set foot on this cured island!"

Orobai arose immediately. Miraanni was already awake and was staring intently at T'inshar. T'inshar was precisely as Lilt'a described – cold, inert, and no doubt close to death if he didn't get some help soon.

"You must do something for him," pleaded Lilt'a. "Help him Mu'shué!"

"I will do what I can – he'll be fine," Orobai assured her in a calm and soothing voice that conveyed a sense of certainty that Orobai did not truly feel. He quickly prepared an infusion of herbs. Slowly they could feel heat return to his body and his color seemed somewhat improved, his cheeks and exposed chest reddening as they flushed with invigorated blood. After a fourth helping of the infusion, T'inshar began to stir and struggled to open his eyes.

"What's happening?" he whispered when he saw his concerned wife leaning over him who cradled his head in her lap. "I feel cold . . . I'm so weak." Shivers ran up and down his body and he looked as though he might vomit.

"You have become ill and Mu'shué is helping you with his herbs," said Lilt'a, trying to conceal her true fear behind a cracking voice that said far more than she wanted.

"It is this place. I knew that we never should have come here," T'inshar said weakly. "I think I'm dying. The spirits of this cursed island are taking me with them . . ."

"I do not think that your illness is what you believe," said Orobai quickly. "I have not felt any ill will from the spirits of this place towards us. I fear that what has happened is the work of the stranger who follows us. Faen saw him pass us by last night, and in a vision I saw him working with krin. It is a sorcerer who follows us. That you were attacked first indicates that he wants to incapacitate us and strand us here. Then, he'll come looking for us."

"You have to do something," pleaded Lilt'a. "You have to stop him!" Panic was welling up within her. Lilt'a's eyes darted back and forth, as though she might see something that would help them, but of course, nothing was there that would be of any use. She felt trapped. If Orobai didn't act soon, she might lose all self-control.

Right at that moment, Orobai heard a voice, as clearly as if someone were speaking directly to him. Yet no one in their small kughain was making a noise, other than the labored breathing of T'inshar. In perfect Illanii the voice commanded, "Hold me over him." The directness of the voice startled Orobai. Looking about him he saw Miraanni sitting up, looking at him with her intense gaze. Again the voice repeated, "Hold me over him." Orobai then knew for certain that the command was none other than Miraanni's.

Doing as she wished, Orobai held her aloft above the ill man. His vision immediately shifted. He no longer saw the child in front of him but rather saw T'inshar from Miraanni's perspective. *I'm seeing through her eyes!* When he moved Miraanni, his own vision moved with her as he passed her over T'inshar's body.

At first he only saw T'inshar before him, much as he did when looking with his own eyes. Then the sight before him changed and it was as though he were looking directly into T'inshar's body. But it was not T'inshar's physical body into which his vision penetrated. Rather, it was his subtle body, the spiritual energy that lay beneath the surface of the coarse physical nature of his being. The energy flowed in intricate patterns and channels that gathered into knots along the spine and brain and radiated out into the extremities of T'inshar's body. There were five such knots in all. Near the heart the energy was tight and constricted. Something prevented the energy from reaching out into the muscles of the body, the limbs, and the vital organs.

The vision becoming even clearer, Orobai could then distinctly see that behind the energy knots was something that should not be there. There in T'inshar's body was sorcery made visible. Reaching around T'inshar's heart with long dark legs was an evil looking spider, quickly spinning its deadly web about his heart. From there the webs of the grotesque spider stretched out through T'inshar's body, drawing all the energy to it, pulling his life-force away from him, devouring it and making it a part of itself as it grew larger and T'inshar grew weaker. If they did not do something about the spider immediately, it would devour his spiritual essence, leaving him a hollow body, drained of all that gave it life.

Orobai could only stare for a moment, watching the spider grow larger before his eyes. Its legs reached all across T'inshar's body now, and it began to vomit a rank, vile poison into the very core of his being. T'inshar started shaking uncontrollably and lost consciousness again as Lilt'a cried out, barely holding on to her composure and sanity.

"You must do something! Mu'shué! Sará'é!" she cried, her voice cracking. "Help my dear husband before it is too late."

Orobai heard a clear command in his mind in Illanii. "Sing," it said with a firm sense of authority. An outside force that Orobai could only assume was Miraanni compelled him to do as the voice had commanded. His rich voice flowed out of his mouth and poured over the shaking man. The Altfein came to life and Orobai could feel their power coursing through his and Miraanni's bodies, which now felt as one.

The small child became stiff and her eyes rolled back into her head as she entered a deep trance. Looking into her through his own eyes now, Orobai could see the subtle wheels of her energy begin to spin wildly as the power of the Altfein flowed through her with astounding intensity. She too then sang as her eyes focused once more on the body of the ill man before her. Again Orobai could see through her eyes into T'inshar's body. There the hideous spider seemed to recoil from the sound of their combined voices as it desperately tightened its grip on T'inshar's weakening heart.

Orobai held Miraanni out a little farther. With her gaze fixed firmly on T'inshar's breast, she opened her mouth wide as Orobai placed her directly against the sick man. Immediately he reacted to the touch of Miraanni's lips against his bare skin as he convulsed wildly, thrashing violently up and down. Miraanni's mouth was firmly locked to him, however, and nothing could dislodge her. Lilt'a stared on with a desperate mixture of hope, terror, and disbelief, her teary eyes taking in the bizarre scene before her.

Orobai now had the full burden of carrying the song. He sang more firmly with great conviction as he could feel Miraanni's power respond to his voice, the Altfein coursing through their bodies. Miraanni sucked at T'inshar's chest above his heart as he thrashed about. The more he convulsed, the harder she pulled with all the force she could summon and the harder Orobai sang.

Slowly, their combined efforts weakened the grip of the spider. Orobai could see the venom of the horrible creature absorbing back into itself. The webs it had spread throughout T'inshar's body loosened and he groaned loudly as he regained semi-consciousness. Harder now Orobai sang as Miraanni sucked with such force that T'inshar's shaking body rose completely from the ground, suspended a few inches above the floor.

Orobai could now feel Miraanni pulling on the spider, tearing it free from T'inshar's heart. T'inshar began to vomit and from his mouth came a stream of spider webs encrusted with vile phlegm and puss. With its entire web gone, with one last violent pull, Miraanni tore the spider free from the sick man's heart as he fell back to the ground with a dull thud.

Miraanni had taken the spider into her own body. The energy coursing through her wrapped itself about the creature, crushing it. Then, Miraanni suddenly stiffened as she vomited what remained of the spider into the fire, exploding into purple flame and repulsive smelling smoke.

Lilt'a fell back in horror at the sights before her, having to turn away from the force of the flames as the smell of the burning remains filled her with the overwhelming urge to vomit herself. Struggling to pull herself together, she reached down to T'inshar who was now regaining full consciousness. Weeping over him, Lilt'a stroked his face and kissed his forehead. Slowly T'inshar opened his eyes and met Lilt'a's fearful gaze.

"He is healed, but he will need time to rest," the voice said in Illanii once more to Orobai as he fell back, exhausted, with Miraanni still in his arms.

"Thank you. Thank you Sará'é. Thank you Mu'shué," said T'inshar weakly, struggling to regain his strength and composure after their combined ordeal.

"Rest now," was all Orobai could manage to get out before falling into a deep sleep, no longer able to stay conscious.

* * * *

Orobai awoke several hours later to find Lilt'a caring for a still weak, though clearly much improved, T'inshar. The two children were fine and all seemed surprisingly well, given what had happened just a few hours earlier. Lilt'a was composed, though still obviously anxious about her husband's sickness. Seeing that Orobai was now awake, T'inshar spoke.

"Thank you, Mu'shué," he said weakly, but with an underlying vibrancy.

"You're welcome," replied Orobai, still trying to assess their situation. "I trust that you are feeling somewhat better?"

"Yes, though I am still weak."

"You must tell us what it was that Sará'é did," said Lilt'a with a mixture of disgust and curiosity. "What was that thing that she spat into the fire? It looked horrible."

"As best I can tell it was sorcery, Lilt'a," said Orobai. "I have seen the Want'né remove such things from people before, though I have never seen something like this actually inside a person myself, until now."

"But what was it?" asked T'inshar still unaware of precisely what had happened to him.

"A spider," Orobai said flatly. "A large and hideous spider. I don't think it was a real spider, however, at least not in the sense that we might normally understand it. It was a negative force or ill will that had wrapped itself in the symbolic cloak of a spider. It was Sará'é who knew it was there and what to do about it. I was merely the helper. When I held her over you, I was able to see it in you. It had wrapped itself around your heart and spread its poison throughout your body. I am sure that if we had not removed it that you would have died, probably by this night even, if not sooner."

T'inshar shuddered to hear of the grotesque being within him.

"How did the child know what to do?" asked Lilt'a.

"To tell the truth, I really don't know," answered Orobai. "She has many strange abilities and clearly knows more than she should of many things. It is perhaps best for us to think of her as a child in body only, but not in mind or spirit. I myself have never known the art of removing sorcery objects, though I have seen your uncle, T'lan, and many others do these things among your people. I do know, however, that such things enter into one's body intentionally and at the will of another. This was no accident, and it was surely not the spirits of this place that caused this. This illness was specifically meant for T'inshar. It is most likely that the perpetrator will now attempt to seek out the rest of us, thinking that we are incapacitated."

"Then we have to do something," said Lilt'a anxiously. "My husband is still weak and I can't protect us. And what if you or Sará'é becomes sick? What will we do then?"

"I don't think we have to worry about that," said Orobai calmly, trying to ease Lilt'a out of her growing panic. "If whoever did this could affect Sará'é or myself, I suspect that he would have done so from the beginning. He' just trying to get you two out of the way so that he can deal with my sister and me in a more direct way."

"So what would you have us do, Mu'shué?" asked T'inshar, struggling to lift himself up on his elbows but only falling back to the ground. "We cannot just wait for this sorcerer to find us and do what he will. I cannot lie here like an invalid while my wife and child are in danger!"

"No, you are in no position to fight, and you will not need to. I believe that I have a way to change this sorcerer's mind," said Orobai.

"But how?" asked Lilt'a. "We don't even know who is doing this to us, let alone where he is."

"Though I am not certain, I do have a good guess as to who our assailant is, and perhaps you can guess too, Lilt'a, for you were there," said Orobai.

"T'urk'nan. It must be T'urk'nan," said Lilt'a with a sense of realization.

"My suspicion exactly," agreed Orobai. "Jinru warned me that T'urk'nan would not be content to leave us alone. And after that encounter with him on the last night of the Ceremony with the issue of the krin, it would only make sense that he is attempting to use his father's power against us. He is the one who committed the crime he accused me of."

"So, this young Want'é would use the very power of the Yu'rindah against Sará'é and those who would protect her!" said T'inshar incredulously. "How could any of our people have such malice?"

"Though it might be difficult to understand," said Orobai, "it may not truly be malice. Jinru told me that T'urk'nan's has a deep love for his people. He fears that the child and I are seeking to deceive you and have staged her powers to manipulate you for our own ends. I am sure that he feels justified in using whatever means he may have at his disposal to remove what he perceives as a threat to the sanctity of his culture and traditions. Though he has gone beyond the realm of what most Yamné would find acceptable, he acts out of a sense of purpose. And this makes him dangerous, for he has shown that he is willing to step outside of his culture to save it. He is unpredictable and could prove a danger to others, and not just our immediate company. But perhaps there is a way that we can dissuade him from further rash action against us right now."

"What did you have in mind?" asked Lilt'a, curious. "No offense, Mu'shué, but I don't think that you'd be any match for him, were you to confront him. He'd surely kill you."

"Physical confrontation is not what I had in mind," said Orobai. "I've never been one for violence of any kind, and besides, I'm old and weak. No. I have something else in mind – something more befitting my skills.

"Tell me, did either of you know his father, the one who died in the snowstorm?" asked Orobai provocatively.

"T'inshar didn't, but I knew him," said Lilt'a with a puzzled look, "but I don't see how this will help us."

"Good," said Orobai, not bothering to explain himself or his plan. "I need you to picture him in your mind. Think of the most recent times that you saw him. Think as clearly as you can of his actions, his mannerisms, how he carried his body. Set your mind on what he wore, how he decorated himself. Think also of his choice of words and tendencies in speech. No detail is too small or insignificant."

As Lilt'a followed Orobai's instructions to the best of her ability, Orobai set his mind into a deep meditative state. Once focused, he extended his awareness outwards to encompass his immediate surroundings. In his mind's eye he was able to see himself, the small shelter, his companions, and the island. Opening his mind to the others in his awareness, he began to sense their thoughts and feelings. And not only those immediately present, but he could also sense the inner thoughts of those who had been on the island before, even from long ago. He could see Yamné, the members of the Mo'rinldah, and their thoughts and feelings as they conducted their secret ceremonies on Gu'yel. He could also sense the time they were attacked and the spirits of those whose bodies lay dead on this land.

Not wanting to be distracted, Orobai set aside these dark and disturbing impressions of the past and once again centered his mind on those immediately present. Carefully he sorted through the thoughts, impressions, and sensations, and amid the tumult of other minds, he was able to shut out all but Lilt'a and her thoughts.

Centering his mind on her, Orobai sensed impressions of an old man. Orobai saw him in her mind as she remembered him – the way he moved, the way he spoke, how he looked, and how he made others feel. It was all there for Orobai to absorb and take into his mind.

Orobai sensed much else in Lilt'a. He could feel the overwhelming love and concern she had for her husband, feelings so strong in fact that they began to wash away the images and impressions of the dead Want'é. Sensing this, Orobai withdrew his mind from hers. To stay longer would be to invade her privacy as her deepest inner thoughts were open to him in such a state and he had no desire to violate her trust.

Gently, Orobai centered his mind back into his own private awareness. He could once again sense the confines of his body with the rise and fall of his own breath. Opening his eyes, he emerged from his meditation and spoke.

"Thank you, Lilt'a," he said with a kind and reassuring smile. "You need no longer think of this man, for I have seen your thoughts and now know him as you have known him. This will be our advantage that T'urk'nan will not expect."

The Sorcerer

U rya was sinking fast in the western sky behind the thick veil of fog. Soon it would be dark. There was precious little time before the sorcerer would act once more, working his dark art and malicious ritual. Exhausted by the effort to heal T'inshar, Orobai had slept through most of the day, regaining his strength. In the meantime, Faen patrolled about their camp and Sto'orn flew about, trying to find their adversary.

Time passed slowly in the subdued quiet of the shelter and it seemed a long while before Sto'orn returned and called Orobai outside to speak with him.

"I have found our 'friend,'" said Sto'orn. "He has concealed himself well, but not well enough. His camp is not far down the river on the southern bank, just beyond the eastern tip of the island we are now on. I first found his boat, which he attempted to keep from view by piling leaves and grasses upon it. He was careless, however, and his oar was easily visible, even in the fog, which still remains thick and heavy about the water and the shore.

"His camp is set back a short way from the river upon a ledge. You cannot see it from the water, but from above it is easily spotted. He is staying in a cave in the rocks and I clearly saw his trail leading into it, though this too he has attempted to conceal by brushing over his tracks with a small branch of leaves, which I saw by the entrance. It would seem that he guessed that I might go out to look for him, though he doesn't know how to conceal his markings from an eagle. Perhaps lesser beings might not see his tracks, but such obvious marks could not escape these sharp eyes," said Sto'orn with true eagle pride.

"You have done excellently, my friend," said Orobai. "And tell me, did you see our pursuer, and if so, can you tell me of his appearance?"

"Of that I cannot say," answered Sto'orn. "I saw no sight of him, only his traces."

"Well, that is unfortunate as I had hoped to confirm my suspicions of his identity. But nevertheless you have done well and it will do. It would now be best for you to stay out of sight, but stay vigilant. Keep your eyes trained in the direction of our 'friend' and let me know immediately if you see anything of significance, though I fear that soon we will all be blinded by the fog which worsens even as we speak."

* * * *

Before long a veil of darkness had been pulled across the sky and T'inshar and Lilt'a's anxiety began to grow once more, knowing that sorcery was only practiced after the sun had left the world. Orobai assured his companions that they would be well and not to fear. Both Faen and Sto'orn were still looking out for them all. He explained that he would now have to leave them but he would return shortly. In the meantime he encouraged them to keep their spirits up and not to let fear take hold. "Fear is the sorcerer's strongest ally," he warned.

The night air outside was cold, dark, and wet with fog. The feeling was ominous and oppressive. Orobai was confident, but he was never one for confrontation, when it could be avoided. Now, he knew he had no choice. Changing into a raven, he took to the air and began to fly down river.

Flying was no easy task in the dark gloom, but Orobai managed to find the far shore of the river after flying out to the eastern tip of the island. Once on the shore, he returned to his usual form and quietly made his way down the riverbank until he came to where the land rose to a high rock ledge that fell directly into the water. There he found a boat covered in leaves and grass, just as Sto'orn had described, with an oar seemingly carelessly left uncovered. Such an "accident" was obviously intentional. Clearly, someone had wanted this oar to be seen. Perhaps their friend even desired a visit from them. Orobai would have to proceed cautiously, as whoever was atop the nearby ledge was most likely expecting him.

Orobai changed his form once more and flew to the top of the rocks quickly and quietly. The ledge bent around a large stone outcropping and from the other side Orobai could see the faint glow of a fire through the fog. Listening carefully before moving around the corner, Orobai could hear the faint sounds of someone moving about and what seemed like the soft sounds of chanting or perhaps incantations.

Taking several cleansing breaths, Orobai cleared his mind and focused for a moment on only his breathing. In and out, in and out, feeling every rise and fall of his chest as the air entered and exited his body. His mind quieted and became calm and free of distracting thoughts. His own sense of ego-identity began to fall away. He was now merely the act of breathing, of being in this place at this time. Orobai was empty and ready.

In this utterly passive and receptive state, Orobai's thoughts drifted to the images and impressions of the old man that he had sought from Lilt'a earlier. Once more he could feel the old man, see his actions, hear his words. It was as though the old man were there with him now. In fact, it was as though Orobai were himself the old man, as his character and nature permeated his being. Through the few recollections Lilt'a carried in her memory, Orobai had been able to glean insight into the patterns that were the old man. He had felt his rhythm, his flow, the way he manifested himself through time in thought, action, and word. He had come to understand the music of his being. With such knowledge, Orobai had extended his mind further out to find the residues of his pattern in the fabric of the world. Now there was no longer Orobai with an impression of the old man in his mind, but only the old man remained, and his life was there with his memories, hopes, fears, and knowledge. It was so much more than simply having known the man, or having seen him, but rather Orobai was the old man, for all intents and purposes. They had become as one.

With this shift in identity complete, Orobai softly let the tones and rhythms of transformation slip from his lips. Through these sounds and the power of the Altfein, Orobai lost his own natural form and took on the shape and appearance of the old man, down to every last detail. Not even the man's wife would have known the difference, had she been there to see Orobai now. And certainly the old man's son, T'urk'nan, would not know the difference either. Ready now to confront their attacker, Orobai stepped quietly around the corner.

There in the darkness, crouching by the fire and mumbling softly to himself, was T'urk'nan, precisely as Orobai had guessed. By his side he had a number of objects, most of which Orobai could not clearly make out in the dim light, though he presumed that they had to be the missing krin that T'urk'nan had accused Orobai of stealing. T'urk'nan was the thief. He had taken his father's sacred tools for himself and his own dark designs.

T'urk'nan appeared entranced and fully caught up in the rapture of his sorcery. Just under his breath he murmured the names of the four directions, but in the reverse, witching order. His incantations had just begun.

Orobai shuffled in place, letting his clothes ruffle softly but audibly. Instantly T'urk'nan sprang to his feet, realizing that he was not alone on his secluded ledge. Orobai was still hidden in a shroud of darkness. Only a dark shape loomed in the fog. Lack of vision did not keep T'urk'nan from speaking with certainty, however.

"Is that you, you Black Devil?" asked T'urk'nan scornfully. "I knew my power would draw you to me, and now I will destroy you!"

While speaking, T'urk'nan reached behind himself and pulled a long black knife from his belongings without taking his gaze from the dark form before him. "Do you not realize that I have merely been waiting here for you? What do you think I would want with the pathetic man and his family? It is you and that damned girl who are my concern. Surely the man is now dead and soon the rest of his family will join him. But you and the girl I need to deal with by hand, and now you have delivered yourself right to me. Once you are out of the way, the child will have no hope. Sorcery may not destroy her, but even the great Sará'é needs food, does she not, Mu'shué? Even if I can't find her, she is still sure to die."

Despite his certainty and his ultimate correctness, T'urk'nan recoiled in utter horror and shock as Orobai stepped forward from the darkness to reveal himself in the soft light of the sorcerer's fire. There could be no mistake that T'urk'nan fully recognized who stood before him now, and it was not at all whom he had supposed. Instead of the black form of Orobai, as he had fully expected and desired, there, standing before him clearly and without any doubt, was his dead father. Every detail was correct and spoke of his true nature. There was no way for T'urk'nan to see through the deception, so perfectly had Orobai executed it. Only one equally gifted in the use of the Altfein as Orobai himself would have been able to cast aside the veil and see the true identity beneath this perfect mask.

With a voice filled with a complex mix of paternal sorrow, shame, and anger, Orobai spoke to the sorcerer.

"My son. Oh, my son. What have you done? What have you done to me? To our family? To our honor? And to the Yu'rindah, that great society to which I dedicated my life and work? Speak now and tell me true. What have you done?"

Orobai had captured the essence of the old man perfectly. True to his nature, Orobai spoke the old man's voice with a firm, yet quiet, conviction. He had never been one to call out loudly or rashly, unlike his often impatient and arrogant son, and rather spoke in soft tones, though rich with the expression of his inner emotions. As he had had to do in life, the old man spoke to his son now with a great hurt and disappointment that only comes when a child has truly passed beyond the fears and worries of his parent.

All T'urk'nan could do at the moment was recoil in absolute fear. He tried to turn his face away from the man standing before him, but he found he could not truly look away and always his gaze returned to look upon the image of his dead father. He could see the lines of age and worry etched into his face, his well-worn hands from years of hard work in the forest and on the river. He even recognized that the old man was wearing the very clothes he had worn when he was tragically caught in the snowstorm and perished only a short time ago. Every detail spoke to the authenticity and reality of the apparition and he could not deny that his own father's spirit stood before him now in shame and disgrace for what he had done with his krin.

"Speak, Son, and tell me of what you have done and why. And do not lie, for I have seen and I know. You cannot hide your heart from your father," said Orobai, pressing forward with his questioning, seeing the powerful effect it had on the sorcerer.

Still cowering, T'urk'nan spoke with tears choking his voice, "Father . . . father . . . how can it be you? It has been more than two months since I have seen you with my own eyes, yet you stand before me now as one made whole. Yet you are no longer of this earth!"

"My spirit is strong, Son. You have disturbed my rest and awakened my spirit from its slumber with your sorcery. Speak now and confess to your wrong doings. I see in your heart and know what you have done with my krin. *My* krin! What right have you to disgrace me so?"

"I have only sought to do what is right . . ." stammered T'urk'nan, "what is best for all our people. I thought if you were still here, that you yourself would have done the same. Surely you, a great Want'é of the Yu'rindah, would have spoken out in wisdom against the great folly of our people. They follow a false prophet, father. They are deceived by their own ignorance. I have tried to remove the cause of their delusion. I have sought to honor you by freeing them from their illusions!"

"By stealing my krin? By working sorcery against your own people?" said Orobai firmly. "This is how you would help them and follow in my footsteps?"

"By whatever means necessary, Father," answered T'urk'nan, seeking his dead father's approval with plaintive and pleading tones. "Though I am a Want'é and have sought to walk the path you laid, I have never been as strong and as powerful as you, my father. The spirits do not listen to me as they did you. They do not speak to me as freely. For many years I have waited . . ."

T'urk'nan suddenly trailed off and then started again, now in a more forceful and defiant tone, as though he might blame another for his own faults. "I waited for you!" he said at last. "Long I thought that you would pass your krin on to me to help me become a greater Want'é, perhaps even as great as yourself. But you never had faith in me, Father. Why did you not pass your krin on to me when you could? Why have you made me do this?"

"I have not made you do anything, Son," responded Orobai, the palpable disappointment flowing from his voice. "You and only you have brought this disgrace upon yourself. And now your own actions reveal that I was right in not passing my power down to you. If only the spirits had granted me a son who was wise and humble in the ways of power. But you, son, are impatient, and you take what you feel is your due whether you deserve it or not. For these reasons alone I judged in life that my power was not to be your own and I see now in death that I was right in this decision."

Orobai's words were like a firm hand across T'urk'nan's shamed face. He recoiled with tears in his eyes where a smoldering fire of resentment still burned. "But father, look at what they have done to our people, this black devil and his child consort!" he pleaded desperately. "They have filled our people with false dreams and have used our sacred lore to manipulate us into false belief. Surely it will be the downfall of our people to follow those who are not of our kind. You who are so wise in the ways of the Yu'rindah must surely see that this is true. Do not turn your back upon me, father, nor upon your people! That you are here now shows me all the more that together we can work against this deep corruption among our people."

T'urk'nan was practically crawling on his hands and knees towards the image of his father by this point, desperate for some forgiveness and understanding. But he would not find it in Orobai.

"You will not sway me, Son," said Orobai as he felt the emotional history of the dead man passing through his being. "And you will not use my krin. These are my sacred objects and they are not meant for you. Only by working them backwards are you even able to muster a little of their power, for they are not meant for one of your heart.

"When you were young, I had many hopes for you, but early on you showed your impatience, your haughtiness. Think back on how you behaved towards your siblings and your cousins when you were younger. Think back on how you looked down upon them for not sharing in your knowledge and ability. You used your skills to put yourself above others and to make them feel lesser because of it. No one of this mind is deserving of my krin, for the way of the Yu'rindah is the way of compassion! Did the Kite teach the way of the Ul'mult'ah for her own betterment? No! She taught us of the sacrament so that all might find enlightenment and wisdom, so that none should rule over another nor make choices for them. If our people choose to see something in the stranger that you do not see, then who are you to force things otherwise? What great insight have the Ul'mult'ah given you to pass judgment over others? What vision have you seen that so fills you with hate and fear that you would use my legacy for sorcery, of all things?"

"I have seen, Father, and I do have fear!" choked T'urk'nan. "I fear for our people. While they see light and love, the Ul'mult'ah have shown me death! They walk into their own destruction for strangers! For strangers, Father! If they will not open their eyes, then I will have to force them open."

"Son, have the Ul'mult'ah taught you nothing? Have you never listened to the stories of our ancestors? You take upon yourself a responsibility that does not belong to you. So the Ul'mult'ah have shown you death where they have shown others light. Perhaps they show you true, or perhaps they show you only what is in your heart. As I look into your heart now, I see darkness that is your own undoing. You may have sent your sorcery upon another, but I say that the spider already has its webs upon you and there is rot in your heart!"

"But the death, Father. The pain! You would let this fate befall our people? How can I not take arms against such death?"

"There is no life without death, son. You cannot stop it. All things will pass away in time, just as I have, and just as you will too, someday. We must act from compassion, not fear. This above all is what the Ul'mult'ah show us when they reveal our lives and hearts to us. Were you not so full of yourself and more humble, this you would know . . . indeed, you would have learned this lesson long ago, as all initiates should have. Now I fear you will learn it by force rather than by grace, and it will be your own downfall. We all suffer, Son. Do not take haste to make your own suffering that of others."

"Then I say that you are a fool, Old Man!" said T'urk'nan, becoming righteously indignant. "You are as much a fool as any of the others. You call me arrogant, yet it is all of you who are arrogant, not I. I merely do what none other is brave enough to do. I am willing to risk everything for my people, so great is my love. I am not to fault if they are not wise enough to see this!"

"You only confirm my fears with every word you say. I had thought that perhaps my own passing would have softened your heart, Son, but I see now that this has not come to pass. It is clear that I cannot allow you to continue in your work."

"But you are dead!" cried T'urk'nan, "and you have no power over me!"

"This is true," said Orobai, "but even in death I do carry power over my own krin, and you will not have them."

Upon saying this Orobai removed from a bag the white and black abalone shell that Alu'inir, the matriarch of the Yu'rindah, had given to him before departing. Holding it aloft out before him, Orobai began a secret incantation of the Yu'rindah that he culled from the remnants of the memories of the old man that had left their impression in the fabric of the world. The incantation was one of controlling, where the relic of the society, the abalone shell, gained power over the krin of individual members. Holding the shell in his hands, Orobai could see clearly in his mind when others before him had used the same shell to do likewise against those who had gone astray in their use of power. It was not common, but rather a last resort of the group to exert control over a member who had stepped outside the bounds of the society and had violated their prohibitions, using their krin improperly. Such a procedure was an effective method to gain mastery over the tools of one suspected of committing sorcery or of some other evil and selfish doing. It could also strip someone of spiritual power, though this was a final resort, as anyone completely stripped of power would surely die. Without the help of the spirits, no one could live for long.

T'urk'nan clearly knew all of this given his reaction upon seeing the shell in his father's hands. "No!" he cried frantically, getting down on his knees and holding his clenched hands out to the apparition. "You cannot do this to me! My father! Have pity on me."

Orobai paid the pleading man no heed and continued with his incantation. One by one images of all the objects that T'urk'nan had stolen from his dead father began to appear in the shell. There were feathers of various kinds, special stones and gems, bones of different animals, and other such krin. Looking at the images, Orobai could see not only the krin but the powers that worked through them as well. These were all the spirit powers of the old man. This was what he had used in life to heal and to do good works for his people. Now they were all corrupted through their use in sorcery. Never again could any of these krin, or their spirits, serve to work good in this world for they had been changed by hate, fear, and envy – all those things upon which sorcery thrived. All that was left for such krin was destruction by fire so that they might no longer sow their seeds of destruction in the world.

There was nothing that T'urk'nan could do, despite all his plans and intentions. As Orobai said the secret incantation, all of his father's krin began to smolder. In a burst of flame they exploded into the night in a rush of fire and sparks. Orobai's work had released their energies. All the years of prayer and dedication of the old man went up in flame. All that had made his sacred relics alive and powerful was no longer held within them and was set free into the world without a container to hold it. The evil was transmuted by the fire and burned to ashes and dust, leaving only the refined spiritual essence of their once-great power. And T'urk'nan, the man who could have been a Want'é of his people, yet chose the path of sorcery, was left without tools to work his trade or ply the powers of darkness. He had been left powerless to harm Orobai and his companions by any spiritual means. If he wanted to stop them now, he would have to do it with his own two hands.

All the while T'urk'nan could only cry out, "Father . . . Father," with tears streaming from his eyes and falling down upon his limp and withered body. The destruction of the krin seemed to take T'urk'nan's own power with it and he now appeared as an empty and impotent shell of a being that had lost all purpose and substance. Orobai had not said the incantation to strip T'urk'nan of his own power, though, and it was merely T'urk'nan's reaction to the situation that made him appear so. He was devastated and forlorn, weeping into his powerless hands.

Finishing the incantation, Orobai replaced the shell in the bag he had taken it from. Seeing him do so, T'urk'nan spoke through his choking cries. "And what will you now do with me, Father?" he asked. "What fate will you cast upon your own son?"

"Nothing," answered Orobai. "For you, I have nothing. You will have to live with your shame and fear, but it will not be my own. Though you have used my krin, I have taken them from you and never again will you be able to use my belongings to gain power over others through sorcery. I myself have no punishment for you, other than the disappointment of a father in his son."

"But what will become of me now?" asked T'urk'nan.

"That is for our own people to decide. The man and woman you sought to harm are fine. I have seen to that. I have little doubt that they will tell others of what you have done. Then you will have to face the consequences for your actions and will have to face the fate that they decide for you. And remember this – if you seek to do them any more harm, then you will seek my wrath."

T'urk'nan could only weep. He knew that once others learned of his doings, they would either kill him or send him into exile, homeless, nameless, and lost in the world. Having been so sure of his success, he had never considered such a possibility before, though the realization of his fate now swept over him like a rush of cold water. He would never be able to walk among his people again. He would lose everything – even his name. It was the end of his life, as he knew it. T'urk'nan would be no more.

As silently and mysteriously as he had appeared, Orobai slipped back into the shadows, away from the broken man. In moments he was in the air flying back to Gu'yel and his companions. He had thought of sinking T'urk'nan's boat and oar, but had decided that T'urk'nan should still be allowed to make his own choices. It was unlikely that T'urk'nan would attempt any further harm, for the time being at least, and even he deserved the chance to go his own way. Orobai chose to leave the failed sorcerer to his own devices and his own fate.

Before long Orobai found his camp and returned to his natural form. He was happy to do so as it was never very comfortable taking on the form of another, and it was a significant strain on him in both mind and body. He was tired now and desired only to rest through what remained of the night. Tomorrow they would have to move on and face a new day.

T'inshar and Lilt'a were happy to see Orobai return safely, as were Sto'orn and Faen, who greeted him outside and reported that all was well. The children were fast asleep and the fire was low. The two adults had been unable to sleep in Orobai's absence and they sighed deep sounds of relief now that he was among them once more. They did not ask Orobai what he had done or what he had seen, though they could easily tell by his behavior that all was well and that he had been successful in whatever it was he had done for all of them.

Orobai felt strangely sad. Taking on the persona and identity of the old man had given him a curious perspective on T'urk'nan and his own motives. There were no easy answers here and Orobai could see things from the failed sorcerer's perspective, to some extent. He had felt rejected by his father, a disappointment, unable to live up to his father's expectations. And now, trying to take actions into his own hands, he had brought about his own downfall. It was tragic. Orobai wished that he could have helped T'urk'nan. But it was too late for that now. T'urk'nan would have to face his fate of either death or exile. Perhaps exile would provide T'urk'nan with the perspective he needed to truly change his ways, thought Orobai. It might, ironically, be the best thing for him. He could make himself into a new man with a new life, if he chose the right path. Orobai took comfort in this thought that played through his mind as he drifted off to much needed sleep – perhaps exile would redeem T'urk'nan and give him another chance.

Parting Ways

The companions awoke to a beautiful clear morning. Urya was rising in the bright blue sky with no trace of the enshrouding fog that had been ubiquitous since their departure from Shashun-Olurn. The songbirds were singing in greeting to the morning sun and all seemed well on Gu'yel. It was weather to match their changed spirits.

T'inshar was clearly feeling much better. He had arisen long before Orobai and had caught some fresh fish for breakfast. Orobai was pleasantly surprised to awaken and find hot tea, fish, and some dried fruit. After last night, he would need to take the time and food to regain his strength and build up his stamina. So much shape shifting in one night was hard on him and taxed his resources heavily. And with a healing before that, he was still in need of rest and recuperation. Were he younger, he could manage all these things with ease, but in his "old age," such spiritually draining activities were difficult.

Miraanni was awake as well and was watching Orobai intently when he rose. As he returned her gaze, a moment of knowing seemed to pass between them. Orobai knew that Miraanni was fully aware of what had transpired the night before. She appeared satisfied and did not show any concern for their immediate safety, knowing that the threat of sorcery and violence was no more. Orobai doubted that even Miraanni could know what T'urk'nan might do in the future, but as for the immediate present, she was as relaxed and as confident in their well being as could be.

After breaking his fast, Orobai thought that it was best for him to tell T'inshar and Lilt'a about what he had discovered of T'urk'nan. He did not tell them of the exact nature of their encounter, however. He did not share the knowledge of his shape-changing ability with others openly, as a general rule.

"But how do you know that we are safe from his sorcery?" asked Lilt'a, becoming somewhat nervous at the mention of the topic.

"The krin he stole are all destroyed," answered Orobai without fully explaining what he had done. "He no longer has the needed tools and will be impotent to harm us further in this manner."

Even as Orobai said this he felt a moment of doubt in his own heart, however. Searching his intuition, Orobai felt that there was something yet hidden, something that he had not seen the night before. In his mind he saw again their encounter in the dim firelight and felt the presence of the man who had intended them such harm. As he recollected the various krin, he felt for only a brief instant that there was something more that he should have done. There was perhaps some krin that he had not seen, or was it only a mistaken feeling? Orobai could not tell and only a shadow of some vague possibility rested in his mind. Somehow he knew that the problem of T'urk'nan had not come to an end the night before.

Not wanting his companions to worry, however, Orobai did not share this troubling thought and assured them that all would be well. It was a beautiful day and he was certain that they were safe, for now.

"The elders will exile him," said T'inshar, "or perhaps put him to death. I will see to it that he is punished for what he has done. Why did you not kill him, Mu'shué, knowing what harm he intended us all?"

"That is a judgment that I leave for you and your people," answered Orobai. "I am no judge, and certainly am no executioner. If your Want'né deem that this is T'urk'nan's due, then so be it. I will not be the one to make or carry out such judgment. That is not my place."

"Perhaps that is best," said Lilt'a. "You are wise Mu'shué, and our Want'né will do what is best for us all."

Before long T'inshar had prepared their boat and everything was ready for their departure. As a precaution, Orobai sent Sto'orn out ahead of them to see if he could find T'urk'nan. Sto'orn had nothing to report, however. The boat and oar were gone and the camp appeared abandoned. There was no sign of the sorcerer, either up or down the river, and he had clearly left some time ago. Orobai felt this confirmed his optimism that they were in no danger from T'urk'nan on this day. Feeling confident and secure, all got in the boat and together they set off down river with Sto'orn following above them in the clear blue sky.

* * * *

For several days they floated down the river under T'inshar's direction at the rear of the boat, occasionally correcting their course and paddling vigorously when necessary. In a few places they all had to get out of the boat and carry it through shallow waters. Miraanni enjoyed these times as it gave Orobai a chance to play with her in the water, dipping her feet in the cold flow, or splashing a little on her face. Even the normally reserved Sto'orn became caught up in the carefree and playful mood, pretending to dive down at the young girl and her companions, much to Miraanni's delight. In all, the journey had completely changed its character from those first few days and the darkness and fear they had felt was all but forgotten.

Orobai kept a close eye on Miraanni to see if she showed any signs of sensing anything, but he never saw her worry or become uncomfortable, so as the days passed and the evil they had endured on Gu'yel passed further from them, he too relaxed and simply enjoyed their time traveling together. At night the adults would take turns telling each other stories. T'inshar was fond of singing different Yamné songs for them, and Lilt'a would occasionally join in. Orobai also provided some entertainment by playing a small flute and telling stories of the ancient Yamné and other peoples of Aurduin. He was sure not to sing himself, however, knowing that it would only provoke a reaction from Miraanni.

Miraanni seemed to be changing with every day. Though now only roughly a month old, Lilt'a judged that she had the appearance and mannerisms of a child at least four times that age, and at times seemed even far older and wiser than that. She had gained much in size already and was able to hold herself up and manipulate her extremities with the abilities of a child significantly beyond a mere month. Lilt'a was sure that she would be speaking by one year of life, if not much sooner. Orobai marveled at all this, though by now he was not very surprised. Miraanni was clearly extraordinary in every way, so why should it be strange that her development was far accelerated? However, Orobai pondered that perhaps there was more to this than simply growing quickly. *Is she rushing to meet the future? Does time run out?* Orobai could not answer the questions that passed through his mind.

Most of all, Orobai enjoyed Miraanni's pleasure. Through her, he found that he saw the world anew. All things ordinary and usual were a new discovery, a new sensation, and a new joy. Miraanni watched the landscape intently as they passed down the waters of the Black River. She watched the birds, animals, and paid careful attention to the shifting colors and textures of the sky above her and the subtle reflections on the surface of the water. She took it all in with a pure joy and pleasure that was obvious in the simple, yet deeply satisfying, smile that seemed to only rarely leave her bright face. It was as though she looked upon all things in the world with love and that her empathy extended outward from a radiant source within her being that encompassed all of Aurduin. And not only did the child smile upon the world, but the world seemed to smile back upon her. Birds greeted her upon seeing her. Flowers bloomed in her passing. Fish leapt from the water to catch a glimpse of her. Even the trees seemed to reach out over the river to give her a bit of shade in the midday sun. Enchanted, she seemed, and the world about her was as a blessed land. Truly the strange child moved in beauty in a world of wonder.

After several days of such happy travel, the Morianithanlim-Gathr finally began to loom on the southeastern horizon. As the mountains grew in size and came more fully into view, Orobai could easily make out Arnthanlim-Zan where he had met with the council of the Arnyar only a few short weeks ago, though it now seemed long ago, after all that had happened in such a short time.

T'inshar and Lilt'a knew the mountains by their Yamné name, T'unmo'rinlgult', the Salmon Teeth Mountains. The village where they lived was not far off now and they would be there in only one more day. To get there they would have to take one of the tributaries of the Nordlith that fed into it from the north. The Yamné called this smaller river Ghu'n't'il due to its red color that came from the soil created by the tall redwoods of the Northern Forest. In fact, many of the tributaries to the Black River had a similar red hue for this very reason.

The companions made their camp at the confluence of the two bodies of water for the night as the distance left was too far to make in what little remained of the day. It was an ideal place for a camp, with spectacular views of the jagged T'unmo'rinlgult', whose dark sharp tips cut into the sky. Clouds were gathering just to the south of the mountains. Against the white backdrop were the distinct silhouettes of several Arnyar flying about Arnthanlim-Zan. Orobai thought that he should send Sto'orn off to investigate as perhaps they had some news. He also instructed Sto'orn that he should inform the Arnyar of both the sorcery attack and Miraanni's healing ability, for surely they would be greatly interested in hearing of these things, if they did not already know through their own means. Sto'orn gladly agreed and set off at once.

In Sto'orn's absence another group of Yamné who lived in the same village as T'inshar and Lilt'a, who were also making their way home, joined Orobai and the others for dinner. These new arrivals had come in four longboats and were a mixed company of young and old, men and women. They all seemed delighted to have found T'inshar and Lilt'a with their special companions and were surprised that they had not yet completed the journey home, as they had left well before the others. Orobai advised his two companions not to speak of T'urk'nan yet and to wait until a council could meet at the village among the elders. All agreed that it would be best not to stir up passions unnecessarily, especially as there were some young men in the group who would likely be eager to take immediate action against T'urk'nan for his grave offenses.

Sto'orn returned just as the evening meal was ready. So that he might speak with the eagle privately, Orobai took leave of the others and walked off some distance.

"What news do you bring from the Arnyar?" asked Orobai.

"They have gathered to consult with each other regarding knowledge of Miraanni among the different peoples of Aurduin," answered Sto'orn. "They say that word has now spread all throughout the land that the 'Black One' is abroad with a strange young girl with miraculous powers. Stories are circulating from culture to culture, they say, some of which were based on fact, others on pure rumor and speculation. Miraanni has quickly passed into legend among the various peoples of Aurduin, say the Arnyar, though most do not guess her true relationship to you, Orobai, an ignorance for which the Arnyar were thankful. Mostly they are concerned that word of the child has definitely reached the far west and they urge your continued haste."

"And what of our incident on the island?" asked Orobai. "Did they know of it, or did you need to tell them?"

"They had a sense that something had gone wrong," answered Sto'orn, "but they did not know anything specific until I told them."

"And?"

"And they said that you should have killed the man."

Orobai nodded. He knew how the Arnyar thought. They were hunters, after all. Orobai was not, however, and he made his own choices.

"They say that if they find him, they'll take care of him in their own way," added Sto'orn.

"No doubt," said Orobai. "And did they say anything else?"

"Only that spring is on its way, and that you need to hurry. They say that if you don't start your pilgrimage before the spring equinox, you will have to wait for the next year. They wanted you to understand how displeased they would be."

"Of course," said Orobai. "I would be as well. I have every intention of getting to Laftandiar-Urya and starting my quest as soon as possible. There's still time."

"Only if you see to it," said Sto'orn. "Don't let these people hold you up any longer. We've already wasted enough time among them, and they almost ruined everything."

Orobai returned to his companions. By now they were telling stories and arranging their camps for the night. Lilt'a was giving Miraanni one last feeding before bedtime. One of the elder women who had arrived with the newcomers was just finishing telling a story of one of Raven's many exploits as a trickster and fool. At the conclusion of the story the old woman looked up at Orobai and requested that he now provide them all with some music before bed. Orobai agreed, but first he desired to eat a little food as he had stepped aside right when they had begun eating. The old woman thus broke into another story about Raven, this time telling of the time that Raven changed into a fish and was caught by an unsuspecting fisherman who then, through various trials and difficulties, learned the true nature of his catch after being confounded by his inability to cook the seemingly magical fish.

By the conclusion of this story Orobai had eaten his fill and was now ready to offer some entertainment. As he had done over the previous nights, Orobai took out his small bamboo flute. The music was beautiful and filled with subtle shadings of emotion, wisdom, and power. All who heard his flute playing marveled at his ability, for even without the evocative power of the Altfein, which only responded to his singing, his flute playing still had the power to conjure up exquisite visions and images in one's mind, as though one were looking out upon a scene of great beauty and depth.

Before long all the children had passed into sweet dreams listening to the soft sounds of the flute. Orobai then played a short while longer as some of the adults softly hummed along with his plaintive melodies as one by one, they all drifted off to sleep.

* * * *

In the morning all the company packed up their belongings and, as one large group, all set out up Ghu'n't'il. One of the young men from another boat traded places with Orobai so that he could help T'inshar paddle. As they went, the men and boys sang rowing songs, which inspired everyone to make the journey quickly. It was another beautiful day with the sun above them and a deep blue to the sky. The T'unmo'rinlgult' were lost in clouds that morning, however, and when the clouds moved on later that day the mountains had a fresh dusting of white snow that sparkled in the afternoon sun.

That day they saw a number of osprey on the river, which all took to be a clear sign that spring would soon be coming, as the osprey always marked the transitions of the seasons as they migrated about Aurduin. Sto'orn even joined the eagle-like birds in their fishing along the river, though the smaller osprey found the eagle's size and presence intimidating. Watching the birds of prey, some of the Yamné commented on how they would soon begin to see many of the migratory waterfowl come through such as herons, egrets, ducks, loons, grebes, and many other birds. All the signs pointed to a good spring with a great abundance of life. Many comments passed around the group praising the power of the Iryuah'eeh'né in assuring that the world would be beautiful and teeming with life for another year.

As evening arrived, the group of boats finally came within sight of their village, Ashu'n. It looked much like any other Yamné village with many kughain with smoking fires, meat hanging out to dry, children playing, and the occasional dog running about and barking. While many of the villagers had gone to Shashun-Olurn to attend the great feast, others had remained here at their home and thus the village was not completely empty. Some of the elders were no longer able to make the trip and they had stayed with some members of their families to watch over them. And some families with young children who were either beyond their first year, or too young for their initiations, had also stayed at home.

Word had already reached the village of Mu'shué's having brought a strange young girl to the Winter Feast. Upon seeing the approaching boats, a greeting party was quickly formed. By the time Orobai and his companions pulled their boat up to the shore, curious individuals had surrounded them. All eagerly awaited an opportunity to meet the now-legendary Sará'é and perhaps receive a blessing from her as they had heard had happened for the others at the lake.

Not wanting to disappoint or offend anyone, Orobai graciously presented Miraanni to the public. As at Shashun-Olurn, the people quickly lined up to come forward and make a small offering, say a prayer, and if possible, touch the little girl. Miraanni seemed pleased with all the sudden attention, which she had perhaps missed since leaving Shashun-Olurn, and smiled joyfully at the supplicants before her. Other than the good feelings shared by all present, there were no miraculous feats or unexplained phenomena surrounding the peaceful child. The Yamné of the village seemed content merely to have her in their presence.

That night the villagers held a great feast in Orobai and Miraanni's honor. Food, songs, and stories were all plentiful, along with dancing, laughter, and positive thoughts. After several hours of this, the weary travelers took their leave of the others and began heading to their private camps. As Orobai was getting ready to retire, T'inshar came forward to speak with him.

"Before you sleep, Mu'shué," he said, "I would ask on behalf of the Want'né that you meet with them in council to discuss the case of T'urk'nan."

Orobai was not eager to do as T'inshar requested. He had hoped that T'inshar would deal with this sensitive issue after he had left, but apparently the burden of carrying such knowledge was too much for T'inshar to keep to himself, understandably, and he had already sought action on the matter. Reluctantly, Orobai agreed as T'inshar escorted him to a kughain somewhat on the outskirts of the village. There, several elder Want'né had gathered, both male and female, to hear of what had happened. Lilt'a was already there as well and seemed ready to speak. T'inshar and Orobai sat down next to her and looked to the elders to begin.

"We do not wish to keep our honored guest long, for we know that you must be tired and desiring rest and the comfort of a warm bed," began Ush'molgu, whom Orobai recognized as head Want'é of the village and one of their wisest elders. "However," continued Ush'molgu, "we must forego some comfort for but a while so that we may come to understand what has passed. It is our understanding that some evil has occurred and that our own T'inshar here was the victim of sorcery. Can you confirm this, Mu'shué?"

"Yes, I can," replied Orobai, "and I can speak of the perpetrator of this act as well."

"Very good," said Ush'molgu. "T'inshar and Lilt'a have both said that this sorcery, which T'inshar suffered though, was committed by the young Want'é, T'urk'nan. You have confirmed this?"

"Yes, I have, though I am the only member of our party to do so," explained Orobai. "I confronted him directly and caught him in the act of committing sorcery against T'inshar and Lilt'a. Both the eagle and wolf saw him as well," added Orobai, "though I know that does you little good for you cannot speak to them as I can."

"We understand," said Ush'molgu. "You need not worry about this, for our own insight and dreams will reveal the sorcerer to us. What we want to know is what happened to his krin and whether you have direct knowledge that he used these krin in the sorcery."

"The krin belonged to T'urk'nan's father. I made sure to destroy them properly. Had I not, I believe Lilt'a herself would have become ill as she was the next intended target, after T'inshar."

"Yes, we have heard of what occurred at the Feast and how T'urk'nan accused you of taking his father's krin. You are certain that these were indeed the krin in T'urk'nan's possession?"

"Yes. I am certain. He admitted as much when I confronted him."

"Thank you," concluded Ush'molgu, seeming satisfied with Orobai's brief answers. "You may leave us now as we have much to discuss concerning T'urk'nan's fate. These two, T'inshar and Lilt'a, should be able to answer any further questions we may have."

Without anyone else speaking, Ush'molgu dismissed Orobai from the council. He was glad that they did not press him about how he had destroyed the krin or how he was so certain of their origin. It seemed sufficient that he was sure in his judgment. Orobai always liked this trusting and respectful nature of the Yamné, who were ready to take someone at his word rather than press into his private doings and thoughts. He had expected more questions, however. Orobai supposed that they may have already had such thoughts and concerns about T'urk'nan before now and this was only a confirmation of their fears. Regardless, Orobai was tired and ready for rest. He found the kughain that someone had prepared for him and quietly joined Faen, Fenruk, Elkil, and Miraanni in blissful sleep.

* * * *

Come morning, many people were already gathered to see Mu'shué and Sará'é off on their continuing journey to the east when Orobai arose. Some thoughtful individuals had prepared a smaller boat for them that was well stocked with necessary supplies of food, clothing, skins, along with many of the gifts that Orobai had brought from Shashun-Olurn. It was apparent to Orobai that he would again have to manage several more gifts as those awaiting their departure had their own offerings intended for his small companion.

In what was now a common sight for Orobai, numerous people flocked around him as he brought Miraanni out to the boat. Among them were T'inshar and Lilt'a, as well as many of the Want'né, including Ush'molgu. The sun was out, the birds were singing, and the light of the new day played upon the surface of the red waters of Ghu'n't'il. The village of Ashu'n seemed a place of perfect peace and serenity to Orobai, now that he was leaving the Yamné behind him. *If only I could stay among them for a bit longer and get a truly good rest*, he thought to himself. But alas, the Arnyar would have none of that, especially now with word of Miraanni having traveled far to the west of Aurduin. He and his sister must press on and comfort could not be a concern now. And what was more, he would have to be on Norgath by the spring equinox if he was to properly carry out the dictates of the Arnyar. There was no time to waste for they still had a great distance to travel down the Nordlith before they would reach Laftandiar-Urya, the City of the Rising Sun.

Ush'molgu was the first to greet them, saying, "Mu'shué and honored Sará'é – we, the people of Ashu'n village, are sorry to see you leave. Are you certain that you cannot stay among us longer and bless us further with the presence of the Sacred Child?"

"No, we cannot stay," answered Orobai. "Though we thank you for your invitation and kind generosity, we must continue. Should Goar Saum smile upon our fates, we will meet again before the waters of time flow far beyond us."

"Very well," said Ush'molgu, rather formally. "We shall not stand in your way nor keep you any longer. By the powers of the directions and the Want'shan, the Sacred Seven, may your journeys carry you safely to your destination. You will walk in beauty, with beauty above you, below you, in all directions, and within your hearts. The light of the heavens shines upon you and your path is marked with pollen."

With the reality of their departure now inevitable, Lilt'a began to cry. For nearly two weeks now she had been a mother to Miraanni. She had grown truly fond of her and her love for the little girl ran deep. Having to part from her now was almost more than the woman could bear. T'inshar comforted her and reminded her of her own family and her duties in her village where she was needed. Orobai assured her as well that in time she would be with Miraanni again and that her ritual bond of mother would never be forgotten. All this was little consolation for a mother who felt as though she were losing one of her precious children and her pain ran deep into her heart.

Miraanni looked deep into the eyes of the woman who had given her nourishment, love, warmth, and had seen to her every need over the past two weeks. Her own love for the motherly figure of Lilt'a was obvious to all as the child gazed upon her. From deep within the heart of the small child a wave of love began to radiate outward and encompassed all present so that all felt their entire beings saturated with this love of a daughter for a mother. It was as though for a brief time there were only these two and all others were merely passive witnesses to their love and devotion for each other. Lilt'a could only weep harder and more profoundly, though now the tears had changed from bitter sadness and loss to a satisfaction of mutual love and need as recognized by the special child. Miraanni let Lilt'a know as clearly as she could that she returned her love and that she would not forget her. And with this knowledge, Lilt'a was able to let her go willingly into an unknown future and an uncertain fate beyond the reach of the Yamné and the safety of their traditions, ceremonies, and knowledge.

When the moment between Lilt'a and Miraanni had passed others began to step forward, again giving gifts and offerings to the sacred child. Orobai graciously accepted all these tokens and added them to the quite large collection in their now seemingly too small boat. Once all had had their chance to make their offerings, Orobai helped Faen and the cubs into the boat. He then strapped Miraanni about his chest in the sling he had used previously, got into the boat, and with his oar, pushed off from shore. As they gently floated down the smooth waters, the adults stood at the bank and waved good-bye while the children ran out into the water and down the riverbank. In only a few moments their boat slipped out of sight around a bend and Orobai and his companions were left alone upon the red waters with the sun rising in the sky, the Morianithanlim-Gathr before them in the distance, and the eagle soaring high above their heads on the warming currents of morning air. Laftandiar-Urya awaited them and they were once again upon their way.

The Seeker

I t was already late afternoon on a cold and wet day by the time Orobai and his companions reached the confluence of the Red and Black rivers. The rain had begun around midmorning and was only now showing signs of letting up and giving Urya the chance to show its face in the last light of the day.

The going was slow, despite the smaller boat and fewer passengers. Now it was up to Orobai to steer and paddle. Given his generally tired state, this was no simple task. He thought to himself how much he would prefer to simply fly, rather than be confined to such a slow method of travel, but there would be no point in going on if he did not have the child with him, and he would not be flying with Miraanni anytime soon.

As the clouds began to break and the rain subsided, the Morianithanlim-Gathr emerged from the veil of clouds, now thoroughly covered with fresh snow that glistened in the slanting light of the late afternoon sun. Lower down, the world reflected the light in a lustrous wetness from the fresh rain and all appeared clean and as though everything was new.

Orobai let his small boat out near where they had camped on their journey upstream, thinking that they could stay there for the night, and most importantly, get a chance to rest his weary body. At least they would only be going downstream, Orobai thought to himself, thankful that he did not need to struggle against the strong currents. And now, being far away from where anyone might see him or what he intended to do, he could take care of the gifts received during their time among the Yamné, which only weighed them down considerably and slowed their journey.

Before taking care of all the gifts, Orobai made sure that there was a dry spot for Faen and the cubs where Miraanni could cuddle up with the wolves and nurse. Orobai had been concerned that Miraanni would not take to returning to her wolf mother after having had a human mother for the past few weeks, but she went to Faen gladly and seemed to be taking in enough nourishment to get by without complaint, so his worry quickly faded away. Faen was happy to have the child back in her care, for indeed, that is why she had come on the journey to begin with and was pleased to have regained that usefulness for which she was originally employed. Orobai built them a small fire and a comfortable lean-to and then set about taking care of the abundant gifts.

In a short time Orobai had everything sorted into what he wanted and thought they might need and those things he judged they could do without. Orobai repeatedly called upon the power of the Altfein to dematerialize the objects before him and have them rematerialize in his storage room back home by Golgath. Unlike the ritual actions of the Yamné and the other peoples of Aurduin, Orobai's "magic" did not depend on words, incantations, prayers, or other verbal formulas. Instead, as with all things regarding the use of the Altfein, he accomplished this merely through the precise and predictable manipulation of tones, patterns, and stress of his voice. The distance itself didn't matter and Orobai presumed that material could theoretically be sent over an infinite distance. As he understood it, the objects did not in any way traverse the intervening space – they simply disappeared from one place and reappeared in another. The only limitation for him was size, as it took energy and spirit from the Altfein to accomplish such a task and try as hard as he might, Orobai had never been able to dislocate large objects in this manner.

In theory, he supposed that one could do such a thing with sufficient vocal stimulation and enough Altfein. According to the Arnyar, this was how the Illan had managed to reorganize massive amounts of matter in the creation of Aurduin such as the rivers, mountains, and all other beings. With their power, they simply rearranged physical matter and the spirit that resided within it to bring life and substance to all things. This was not Orobai's power, however, and he was limited to rather small but nonetheless astonishing accomplishments.

Now, however, even this relatively small collection of objects was proving difficult for Orobai to send away. It took a great deal of strength and stamina on his part to keep up the proper tones with his weary voice. And the more he sent, the more he had to strain and concentrate the power of his singing. He knew that this could only mean one thing – the Altfein were running dry.

While these special stones held strange and wondrous power, this power was not unlimited. The spirits within them became spent through use. Once dissipated, the Altfein were little different from any other jewel or gem, despite their unusual beauty. Their unique light would fade and they would no longer reflect the light around them in the preternatural way in which they did when new. Slowly but surely, they would fade away and become but an empty shell of the power that once resided within them.

Such was clearly happening now. It occurred to Orobai that he had not sought to replace his Altfein since before returning from Jeaniaurduin, when he first found the radiant jewel that had become Miraanni. Much had occurred since then and he had used the Altfein a good deal, especially at the Iryuah'eeh'né and in the ordeal with T'urk'nan. These Altfein were now spent and Orobai would have to find new ones, and quickly, for there was no telling when he would need their unique powers once more.

Fortunately, it was not difficult for Orobai to find the sacred stones. Though not ideal, he knew a good place to find them in the Morianithanlim-Gathr that was not too far from where they were now. To find the best Altfein, he would seek them out on the Goargathr at the proper times of year, such as he was planning to do once Miraanni was secure in Laftandiar-Urya. However, he knew how to find them on any mountain, even if the situation was not preferred, and for the time being, the Elk Horn Mountains would do. Orobai had used their Altfein before, and aside from the Altfein of the Goargathr, these were the strongest among the remaining mountains of Aurduin.

In the morning, after a good night's rest, Orobai put out their small fire and quickly packed up the boat, launching them down the river once more, this time back in the waters of the Black River headed to the southeast. Early that afternoon Orobai found a small tributary that led south into the mountains. It entered into a canyon with steep walls, as were common among the features of the Morianithanlim-Gathr. Nestled in among the bases of the high cliff walls were small sandy beaches that tended to catch driftwood traveling downstream and were ideal for many herbs and other medicinal plants. Orobai found a beach that was somewhat hidden from view due to the surrounding rock walls and had enough wood for them to have a fire and erect their small temporary shelter of branches and animal hide to keep them out of the rain and cold.

Orobai worked quickly, despite his fatigue. He hoped to be able to look for the Alkeinfein that very night so that in the morning he might find the Sarnfein and then move on. He first made a fire to give them light and warmth and then put up their small skin and branch shelter that would be just large enough for him, the child, and the wolves. There they could huddle together in warmth and dryness through the night, though it left little room for anything else of their supplies, the remainder of which he carefully placed under the upturned boat.

Faen assured Orobai that she could watch after their camp and would care for Miraanni while he searched for the stones. Orobai set out at once to seek the Alkeinfein, for he could see by the subtle lightening of the eastern horizon above the rock walls that Ranya would soon be shining down upon them and the precious stones would then make their presence known. With what little power was left in the Altfein that Orobai had with him, he took to his raven form and quickly flew up the canyon.

He didn't have to fly far before he reached Maugu'in Falls, as it was called by the Yamné, a high waterfall in the face of a sheer rock cliff. Orobai did not know what this name meant in Yamné, and in fact, the original meaning of the name had even been lost to contemporary Yamné who no longer used this place as their own. In Illanii, the falls were named after the surrounding cliffs, Zallur, which meant something like "Water Falling over High Rocks." The name, like many Illanii words, was essentially descriptive.

Orobai flew up to the top of the falls where he could get the best view of the pools of water both above and below the cascading water. Ranya was now climbing over the surrounding rocks and the light of the full moon glimmered in sliver rays about the falls. From this vantage point Orobai could look out to the north and see the winding trail of the Nordlith as it made its way east in the moonlight, the tall trees of the Northern Forest, and his small camp down below, glowing in the soft yellow-orange light of an intimate fire.

Turning his attention back to the water, Orobai began to scan for the sacred stones. For those unlearned in the Altfein-Aryat, the glittering light of the Alkeinfein appeared merely as the playful dance of moonlight across the surface of the water, just as the Sarnfein would appear as the shimmering of the sun in a watery reflection. For one such as Orobai, who looked with knowing eyes, the difference between water-reflected light and Altfein-reflected light was subtle, but obvious. Whereas water reflected light according to the patterns of ripples of the movement of water, the Altfein organized the light of Urya and Ranya into their own distinct patterns. They thus did not merely reflect light, but rather they reorganized it into living, organic patterns, just as all life takes energy from the environment that surrounds it and reorganizes it according to its own living rhythms.

Complex patterns of energy in space and time – this was the basis for all things in the changing world and one of the fundamental teachings of the Altfein-Aryat. The world was made of ever-changing rhythms of life in an ongoing dance of birth, life, death, and renewal. In many ways the Altfein were crystallizations of this process and power. They naturally drew life-giving power to themselves and those with the proper knowledge and ability could direct their unique potential to create and give life. Yet this was a power that Orobai had never had – not until now, and the appearance of Miraanni. Clearly they did have this power, this power of true creation and the power of life. Together, when they used the Altfein, they manifested the power of the Illan, though in far more limited form.

Orobai began to sing in order to make the self-organizing patterns of light of the Alkeinfein more apparent so that he could easily find them. Orobai knew that success was all in the tones and patterns of voice that he used. There were different such tone-patterns for the Altfein according to when he sought them, related to the time of day and time of year in the cycles of the moon and the sun. It being a full moon now, Orobai needed to use the Lumran tones. Calling up these tones was easy for Orobai to do, being intimately familiar with them, though the uninitiated would find them nearly impossible to duplicate.

Instantly the light of Ranya began to organize into the unique and distinctive arabesque patterns of the Alkeinfein under the light of a full moon at the sound of Orobai's rich and resonant voice. As Orobai looked down upon the pool of water, he could see that deep within the waters there were several Alkeinfein of greater and lesser potency. Orobai set clearly in his mind where the best were, and drawing upon their power, glided down to the water's surface in raven form and just before touching the water, slipped effortlessly into the form of a river otter and dove into the cold darkness. In only a short time Orobai had retrieved several of the most powerful stones from the water, which he pulled from the bottom with his otter paws and set out upon the bank. These would be sufficient to at least get him to

Norgath, where he could find the truly powerful stones. And some would be for his sister, who, like himself, should keep her own stones about her so that she could always access their power at will. Now he would only need to do the same procedure in the morning, and under the light of the morning sun, find a few of the Sarnfein. They would then be able to continue on their way with the secure knowledge that they had the sacred stones and would be able to meet whatever unknown challenges lay before them.

* * * *

That night Orobai had a strange dream. The dream started with Orobai sitting next to T'lan. He was handing Orobai the gift of the Ul'mult'ah, just as he had done when they left the lake. Orobai could hear T'lan telling him again how the talisman would warn him of danger, and show him difficulties that lay ahead.

The dream then shifted. Orobai, Miraanni, and the animals, much as in waking life, were traveling down the river. A feeling of dread and fear started to overcome Orobai in the dream. He felt that there was something coming after them, pursuing them. At first it was an oppressive intuition that something unknown was out there, lurking just beyond the horizon. Even in the dream Orobai considered whether this was a residual feeling from having been pursued by T'urk'nan or if the sorcerer had unexpectedly taken up the pursuit once again. Orobai's dreaming mind dismissed this thought, however, as the feeling left the unmistakable impression that the pursuer was someone or something new, something outside of his experience. And what was worse, it almost seemed to Orobai as if the pursuer were somehow responding to Miraanni in a way he could not yet understand, as though there was a subtle connection between them. Something was drawing near.

Orobai had faced many difficulties and challenges in his life and fear and anxiety did not come easily to him, yet here, the feeling threatened to stop him in his tracks. Orobai knew that they had to hide and that their fates depended on it.

It was then that he saw it. It flew in the air, somewhat like a bird, though the shape and look of it reminded Orobai of a stingray. It was not as large in breadth as a true Arnyar, though it certainly was larger than any other creature Orobai had ever seen in the air. It flew relatively low to the ground and produced a strange humming sound unlike anything Orobai had heard before. At the forefront of the flying thing there was a strong light that pointed in different directions, seemingly at will, as the strange metal creature moved about in the dim light, searching the ground beneath it.

Intuitively, Orobai knew that the strange thing could only fly over relatively unbroken ground or calm water, and thus he quickly sought to move himself and his companions onto rough and uneven ground with deep fissures and cracks accentuated by large boulders and other obstructions, shifting his dream from the environment of the river to the land. It was then that Orobai realized in the dream that he was now with others who were strange to him whom he did not recognize. Together, they moved across a flat and open land on painted horses and seemed to be running through snow. The movement exposed them however, and the blinding light of the flying thing reached out through the darkness, capturing them in its searing beam. A terrible flash of light shot forth from the flying thing, accompanied by the sound of ferocious thunder, and Orobai could smell the distinct odors of burning human flesh and seared horsehair.

In a bolt of fear, Orobai awoke. He looked and listened, but nothing seemed unusual or gave cause for alarm. Seeing that light was coming into the sky, Orobai quickly got up, remembering why he had come to this place, and within minutes was waiting atop Zallur for Urya to shine down upon the water below, the ill foreboding of the dream gently slipping away.

It was not quite yet daylight, so Orobai sat down by the cliffs and took the time to meditate, center his mind, and renew his spirit. But as he did so, his concentration was soon broken by a faint, yet distinct sound, a sound that was out of place. Initially, Orobai merely puzzled over the peculiarity of the sound, not recognizing it. The more he listened, however, the more he felt that there was something familiar about it, though, despite its strangeness. Then Orobai knew. It was the sound from his dream.

Instinctively, Orobai withdrew from the lip of the falls into the nearby brush as his eyes scanned about, seeking the source of the strange sound. Then, looking out upon the Nordlith, he saw it. Indeed, it appeared as some kind of metal bird that didn't need to move its wings to fly, or perhaps a large silvery stingray, floating through the air. The sound it made was distinct for its uniqueness and the sense that it was fundamentally out of place, but it was neither loud nor obtrusive.

The strange metal bird glided along not far above the water in the morning twilight with the yellow-orange hues of the rising sun reflecting off its smooth metallic surface. It actually looked beautiful, in a way, Orobai thought as he gazed down upon it. There was an elegant and aesthetic appeal to the design and its novelty intrigued him. *What is this thing and how does it work? Is this one of the creations of the west the Arnyar mentioned?* Orobai thought back to his earlier dream he had had in Jeaniaurduin of the strange animal-like machines digging in the earth. *They must be related. This must be from the west.*

The flying machine appeared to be searching for something, and if Orobai's dream was any indication, that something was him and his companions. Orobai grew anxious as the metal bird drew closer to the tributary where they were camped, but then breathed a sigh of relief as it continued on up the river, not noticing them or their well-hidden camp.

Despite the fact that the strange flying thing had done nothing threatening, nor made any advance towards them, Orobai felt exceedingly disturbed by this sight. Something as yet unknown had burst forth from a dream into life and what it was or how it worked, Orobai had no idea. This in and of itself gave him pause, but the inescapable intuition that the thing sought him and Miraanni made the feeling all the worse. It was rare for Orobai to catch glimpses of the future, and the fact that he had seen this first in a dream was disturbing. It meant something, but what? Was the remainder of the dream to manifest into reality as well? Orobai knew the answer that T'lan would give. He felt the small bag containing the Ul'mult'ah talisman with his thumb and forefinger.

Orobai had to learn more of these, and what they were capable of. He decided right then that he would fly to Arnthanlim-Zan that day, as soon as he was finished here, and see what he could learn from any Arnyar who might be there. They should tell him what they knew, and surely this was something they would have some knowledge of, for the Arnyar saw all, Orobai reassured himself.

With the strange flying machine gone, Orobai relaxed and could once again concentrate on his task of finding some Sarnfein. Once Urya rose high enough in the sky to reflect on the pool of water below, this task proved as easy as finding the Alkeinfein the night before under the light of Ranya. Singing the Omur tones, Orobai picked out a few of the most potent Sarnfein and gathered them once more as a river otter, some for him, some for Miraanni, leaving the rest behind for perhaps another time.

When he rejoined the others, Faen, the cubs, and Miraanni were awake with the young ones nursing. Sto'orn had joined them as well, wanting to speak with Orobai.

"You have seen the strange metal object that flies low to the ground and over the water?" asked Sto'orn anxiously.

"Yes," answered Orobai. "I saw the metal bird from atop the falls."

"I don't know what that thing was," said Sto'orn, "but I can assure you that it was no bird."

"Of course," said Orobai, "but I must call it something, not knowing what it truly is."

"What do you think it was after?"

"Us," Orobai answered tersely. "That is one thing that I do know. I must seek out the Arnyar who perhaps know more of this."

"But what of the girl?" asked Sto'orn, knowing that Orobai would have to leave Miraanni and the wolves behind.

Indeed, what to do with them? What if the thing returned and found them here, unprotected and exposed? He had to do something to ensure that they would not be discovered in his absence. Orobai pondered the situation for a few moments as he looked at Miraanni, who patiently stared back up at him. It suddenly occurred to him that she was perfectly aware of what was happening and was merely waiting for him to make a decision. Realizing this, Orobai thought that he could make a demonstration for the small child that she might understand. He began to sing, making the proper tones to bring the sacred stones to life. Doing so, he created an illusion of stone and sand so that anyone looking upon him would not see him – all that appeared there on the small beach was the surrounding landscape and no sign of the old being remained. Then, as quickly as he had disappeared in the Altfein-generated illusion, Orobai stopped singing and he immediately reappeared.

Initially Miraanni stared and giggled with a child's delight and wonder at this sophisticated disappearing act, but once the novelty wore off after a few repetitions, she began to understand that Orobai was showing her what she should do to conceal herself within her surroundings. It was a relatively easy procedure for it was a simple illusion of wrapping the landscape around oneself. This was nowhere near as complicated as transforming, which actually involved reorganizing matter, or producing illusions of objects, scenes, and events that were not present. One merely needed to blend into the background. It was a trick that Orobai had found useful many times throughout his long life and never once had anyone discovered the illusion when he employed this technique. Now it would be Miraanni's turn to try.

Orobai could feel Miraanni's presence within his own mind. It was a connection between them that had been consistently growing stronger, though Orobai only truly noticed it when he directed his attention to it consciously. Otherwise, her presence was more like the comfort of knowing that he was not alone and had a companion and confidant when needed, though not necessarily engaged with at every moment. Now that he was concentrating on the small child with all his attention, he could clearly feel her presence within his mind and being. Her own awareness was part of him now and when intended, his thoughts could be her thoughts, and hers his. This was a talent Orobai had first learned through the instruction of the Arnyar as such mind-to-mind transmissions were how they imparted their most esoteric knowledge to him.

Though Miraanni had not yet learned this skill of mental sharing directly, she seemed to have a natural talent for it and an uncanny intuitive understanding of the practice. Orobai suspected that Miraanni had this ability with not just him and his own knowledge, but with others as well, given her proclivity to react towards people precisely as they would desire her to act – the Yamné being a case in point. Orobai also suspected that just as with him, Miraanni had the ability to absorb information from the surrounding environment and could read the subtle signs of the past that gravitated around places and times. She too could find the secret patterns of manifestations and the knowledge and wisdom encoded within them.

Now she would have to turn these skills to her own protection. It was imperative that she understood fully what she needed to do and how to use the Altfein on her own without Orobai's instruction. This was perhaps dangerous, for there really was no telling what she would be able to do with the stones outside of Orobai's supervision. It seemed a necessary risk however, and if Orobai's intuition was correct, for her to truly activate the power of the stones as she had done back at Shashun-Olurn, for example, she would need him as well. Orobai was therefore confident that at least she wouldn't accidentally sing anything into existence.

To communicate to Miraanni what she must do Orobai first brought forth a vivid recollection of his dream. He could feel Miraanni in his consciousness like a witness to the events playing out in his mind. There she could see the strange flying thing and feel Orobai's anxiety over it finding them. He was also sure to concentrate carefully on the peculiar sound of the machine so that Miraanni might know of its approach from a distance and take preventative action against discovery.

Next, Orobai concentrated on the sight from earlier that morning of the very thing from his dream flying low above the river, clearly searching for something and the feeling of menace that it brought with it. Orobai held these thoughts distinctly in his mind until he was satisfied that Miraanni understood his intent.

He then shifted his thoughts to what he had just shown her about using the surrounding environment as a cloak of illusion. He showed her how she should use this if she felt threatened or exposed in any way, and especially if the flying thing should return.

Miraanni understood what she was to do. Orobai had successfully communicated to her what the danger was and what the solution could be. To show that she understood she looked up at Orobai knowingly, opened her mouth, and began to imitate the tones he had produced earlier. In an instant the girl, along with the three wolves, the boat, their belongings, camp, and campfire, all disappeared. Looking about him, all that Orobai could see was an empty sandy beach with scattered herbs and plants, some driftwood, and gray rock walls. No visible presence of the girl or any other sign of their presence remained. Only if listened to very carefully and with a knowing ear could one detect the soft and subtle sounds of a child's voice somewhere within the illusion.

"Excellent," exclaimed Orobai proudly at the masterful work of his young apprentice. Upon hearing his voice Miraanni ceased the illusion and reappeared before him, looking up with a gleeful smile spread across her shining face. It seemed to Orobai that she enjoyed this newfound skill. Now he could only hope that she would use it wisely and cautiously. It would have to do, regardless. Orobai had confidence in his young apprentice, however, and felt that leaving her behind for a short time would come to no ill, given her constantly surprising wisdom, skill, and talent. Truly she was blessed in the ways of the Altfein-Aryat and would use her skills wisely in his absence.

"This is my own initiation for you," said Orobai, reaching into his things and pulling out a small leather bag attached to a string. From his collection of newly acquired Altfein, he chose two small ones and placed them in the bag, sealing it tight. Next, he tied the string about Miraanni's neck, making a necklace of the small bag.

"Now these are your stones," he said. "They're sacred, just like you. And now, just like your elder brother, you'll be able to call upon their power whenever you need to. Use them wisely and with full knowledge of their power and purpose."

* * * *

The flight up to Arnthanlim-Zan was long and arduous for Orobai. It seemed to him an eternity before he finally reached the high peak where the Arnyar met in council. His repeated glances behind him slowed his flight, constantly scanning the vista below for any sign of the flying thing, or anything else that might threaten his dear little sister. He saw nothing of any concern, however, and continued on his way. At times he thought he caught a glimpse of light reflecting off a metal surface, but he was never sure.

Upon reaching the place of council, Orobai was surprised to find no Arnyar there, as Sto'orn had visited with them here only a couple of days previously. Orobai did see one of the lesser eagles circling above overhead, who initially took no notice of Orobai, not being concerned with a mere raven. When

Orobai changed back into his usual form, the eagle flew down right away, knowing who Orobai was and the importance of his arrival.

"Atluin, Grundin," said the lesser eagle rather formally.

"Atluin," replied Orobai. "It is imperative that I speak with one of the Arnyar directly. Please do me the service of calling one here to me. I would seek them out myself, but I am tired and am in need of your quick assistance."

The lesser eagle flew off without hesitation or question. Before long Orobai could hear the heavy flap of wings that could only be a true Arnyar as one of the great eagles crested over a ridge just to the west and swooped down, landing suddenly in front of Orobai, who, as usual, felt dwarfed by the great bird.

It was Utra'a'ki from Avengath in the west.

"So, you have seen it?" said the immense bird knowingly.

"If you mean the strange flying thing, then yes."

"But it has not seen you or the girl?"

"No."

"Good. If fate is on our side, then so it will remain."

"Do you know what it is?" asked Orobai.

"Yes, and no," said Utra'a'ki cryptically. "I know of these things, and others like them, but I cannot say honestly that I know fully what they are or how they work."

"Please, Great Eagle, tell me of what you know," Orobai requested, hoping that the eagle might be able to give him some genuine insight into this strange new thing.

"What you saw is no bird, as you might have guessed," said the eagle, starting with the obvious. "It is one of the machines that the people of the west have made. These are the same people who dig up Jeaniaurduin. They make these things out of metal and ore that they take from the body of Eyar. There is some source that powers them that they also dig from Eyar, but we do not know what this is or how they derive power from it. But we do know that these people have many such machines – things that go about in the air, on the land, and even in the sea where they live among the western archipelago. Though you cannot see them, there are men inside. They wear the metal beasts like some great skin."

"Are they dangerous?" asked Orobai, feeling that the answer to this too was perfectly obvious.

"Yes," said Utra'a'ki gravely. "It was from the very same weapons that are on these flying things that we lost Tur'orn and Ya'lan, the previous Avengath Arnyar. They are deadly, Orobai, and their power is a terrible one. It is as though they can call up lightning at will and direct it wherever they desire, within a certain range. If it makes contact with you, this lightning will incinerate you in an instant and there will be nothing left of you to mourn. I would confront the machine only if absolutely necessary and it should be avoided at all costs. I do not think that there is any protection from its weapons, other than secrecy and concealment."

Utra'a'ki broke off for a moment, gazing out over the horizon, as if he too were looking for the thing below. After a moment he continued.

"I followed this one here from Avengath at a distance, and from watching it carefully, I have learned that it does have limitations. It can only fly over unbroken ground or calm waters. It cannot fly high in the air as we do, nor can it soar to the tops of the mountains when the sides are steep and broken by rocks and cliffs, though smooth and gradual inclines are not a sufficient barrier. These limitations are fortunate, but as long as you and the girl travel the river you are within its reach. Water, in and of itself, is no obstacle for such a thing. It can even travel on the open ocean, provided that the waters are calm enough."

"And how long have the Arnyar known of these things?" asked Orobai.

"We have known for some time now that the people of the west have been building such machines, though we did not know of their real danger until we lost Tur'orn and Ya'lan. The machines and the weapons have grown more complex and powerful in time. I know that you, Grundin, have not been among the people of the west for some time. They have grown clever and cunning in their design and use of such things. It drives them on and they seem to think of little else. For the construction and use of these things they abuse other peoples of the west. They destroy the land and seek only their greater power, control, and dominion. It is as though it were a kind of addiction to mechanical innovation and the resultant power and authority that accompany it. In their wake they have left unimaginable suffering and destruction, though they show no concern. Only more power, more control, more innovation of the instruments of power – that is all that drives them on. They are singular in purpose, Orobai, and they have no mercy.

"It is for these reasons that we Arnyar believe that they would seek to use the girl for their own destructive ends. They have shown no concern for others and think only of themselves. Think of what they might do if they could harness the power of the girl! This is why we must keep her from them at all costs."

Orobai nodded. It seemed that things were worse than he had imagined in the west.

"Is there no way to stop these machines? Do they have any weakness that you know of?" asked Orobai, hoping for some positive answer.

"Only that they are controlled by people," answered the great eagle. "These metal beasts do not live, do not breathe or think. They are under the control of a person inside them who must come out sooner or later. When there is no person within, the things are lifeless and do not move or act. Remove the person and you remove the threat. I know that this is not of much help, but perhaps you may find this useful at some point."

"Perhaps," said Orobai. "It is good to know that beneath all that metal skin and bones there is one of flesh and blood and reason. At least some mystery is removed in my own understanding."

"Very well," said Utra'a'ki, "but do not assume that flesh and blood equals reason. The things they have done . . ."

For a moment the great eagle was lost in thought. His eyes stared away into the distance. Orobai opened his mind to him and caught fleeting glimpses of what the eagle had seen in the far west. It made Orobai shudder.

"I have told you what I can of this thing that now seeks you out," said Utra'a'ki, returning from his thoughts. "Beware, for it moves quickly and does not need to stop for weather or time of day or night. Remember that it can only fly over unbroken places and that it is deadly should you need to confront it. If so, you will be hard pressed to prevail against it. Avoid it if you can. We will be watching, but there is little that we can do against it. It is up to you to use your skill and wisdom as best you can and get the girl to Laftandiar-Urya with all due haste. I am certain that it cannot cross the mountains surrounding the city and the journey along the coast would be perilous for it. Laftandiar-Urya is your best protection. Speed and secrecy are your allies. Do not squander them."

* * * *

It was late afternoon by the time Orobai arrived back at their camp at Zallur. He found his companions well. Sto'orn reported that the flying thing was neither seen nor heard and that they had all passed the day without worry. Orobai was glad to hear it, though he felt strongly that this was not the last they would see of the thing on their journey down the river. They would have to keep up their guard and be ever watchful.

There is still more to the dream that has yet to come to pass. We will meet again.

Turning from the Path

D ays passed with no sign of the flying machine, that great silvery bird that
brought such menace and dread. They had now traveled well beyond the
reaches of Yamné territory. In years now long gone by, this land too had
been the home of the Yamné, when their culture had stretched all the way from
Golgath to the great eastern seas. At that time they had been larger in number and
more defensive of their lands. Now they were fewer, though still strong in numbers,
and their land base had shrunk accordingly.

Now the northern bands of the Djinari and the southern Tolguin, two
cousin cultures who lived on the southern and northern sides of the Nordlith,
respectively, occupied much of this land. Unlike the Yamné, neither the Djinari nor
the Tolguin used boats, and instead were horse-based cultures. Here the great
Northern Forest of towering redwood trees and pine groves emptied out to open
plains and rolling savannas where, on horseback, the Djinari and Tolguin hunted the
northeastern bison herds who migrated in and out of Jeaniaurduin. The northern
bison traveled by way of Northrun, the Black Valley, which separated the far
eastern reaches of the Morianithanlim-Gathr from the thick ring of mountains that
bordered the bay at Laftandiar-Urya.

It had been some time since Orobai had passed through these lands, though
he still knew them well and was still remembered among the people here. However,
he was not on the same terms with either the Djinari or the Tolguin as he was with
the Yamné, and thus was a bit apprehensive about how they would receive him, if
their paths happened to cross. Neither culture was fond of strangers and both were
protective of their lands. And what was more significant, Orobai had a reputation
among them as being a sorcerer. Be that as it may, Orobai was not overly
concerned and thought it likely that their passage through these lands would go

without challenge. He was far more concerned about the possible reappearance of the flying machine from the west.

Here, well into Tolguin and Djinari territory, there were many places where the Nordlith became wide and shallow. It was these fords that, particularly in the dryer seasons, permitted the mighty bison to migrate back and forth across the river. Now they would be in Jeaniaurduin and would be making their way back across the river as spring and summer came upon the land. A much larger herd of bison also roamed the western reaches of Jeaniaurduin on the great plains of the west, Nulthali. They were somewhat smaller in stature and size than the northeastern herd and would winter towards the southwest and enter Jeaniaurduin in the spring.

The towering redwoods of the Northern Forest were now mostly behind them with the large trees giving way to the more open grasslands and smaller trees such as oaks with their twisting limbs, birch, sycamores, and the occasional coastal pine, which would become more common the closer they drew to the coast. Here there were also willows and cottonwood trees lining the creeks and streams that emptied into the Nordlith, all of which were just beginning to bud. In all, it was a beautiful land, just as was all of Aurduin, and Orobai always enjoyed the scenery, especially now with hints of the coming spring showing all around.

Orobai was ready to be done with the boat, as he was tired of all the paddling. Thankfully, they had been traveling down-stream, but it was still a good deal of work. It would only get worse, however, if they were to follow their current course. To actually arrive at Laftandiar-Urya they would have to make a choice. One was to attempt to travel overland. This would prove difficult as they had much to carry, including Miraanni, and the terrain was hilly and broken, eventually rising up to a ring of mountains that surrounded the bay where the large urban community of Laftandiar-Urya was located.

The other route, equally difficult, would be to travel out the mouth of the Nordlith and pass around the northern edge of the mountains and enter the bay from the east and the open ocean. This would be possible as the current tended to flow southward along the coast, but the waters were often rough from the winds of the open sea. And what was worse, coastal fog could obscure the ragged and rocky shoreline, where a small boat such as theirs could easily be smashed to pieces.

Orobai would have to decide soon which way they were to go. Shortly they would be at the opening of the Northrun, which would provide them with the easiest passage into the mountains. They would need to choose then which path they would take. Both were uncertain. To go by water would be quicker, but more dangerous. To go by land would be exhausting, and Orobai did not know the way well, for he had never had to walk it before, having always flown to Laftandiar-Urya whenever he visited. The mountains of Laftandiar-Urya were difficult to cross. They were often broken by volcanic rocks, sharp precipices, and nearly impossible to navigate stone labyrinths. There was a trading route, but to reach that Orobai would have to travel farther to the south around the mountains, and in the open.

As fate would have it, late one afternoon, the decision which path to take was made for Orobai. They rounded a bend to find one of the many shallows of this portion of river. Orobai carefully steered the boat as far as he could, but soon found that he would have to walk alongside the boat through the shallows, if they were to continue. Even on land he needed to use his staff for support and thus managing both himself and the boat without help would prove difficult. It being near the end of the day, Orobai thought that perhaps they should just make their camp there for the night. He was not eager to haul all their belongings around this shallow bend only to do the same to camp an hour or two later.

Faen agreed that they should make camp so Orobai pulled the small boat up to the shore on the southern bank and began unloading their belongings. While doing so Orobai noticed that Miraanni suddenly became alert and gazed intently across the river to the northeast. Orobai's first anxious thought was that Miraanni could hear the flying thing approaching just over the crest of the riverbank. He strained to listen, but did not hear the distinctive, odd sound that the machine made. Then, almost hidden in the sound of gurgling waters, he was able to distinguish the sound of what could only be horses. He relaxed a little with the knowledge that at least whoever was approaching was not their hunter. Looking back to the child, he saw that Miraanni did not seem concerned, and to the contrary, stared across the river with a look of interested anticipation. Once again, the thought crossed Orobai's mind that Miraanni always seemed to intuit more about their situation than even he.

Moments later a small group of horsemen appeared atop the lip of the ridge. Seeing Orobai and his companions, the group halted abruptly and looked out upon them, most likely to judge whether they were friends or foes. It was a tense moment and Orobai thought of the possibilities of what might go badly from this encounter. It was not too late for him to use the Altfein to create some illusion or deception that might drive the horsemen away, but he felt that such would not be necessary. It even occurred to him that Miraanni might have intuitively used the skill he had taught her if she had sensed any danger from the group. That she hadn't was a good sign. In fact, it was almost as if Miraanni was expecting these horsemen.

They were either Tolguin or Djinari. In this light and at this distance it was not clear to Orobai which they might be. Regardless, they were an impressive group with painted horses, long lances, sturdy bows, and elaborately decorated bison skin clothing. Both the Tolguin and Djinari were larger in height and stature than the Yamné and in general had greater physical strength. Their silhouettes on the bank gave the impression of authority and power that should not be challenged, although they were only seven or eight in number. Without saying a word, the group, who appeared to all be young men, quietly and swiftly descended the bank and began to cross the river, coming directly towards Orobai and the others.

As they filed down from the ridge Orobai could see that the group was indeed eight in number and was evenly comprised of four Tolguin and four Djinari men. Their cultural affiliations were evident by the use of face paint and subtle differences on the designs painted on their horses. The Djinari tended to use somewhat darker tones as they collected their paints mostly in the vicinity of Norgath, and the Tolguin's colors tended to be slightly red-tinted, as was much that was found in the Northern Forest with the giant redwood trees. Also, while their symbolism was clearly related, there were some differences in style and iconography between the two cultures.

These young men here seemed to be a hunting party, by the look of them. They carried long spears and full quivers with their finely worked arrows. Orobai guessed that they were probably making their way to Jeaniaurduin for bison. The leader of the group rode a few paces before the others and had an air of authority about him. His face was stern under his long hair and he looked about him with a skill of observation of one who thinks of those in his care, much like Orobai, assessing dangers and threats, opportunities and advantages, before confronting them.

The group rode up close before speaking. They halted at the water's edge and looked carefully upon the odd collection: the ancient, black being, stark white baby girl, wolves, and eagle. They stared silently, taking in the unusual sight.

It was the young leader who spoke first, breaking the tension, projecting his voice authoritatively over the sound of lapping water and the occasional clop of a horse re-securing its footing on the rocky river bottom.

"Maku, Oguantun," he said, greeting Orobai in a way that clearly communicated that he knew who Orobai was, for he had called him "Old Sorcerer." This choice of words forcefully reminded Orobai that among the Djinari he was first and foremost a "sorcerer," indicating their superficial familiarity with him, and their subsequent distrust and wariness. Though the young man had correctly guessed his identity, Orobai was not familiar with him, which was no surprise. He knew very few Djinari, but Orobai felt he looked strangely familiar.

"Maku," Orobai answered, thinking that at least the young man recognized him and gave him a standard greeting rather than open hostility, as the Djinari often did with strangers.

"This must be the Oguantashi we've heard tell of in the forest," said the young man, indicating Miraanni, who looked up at him with fearless and curious eyes.

"I suppose that she is no doubt the very one," replied Orobai, thinking of how the Arnyar had been correct in saying that word of Miraanni had spread quickly about Aurduin.

"I see you have one of those fish-eating people's boats," said the young man, somewhat mockingly, showing his Djinari pride of being a horseman and his dislike for the ways of the Yamné. "You intend to take the Oguantashi through our country with this?"

"We travel to Tushanali-Aka," said Orobai, naming Laftandiar-Urya in the young man's own language. "We have not yet reached a decision whether we will travel the rest of the way by water or by land. Thus far we have trusted our journey to this sturdy boat. The passage to Tushanali-Aka is difficult however, regardless of how we approach it. Both ways are open to us, I hope."

"Over the waters is not good. The waves are strong and the sea is high now. Choose the way of water and you will find your end on the rocks in the fog. Land would be safer for you and your beasts. We can take you over the mountains quickly and safely. This being our land, you should not pass through unescorted," the young man was sure to add, not letting his authority slip for even a moment.

"Surely you are right and we thank you for your offer of passage," said Orobai graciously. "We do not seek to burden you, however, and would not ask any favor of you except to journey peacefully through this land."

"We will grant you that. We would not seek to hinder the Oguantashi, the little sorcerer girl. We can be of more help than that, however. Camp here this night and await our return. Our camp is not far and we will come in the morning with fresh horses to take you and your belongings. It would be no burden to us. What is more, my grandfather expects you, and I have my instructions," said the young man resolutely, showing he would not tolerate any disagreement.

"Very well," responded Orobai, curious about the last reference. "Here we will sleep this night and will look for you in the morning. You have my word."

At that the young man abruptly turned his horse aside and trotted off with his companions filing behind him. As they passed before Orobai and Miraanni, Orobai could see the curiosity in their eyes as they studied him and Miraanni intently with a mix of awe and fear. Their looks said that they would have been happier to merely leave these strange ones behind, but now their leader had obligated them to give some service to the strangers and there would be no breaking ranks among these hunters.

In only a few moments the group of young men had disappeared from sight and there was no trace of their passage.

"What did he mean that his grandfather expects us and that he has his instructions?" Orobai wondered to himself out loud, looking at Faen and Sto'orn. They had clearly heard of Miraanni, and they did not react with any surprise upon finding them here along the river. Was Orobai mistaken in judging that they were a hunting party? Indeed, it almost seemed now that they had been looking for them. Hopefully, they would learn more about this tomorrow.

Orobai had a camp set up before long with a nice fire burning and water heating for tea and a bath for Miraanni. It had been some hours since he had attended to Miraanni, so he sifted through the child's supplies and began unwrapping Miraanni so that he might clean her and freshen her up. It was then that Orobai realized that he had overlooked something he had seen before, but had not truly noticed, until just now – the silver four-pointed star, which had been taken as such a prophetic sign by the Yamné, was no longer visible on Miraanni's breast.

"Where did your star go, Little One?" Orobai asked Miraanni playfully, making a game of looking about her body and her belongings, as though the mark could have simply fallen off. Miraanni giggled at Orobai's game, and though playing along, Orobai thought of the profound impact of this discovery. He had first seen the star at Shashun-Olurn when Lilt'a had pointed it out to him, and now that they were far from the Yamné, it was gone. It was only present while she was among the people for whom the sign had meaning. Would it reappear if he were to take her back among the river people?

Orobai suspected that it would, but why? Was it her choice, or something else? It was certainly interesting that now that they were to be with the Djinari, for whom such a sign would not have any particular meaning, it had disappeared. Would a new sign come in its place? Orobai suspected that in some manner, she would fit into their lives, but how?

"You are wrapped in mystery," said Orobai as he replaced the warm bear fur about Miraanni, holding her close before the fire.

* * * *

Before long night had come. Ranya was waning now so there was not much light aside from the small fire. Miraanni was having her last feeding before Orobai would put her down to sleep. Orobai and the others were well relaxed when suddenly Miraanni became stiff and alert, raising herself up to look intently to the west, staring back up river from where they had come. Orobai looked carefully as well, but saw nothing. Still, he knew that something must be wrong.

To his surprise Miraanni began to sing the tones that he had taught her back at Zallur. Immediately, the Altfein reacted to her voice, and within moments, all present washed away from sight in an illusion that left nothing except the water, shore, stones, and plants. Not even the light of the fire escaped the cover of the illusion and there was no trace of the old Black One, his young companion, or the animals. Such an illusion was so effective, in fact, that those who were hidden by it could not even see themselves or the others whom they were with. It was as if they were not there or did not exist, for only physically touching one so hidden would reveal a presence.

Moments later a bright light shone out from darkness to the west. It was then that Orobai heard the distinctive sound of the flying machine that he had seen a few days earlier. This time it was coming back from the west to the east, following back down the river it had previously flown up. Not having found Orobai and Miraanni up the river, it was now retracing its path. It had not given up and had not gone home as Orobai had hoped, and had even begun to think, given that they had not seen any sign of it since Zallur.

There is still more to the dream. Riding painted horses in the snow. I know it now. The young man we met today. He was in the dream. He will take us over land, and here is our pursuer.

The bright light at the front of the flying machine swept back and forth slowly before it as it flew low to the ground, scanning the edges of the river for perhaps a boat or signs of a camp. Orobai thought to himself that Miraanni must have intuitively known that it was approaching, or perhaps her young ears had heard the thing before he had. Regardless, she had known and done precisely as he had taught her to protect herself and her companions.

The thing came closer now, slipping over the lip of the ridge along the riverbank behind them, gliding down across the water. Realizing it seemed to be coming directly towards them, Orobai's heart began to quicken. The sound of it grew louder as it approached until it was directly over them. Should Miraanni's illusion fail, they would be discovered immediately.

Though it was not high above the ground it was out of Orobai's reach when he stood up to get a closer look at the thing, reaching out towards it, curious to feel it with his own hands. It was clearly made of metal and some unknown means powered it from within. Being directly underneath the thing produced a very odd sensation throughout Orobai's body, as though some force were flowing through him and kept the thing from touching the ground, almost like the repulsive feel of magnetic stones. Somehow the thing was pushing itself away from the ground through this field of energy. Orobai thought that this must be why it was unable to fly over rough or broken ground and had to stay on either relatively smooth ground or water. Small cracks, stones, or perhaps even smaller trees would not be an issue for the machine, but it would not be able to propel itself over canyons, crevices, or areas that were not properly shaped to give an even resistance to its downward force.

Orobai wanted to examine the thing more thoroughly, but he did not have a chance as, just as quickly as it had come, it slipped away into the night and within moments had passed beyond sight and vision, though Orobai did occasionally see flashes of light in the distance as its beam of light adjusted or reflected off some surface. Before losing sight of the light he saw that the flying thing had curved around and ended up following the direction in which the eight young men had gone earlier that evening. Orobai could only hope that it would leave them alone and do them no harm, as they were surely not what it sought.

Once the thing was gone, Miraanni let her singing die away and in a few ripples of light the illusion washed away, leaving them exposed once more to the darkness of the night and the soft glow of their fire. Miraanni had an air of pride and satisfaction about herself, having successfully put Orobai's lesson into practice. She also appeared thoroughly unconcerned about any further danger or threat, as though the entire event had been something of a game or farce. She merely smiled up at Orobai, beaming in pride and joy for playing her game so well and confident that there was no cause for worry. She immediately turned back to Faen to finish her evening meal and soon was asleep. Orobai did not slip into sleep so easily, however, wary that the thing might return and he stayed up many hours, keeping guard over his little charge.

* * * *

The young Djinari man returned very early the next morning, even before the light of Urya completely filled the world and only the song birds were awake, calling out their joyful songs of morning and the new day. Never having truly gone to sleep, Orobai greeted the young man who now came with two extra horses. In addition there was one of the young men who had been with him the day before, and a striking young woman who had a maternal presence about her who looked intently at Miraanni upon catching sight of her.

"Maku," said the young man. "We have come to take you with us. We must move quickly. Wiko here will see to your belongings and Ashi will take the girl," he said, referring to his two companions. "It is better for her to be with a woman and not a beast."

"Thank you kindly," said Orobai. "Now that I know the names of your friends, will you not tell me yours?"

"You can call me Anlin," said the young man. "Now let us hurry. There is no time to waste. The others have already moved on and we must move quickly to join them."

The three Djinari all went about their business quietly and soon had all the belongings arranged and packed on horses much more quickly than Orobai would have been able to do single-handedly. Seeing their behavior with each other, Orobai decided that Wiko and Ashi must be husband and wife. There was a quiet sadness about the young couple. Behind Wiko's stoic expression there was a deep sense of loss and Ashi wore her pain in her soft brown eyes. *There has been a death.* Orobai knew this to be true. Looking them over, he saw no obvious signs of mourning that he was familiar with from Djinari culture, however. Then the answer came to him. *Their child has died before they could give it a name – it was less than four days old. An unnamed spirit cannot be mourned.*

Orobai had to take Miraanni from Faen to hand to the young woman, Ashi, as the Djinari had a strict taboo regarding wolves, coyotes, or even foxes. The Djinari considered wild canines to be so highly potent spiritually that they could cause disease and misfortune merely from contact or even being near them, and they avoided them whenever possible, even going far out of their way to avoid wolf packs or fox dens. That they were even here now, given Faen's presence, told Orobai that Anlin's grandfather must carry great authority. It surprised Orobai that the young woman, Ashi, even took Miraanni into her arms, as she had been nestled up with Faen, thereby making her contaminated in Djinari eyes.

Orobai knew well that the passion of motherhood could overcome any taboo, however. This one here was grieving for the loss of her own child. And now, in her darkest time, after the death of her own infant, she was presented with the chance to mother Miraanni. It made sense to Orobai that she would be willing to risk her fears for this opportunity, even not knowing Miraanni. Here was a grieving mother, drowned in sorrow, and Miraanni was a serendipitous lifeline to a happier heart.

Ashi struck Orobai as a beautiful young woman. Though quiet, as Djinari women tended to be, there was a sense of strength and determination about her. Orobai could sense something of the spiritual potency that the great healers of the Djinari shared, but he could see no signs about her of being an Ohuan, which would be uncommon for a Djinari woman anyway, as most of their holy people were men. Her dark hair framed a smooth face with dark brown eyes and high cheekbones with thin lips and a finely shaped mouth. She was young, but not naive. Anyone who knew death like she did could no longer afford youthful illusions. She brightened when Orobai handed her Miraanni, whom she took gently into her arms. She even smiled at Faen, almost as though thanking the wolf for watching over the child. She seemed to show no fear of the wolf or her cubs.

Look at how she watches them. Her curiosity is stronger than the taboo. She has power, but she doesn't know it yet. She has yet to know who she truly is. Why is she so familiar? Was she the one in the vision of the boat on the lake?

This young Djinari woman intrigued Orobai. It seemed more than luck that she and Miraanni should meet here, just after the death of her own child. Once more, Orobai felt the strange and uncanny pull of secret currents running just beneath the surface of the world. Orobai was never one to believe in coincidences, and every passing event only served to reaffirm his faith that all things happened for a reason.

There is some power at work here, but what, and why?

Kulan's Prophecy

For several days Anlin led Orobai and the others silently through brush and trees, always making sure to keep them well out of the open, hidden from view. They stopped in freshly abandoned camps, giving Orobai the impression that they were not far behind a larger band of Djinari who were also traveling secretly to the same destination. Though no one said so, Orobai suspected that this secrecy was due to the presence of the flying machine.

Orobai hoped that Anlin was taking them to see his grandfather, but given the young man's perpetual silence, he couldn't be certain. Even for a Djinari, Anlin could be rather stoic and did not let his thoughts stray far from his private interior unless necessary, or so it seemed to Orobai.

On this day it was cold and dark with heavy clouds and strong winds. The companions rode quietly, tightly bundled in skins and furs to keep out the cold as best they could. Here their trail turned along the eastern point of the mountains and began to move back west along their southern side. Anlin broke the silence in midmorning to inform Orobai that they would be at the main camp by mid-afternoon.

Anlin's prediction proved correct by Orobai's estimate, though they never saw Urya that day. The sun was always hiding behind thickly overcast skies, making it difficult to be precise about the time. The Djinari camp was tucked away between two folds of the mountains, secreted away among the trees and hidden hills. Lost in the clouds above were the rough rock cliffs that were so characteristic of the Morianithanlim-Gathr.

Like all Djinari villages, this one was temporary, housing the wandering Djinari for only a short period before they would move on in their constant search for game. Despite their cultural differences, Djinari homes, or wintado, were similar in appearance to Yamné kughain and easily transportable as well. Whereas kughain were made of elk hide, wintado were of bison hide and were more conical than the Yamné structures, which tended to be more rounded at top. Also like the River People, the Djinari painted their wintado with designs and symbolism that was particular to Djinari culture and religious beliefs, with images of bison and horses being the most prominent. Other more abstract designs were present as well, such as the horned moon, a crossed sun, iconographic and stylized mountains, and other esoteric designs whose meanings were known only to particular owners and perhaps close relatives.

Anlin took Orobai directly to one such wintado at the far edge of the encampment, nestled deep within the folds of the mountains. Passing through the village, many Djinari came out of their homes to watch the strange procession of sorcerers and beasts. Not surprisingly, many parents pulled their children back and sent them inside out of fear upon seeing Faen, whom Orobai instructed to stay close by his side.

The lodge that Anlin was taking Orobai to was clearly that of an Ohuan, a holy person and seer, as was evident by its use of color and design. Prominent among the symbols was a four-pointed mountain-like design with a dark diamond shape in its center and a stylized eagle above with outstretched wings. Below all this were four bison painted in black, green, yellow, and white. Each bison had a jagged line emanating from its center connecting it to the other three. Beneath them was what seemed to Orobai to be stylized images of water, at the center of which was a white circle bordered by a larger black ring.

Anlin indicated for Orobai to stop and wait as he rode directly up to the wintado. When he called out, a woman who seemed to be old and weathered beyond her years stepped out and spoke to the young man in a low voice so that Orobai could not hear. After a few moments discussion, Anlin turned around and motioned for Orobai to come forward.

"The Ohuantun will see you now," said the young man as the old woman turned and walked away, glancing warily at Orobai and leaving the entrance to the lodge open. Orobai dismounted, gave the two cubs he was still carrying over to Faen, and stepped to the entrance of the lodge.

It took Orobai's eyes a few moments to adjust to the darkness of the interior of the old man's lodge. At first he could only dimly make out the image of an old and weathered man, clearly older than even the woman who had just left, sitting towards the rear of the lodge, lit by the embers of a low fire. As more came into focus Orobai could see the common trappings of a holy person and seer – feathers, bones, skins painted with esoteric symbols, stones, and shells. There were also bison skulls located at each of the four cardinal directions. Each skull was a different color with black in the east, green in the south, yellow in the west, and white in the north. Though difficult to see, Orobai could also vaguely make out designs on these painted skulls.

The air in the wintado was smoky from the fire as well as from a small stone pipe that the old man was smoking. Orobai recognized the scent from many years ago and knew that the Djinari were still smoking the same particular mix of herbs and roots that they had smoked when he had been among them a few generations past. Seeing the old man now and smelling the familiar scent, Orobai thought to himself that this old man would have been a child the last time he had spent any real time among the Djinari, if he had even been alive yet at all.

The old Ohuantun motioned for Orobai to enter and sit. As Orobai did so the old man tapped out his pipe and refilled it from a small leather bag decorated with various beaded designs and small shells that Orobai recognized as being from the coastal waters of the eastern seas. Having filled the pipe, the old man lit it once more with a stick from the fire. He first blew smoke to the four directions, saying something low and nearly inaudible under his breath. Once having done so, he passed the pipe to Orobai, indicating through his gestures that he should smoke.

To show respect for the old seer Orobai obliged and took the smoke into his lungs. The effect was mild and Orobai could detect the different earthy tones of herbs and roots. Long ago he had collected such herbs for the Djinari. There were four herbs and roots in all. Each one grew at a different elevation. Not all mountains would have all four, though one could easily find the necessary plants when searching in the vicinity of Norgath and the mountains about Laftandiar-Urya. The fourth root was the most difficult to obtain. It only grew at the highest reaches of the mountains at the timberline, usually among aspen trees. Its fragrant smell tended to be strongest after a light rain and one could easily find it by scent alone at such times.

Smoking the mixture now, Orobai eased into the relaxed comfort of the long absent yet familiar feelings of Djinari culture. The old man sensed this change in Orobai and seemed pleased as he waited in silence, not appearing to focus on anything aside from his own thoughts. In his mind Orobai could see those years long ago when he had climbed Norgath searching out the proper plants with a friend, Ikudano, who had himself been an Ohuan, a Holy Man, of the Djinari. They had shared a special friendship that Orobai had not had among the Djinari either before or since. It had been many years since his friend had passed away and since that time Orobai had not come among these bison-hunting people other than quietly and secretly passing through while wearing black feathers. He had never really been accepted among them and they had never thought of him as anything other than an Oguantun, an "old sorcerer," who should be kept at a careful distance.

The old Djinari Ohuantun before Orobai now did not seem to share this view, or at least had overcome his reservations for some purpose. Orobai studied him discreetly. The man was well weathered with thick, creased skin from many years of exposure to the winds and sun. His hair was long and gray, tangled into thick locks of matted hair, as was common among the Djinari Ohuan. His hands were worn and Orobai thought of how many bison he must have cleaned and skinned in all his many years. Two of the old man's fingers were missing from his left hand. An intuition came to Orobai – *He did this to himself.* It had been no accident but an act of spiritual dedication. Here was a man who was not afraid to suffer for his faith. Orobai could also see by his mannerisms and the cloudy white cataracts in his eyes that the old man was thoroughly blind. The only sight left to him was that of his inner eye.

At last the Ohuantun spoke in a raspy yet subtly strong voice that carried conviction, age, and a deep spiritual authority with it.

"I was but a young man when my first great vision came to me," began the Ohuantun. "I had not even been hunting with the men yet, for I was still too small and not yet a hunter. I had never killed a Wakintunlan. I had never been with a woman. I was but small and weak, merely a boy. Though my body was small, my spirit was large. Though my body was weak, my spirit was strong. My Heya was Uandi.

"My family has always been Ohuan. My grandfather was Ohuan, as was his grandfather before him, and his before him. Long has it been our legacy to learn the Uandigu, the Holy Ways. We know of the sacred lands, the Sacred Mountains, and we have spoken Gadun, the Ancient Tongue.

"It was my grandfather who first told me of Nori, the Black One. He knew you and considered you a friend, despite the knowledge that many of our people looked upon you with fear and mistrust. He befriended you and kept your counsel. He was called Ikudano and his power was strong. The Djun spoke to him and they told him you were holy, that within you lay the power of life.

"Only once did I see you while my grandfather still walked in the daylight of this earth, upon the flesh of Makadun. We were camped by Kordjuni, the Black Mountain. In the early morning I saw you come to my grandfather and together you walked upon the Sacred Mountain and talked of many things. Though my grandfather told me not to fear you, I hid anyway, for I was afraid. I had only seen the sun return from the south four times. Only four winters could I count in my life. I was only a boy and my fear was strong for you were strange and filled me with wonder and awe. Soon after this time my grandfather left to walk in the daylight of the other earth and you came no more among our people.

"It was a few years later that my people were running from our enemies. We had to flee for our lives. Many of us were killed. Mothers were separated from their children. Elders could not keep up as the younger people fled. There was much sorrow in our hearts. We had to do what we could to save our lives and the lives of our families.

"In the confusion of battle, I became separated from my people and was lost, alone in the forest. It was then that I went to Makadun-Shiodjan, our Grandmother's Bones, and it was then that my first great vision came upon me.

"I had only seen nine winters and I was still young. Being alone, with no protection, I sought the help and guidance of Our Grandmother, Danmakadun. I went to the holy place, the sacred place, Shijusha. It is here where the Wakintunlan first came out of the body of Our Grandmother and it is where our ancestors first emerged as people upon Danmakadun. This place is holy to us for it is the place of our birth and the place of the birth of our relatives, the bison, who are the same as us for our lives are one. From there Our Grandmother gives life to all things.

"It was night when I came upon Shijusha. Alone I entered and walked deep within the cave. Through the diamond shaped opening I went with prayers in my heart that Our Grandmother might protect me and save me from our enemies. I prayed that I might find my family with the coming of the new day. And I prayed that I might be given life so that I could take vengeance upon those who killed my family. There I fell asleep, without food, without fire, without water. Still a young boy and not yet a man, I was alone.

"As I slept a spirit came to me. It touched me on the head and told me to awaken and not to be afraid. I stood and faced the empty darkness. Again it told me not to be afraid and instructed me that I was to look.

"Peering into the darkness, I heard the sound of the Wakintunlan; their heavy breathing, snorting, and stamping on the ground. Then out of the darkness a large black female came charging at me. I prayed in my heart and held out an eagle feather that I took from my hair. And as I prayed the cow ran and passed through me and I was unscathed.

"Next a large green cow came at me. Again I held my eagle feather aloft and prayed with my heart. The cow passed through me and I was unharmed.

"Then a large yellow cow came towards me. She too passed through me as I prayed.

"Last a large white cow rushed upon me. As before I prayed with my feather and was unhurt.

"Having proved myself and the bravery of my heart, Our Grandmother, Danmakadun, came to me and blessed me. Again the four cows stood before me, each of its own color. They faced each other from the four directions and all at once they rolled towards the center. When they met, they merged into One, and from this One came Our Grandmother.

"She stood before me just as you are before me now. Her face was old and her hair long and gray. There was a kindness and caring about her so that I knew I was safe and that no harm or danger would come to me in this sacred place, though she was terrifying in her power and there was a look in her eyes that I had never seen before or since.

"'Grandson,' she said to me, 'you have proven yourself through your prayers and your bravery. Now you must follow me and I will show you many things.'

"She turned from me and walked deeper into the cave, turning only to show that I should follow her. As I went, the rock beneath my feet turned to a narrow bridge and we crossed a great chasm. I could not see the bottom, and though I was afraid, I continued on, always behind Our Grandmother.

"On the far side of the bridge stood two great serpents of a kind I have never seen nor heard tell of. They were great and fierce with fire in their hearts and eyes and when they looked upon me I felt as though it would be my death. But Our Grandmother turned to me and told me to fear not, and she passed safely between them, so I followed on.

"Next we came upon two rocks that clashed and ground together, and all that came between them was utterly destroyed and ground to dust and ash. Again Our Grandmother told me not to be afraid and we passed safely between them.

"After, we came upon a great fire with a heat greater than that of even Our Father the Sun above us and it incinerated all before it. But Our Grandmother told me not to be afraid and we passed through it. And though I had earlier felt the intense heat, now it only seemed as though it were clean cool water against my bare skin.

"Then Our Grandmother turned to me, saying, 'My Grandson. You have proven yourself to be of steady mind and heart and strong of body and spirit. Though you were afraid, you continued forward. You are not ruled by your fear and instead seek strength in your prayers and your faith. For this you will be rewarded.'

"Saying this, Our Grandmother once again returned to the form of the four colored bison who stood guarding the four directions. It was then that I noticed that I was in a high place and could see about me in all directions. I could see Our Father the Sun, and though they are far apart, I could also see the Four Mountains, the Hindjuni. All around me there were many herbs and flowering plants, though it was not yet spring. The Wakintunlan from the east, the black one, came to me and told me that in time I would learn the uses for all the plants that I saw there before me and that through these I would heal many people. It also told me that it would be many years before this power would come to work through me and that I must be patient.

"Next the green Wakintunlan from the south came forward and told me that I would know the ways of the beasts of the earth and that I would always be successful in the hunt. It said that my family would never want for the meat of the Wakintunlan, for they would be as friends and companions to me.

"The yellow Wakintunlan from the west then came forward. This one told me that my dreams and visions would always be strong and that through them I would know many things. The future, the past, the present, all these would be open to me and would come in signs.

"Last the white Wakintunlan came from the north. This cow at first said nothing. Looking upon it I saw that in its heart was a great stone of radiant whiteness such as I have never seen since. My gaze became fixed upon the great stone so that the cow was lost to my sight and all that was before me was the radiance of the thing. And within the radiance a shape and figure began to immerge.

"Slowly it came into focus. At first I did not know what it was or could be, for it was strange to me. Despite its strangeness, the closer I looked, the more familiar the image became. Looking upon it I reached back into my mind and there was the image of my grandfather, and with him was the Black One, and I heard the word 'Nori' in the Old Tongue in my mind as the recognition came upon me. It was you, Oguantun. You were the Black One.

"The vision now moved as though backwards, as though time had turned around. I could not tell if it was the beginning of things or the ending, if it was the past, the present, or the future. And it was in this confusion that I saw them. They were Hindjun, four Spirits of the Mountains and they spoke to me in the Old Tongue, Gadun. Though I looked upon them, they were not clear to my eyes. Light shone about them of the four colors and their voices were a music of a kind I had never heard. They told me of you, the Black One. In their own language they told me and I understood, though I could not speak it myself. They said that in the time when strange lights move in the sky and over the ground, and when the Wakintunlan become ill and begin to disappear, that I must help the Black One. At this time I would need to use my Heyadani, my Spirit Power, to aid the Black One in his task. His task would be great, they said, and that all beings of this earth would depend on what he sought to accomplish, though this was not yet known to even him. In the vision I saw you, Nori, and you sang and in your voice were many notes at the same time and it was as the sound of the voices of the Djun.

"Then in the vision the Wakintunlan began to sing. Not in words, not in either the Old Tongue or Djinari, but only with music and sound. From the four directions they sang, and through their song all was made Holy and there was great beauty all around. Though it was not clear, I knew then that I would have some part in this great music of the Wakintunlan, but I did not know what my role would be. I still do not know, though I have thought on this for many years – for a lifetime.

"As the vision began to fade I lost sight of you and all that remained was the white stone of radiant light and great beauty that brought peace with it. I searched with my inner eyes and looked to the four directions. I looked to the sky and I looked to the earth. But there was no trace. The Black One was gone.

"The vision ended when one of the great eagles, all white in color, descended upon me. Its great talons reached down and clasped me so firmly that I thought surely I would die. But I did not. Instead I was taken aloft and we flew through the air with the ground far below us. In only moments I found myself not far from where we are now. I then awoke and saw that I was with my family. They told me that I had come to them, though I had been lost for four days.

"As my grandfather already walked in the light of the other world, I had no one to tell of my great vision. My life has been long and I have seen many things, healed many people, and my Heyadani is great. But I have never told this story until now. I tell you as it concerns you and your Heyadani as much as it does mine.

"I began to think on this vision when I heard through the forest and across the mountains that the Black One was coming and that he had an Oguantashi with him, a small sorcerer girl of great power. Hearing of her great beauty and her radiant white skin I thought of the stone in my vision. I thus told my own grandson, Anlin, that he should keep his eyes open for you and the girl and that he should bring you to me, if possible. Then, when the lights came in the sky and moved across the land, just as they had in my vision as I had been told of in the Old Tongue, I knew that we must meet. Here now we sit together and we speak of things Holy and Sacred. Tashu."

Orobai had listened carefully to the old man's story of that vision granted to him so early in his life that was, in part, only now coming to fruition. He reached back in his mind searching for any image or memory of the old man when he was a boy. Orobai thought back to the times he had spent with Ikudano and any memory he might have of his family. Faces, names, images, all flowed through Orobai's mind in a stream of associations and feelings of familiarity. From all the many images of those people from long ago Orobai isolated the image of a watchful young boy. The boy kept his distance, yet still watched his grandfather and the Black Stranger carefully. In his eyes was the look of a seer and one who would come to know many things that were secret and hidden. *What was his name?* What had Ikudano called the boy?

Kulan. Kulan had been his name. Was this the same one here before Orobai now, aged through time and weathered through many seasons? Looking at him now, Orobai could almost see the face of the curious and fearful young boy in the visage of the old man. Somewhere beneath the worn and wrinkled skin remained the youth with the burning fire of a true spiritual gift. Through all that time something of the boy had remained, dormant, waiting for this time, for this moment, to reveal to the stranger, the Black One, what had happened to him in that sacred place and the prophecy that had been granted to him. Orobai could see that this was all true. Kulan had told no one the full story of this vision, though surely parts were known for it was from this that he first became a healer. But that which the Illan had granted him he had kept safe within his heart for a lifetime, only to reveal it now, so very close to the end.

"I see in your heart that you speak the truth, Kulan," said Orobai, confident that he had guessed the old man's identity correctly. "The Djun have blessed you with their knowledge and I thank you for sharing it with me, and for keeping it safe for these many years. This must have been a special burden on you, not to reveal for so long what was shown and not to have your grandfather, Ikudano, present to share in his wisdom and advice."

Kulan took the use of his name casually and easily accepted the fact that Orobai knew who he was, though he had not revealed himself directly. He merely nodded his head to Orobai's comments, assenting to their truth and accuracy. As the pipe was now empty, he took it up once more and filled it with the mix of herbs and began to smoke as the two old ones sat in silence in the dim light of the fire.

"Tell me, if you would, Kulan, what you take to be the significance of this vision?" asked Orobai after the old man had prepared his pipe and lit it.

"Its meaning is deep and subtle," responded Kulan meditatively. "For many years I have prayed over this and have sought to reveal the depths of what I was blessed to see. I fear that the meaning is not altogether good. The Djun told that the Wakintunlan would become ill, and this I have seen come to pass. Many of my people are not yet aware, especially the younger people. But there has been a change. I fear that something has come from the body of Our Grandmother that has a dark power. It is this that makes the Wakintunlan sick. The eastern herd that we and the Tolguin hunt is still strong of body and heart, but I have heard from the birds and the winds that those of the western herd are growing weak and that many have become ill and die. The Wakintunlan of the west have always been smaller and less stout than ours in the east, and perhaps it is because of this that they are more affected. And this I know as well – it is from the west that this darkness comes. The light that my people have seen in the sky was not from here. Its home is in the west. And I have heard from the Absokale and Zhinjan of invaders from the west, coming to dig up the land. All these things are connected.

"I have thought about the Oguantashi who travels with you," Kulan continued, "and what part she may have in these things. From my vision, I think that the radiant gem is this very child, though this was not shown directly. There was a great power in the stone and through it all things were restored to balance and harmony, but not before much pain. She must be protected. All of our fates could rest upon her, and you, Nori. Though I think it strange that the girl was not within the vision itself – with so much revealed, why was the girl not there? I have thought much of this since hearing of her."

"You are wise, Kulan," said Orobai. "Your meditations say much and my heart is in agreement with yours. There is trouble in the west that I myself desire to learn more of. But before I do, I seek to ensure the safety of the girl, who is perhaps the most sacred thing in all the world in these times."

"Yes . . . yes . . . the girl. She is the key, I think. I am only beginning to see this now that she is here among us," said Kulan, becoming somewhat animated by his own thoughts. "I can feel her power. Even if I had not heard that she was among us I think that I would know it. You know this too, Nori. You feel her. She is a part of you. I feel it in you. I would have known right away. You are not the same being you were when I last saw you when I was but a boy. Your being and hers are part of the same whole. Perhaps this is part of what the vision meant with the stone remaining in your absence. The girl will carry on the power and purpose that makes the both of you and binds you together. Perhaps just as with myself, your time in the daylight of this earth is soon coming to an end . . . and hers is just beginning."

Silence descended upon the enclosure of the lodge with the speaking of these fateful words. Orobai considered them carefully and again saw Kulan's wisdom. *Perhaps . . .* , he thought silently to himself. He had not truly considered this possibility before this moment, but now that it was spoken, there was a sense to it, and it even seemed to fit well with the revelations of the Raven and Kite societies of the Yamné. But much was unclear in the old man's vision and there was still much that had to be revealed before Orobai could be certain of what was to come. Only the task the Arnyar gave him would truly reveal their fates, Orobai thought. At least he hoped it would. The Arnyar had given him this task with utter certainty that once completed, the Illan would make themselves and their will known. Then, and only then, could Orobai be certain of what would be and what he was to do.

Breaking the silence, Kulan spoke at last, saying, "It had been my hope that just as I had continued the Uandigu as an Ohuan, as did my grandfather and his before him through time immemorial, that my own grandson, Anlin, would learn these ways. When he was born I had thought to myself that now the spirits would bless this young one and he would learn the Holy Ways, the Uandigu, and that they would give him a great vision of his own to carry on this work. Then, I thought, I would have someone to share these things with who might be able to add his own insight and wisdom. But such was not to be. Anlin does not have the Heyadani about him. Our line has come to an end and it will pass from this life with me, I think. My granddaughter, Ashi, is of strong spirit. If only she were a man and not a woman. Then I would have someone to carry my power, but wishing will not make it so. We all must accept that all things come to their end."

The two sat in silence as the old man contemplated the fate of his family lineage. Clearly this saddened him, but he had come to accept it.

Breaking the silence once more Kulan eventually said, "But surely you are tired and hungry and desire rest. I have been inhospitable to call you to me so suddenly, without showing the graces that all honored guests are due. I have kept you too long now. The day grows late and we will have time to talk of these things further another day."

Kulan then abruptly stood up and motioned for Orobai to follow him out the door of the lodge. Orobai was impressed at how well the old man navigated his way about the lodge despite his total lack of vision. If it were not for his visible cataracts, one might never know he was blind.

The two stepped outside into a darkening world. Someone had erected a wintado close to Kulan's for Orobai and Miraanni. In the center of the camp there was a large fire where people were gathering to visit and enjoy the warmth. Taking Orobai to his lodge, Kulan showed him that meat and drink were available along with a bed of warm bison hide. Orobai was thankful and went inside to rest. Faen was already there, curled up with the cubs.

A few minutes later Ashi appeared at the door with Miraanni, who seemed happy and well cared for. Orobai smiled, glad to see that Miraanni was content. For the first time Ashi spoke directly to Orobai.

"I want you to know that I do not consider the girl as Oguantashi," she said. "I know that that is how people speak of her, but it is not so. I have no fear of her and I know that she intends no harm to anyone. I have spoken with my sisters, and having seen the girl, they feel the same way. She is not Oguantashi. She is Ohuantashi – not a sorceress, but a holy being. Though I do not know you, I think that you are perhaps Ohuantun as well."

Orobai was caught off guard by the young woman's peculiar mixture of confidence and shyness. There was something about her he couldn't quite grasp, like a flower gone to bud that had not yet revealed the true complexity and artfulness of its coming petals. *What is it about this woman that makes her so special?*

"Thank you. You are kind and have a good heart," said Orobai as he accepted the proffered child from Ashi's arms.

"I would know her name," said Ashi. "What do you call her?"

"I call her Miraanni," answered Orobai.

"Does it have a meaning?"

"Yes. In the Old Tongue her name means 'Mysterious Girl-Child.' I gave her this name as she was strange to me at first, just as she was for you."

"That is a good name, but it sounds strange in our tongue. If you do not mind, I would call her Ali. In our tongue it means 'kind,' for she has a kind heart."

"You choose well," replied Orobai.

Pleased at Orobai's approval, Ashi left with a smile and a bounce in her step, as though something about her had been validated in her giving Miraanni a name that Orobai approved of.

For his part, Orobai couldn't shake the feeling that there was truly something special about this unassuming woman. Despite the depth of what Kulan had revealed to him, Orobai found that his mind could focus on little else than the perplexing enigma of Ashi. Though he respected the old man, Orobai felt certain that Kulan was wrong to dismiss Ashi for being a woman. Her spirit was strong, and her future seemed heavy with the weight of destiny.

Riding into a Dream

Orobai awoke in the morning to find that the earth was covered with freshly fallen snow. The bulk of the storm had passed by daybreak. Only occasional drifts blew through the Djinari camp, adding to the soft white blanket the late winter storm had left in its passing. Though unusual, there had not been much snow this winter at such low elevations. Orobai was thankful that he was here in a nice warm lodge and not out on the exposed waters of the Nordlith, nor trying to battle the stormy gusts of the eastern seas. Had he continued on the path of the river, they would have been where the river meets the sea by now and would have been caught in the full fury of the storm that came in from the open ocean.

As Orobai stirred he thought over his meeting with the old Ohuantun the night before. Orobai could see how these visions from the old man's youth fit well within the unfolding revelations of Miraanni's fate and his own, but many questions still remained unanswered. There was much that was surprisingly consistent with what he had learned among the Yamné, though there were particular aspects of Kulan's vision that seemed to be unique to him and his own insight. Something particularly interesting was Kulan's prediction that Orobai was nearing the end of his life and that whatever power created and sustained him through these many years would pass on to Miraanni, who would, in some sense, take his place. Would Miraanni be the new steward of the Altfein-Aryat? Was that her fate and purpose? And had the Illan intended this to be so from the beginning? Or was Kulan mistaken, and was there another interpretation? The more Orobai learned of the puzzle the more perplexing it all became.

More practical issues were at hand, however, and Orobai's thoughts soon moved to other concerns. There would be time to ponder later. Now, Orobai needed to arrange for passage across Northrun to the mountains. The longer he lingered here, the more he felt the urge to move on press upon him. Miraanni was still not safe and the flying machine was lurking out there somewhere. The sooner they got to Laftandiar-Urya the better.

Orobai found some of the Djinari milling around outside going about their morning routines as he came out of his lodge. The air was brisk and he could see the trace of his breath and of the others who walked about in the cold morning air. The casual glances his direction did not seem as harsh as they had the night before, as though something had softened during the night – not completely, but enough to make Orobai feel a bit more comfortable among the people. Perhaps opinions were turning, he thought to himself.

Anlin, who was outside tending to some horses, noticed right away when Orobai came out and came to him directly.

"Good morning, Nori," Anlin said cheerfully. Seeing Orobai's reaction, Anlin added, "My grandfather has told me that I should not call you Oguantun. He says that in the Old Tongue you may be called 'Black One.' He says that I should honor and respect you, and the girl as well. If it pleases you, then I will use this name. And I have heard from Ashi that she calls the girl Ali and that you approve. Do you agree with this?"

"Both names are fine," said Orobai. "I have been called the 'Black One' many times before and it is nothing new to me. As for the girl, you are welcome to call her Ali, as Ashi has chosen. She knows her best here and I trust her choice."

"Good," said Anlin. "My grandfather is a wise man and I follow his instructions in all things. He thinks much of you, Nori. I do not know why, but you are important to him. Though he has not spoken of you before, it would seem that he has kept you in his thoughts for many years. Among our people he is known as a great Ohuantun. All Djinari give him their respect, and many of the Tolguin know of his power and respect him as well. If he says that we are to treat you with respect and honor, then it will be so. He would have us help you in any way that we can."

"For this I thank you," said Orobai. "All that I will ask is what I have mentioned before – we seek passage to Tushanali-Aka. Though the snows may be heavy and the way difficult, it is the course of our path. You and your people know the way best, so if you can help as guides, we would be indebted to you."

"My Grandfather has already decided who will attend to you. If you choose to leave today, we can have horses and supplies ready. We had intended to hunt the Wakintunlan in the southwest, but now we go where you go, until you need us no longer. Though we need the meat to feed our families, my grandfather tells us that your need is greater. He has seen much and the spirits bless him with wisdom. I will do what he asks of me."

"Then we should leave today, if possible," said Orobai decisively. "I will speak with your grandfather and see what his heart tells him."

This was an offer that needed to be acted upon immediately. It was perfectly clear that while Anlin respected his grandfather and would obey his wishes, this was not his choice, and most likely not the choice of others. The offer to help might grow cold with time. The moment to act was now.

Anlin nodded in assent and directed Orobai to Kulan's wintado, opening the door flap for him and calling out to alert his grandfather of his visitor. There Orobai found the old man sitting before the fire with the old woman by his side, who now looked upon Orobai differently than she had the night before, though still a hint of mistrust and caution rested deep within her dark eyes, much as was true for Anlin.

"Do not mind my wife, Nori. You see, she is cautious," said Kulan, listening carefully to the silence. "She is a good woman and intends no disrespect. Despite what I tell her, you must understand that we are all wary of anyone who keeps the company of wolves. Such things are not done among our people. We fear wolves and their power. You, however, have made a friend of their kind and I understand that you can speak with the wolf and her pups. This is a strange power to us and your ways are unfamiliar. For us, the wolf can bring disease and misfortune, but for you it is not so. And I know that there are now greater things to fear in this world and we must overcome our prejudices."

Somewhat hesitantly, the old woman offered Orobai some food and drink to break his fast, which was gladly accepted. After eating, Kulan lit his pipe once more and again spoke with the same sense of importance as he had the night before

"If things were otherwise, I would keep you here longer, Nori. There is much that I would like to ask of you and learn of your ways and your knowledge. My grandfather told me when I was a boy that Holy People should always seek to learn from each other. He told me that Power is not a competition, nor is it a game. Those with the gift must seek to use it wisely and true knowledge can be shared. Today, too many try to keep their power or their ways secret. We hide too much. Perhaps we trust too little or we think too much of ourselves and our reputations. I feel that we could learn much from each other. If only this were another time. Had we met earlier in our lives, perhaps our friendship would have been as great as that which you shared with my grandfather, or even greater. But time moves ahead quickly now, and the pace of things speeds upon its course to an end that we cannot yet see and only now feel in our hearts."

"You speak wisely," said Orobai. "I too feel that our friendship could have been great and that there is much we could share. You have already graciously shared much with me, yet I have given you nothing."

"What you have to give you will give to everyone," said the old man. "I would be selfish to seek to keep you and your gifts now. Greater things move upon us. You must continue."

"Yes," affirmed Orobai, seeing his opportunity to secure their passage. "Tushanali-Aka is our destination. We are hunted and must move on."

"Hmmm . . . The lights . . . they are seeking you out. We saw them come through the sky and we heard their strange sound. The lights shone down upon us, and my people were afraid. This is why we came here, to these folds of Our Grandmother's flesh. Here we are safe, I think. But you must travel out into the open. You must cross the valley before you reach the mountains on the other side where you can hide once more. Because of this, I have instructed the young men that they should go with you to protect you and the girl, if needed."

Orobai protested that only a guide, a horse, and some provisions would be necessary and that they need not send their young men, especially as they were themselves in need of bison meat and had intended to hunt.

"These things can wait. If you have more with you, I think you will be better served," insisted Kulan. He had already discussed with the young men that those who first came upon Orobai and Miraanni were to take them. Even the Tolguin had agreed to do so. Eight was an auspicious number, and as fate had decreed that they were the first to find Orobai, they should be the ones to take them farther. Respecting Kulan's wisdom, they had all agreed to sacrifice their time on the hunt to take their special envoy across the mountains.

Orobai graciously accepted Kulan's arrangements. Briefly taking leave of the old Holy Man, he went through his belongings and returned with some of the best eagle feathers the Yamné had given to him and Miraanni, along with some of the precious stones that he had collected. Kulan was especially pleased with the eagle feathers, which he touched delicately with his rough and well-worn hands, stroking the feathers from base to tip, all the while saying quiet prayers.

Within an hour all was nearly ready for their departure. They would need at least a full day to cross the open valley, Northrun. Once they reached the foothills of the mountains on the other side, they would be able to find trees for the lodge cover they would bring with them. To travel light and quickly was their aim.

The men worked quickly and to Orobai it seemed hardly any time at all before they were about to move out. Being nomadic peoples the Djinari and Tolguin had perfected their art of travel and could be ready to depart in only a few moments notice, as was the case now.

Orobai was about to mount his horse, ready to accept Miraanni from Ashi, when the young Djinari woman suddenly spoke up.

"I will go with you," she said, looking to her cousin and her grandfather.

"No," said Anlin. "It is too dangerous. These two are hunted, and we have to travel in the open."

"Anlin is right," said Wiko, Ashi's husband. "Stay here where it is safe and warm. Nori will care for the child and soon we will return with much bison meat to feed our people. Stay here with your sisters and be well."

"I will go," said Ashi defiantly. "I will care for this child. None of you men have any idea what this child needs. I do, and I will care for her."

Not knowing what to do about the obstinate woman, Anlin and Wiko looked to Kulan for direction. Without giving him a chance to speak, Kulan's wife came forward and spoke for the first time since their arrival. Quite surprisingly, she gave her unequivocal support to Ashi. "A child needs a mother, not a wolf!" was all she needed to say.

Kulan knew better than to argue with his wife once she had made up her mind, and an elder's word was final. "You will go with them, and care for the child, my granddaughter," Kulan said. "It is the way it is supposed to be." It was a pronouncement no one could argue with.

Not surprisingly Ashi had already packed and was prepared to leave immediately. She had a horse ready and took Miraanni into her arms, keeping her safe and warm. Ashi's sisters, Ohada and Nuya, came forward and wished both her and the child well. Orobai could see that they all had bonded quickly with Miraanni, who had easily charmed all of them with her unique ways. The sisters kept their tears back and Ashi assured her two younger siblings that she would return to them as soon as she was able.

"We will meet again," said Kulan as Orobai and the others rode off, "I have dreamed it and it will be so . . ."

As they passed from the encampment, the old man stood in the center of the camp with his wife at his side. He stood with his arms open and raised to the sky as the sound of a traveling song came to Orobai over the bitter wind. "They travel across Our Grandmother. They travel in a Holy Way," Orobai repeated the refrain of the song to himself quietly. "They travel for a great purpose. May all their paths be lined in Beauty . . ."

And it was beautiful, and that thought would have stayed with Orobai if it were not for one thing. Now that they were all traveling, he could easily recognize this situation.

This is the second part of my dream . . . painted horses, riding through the snow. We will be hunted.

Tracks in the Snow

Out on the open plain of the valley of Northrun, or Wakintunlan-Dashikital, as the Djinari called it, the cold wind blew fiercely. More snow came in from the east, though not enough to cover their tracks. The farther they went, the more it looked to Orobai like his dream of the flying machine from the west. He looked at his companions. Though he could not be certain, he felt strongly that these indeed were the strangers in his dream. They could turn back, thought Orobai, but what then?

There was no sign of the flying machine, though all were busy looking. Yet all they could see was the white of the snow, the gray of the cold sky, and the gusts of wandering snowflakes through the air. Orobai listened as well, searching for that distinctive sound, but all he heard was the whistling of the wind and the sound of horse hooves crunching in the snow.

Maybe the dream was wrong?

The going was slow as more snow had fallen on the valley plain than at the camp by the mountains and the cold, white snow was growing ever thicker about them. Faen had to struggle to keep up, having much shorter legs than the tall horses. In her younger days Faen would have had an easier time keeping up with the stout horses, but now, like Orobai, she was old. Her joints ached in the cold and she was no longer the agile young wolf she had once been. She was proud and determined, however, and trudged on without complaint or rest. Sympathizing with his companion, Sto'orn dropped back with the wolf, who was consistently falling farther and farther behind.

Despite the fact that Faen was Orobai's companion, Anlin and the others would not wait up for her. And though concerned, Orobai pressed on with the others, ultimately more concerned with getting Miraanni to the other side than anything else. He glanced back often, making sure she was still following along. By midday she had nearly passed out of view of those on horseback, causing Orobai to linger at the back of the group, torn between his concern for his friend and his sense of urgency in getting Miraanni to the other side of the valley and hopefully out of immediate danger.

Orobai's feeling only grew worse. With each passing step it seemed to him that they were more in the dream than ever. But still, there was no sign, and they pressed onward.

As evening drew on, the riders began to approach the mountains on the eastern side of the valley where the land rose up to greet the foothills and folding canyons of the watershed. Not far beyond these low hills, the mountains surrounding Laftandiar-Urya rose to the sky with sharp and jagged volcanic rocks, proving difficult to pass through unless one knew the way. Two of the riders went ahead to scout out a campsite and find trees that they could use to construct their lodge. It would be dark by the time the rest reached the camp, but by then hopefully all would be ready and they would have a warm lodge to greet them with a welcoming fire.

By now Orobai could no longer see Faen, though he occasionally caught sight of Sto'orn circling above where the wolf had to be, lost in the white blur of the gusts of snow. He trusted that they would find their way to them easily enough with Faen's nose and Sto'orn's eyes – they were animals, after all, and did not need anyone to look out for them. And besides, their trail in the snow was clear enough. Too clear, in fact, thought Orobai as he looked down at their all too easily seen tracks.

Then it happened and unspoken fears were made real. Suddenly a clash of thunder and lightning broke the monotonous sound of the constantly blowing wind. Startled, the company quickly halted and spun around, looking in the direction from where the sound had come. Another bright flash of light filled the sky, reflecting off of the snow, clouds, and blowing drifts. It seemed to be a flash of lightning by the look of it, and a sound like thunder came rippling on the wind once more with only a slight lag time behind the light. Perhaps if it had been raining or if the clouds had been thunderheads, then no one would have thought much of the lightning and thunder, but these were snow clouds and were not electrically charged. Silent, knowing looks passed among the travelers. Whatever was causing this was not natural, and it was certainly not good.

Another crack rendered the sky in bright white and blue light as once more the sound of thunder and electricity crackled in the ears of the onlookers. This time they could see the electricity itself in the sky and not just the ambient light it produced. There was the silhouette of an eagle against the bright background of light and electricity that disappeared into darkness as quickly as it had appeared. Then, rising above the mists of the horizon came lights in the sky with a blinding searchlight at the forefront, scanning the ground and the area around where the lightning had just been. It was the flying machine. It had followed their tracks in the snow and had clearly located Sto'orn and Faen. Now the flying machine would no doubt come for them.

The Djinari and Tolguin men flew into action immediately without any need for commands or counsel. They all took spears and bows in hand. While effective against game animals or other similarly armed enemies, their weapons would be little use here. It was all they had, however, and their bravery and honor would not let them do otherwise than confront the threat head-on.

Two of the young men broke off from the group and charged towards the machine, which now drew closer, scanning their tracks on the ground with its strong front light. Anlin called out to them, but they had rushed off with such speed and determination that they gave his urgent call no heed.

"Run to the hills!" shouted Anlin to the others, not waiting to see what would become of the two who had rushed off. "We're closer than you think. Ride!"

As the group rode frantically to the hills, they heard behind them the crackle of lightning once more and the roll of thunder rumbled through the air as a powerful electrical charge coursed from the machine to the valley floor below it.

Thunder, then silence. The machine did not stop. It came on faster now, spurred on by a fresh trail and having encountered prey. It sped forward through the darkening sky with its light shining before it like a powerful all-seeing monoscopic eye.

If it relies on vision, then let us give it something to see.

Yes, Brother. An illusion.

Their minds joined, Orobai and Miraanni simultaneously began singing the sacred tones that would bring the Altfein to life. In an instant, the entire company of riders suddenly vanished into the illusion the brother and sister created of snow and darkness. The trick had worked on the flying machine before. Orobai doubted it would be enough this time.

The startled Djinari and Tolguin all called out to each other in fear and amazement, never having experienced such a phenomenon of having everyone about them suddenly disappear, along with any sight of their own bodies.

"Be silent!" called out Orobai, letting Miraanni sustain the illusion. "It is only a trick. We cannot be seen, but we can be heard, so be silent."

The others obeyed and watched warily as the seeker approached in the air above them.

The bright light of the flying thing seared down upon them as it came to a sudden halt. The light turned back for a moment as if checking to see if indeed the tracks in the snow led to this point here. It slowly circled around. Orobai could feel the same strange magnetic force as when it had passed over back at the river. Everyone below held their breath as they too looked up at this strange contraption made by people far to the west and even further from their knowledge of the familiar or the possible.

It paused for a few moments directly over those hiding below and then began to move off in the direction in which they had been heading. It occurred to both Orobai and Anlin simultaneously that they themselves had been following the tracks of the two who had gone to set up the camp and that the flying machine could follow these tracks just as easily as they. Anlin motioned as if he would fly upon the path, but Orobai stayed him and kept him within the reaches of the illusion. Orobai then changed his tones, however, as Miraanni continued her part to maintain the illusion. The flying machine suddenly swerved from the path and started to circle back to the valley.

"What have you done?" Anlin asked Orobai, amazed that the machine was actually flying away.

"I've given our hunter some new prey," answered Orobai quickly. He had created an image of themselves, riding at full speed across the valley. Only now the seeker was chasing illusions and ghosts.

Taking immediate advantage of the situation, Anlin called out for all to ride. As they broke into a fast gallop, Miraanni focused her abilities to add to the illusion that Orobai had created to draw the machine away from them. Together they focused their minds so that they could see what was taking place in the pursuit, as though they were there from the same vantage point in space. Intuitively, they knew each other's thoughts and were able to work together to further the deception. Now it appeared as though some had broken away from the others and there were two groups to pursue. In one, an image of Orobai fled to the north. In the other, Ashi, carrying Miraanni, fled to the southwest. If the flying thing truly knew what it was seeking, it would have to choose which its main aim was.

The choice became clear – the seeker let the image of Orobai go, after sending one careless bolt of electricity in its direction. Instead of pursuing the black rider, the machine flew after what would have been Ashi and Miraanni, while attempting to blast the other riders from their mounts and remove what little threat they presented to capturing its target. But all was done for nothing, for it was merely an illusion and the seeker chased only phantoms and shadows across the wind-swept snowfields of the valley.

It was enough. The group of riders escaped into the folds and deep crevices of the hills where the seeker would not be able to follow. In fact, they had been closer to the hills than they had originally judged and they felt securely out of range in what seemed only a few moments.

Safe now, Orobai and Miraanni ceased the illusion. The flying machine reacted with a flurry of electric bolts as lightning once more filled the space around it, only now it truly had no target, not even an illusion, for the trick was revealed.

It circled back, returning to the original trail once more. Using a different tactic, Orobai quickly began to sing again with the hope that Miraanni would understand and add her power and ability to his own. Instantly, Miraanni knew Orobai's intentions, and together they called up a great snow that came upon them all in a fury from the east. In just a few moments, all was dark with a blinding flurry of white snow whipping about them. It was their only hope to cover their tracks, if only the snow could conceal them quickly enough. However, this meant that the two men whom they had left behind would not be able to follow their course to the mountains, and neither would Sto'orn or Faen, if indeed any of them were still living.

In only minutes several feet of snow had fallen on the valley floor. No trace was left of their tracks under the cold, white blanket. The now distant lights of the flying machine swept randomly across the horizon, indicating that it had lost their tracks once again. The snow had covered their traces and they would be safe.

For those they had left behind, there was nothing any of them could do now, so they pressed on, making their way to the camp where they would spend the night, wondering about the fate of their companions.   In the morning, with the coming of the new day, they would seek them out, but for now they would have to hide in the safety of the mountains with the anxiety of the unknown fates of their friends filling their hearts.

Orobai's dream had come to pass, and with it, death had surely found them.

From the Ashes

It was a fitful night in the wintado. Everyone was concerned for those they had abandoned, waiting for morning and the chance to attempt a rescue. Vengeance was sworn and passions ran high. Ashi cared for Miraanni, singing soft lullabies, and Orobai did what he could to care for the two wolf pups, anxious for their mother. Finally, sleep came over the weary group and all was silent but for the sound of the cold wind and the soft and plaintive whimpering of the cubs that lasted even into their dreams.

All awoke at the first light of dawn. The clouds had mostly blown away and a mist hung about the valley in a gray shroud. Miraanni, Ashi, the cubs, and several of the men were to stay at the camp. Anlin, Orobai, and the others were to go and try to find their companions in the valley below. Anlin and the other men left on horseback with Orobai saying that he would make his own search for the eagle and wolf.

When the others were out of sight, Orobai changed into his form as a raven and took to the air. As he climbed upwards he scanned the horizon for any sign of the seeker. Nothing seemed out of the ordinary and he could find no trace of the thing. It could still be hiding in the mist, Orobai thought to himself, so he must be cautious. At least it was not simply waiting for them openly. Perhaps they had convinced it that it was only chasing illusions here and it had decided to continue the search elsewhere, or even return to where it had originally come from, traveling back across Aurduin.

Orobai circled through the air for what seemed an eternity, always scanning the ground below for any sign, anything that might show him the location of his friends. He found no tracks, not even ones that might be fresh, and his heart grew darker with the knowledge that his companions most likely did not survive the sudden attack of the night before.

As hope faded from his heart, Orobai at last caught a glimpse of something below him. At first it seemed to be only a black spot upon the snow, but as he flew in closer, Orobai saw what was unmistakably the tip of a primary feather. Singed and ragged, the tip of the feather extended just above the snow, pointing towards the sky.

Orobai immediately flew down and came to rest by the feather. In his own form now, reaching into the snow, Orobai could feel a wing. It was Sto'orn. Orobai began to dig furiously into the white powder. Though his hands stung from the cold snow, he dug deeper. Slowly the body of the eagle began to emerge. Much of one wing and part of Sto'orn's body was badly burned to the point that most of the feathers were gone and the skin was charred and cracked with pus and blood. As Orobai dug, the eagle did not stir or make any sound or movement. Sto'orn seemed lifeless, there in the cold snow stained with blood. He was even cold to the touch and the feathers that had not burned were now frozen with ice. It seemed hopeless.

But then came a faint sound. Bending down to the eagle's head Orobai heard what was unmistakably breathing. Sto'orn was alive, but barely. Without immediate help he would surely be dead before midday.

"Wake up!" Orobai shouted at the eagle. No response. "Sto'orn! Open your eyes." Still no response. At least he was breathing. There was still some hope.

There was nothing that Orobai could do for him now, except to chew some healing herbs he had with him and place them as a salve on some of the eagle's worst wounds. He had too few herbs to be of much help, though, and if Sto'orn were to survive, other, more profound healing would be necessary.

"Faen!" Orobai called out. He listened. There was no answer. Looking about, he saw no tracks or signs. She had to be close, but where?

As Orobai looked around he noticed that a little way off the snow fell into a strange depression that was lower than the surrounding snow. The area was oddly circular, in contrast to the generally flat and smooth contour of the valley floor here. *The snow was melted there. Lightning struck that spot.*

Orobai walked to the depression and felt about it by pushing his staff through the snow. As the snow was powdery, he was able to push it all the way to the firm earth several feet below him. Nothing. But there was a feeling about this place that drove Orobai onward in his search. He could sense Faen. Focusing on these sensations, he could feel Faen's struggle through the snow to keep up with her companions. He sensed her thoughts and how her mind was centered on her responsibility to her cubs and Miraanni.

The Old One used this intensity of sensation to search further, deeper into the memory impression that had welded itself to that place. Orobai could feel a sudden shock and panic in the memory-feeling of the old she-wolf. Her heart raced and suddenly she was lost in silence. An abrupt and sudden end. The memory-feeling was no more. The final thought had been for the cubs and Miraanni and their safety.

She was a mother until the end. Her last thoughts were for them.

Orobai began to dig through the snow once more, despite the biting cold. He knew this was the place. It was almost a curse, this gift he had of sensing the dramatic memories of a place. Memories and feelings, locked forever in space and time, echoing the trauma of what had passed for eternity, calling out for a witness. Orobai was glad that it was only he, and not Miraanni who had to experience this now.

Finally, he reached the ground. Here the ground was not green, but was charred and burned to a deep blackness so that there were no remains of the grass and plants that should have been there. Instead all was ash. There was nothing else.

Orobai cleared away more snow. He only found more of the same burnt ash. He sifted through the ash and burnt remains with the end of his staff. A feeling of hopelessness came over him. There was nothing left of Faen.

Then he saw something unmistakable. There, amidst the snow and ash and burnt embers, were teeth, wolf teeth. The truth of the scene was now irrefutable. Faen had been utterly burnt, and now all that remained were her teeth, whose strong enamel had perhaps protected them. The old wolf was dead.

Orobai's heart sank. Though a wolf's life was short in comparison to his own, Orobai felt that he had known Faen for a long, long time. He had known her since birth. He had seen her grow, raise children of her own, and now his old friend and companion was gone. Though all things must pass, it was still hard for Orobai to let go, knowing that Faen had only come on this journey for him and for Miraanni, and now her two cubs were left orphaned. Orobai pledged to himself there and then that he would ensure that the cubs would survive and would grow to be wolves that would have made their mother proud.

You have my word, old friend.

The Old One reached down and gathered what he could find of Faen's teeth. As he did so, he thought back to what the Arnyar had said about Tur'orn and Ya'lan, the two Arnyar from Avengath. They two had been killed by the same kind of weapon. Was this how it had been for them? Were they struck down from the sky in a burst of artificial lightning that consumed their bodies and left nothing but ash? Had there been no remains of them at all, or had some broken and burnt part of their bodies survived – a feather, a talon?

Orobai put the teeth away in one of his bags after saying a prayer for Faen's spirit. His thoughts then turned to Sto'orn. There would be time to think of the dead later. He had to do something, and quickly, if the golden eagle were to survive. Going with his first intuition, Orobai began to sing, transforming himself into a massive Arnyar, all black in color. He would carry the dying eagle back to Miraanni, and together, they would do what they could.

The dark eagle reached out with his massive talons and gripped Sto'orn delicately, but firmly, so as not to drop him. He then rose to the sky in a great lift of wings and feathers, carrying his dying companion aloft. As he did so, Orobai called upon the power of illusion and they passed through the sky as a cloud or mist so that none might see the magnificent form of the great eagle, which would surely prove an attractive target to the flying machine were it still nearby. Quickly Orobai flew, knowing that his friend did not have long to live in this world and that time was now of the essence if he were to survive.

It was not long before Orobai found their camp. Those who had stayed behind saw only a strange mist descend upon them in a great rush of wind and sound of feathers, and as the mist dispersed, there stood Orobai with the broken eagle in his arms. Wasting no time and not offering any explanation to the amazed onlookers, Orobai carried the eagle into the wintado where he found Miraanni sitting up, awaiting their arrival, anticipating their need. Ashi was there, too, and merely looked on, waiting to see what would happen.

No one else entered the wintado. Orobai set the burnt eagle upon the floor of the lodge before Miraanni, who looked over his body, judging the severity of his wounds. She then held her two small hands out before her and began to sing. It was a complex mix of tones and shifting intonations of polyphonic chanting. Orobai only had to listen for a moment before he understood the logic of the sound and was able to join in with the small child. Together, their voices became strong and joined as one voice, calling the Altfein to life in a burst of white-blue light.

The light enveloped Sto'orn's broken body and flowed over him like water. It moved about his wounds and passed through his feathers and singed quills. It poured into his mouth, and like a great wind, filled his body. As it did so, the wounds on his body began to heal, the skin and flesh regenerating. And the feathers straightened and new quills emerged that unraveled into beautifully formed feathers of banded gray and dark brown with the characteristic markings of a golden eagle. Sto'orn once again began to resemble the eagle that he had been as all trace of the horror that had befallen him left his body. Slowly, his breathing became stronger as well, and he began to move his wings, tentatively at first and then stronger and more confidently. At last he opened his eyes to look up at those healing him.

"I am not dead?" he asked, weak and confused.

Orobai only shook his head, not wanting to break the chant and its power. Sto'orn rolled back and let them do their work, occasionally groaning with the aches and pains of healing with his wings spread wide. Gently, Miraanni began to trail off with her song and Orobai followed her lead. Sto'orn managed to say "Thank you," before he fell into a restful healing sleep there in the wintado.

Orobai leaned back against the wall of the wintado in exhaustion. It was so much effort and he was so tired. He could have fallen asleep right then, were it not for the sound of the others arriving back at camp with either survivors or more bad news. By the sound of it, Orobai judged that it was a mix of both. Orobai steadied his mind and body and went to see what had happened, following Ashi out of the wintado.

Anlin and his companions were just coming up to the camp. One horse carried two men with one of them slumped over the front before the rider. As Ashi rushed to the limp body, Orobai realized for the first time that he had not seen Wiko since all the chaos began the night before. He now understood that it had been

Ashi's husband, Wiko, and one of the Tolguin, who had rushed off so quickly to meet their fate with the seeker as the others sought refuge. Like a true Djinari woman, Ashi had been stoic in the face of her husband's uncertain fate. She had not grieved and she had not complained, and instead had sought to comfort and care for Miraanni in her husband's absence. But now that she could see that the body carried on the horse was not that of her husband, she could no longer hold back her tears as she turned away to hide her face and sorrow.

"He is not gone, yet he is near death," said Anlin somberly of the man slumped across his horse.

"And what of Wiko?" asked one of the Djinari men who had stayed behind at camp, glancing over at Ashi, and then back at Anlin, asking the question Ashi could not bring herself to ask.

"There was no trace of him, except these," said Anlin, holding out a collection of teeth in his hand. "It was the same fate for his horse. Nothing was left but teeth."

Then, looking at Ashi, he added, "I am sorry for your loss. There is nothing we can do."

Ashi wept in anguish.

"Nori," said Anlin, addressing Orobai now, "tell what you have learned of the beasts."

Orobai did not have a chance to answer before one of the men who had stayed behind called out, "He came out of a fog carrying the eagle and took it to the wintado. A strange singing came from within."

"This is true," said Orobai. "The child and I have healed the eagle, though he was close to death."

"And the she-wolf?" asked Anlin.

"She is gone."

"My brother," said one of the Tolguin men, pulling the wounded man down from Anlin's horse. "If you could save the bird, then save my brother!"

Orobai looked at the inert body now resting in the man's arms, slumped as if already dead. His hair was burned from his head and his body reeked of burnt human flesh. At least half his body was black and charred down the right side and his face was hardly recognizable. Most of his clothes had burned off his body entirely and he lay before them now naked and moaning in terrible pain.

"Take him to the lodge," said the exhausted Orobai. "We will see what my sister and I can do for him."

There they found Miraanni with an expectant look in her eyes as she watched them place the man's body before her on a bed of bison fur. Gently, Miraanni began to sing once more as she held her hands out in front of her over the man's aching body. Orobai too began to sing. Once more the white-blue light came from the Altfein and coursed over and through the burnt man's body. It seemed to lift him up from the ground as it encircled him, making him new again.

"What is your name?" Orobai asked the man when he finally opened his eyes.

"Washon," answered the Tolguin. "Where is Wiko?" he asked, turning his head from side to side, looking for his companion. When no one answered him, he knew.

Ashi stepped forward, holding the teeth of her dead husband in her hand. Her fragile voice held a glimmer of hope within it. "My husband was a good man," she said. "Can you not do for him what you have done for this one here? Can you remake him from these remains?"

Even though this skill was new to Orobai, he knew that what Ashi asked could not be done. "I am truly sorry for your loss, Ashi. I wish that this had not happened to your husband and that he was still with us now. Healing is one thing. To take a man who has been wounded, even to the point of Washon here, this can be done. The body is still alive and the spirit is still present. But death is another matter. To call someone back from the dead and to remake a body . . . such is not possible, I fear. One day, death finds us all, and from this there is no return in this life, or in this form. All spirits must eventually pass from this world to the next. What may happen then, I do not know, for death is unknown, even to me. But I cannot do this thing that you ask. I cannot bring back one who has been lost."

Ashi was inconsolable now and she wept openly for the loss of her husband. The others tried to comfort her, but she pushed them aside and went to Miraanni, picking her up and holding her tightly to her breast as she cried.

She has lost much. First a child, now a husband. Will Miraanni be comfort enough?

Now Orobai was truly utterly exhausted. He would have fallen asleep right then and there but he noticed Miraanni looking at him intently as she nestled in Ashi's arms. Sitting on the floor of the wintado, he moved over to them and leaned in close. Miraanni reached out her hand and grabbed at one of Orobai's bags that he kept about him. It was the bag in which he had carefully placed Faen's teeth – all that now remained of his old friend. Orobai removed it and cradled it in his hands as Miraanni reached out for the leather sac.

"Yes, she was like a mother to you – the first one you knew to nourish you and comfort you with her own life and substance. Like a true mother, she also gave her life for you, and I can see you understand this. I think that perhaps this should be yours," said Orobai as he tied the small leather bag around Miraanni's neck. "Here you can keep the remains of your first mother close to your heart, always."

Orobai watched as Ashi opened her own hand, looking down at all that remained of her husband. Teeth mixed with ash. She closed her fist, fighting back the tears, wiping her eyes with the back of her hand. She held Miraanni tighter and softly kissed her upon the head. Now, after so much suffering, Miraanni was all she had.

Ashi's Choice

The next few days were difficult for the band of travelers. Both Washon and Sto'orn were healed in body, but not necessarily so in spirit. Washon in particular felt undeserving of his own good fortune at having returned from a state so close to death while his companion, Wiko, was now nothing more than a collection of teeth and ashes. There was not even a corpse for them to bury and mourn properly. Both the Djinari and Tolguin could face the reality of death, but to be left with so few tangible remains was hard for them. Their shared funeral customs dictated that bodies must either be buried in the ground facing upwards, or alternatively, placed in a scaffold in a tree where they could slowly return to the elements of the earth. Only by following the proper funerary customs could the dead person's spirit return to his or her people in another form. In this way loved ones might not be truly lost into the abyss of the unknown. But Wiko's fate was beyond any ceremony or ritual now and it wore upon the company of Djinari and Tolguin. Washon was wracked with guilt that he should be blessed with life anew when the man who had stood by his side was lost forever, his spirit condemned to wander in the darkness.

There was no further sign of the flying machine that had brought so much sorrow to them. Despite its sophistication, traveling over steep mountains and canyons was beyond its ability and it had to give up the pursuit. Orobai could only hope that it had not gone around the mountains along the coast and try to meet them on the other side. His suspicion was that it had returned to the west, empty-handed.

Still, he was puzzled that it seemed to know precisely what it was looking for. Even if those in the west had heard of Miraanni, how could it be that they knew so much, so quickly? It was disturbing, but Orobai could think of no clear answer.

At least the weather had been kind. The wind had warmed and brought with it some rain, but no more snow, and eventually several days of sun and clear skies. The warmth and beauty made it seem as though they could put some of their sorrow behind them, at least for a little while. Spring felt not so far away now and Urya traveled further north each day, making the light longer and the dark shorter. Every day brought a little more hope.

After many days of traveling, their goal seemed within reach. The City by the Sea was close. It was midday when they crested a ridge and looked down on Laftandiar-Urya below them. All stopped and gazed out in wonder at the beautiful communities of high buildings and intricate architecture. The tones were of the earth and sun with buildings washed in earthy yellow with red tiled roofs, grand arches, elaborate towers and staircases, open courtyards, gardens, and located strategically about the villages, numerous large sails atop the highest buildings that turned with the ever-present wind from the northeast that blew through the bay and on into the interior of Aurduin.

From these shimmering sails the people of Laftandiar-Urya drew power from both the wind and sun. They made many sophisticated devices that used this power to make their lives easier and more comfortable. In many ways these inventions were similar to the flying machine that had hunted the travelers. The Ulusi-Rata used their technology for the betterment of life and work, however, and not for war and death. The casual visitor might not even really notice such machines in Laftandiar-Urya, so subtly had the Ulusi-Rata integrated the mechanical inventions into their lives. Ulusi creations did not dominate them and the Ulusi did not use them to dominate the land or others.

With a history rooted in seafaring, many of the people of Laftandiar-Urya still made their living upon the sea in boats of countless shapes and sizes, which dotted the shimmering waters of the large bay. The smaller boats rarely left the bay, but the larger boats would travel out into the open sea and there seek the large fish of the deep waters, but they never went so far as to be out of sight from the shore. In these sea-worthy boats the Ulusi-Rata also traveled to the south where there were more villages along the coast beyond the bay. Some would travel farther down the coast to trade with other peoples, or venture up the Durndlith to Mwataan Agdlan, the Temple of the Serpent King.

Looking out over the bay and the elaborate architecture, Orobai thought of the history of the City of the Rising Sun and how it had become what it was now. Like so much of Aurduin, Orobai has seen this place change dramatically over the centuries. Long ago the bay had been a refuge for the birds and animals of Aurduin, for no people had lived there. Orobai could remember those times for he had lived not far off at Norgath, his very first home. The rugged mountains and difficult passage into the bay from the coast had probably kept most people out. Orobai had wandered there alone with his thoughts and music. At that time the Arnyar of Norgath used to hunt the waters of the bay where they would dive for seals and sea lions, as well as any large fish that might unwarily swim too close to the surface. However, when people came to the bay and began sailing their boats upon the waters, the Arnyar retreated to the Black Mountain, for the Arnyar never desired to live with people and instead preferred solitude. Now, when the Arnyar of Norgath wanted to hunt they would fly to the open ocean.

It was people from the far west who had eventually populated this bay. Orobai had seen it happen. Along the western coast of Aurduin people had long used boats to travel among the numerous islands of the warm western seas. After a period of religious and social upheaval and change, some had chosen to leave the western archipelago and traveled farther and farther around the southern cape, establishing villages and towns along the tropical southeastern coast. Eventually they came to this bay and built their cities and towns, never venturing farther north. It had been the greatest migration of human culture in all the history of Aurduin. In the process, the Ulusi-Rata had come to be as a people.

Orobai had seen it all, in bits and pieces, over the centuries. He had seen the peoples of the west develop and grow and venture ever farther to the south and then back to the north. He had seen their cultures, religions, languages, and customs change with their shifting identities and sense of place in Aurduin. New places had become sacred to them as old places were forgotten. Old religions became myths and new stories replaced the old. As they discovered new lands and new plants, animals, and birds, ceremonies and practices changed accordingly. Languages were born and languages died.

The people of Laftandiar-Urya still knew of their distant origins however. As the migrants had long ago invented a sophisticated writing system and special scribes had the duty of recording and passing on the history of the people. The earliest histories were filled with many religious rationalizations and explanations for why the migration was taking place, but as time wore on, the histories became increasingly secular and less couched in religious doctrine. The old religion, called the Tal, faded away and new, more experiential and methodical approaches to spirituality supplanted the earlier myths. This process eventually became the foundation for the Ulusi educational and social system, which was based on an intricate understanding of both the science of the mind and of the physical world.

Here in Laftandiar-Urya, great schools were built for the teaching of accumulated knowledge and traditions. These schools emphasized various skills such as art, music, meditation, mysticism, healing, philosophy, and the technical arts such as mathematics, astronomy, ecology, and architecture. It was in these schools that the leading Ulusi-Rata thinkers honed their skills and practices, always striving to push the limits of knowledge and practice. In all, the Ulusi-Rata had a rich and varied culture.

Orobai had seen all of this develop with great fascination. From what he knew of the Illan from the Altfein-Aryat, he saw many similarities between these peoples and the Illan. This was not to say that other peoples were not wise and learned and greatly skilled in their spiritual and philosophical development, but in terms of society and organization, this seemed somewhat similar to him. Orobai imagined that the Four Temples of the Illan must have been something like the great centers of thought and learning among the Ulusi-Rata and their prestigious schools of higher learning.

The educational system in Laftandiar-Urya was almost exclusively run by women. In fact, highly spiritually developed and gifted women administered most of the city. The Ulusi generally believed that women naturally had a greater capacity for spiritual development than men. This was a bias that they had carried with them from the west and therefore was foundational to their society. The wise carefully watched children of both sexes from a very young age and selected youngsters for different schooling programs. Girls were chosen for the higher spiritual arts more commonly than boys, though no aspect of life was shut off from either as a rule. Yet by custom, there were important differences in gender roles in society, and especially in spiritual matters, more trust and confidence was afforded to women.

These were all reasons that Orobai had first thought of when deciding to bring Miraanni here, to this City of the Rising Sun. Aside from the fact that it was far from the west, as the Arnyar wished, Orobai knew that here Miraanni would be in the best possible hands in all of Aurduin. Here the people would nourish and cultivate her special gifts in a safe environment where Orobai need not worry about her as he completed the task the Arnyar had given him. He still had a long and difficult journey ahead of him and he would soon need to begin his pilgrimage to the Goargathr. He could leave Miraanni in the safe care of the wise women of Laftandiar-Urya. In particular, Orobai wanted to leave her with Nataali-Wantalth.

Nataali-Wantalth was the head mother of Hyanchalth-Murira, the Advanced School of Mystical Arts for Women. The prestigious and highly influential school was nestled back into the mountains away from the city proper, closer to their sacred mountain of Norgath. Nataali had been head mother ever since she had replaced her own mother, Ulanishar, who had held the reins of the flagship school for a generation. Orobai had long been friends with Nataali's family and had known her since birth. She was a rare friend with whom Orobai felt he could truly share anything. He was excited to share his young sister with her now. Nataali was like family, and Orobai's thoughts had turned to her almost immediately upon Miraanni's unexpected entrance into his life. Orobai wondered now if perhaps Nataali was expecting them, for she was one who knew many things.

"We'll make camp here," said Anlin. "This city dwellers keep a careful eye on their borders. They'll come and greet us soon enough."

Indeed, Anlin was right, for he had come here before to trade and knew a little of their ways. The Ulusi-Rata were not unwelcoming, but they did maintain careful watch on their bay and while people were free to travel and trade as they saw fit, it was rare that anyone would come and go unnoticed.

As the men set up camp, Orobai and Ashi went to sit in an open meadow overlooking the scenery of the bay while they played with Miraanni and the two cubs tumbled and chased each other nearby. Ashi took the opportunity to speak privately with Orobai, something she had not had a chance to do as of yet.

"Is it true what the men say of these people?" inquired Ashi, who had heard the men talking among themselves of the 'backwards' state of Ulusi-Rata society. "It is true that these people are led by women who have great spiritual powers?"

"Yes, it is true," answered Orobai, studying Ashi's reaction. He could see that she was greatly intrigued. Perhaps it had never occurred to her before that women could be powerful leaders and wield true spiritual authority. Such was largely not the case among Ashi's own people, the Djinari. Authority was almost exclusively male, in her world, and women spiritual leaders were exceedingly rare. The fact that Kulan overlooked Ashi as a potential recipient for his spiritual knowledge was a case in point.

"It has been this way ever since the Ulusi-Rata left the west," continued Orobai. "As a culture, the Ulusi-Rata have decided to place more trust in women than men when it comes to leadership and things sacred. According to their myths, many thousands of years ago, their male leaders betrayed them. There was a religious war and it was the holy women who led the people through the destruction and corruption. It had a profound impact on how they saw themselves, and their hopes for the future, at least according to their myths."

"Why did they leave the west?" asked Ashi, growing even more curious.

"Desire for a new life, perhaps," answered Orobai, not knowing what had truly led them onwards. He knew some fragments of their long and complicated history, but he had to admit, he never known what had motivated them to leave in the first place. Given the highly religious and mythical nature of the early histories, it was difficult to distinguish historical fact from legend, even for Orobai.

"Sometimes I think of faraway places, of finding a new life," said Ashi, gazing out towards the horizon, feeling empathy for those long-ago pioneers. "Sometimes, it feels there is nothing for me back home, besides my sisters . . ." She fell silent, staring off into space.

Beneath her sadness there seemed a deep longing and a steady, if unexpressed, passion. The young woman wanted more. It wasn't merely a matter of having lost her child and then her husband. These tragedies contributed to this restlessness, no doubt, but there were other currents that ran through her heart, even if she didn't understand them or know how to let them come to fruition.

Orobai could see it. He could see the struggle and dissatisfaction within her. It seemed clear to him that even if her child and husband had not met their untimely fates, she still would feel this subtle yearning.

Ashi eventually returned from wherever she had gone in her mind. After a long silence she said, "And you think that these women here, these women with strong spirit power, will care for Ali?"

"Yes, I know they will," answered Orobai confidently, as though there were no point to even asking the question.

"Why?"

"They will recognize her for what she is and that will be important to them. They will know that as time grows, she will be able to teach them more than they can teach her. This will be of great value to them and they will treat her well. Here they study all children carefully to assess their potential so that they can reach their highest level of achievement and personal fulfillment. They will have never seen a child such as Ali. She will be the greatest marvel and they will do everything they can for her.

"Besides all that," added Orobai, "they are my friends. They will want to help."

"Will you not return for her? Is this to be her home forever, raised by these women?" Ashi looked forlorn at the thought.

"Of course I will return," Orobai assured her. Then with a deep sigh added, "There are things that I must do, however, and the child must be kept safe. This is the best place for her. I may be gone for some time. I have a difficult task ahead of me."

As Orobai was speaking, Elkil and Fenruk carelessly tumbled directly into Ashi and quickly dashed away, continuing to play and roll as young cubs do. To Orobai's amazement, Ashi did not react. In fact, she hardly seemed to notice and only half glanced in the cubs' direction and smiled.

"You're not like the others with these two," Orobai said. "Are you not afraid of the wolves?"

"I was a little at first, but not anymore," answered Ashi. "At first I was afraid and only wanted to stay away from them. But I have seen how Ali loves them, and how they love her, so I know that they cannot be bad. Sometimes I wonder if our fears are just limits we impose upon ourselves," she said, philosophically. "And besides, we all have something in common now . . ." As she trailed off, Ashi looked at the small bag around Miraanni's neck with Faen's teeth inside. She then looked down at her own collection of teeth from her husband that she too had placed within a small leather bag.

Just then the two cubs came bounding back and hid behind Ashi with a whimper. Out of the forest a group of men on horseback emerged and came directly up to Ashi and Orobai in the meadow. They were Ulusi-Rata. They carried long swords of tempered metal and wore intricately embroidered clothing with subtle colors and textures. Despite the swords, they were more formal than actual soldiers of any sort, as the Ulusi-Rata were not generally a militaristic people. Orobai could tell by their decoration that they were an escort for a sister from Hyanchalth-Murira, Nataali's school.

Orobai and Ashi stood. In the back of the group, on a large red horse, was a beautiful woman with an elaborate crown of scarlet feathers. She wore a green silk gown with golden embroidery and high leather boots, the standard riding uniform of a sister, a Lalntalth, and the feathers indicated that she was a high-ranking instructor. Seeing how well she managed the large horse and seemed to exert a subtle control on the other animals, she was skilled in the art of animal empathy.

Ashi noticed this as well. She gazed up at the regal looking woman with the male guards, a look of wonder passing over her. Ashi stared unabashed at the woman's clothing and her poise, like a child discovering something new and profound.

Ashi's admiration was evident to the woman on horseback, who seemed to issue some silent command so that the men quietly slipped to either side, leaving her in plain view. The effect was such that while she herself had not appeared to move at all, she now stood directly before Ashi, presenting herself to the young Djinari woman. The rider looked Ashi up and down with a powerful and commanding gaze that Ashi met equally. This was impressive for even powerful men would often lower their gaze when confronted by a sister from Hyanchalth-Murira, whose eyes bore deep into a person's inner self. With just a look they could make a person confront his or her own limitations and weaknesses, and many did not withstand the test gracefully. But Ashi was not intimidated and looked on only with greater curiosity as she stood firmly in her place.

Taking her eyes away from Ashi and meeting Orobai's gaze, the woman spoke.

"Atluin, Grundin," she said with a nod, greeting Orobai in his own language. Like her other sisters at Hyanchalth-Murira, she obviously had some knowledge of Illanii. The sisters would learn bits and pieces of the language in trance and meditation during their mystical raptures. Some only knew the sounds of the language, but others were able to discover something of its meaning. Those who were truly advanced, such as Nataali-Wantalth, could even write the language in their own script. In fact, these mystical women were highly gifted with language in general, and those who had received the language empowerment could essentially become fluent in a language after being exposed to only a few words. It was a power and skill that baffled and amazed those who witnessed it directly.

"Atluin, Lalntalth," responded Orobai, nodding slightly and making a sweeping motion before him with his hand.

"The Mother expects you," the woman said, referring to Nataali-Wantalth. "She has dreamed of this time, and I see that her insight has come to pass."

"Of what has she dreamed?" asked Orobai, curious, but not surprised.

"She dreamed that the Gem Seeker would come among us with companions. He would come with a wounded eagle that he bore upon his shoulders, she said. And in his company would be a woman with child, though the child would not be her own. And this child would be sister to two wolves who had no mother."

Orobai smiled. It sounded just like Nataali – recounting her dreams in riddle-like form. Orobai glanced at Ashi. Her mouth had dropped open slightly. She was clearly awed.

"Indeed, she has seen much. The Mother is wise," said Orobai with another nod and bow.

"It is time to leave your escorts behind, Grundin. You are our guest now. We are ready to receive you at Hyanchalth-Murira."

"Yes, but first I must say good-bye to these good people. They have sacrificed much to bring us here," said Orobai, looking back toward their camp.

"Very well. We have seen their camp above us on the hill. Go and bid them farewell. They are welcome to stay in this place tonight, or longer if they wish," said the woman, "though I think that they will soon choose to go elsewhere."

Orobai did not need to return to the wintado, for the others had now come down to them, having seen the regal woman and her escorts from above. The men carried their spears, though not brandishing them in a threatening manner. Orobai watched as the men looked upon the sister and her guards. Like Ashi, clearly they too had never seen a woman such as this before and all but Anlin glanced away as she looked at each of the men in turn.

"This one has come to take you and the girl?" asked Anlin authoritatively, stepping forward and physically separating himself from his companions as if to make a statement before the powerful woman that he was in charge and would not be intimidated.

"Yes, we will go with her now, but I would not leave without bidding you all farewell," said Orobai. "I owe you much for our safe passage. You have all suffered because of us and for that I am sorry."

"You owe us nothing, Nori," said Anlin. "We came of our own choosing. The Djinari and Tolguin are free people and we expect nothing in return for the consequences of our actions. We are sad for our loss, and for yours. We also thank you for what you have done for Washon, for surely he would have died, had you not helped him."

Saying this, Anlin came forward and surprised Orobai with a firm embrace. He then instructed one of the others to come forward bearing Orobai's belongings. One of the woman's guards jumped from his horse and quickly took the items from the other man's hands. Anlin then turned to Ashi and quietly told her that it was time for her to give the child back to Orobai.

The guard who had taken Orobai's things went now to a riderless horse. There was not one horse without a rider, but two. Had the two horses just arrived, or had they been there the entire time? Orobai was not the only one to notice, and Anlin looked on with suspicion.

"What is this?" Anlin asked Orobai.

"I am not sure," answered Orobai honestly, looking up at the woman for some indication of what they intended.

It was Ashi who supplied the unexpected answer.

"I will go with the girl."

Her words evoked a profound silence. Anlin stared at her in disbelief.

"I am sorry, Cousin, but this is my choice," said Ashi. "My husband is gone and my obligations are broken. I choose now to go with Ali."

"Our grandfather would not like this!" said Anlin forcefully, glowering at his cousin. He had a look of someone considering various options in his mind.

"Who are you to say what he would or would not like?" retorted Ashi, with a surprising directness and outright challenge to his authority. "He would have liked you to follow in his path, but you have broken with our family's tradition of having an Ohuan. So how do you know what he wants? Would you share in his blindness?"

Ashi's words and demeanor startled Anlin for never had she been as outspoken as this. He made a move to come forward and take her with him by force, if necessary, but all it took was one glance from the woman on the tall horse to restrain his will.

"This young woman is coming with us," said the sister, surprising all but Orobai by speaking fluent Djinari. "It would be better for you to part in a good way."

Anlin could not resist the sister's will. The others watched on in stunned silence as Anlin gave up without so much as a protest against the strange woman.

With a silent motion he sent off one of the others to fetch Ashi's belongings. She did not have much, and in moments the other horse was secured as it waited patiently for a rider.

Recovering his composure and will, Anlin spoke to Ashi softly. "Very well. Go with them and may the blessings of Our Grandmother go with you. It is your right to choose, though I would have you return with us. Know that I think this is a strange choice that you make. This will bring shame to our family. It is not right for Djinari to live among strangers. A Djinari woman belongs with a Djinari man among our people. These people here are strangers and their ways are not ours. Though you make your own choice, it will bring disgrace to us."

Ashi said nothing in return. She didn't need to. Anlin knew as well as she that she had no Djinari man to return to.

"May the blessings of Danmakadun go with you on this path," Anlin said at last. "Tashu."

With that, he turned to the others and with a silent motion let them all know that there was nothing more for them here. Without looking back, he walked up the hill to their wintado and began to dismantle it. Several followed, while a few others watched in disbelief as Ashi mounted the horse provided for her. Uncertain, though trusting, she abruptly took her leave of her people and the world she had known all her life.

Thus it was that Ashi, a young Djinari widow and bereft mother of a deceased infant, left her people and joined the Ulusi-Rata, along with Orobai and Miraanni. She didn't know it then, but it was an act that would affect her life in ways she couldn't even imagine. She was leaving far more behind than she realized, and was walking into a new life beyond any expectation or dream, good or bad. Though Ashi never would have guessed, it was a decision that directly affected the fate of all of Aurduin, and was a choice that would bring consequences for everyone.

In a few moments the company of mystical woman, guards, and their new guests, slipped out of sight. The Djinari and Tolguin men quietly returned to their camp, packed their things, and were soon gone and were not seen in Laftandiar-Urya again. Orobai wondered what Anlin would tell Kulan about this turn of events when they returned. What would the old Holy Man think?

As they rode on together Orobai looked carefully at Ashi, still surprised by her unexpected declaration that she would join them. There was something different about her now, as though her taking this action had had an immediate effect upon her. The hidden potential that he had perceived in her was starting to show.

What had Nataali seen of this young Djinari woman in her own dreams and visions, Orobai wondered. He had not expected Ashi to make this choice, but clearly Nataali had, for she had sent a horse for her. Orobai knew that Ashi would never be the same.

Nataali

Once accommodated in Laftandiar-Urya, several weeks passed before Orobai saw Ashi again. One morning, the sisters brought her by for a visit with Miraanni, before beginning their daily routine of meditation, philosophy lessons, mind-body exercises, and everything else that their rigorous curriculum required. Ashi, who was now being called Lalntush, "little sister," the standard designation for new female initiates into the schools of Laftandiar-Urya, looked more like an Ulusi-Rata than a Djinari now.

Orobai thought that the change suited her. Her own people would have hardly recognized her, for she had all the trappings of a student of Hyanchalth-Murira, black silk robe with dark purple hood. Her tall leather boots, which shone beneath her robe, indicated that she had begun her initiation into the teachings of animal empathy, the Ulm-Lanish. In all, Ashi seemed happy and fulfilled in a way that she had not been before. Yet there was still sorrow for her dead husband, her child, and all that she had left behind.

Her life had quickly transformed into something she could never before have imagined. The sisters had accepted her into their school immediately, almost as though they had been waiting for her. According to reports that Orobai had heard, she showed amazing promise and had already demonstrated considerable skill and raw natural talent. She had truly entered another world far from where she had come only a few short weeks ago.

Ashi was not alone, however, in being away from her own people. Laftandiar-Urya was a city of many different peoples from far along the eastern coast to the south. The collective name of Ulusi-Rata indicated as much in that these were the "Peoples of the Sun." No single ethic or cultural group dominated the others. Ashi's peers at Hyanchalth-Murira were from far and wide. Many had left their families for many years to come and study at the prestigious school. Upon graduating, they could choose to go back to the village or town where they once lived, select a new community as their own, or even stay in Laftandiar-Urya itself, as many chose to do and become civic leaders, administrators, and spiritual guides.

Ashi's visit did not last long, for a novitiate's life was busy and rigorously scheduled. Miraanni obviously enjoyed the visit, giggling and laughing in Ashi's arms as they embraced each other. Some of the other sisters who had come with Ashi had seen Miraanni before and for others she was new. They all looked upon her with awe and respect, for they had all heard of her abilities and they knew how the Lalntalthta spoke of her. They also knew that Nataali-Wantalth had given strict instructions to show the girl all the comfort, respect, and hospitality that the school could muster, and they dared not go against the word of the School Mother.

Ashi had to say good-bye when some of the Lalntalthta came by to take Miraanni, as they did every day since Orobai and Miraanni had arrived at Hyanchalth-Murira. What they did with her every day Orobai did not precisely know. He only knew that Miraanni would be returned to him each night clean, fed, and very happy and satisfied. He implicitly trusted that they would only do what was in her best interest and respected the fact that they were curious about her and wanted to learn more of her abilities and uncanny skills.

Other than these daily visits from the school sisters, Orobai was mostly alone. Despite having anticipated their arrival, Nataali was currently on retreat on Norgath. In her absence, she had left instructions that no one was to bother him and that he should feel free to go wherever he pleased. Orobai found this more than satisfactory, for really what he wanted most was time to rest after all his traveling and the difficult obstacles they had overcome to reach this haven in the secluded bay.

Today Nataali would be returning. On Norgath, she had been secluded upon the mountain for a rigorous and demanding month of meditation and contemplation. She had left for the retreat at about the same time that Orobai had met with Kulan and learned of his vision as a child. Sometime before this Nataali had had a dream of Orobai, Ashi, Miraanni, and the eagle and wolves, and had left her instructions as to what should be done with them upon their arrival. Now everyone, Orobai included, was eagerly awaiting her imminent return.

Orobai had known Nataali since her birth. Her mother, Ulanishar, had been Wantalth of Hyanchalth-Murira in her own time. Though such positions were not necessarily hereditary, it was not uncommon for a daughter to follow in her mother's footsteps, however. They could not reach such a high position by default, but rather had to prove that they had the skill and ability, and if so, could be chosen by the Ainchalthta, the Council of the Schools. Nataali had proven her own skill and worth and thus deserved the title of Wantalth, as did all others with equal titles.

Ulanishar had been unmarried but had desired a child. Many of the women who passed through the School of Mystical Arts never took a husband, though it was acceptable for them to do so after their completion ceremonies if they so desired. Those who did not marry, yet wished for children of their own, could choose a mate from Ulusi-Rata society without any scorn or censure from others, and such choices were common. For many of the mystical women, children were desired, but not necessarily a life partner. Such had been the case with Ulanishar.

She had chosen a gifted statesman as mate. Together they had conceived Nataali, and a twin brother, according to Hyanchalth-Murira custom of a sanctified mating union. Nataali had been Ulanishar's only daughter and she had taken great pride in seeing her eventually take her place at Hyanchalth-Murira.

Orobai had known Ulanishar from her own childhood in Jodwan village much farther to the south along the eastern coast among the Shundway people of the Ulusi-Rata. He had been there when the gifted child was selected by a group of sisters from the school who recognized her abilities at the early age of only four. He had watched her grow and develop in the school and finally become School Mother. And already in Jodwan village, her family had had a long history of highly developed spiritual leaders and local healers. Indeed, Nataali came from an impressive lineage.

Under both Ulanishar's and Nataali's leadership, the School of Mystical Arts had grown both in size and stature within the Ulusi school system. Nataali herself was perhaps the most highly respected School Mother of recent memory, and Orobai suspected that her legacy would be remembered for many generations to come. And he was certain that Miraanni was bound to affect this legacy, and perhaps Ulusi-Rata society at large.

A knock came on Orobai's door in the late afternoon. It was still a little too early for the sisters to be returning with Miraanni. Opening the door, Orobai found a young girl dressed in the colors of the Wantalth: emerald green with interlaced geometric patterns of gold and silver. Upon her shoulders was a small cape of iridescent feathers from the tail of the magpie, the emblematic bird of the School Mother of Hyanchalth-Murira.

"Honored Grundin," said the adolescent girl, bowing low to the ground and speaking in a formal register. "Nataali-Wantalth has returned from Norgath, the first of the Four Sacred Mountains, and she requests the honor of your presence in her home. There she hopes that you will dine with her and spend the hours talking. If you would be so kind, please come with me now."

Eager to meet with his friend, Orobai quickly grabbed his staff, told the cubs to wait for Miraanni, and walked along the path to the school with the young girl before him. Finally, Nataali was back.

* * * *

Being head of the school meant that Nataali lived in the Faltuwan, the "Mother's House." This elegant building sat deep within the extensive botanic gardens that wound through gently rolling hills surrounding the school. Here the sisters had collected plants from all over Aurduin. They were arranged in different regional gardens so that one could easily stroll through many of the different ecosystems of Aurduin in a few hours. The sisters also had a garden of mystical plants. Here they had collected as many species of visionary plants as they could discover throughout Aurduin. Many of these were known to the different cultures that made up the Ulusi-Rata and most were from more tropical locations and therefore needed a green house. All sisters were initiated into the use of these plants before their completion, but only a few would go on to truly become masters of the difficult and demanding task of managing the radical and visceral experiences that could so easily catapult one into the farthest reaches of the mind and spirit. For this advanced instruction they would travel to the Temple of the Serpent King in the southern tropical forests, the Mwataan Agdlan, and there study with the highly experienced Sorcerer-Priests.

There were also food and herb gardens that the sisters actively used in creating their own unique recipes. The sisters were particularly fond of herbs and spices and it was something of a competition to see who among them could create the most unique and striking combinations of flavors. It was these smells that came to Orobai's nose now as he walked behind the adolescent girl. He could smell the many variations of basil, thyme, marjoram, sages of all kinds, and the many other exotic odors of the herb garden. There were many other scents that Orobai recognized from the meals he had been served over the past few weeks but could not identify. The light rain that was falling helped to bring out the scents of the herbs and Orobai wished that he could spend hours simply sitting and smelling with his highly receptive nose.

It was here in the herb garden that the Mother's House sat. Nataali's mother had been the one to originally have the house constructed here. Like all the other buildings of the school, it was created in its own unique style. Each school had its own individual look and Hyanchalth-Murira was no exception. A common feature of the architecture of the School of Mystical Arts was high vaulted ceilings with intricate and elaborate arches, grand walkways, open courtyards, and towering spires that reached up into the sky. It was designed to give a sense of transcendent space and openness, even when enclosed or in a small area.

There was also an organic flow between different buildings and areas so that no part felt disconnected from the whole. Buildings were designed to look very different from different angles and perspectives, while simultaneously exhibiting a supreme sense of balance and symmetry. The architecture accented the landscape around the school so that the school itself, despite its grand style, did not dominate the landscape but rather served to accent and highlight it. Neither the mountains nor the bay were ever excluded from view from the most prominent buildings on the school grounds. In fact, with the central courtyard of the school, the perimeter was designed to mimic the ring of mountains around the bay with the central opening to the yard being an exact replica of the eastern opening into the sea beyond. At the center of the courtyard was a crystal-clear mountain lake that itself mimicked the bay. At the far side was the central lecture hall and meditation house that resembled the mountains to the west of the school. There were four main gates to the central portion of the courtyard in each of the four directions. Often students could be found meditating in the peaceful serenity of the lakeshore. It was here that the equinoxes were celebrated, for on these days Urya would rise directly between the mountains that formed the opening of the bay and was mirrored by the wall of the courtyard. The school was a geomantic masterpiece.

Nataali's house shared all of these characteristics though in its own unique ways. One only need look upon it to share in the mystical serenity it exuded and exemplified. Ulanishar had chosen the finest architects for the original construction of the home. Here, Nataali hosted functions with dignitaries from all throughout the reaches of the Ulusi-Rata as well as with ministers of the city of Laftandiar-Urya and important Mothers and Fathers from the other schools. In addition to being located adjacent to the school garden, the home also had its own private garden, meditation hall, ritual complex, music room, and guest quarters. It was one of the finest homes in all of Laftandiar-Urya.

Orobai had been here many times before and each time he marveled anew at the architecture. It was far beyond anything that he would ever desire for himself, but the home suited Nataali well and she moved about it with a grace and elegance that made it seem as though this house were a part of her own body. But then again, Nataali, as with other skilled sisters, moved through any space as though it were her body. One of the first lessons of Hyanchalth-Murira was that mastery of the mind, body, and environment were all interconnected and that none could be achieved without the other. Nataali exemplified this philosophy supremely.

The young girl quietly opened the door to the house and motioned for Orobai to follow. She took his wet cloak and hung it up in a room with temperature and humidity control so that it would be fresh, warm, and dry when Orobai was ready to leave. The interior of the home was fashioned with dark and lustrous woods of many different kinds. The furniture was invitingly comfortable, but not ostentatious. On the wall hung intricate tapestries and images called skrit-yal. These were representations of meditative visualizations, some abstract, some symbolic, but all beautiful and complex. There were also many plants and delicate flowers and the scent of burning jaspin incense wafted through the warm and refreshing air of the house, which Orobai drew deep into his lungs, savoring the unique fragrance.

The sounds of voices echoed from farther back within the house. The conversations sounded important and business-related. The voices grew louder and momentarily a large group of men and women stepped into the entranceway. They wore clothes of different colors with various insignias that let Orobai know that these were all administrative personnel who had no doubt come to Nataali's to discuss important school business. The Spring Equinox was drawing close and there would be many important ceremonies and duties to perform at the school that would require Nataali's supervision and input.

At first no one noticed the young servant girl and the dark figure of Orobai standing quietly by the door. One of the administrative women let out a startled gasp upon realizing that a strange, black, and somewhat ugly being stood before her in the dimly lit doorway. She stepped back, holding her hand to her breast with a frozen look on her face as she stared at Orobai. The others seemed equally startled and clearly looked upon Orobai as some strange and curious sight. Orobai scanned the group and did not recognize anyone. Thinking the situation awkward, Orobai took it upon himself to break the silence.

"Good evening ladies and gentlemen. I trust you are all well?" he asked in eloquent Ulusi.

"Good evening to you . . . uh . . . Sir" stammered the woman who had first noticed Orobai.

"Good evening indeed!" came a voice from the other room. It was Nataali. As she came from the adjoining room to the doorway the others quickly parted to let her through. Though it had been several years since he had seen her, Nataali looked the same as she had for many years. The sisters of Hyanchalth-Murira always aged well and Nataali was no exception. Through their mind-body techniques, called Xhutai-Ku, the sisters manipulated the life force of their bodies and environment to bring them to the peak of physical and mental prowess, a skill that Nataali had mastered long ago. Though she was significantly advanced in years, she still had the appearance of one quite young, and through these techniques would most likely live for many more years in a nearly identical condition.

Nataali appeared now in her usual garb of emerald green cloak that separated at the waist to reveal pants of the same color and material and black-laced boots. Upon her shoulders were iridescent black feathers that shone green, purple, and blue in the shifting light. The dark clothing set off beautifully against her bronze skin, tattooed face, and long dark hair that fell in intricate braids down her back and over the soft feathers.

Without hesitating a moment, Nataali walked directly up to Orobai and embraced him, saying quietly, so that no one else might hear, "It is so good to see you, Orobai. There is much we must discuss . . . in private."

Orobai returned the embrace gladly and whispered back, "Nataali, my old friend," with a warm smile on his dark face.

Orobai could tell by the people's reactions that they had not seen the School Mother embrace too many people before – at least, not any so odd and unusual, for they stared in disbelief, though they were quick to regain their composure before Nataali turned back around to face them.

"Thank you for bringing our guest, Kalisha," Nataali said to her young servant. "And thank you all for bringing your concerns to my attention," she said to the administrators. "I assure you that all will be attended to promptly and with all due consideration. Now, I must ask you to leave, for my guest and I have pressing matters to discuss in private."

At first the others did not move for they were still fixated on Orobai. Seeing the problem Nataali added, "Perhaps you do not know who our guest is? This is the one who brought the gifted child to our school. This is the Grundin, the Gem Seeker. He is an old and trusted friend of mine, and of my family. I know that you will all treat him well as guest of the Wantalth of Hyanchalth-Murira."

"Of course, m'lady," said the group in near unison, who then began to file out the door past Orobai, each giving him a respectful nod or bow on his or her way out while still keeping an obvious distance.

When they had all left, Nataali turned to Orobai with a smile and said, "You must forgive them, Orobai. They work with numbers and books and rules and regulations. Their lives are made of routine and the commonplace. That is why they are all good at their jobs, and schools such as this are in need of people with more mundane concerns. But they are not accustomed to the unusual or the uncanny, despite the fact that they work here among some of the most gifted people in all of Aurduin. They thus mean no offense by their looks and reactions. You are simply outside the bounds of their experience, Grundin, and as such are startling and perhaps even shocking."

"Good! The day I become ordinary would be a strange day indeed," said Orobai laughingly.

Nataali invited Orobai to come inside and instructed Kalisha that she was to have the cooks serve them their meal within an hour. She should also light her sitting room with candles and a fire and then bring them some tea. The young girl quickly rushed off to fulfill her mistress' orders. Orobai appreciated the gesture, for the candles and fire were intended for him and his comfort, and as an added surprise, the tea was the very same Black Tea of the Yamné, which was cultivated in the school gardens.

"You know me well," said Orobai, sitting down in one of the comfortable chairs by the fire.

"I should hope so," answered Nataali. She too sat down and looked intently at Orobai.

"I met the girl today," Nataali continued. "She's extraordinary. Never in my life have a met someone like her. Not even the greatest Wantalth of our school could come close to the skill and power she already possesses, and she is so young, just less than a year, I would guess."

"Far less than that, actually," said Orobai.

"What do you mean?"

"She's no more than three months old. By my estimation, she's growing at three to four times the average rate. I think that by the end of her first year she will have developed to the equivalence of a four-year-old."

"Extraordinary!" exclaimed Nataali. "And what do you think is the meaning of this advanced rate of growth, Orobai?"

"I am not sure, but I believe it suggests that whatever purpose called her into being is pressing down upon us. Perhaps she grows so quickly because she needs to."

"You must tell me everything about her," said Nataali, fascinated.

It was a compelling command. All the sisters had a way of getting any kind of information they wanted out of people, and here Orobai was no exception, though he would not have resisted even if he had been able to. Orobai held nothing back and he told Nataali everything he could about Miraanni: finding the jewel in Jeaniaurduin, the meeting with the Arnyar, Faen's sacrifice, Miraanni's time with the Yamné and the Djinari, her fantastic healing abilities, their struggle with T'urk'nan, their pursuit by the flying machine from the west, and her skill with the Altfein. For hours, Orobai shaped the past few months into a story of the special girl and all that they had encountered and discovered along the way to their destination, this city on the edge of the world by the eastern seas, their last refuge. All the while Nataali sat silently, focused on Orobai's every word. She said nothing, though she occasionally nodded and gently rocked back and forth to the rhythm of Orobai's words. Her eyes, though still intense, were mostly half-closed, as though she were looking with her inner eye and watching the story of Miraanni unfold before her in her mind as Orobai narrated.

By the time Orobai finished, many hours had passed. The food that had been prepared for their supper had gone cold, the fire had turned to glowing embers, and the candles had all but burned down to their bases. Orobai somehow felt relieved at having told Nataali everything he could, as though a private burden had been shared with another sympathetic spirit. His trust in Nataali was so complete that he never gave any thought to the idea that she might abuse the secret knowledge that he had given her. He knew in his heart that Nataali would not reveal to others the true nature of all that Miraanni had done, or was capable of doing, or the special role that she seemed to be playing in the religious and ceremonial lives of the Yamné.

Orobai had lost track of time long ago and suddenly became aware that he had missed Miraanni's return to his guest home in the woods. Breaking the silence that remained at the end of his soliloquy, Orobai said, "It is far later than I had intended, and I fear that I must leave abruptly, for surely Miraanni awaits me at our home."

Breaking from her meditative reverie, Nataali responded, "Not to worry, Orobai. I had her sent back with the young Djinari woman, Ashi, who, by the way, seems to be quite exceptional in her own right. One of our instructors, Shintan-Vur, whom you met upon your initial arrival with the Djinari, says that we are to expect extraordinary things from this one. Yes, it is a good thing you brought her to us along with the girl. I have a very unique feeling about her . . . something I've never anticipated before . . .

"Anyway, Miraanni is in good hands so you can relax," said Nataali, seeming to emerge from a brief meditation. "Come, we must eat."

At that Nataali rang a bell that summoned Kalisha, who quickly came and took the food, reheated it, and had it back for them to eat in only a few minutes. Orobai had not realized how hungry he was until he began to eat the savory food and was thankful that he need not rush off as he had thought.

When they had finished eating, Nataali and Orobai returned to the newly refreshed fire and sat in silence in its warmth for a few moments before Nataali spoke.

"There is much that we still need to discuss. In particular I would like to discuss with you the problems that have been developing in the west, Orobai. This is terribly serious – perhaps more so than any of us yet fully realize. But it is late and I do not want to continue a discussion of such serious things at this time, for surely you are tired and would like to rest. I too am tired and have traveled far this day. Tomorrow I will send for you again. There will be a meeting of the City Ministers and heads of some of the schools in the midday. It would be good for you to attend, for there is much that you can contribute, and probably there is much that you will learn. I think it undeniable that the events that have come to pass are all connected. Things have become imbalanced. All the sisters can feel it, and surely you feel it too, Orobai."

"Yes, I have. I have seen it in my dreams and felt it in my body, heart, mind, and spirit," said Orobai. "And no doubt Miraanni feels it as well. There is something happening in Aurduin. A great change is upon us."

"Yes . . . Here at Hyanchalth-Murira we teach of the Khutan-Scyr, the Dynamic Balance of All Things. As you well know, it is one of our central philosophies. As a guiding principle, it is what teaches us the boundaries and limits of our own uses of power. It is the extension of the Xhutai-Ku to All that Is.

"Mind you, in this, the sisterhood has never promoted a static view of the world, for stasis is not a natural characteristic of the changing world. We cannot stop change, nor should we try."

"Qui ol lqui. Trah ol ltrah," responded Orobai with the ancient Illanii saying. "A note held is not a note. Music held is not music."

"Precisely," said Nataali. "But those in the west have gone too far. What they do now is disrupting the Khutan-Scyr. It is the girl, Miraanni, who will restore the Dynamic Balance, but I cannot say how or why. I know this in my innermost being, however. And from what you say, the Yamné seem to know this as well. And you too, Orobai, are bound to this fate, but perhaps you have always known this. You have always said that Illan created you for a purpose that they could not fully foresee. I fear the time is upon us. The girl is Sarnrhobi, the Harbinger of the New Dawn for Aurduin. It is undeniable. You are right to say that a great change is upon us, but what?"

"You are wise, Nataali, and I know in my heart that you speak the truth," said Orobai. "We will talk more of this tomorrow."

"Yes, my old friend. Now go and rest, or stay and sleep here if you like. It is late."

"Thank you, but I would return to my own quarters. I do not mind the time and will enjoy the walk," said Orobai as he extended his hand for his staff, which he found just out of reach.

Nataali quickly moved to get Orobai his staff. "Can I give you a light or send an escort with you? I can have Kalisha walk you back," she said, helping Orobai rise from his chair by the fire.

"No, my staff will light my way, if it is needed, and I can find my own way easily enough."

"Very good. Until tomorrow then." Nataali escorted Orobai to the door, giving him his warm, dry cloak, and watched as he walked slowly down the path to the gardens, slipping away into the nighttime darkness.

* * * *

The rain had ceased and the clouds had cleared, revealing a starry sky above, unlit by the absent moon. To help him find his way, Orobai set the Altfein in his staff to a faint blue glow to his quiet humming. His own sound was occasionally punctuated by the calls of owls and nighthawks, whose silhouettes Orobai glimpsed from time to time against the background of the starry sky. As he walked, he thought over all that had been said and all that had brought him and Miraanni to this point. Despite the tragedies that had befallen them, all seemed to be proceeding according to a larger purpose. "Dir elan. Goar Saum edi laur," Orobai said quietly to himself, repeating the Illan dictums of philosophical faith in the ultimate interconnection and meaningfulness of all things.

After a long walk, Orobai eventually arrived back at his home. He entered to find Miraanni sleeping peacefully in Ashi's arms, who was asleep in a comfortable chair before a warm fire. Orobai took heart in their comfort with each other. It was good that Miraanni now had someone other than himself that she could rely upon and give her trust and love to. Soon he would have to leave, but at least Ashi would be there for her. Quietly, Orobai slipped into another chair, joining them by the crackling fire, and soon fell fast asleep as the fire slowly burned to embers and ashes in the hearth.

The Council at Kur-Aku

The Council at Kur-Aku had already begun when Orobai, Ashi, and Miraanni arrived with their official escorts. Orobai had been to Kur-Aku before, but never had he felt the air of seriousness and concern that exuded from the participants in the great hall now. There were ministers, officials, and delegates who had come from most of the different peoples and major communities of the Ulusi-Rata, both within Laftandiar-Urya and down the coast as well. They all wore their finest clothing showing their rank, home, skills, honors and awards, which gave the gathering a great sense of formality.

The delegates were all exquisite to look upon. They all had unique attire, yet managed to maintain a sense of unity and cohesion with the others. Each could fully express individual identity within the whole, yet still be contained within the larger social structures of Ulusi society. There was a profusion of colorful dress, elaborate headdresses, feathers of all kinds signifying rank and talent, richly embroidered cloth, intricate hair styles, and for some from the communities further south, complex facial tattoos across the forehead and down the nose. And all the officials came with their retinues of aides, assistants, and underlings. It was a visual feast of color, shape, and form.

The great hall itself reinforced the sharing of power between the different elements of Ulusi-Rata society. The primary officials and delegates, with school heads included, were seated in a three-quarter semi-circle before a large, but not obtrusive, podium where speakers could ascend to speak to the assembled crowd. The interested public could fill in the rest of the circle or could sit in the extensive balconies around and above the delegates. Any who wanted to speak could address the council at designated times after scheduled speakers, sometimes prolonging meetings for hours, or even days. Behind the center circle, the room sloped upwards where lesser officials and delegates could sit and beyond that were the grand balconies under high vaulted ceilings around the outer edge of the circle. In this way the focus was on either the elevated podium at the center or on the collective body of the council itself. No one person, aside from the speaker at the podium, was isolated from the rest of those present, and all were able to easily see and hear the proceedings. The ceiling itself was a large glass dome so that a feeling of continuity with the outside was maintained at all times, symbolizing the importance of official transparency and openness. And as with other aspects of Ulusi-Rata architecture, the primary entrances were located in the four cardinal directions, binding the great Solar Hall to the expanse of Aurduin. Equal care and attention was paid to the messages communicated through the architectural structure of Kur-Aku as to the speeches made within it.

The great hall of Kur-Aku was itself located in the center complex of the governing and social administration center at the very heart of Laftandiar-Urya on the western shore of the bay between the tidal flats and lowlands and the surrounding mountains. Here was where Ulusi-Rata society was organized and centralized into elaborate power-sharing social structures and where commerce, education, social services, and all other aspects of Ulusi-Rata society were administered. The buildings of the complex were grand, elaborate, and renowned as the most magnificent of Laftandiar-Urya. While officials conducted business inside the grand buildings, in the courtyards the people gathered in numerous open-air markets where traders and merchants sold beautifully dyed cloth, intricate jewelry made with the famed Ulusi pearls, artwork and handicrafts, and the products of the agricultural and fishing peoples of the city. Not far to the east of the complex was the main sea port where many of the goods and wares to be sold in these markets found their way into the city from outlying communities. Musicians, street performers, artists, and even healers and diviners would market their services in the open courtyards of the center as well.

The city center reflected the complex and heterogeneous nature of Ulusi-Rata society. Public art in the center contained elements and themes of the many different cultures of the Ulusi-Rata. The architecture incorporated many different elements as well, though sometimes only stylistically, for many of the communities far to the south lived in only temporary structures and did not have grand architectural traditions as in the city proper. While many different dialects and languages could be heard among the people milling about the city center, all the signs were written in the official Ulusi script, which was the unifying language of the Ulusi-Rata. The majority of the sacred documents of the spiritual traditions of the Ulusi-Rata were written in the very same script, though variants existed, and passages of these texts, embroidered in colorful banners, were scattered about the courtyards. There were also oratory gardens where citizens could gather to discuss matters of social import during the day and where performers could practice their arts at night, when the city center was lit by glowing crystals that gave off a mix of hues ranging from green to orange.

Orobai had been to the city center many times. He always enjoyed strolling among the merchants and street performers, sometimes even joining in on a musical performance. On this day, however, he and his companions had hurriedly rushed through the courtyards and gardens not stopping to enjoy the sights and sounds as they were late and the proceedings had already started at Kur-Aku.

The council was expecting Orobai and his companions. Assistants directed them to seats that had been reserved for them with the Hyanchalth-Murira delegation where Nataali-Wantalth and other sisters were seated and fully engaged in the proceedings that were already underway. The meeting itself was run by the four main city ministers, the Orrhutha, who sat in the west at the center of the semi-circle of official delegates. Greater Laftandiar-Urya was broken into four main districts of governance. Each was headed by an elected official whose job was to work with the other three ministers for the purposes of economics, city infrastructure, justice, keeping the peace, and administering funds and resources about the city and bay. They, along with their assistants, were considered the primary representatives of the citizens of Laftandiar-Urya. They met regularly with the different working guilds, schools, and economic factions of the city and worked to ensure that everyone's views and concerns were taken into consideration in the shaping of city policy. Other such ministers who were responsible to their own peoples and interested parties were also present from the outlying communities to the south.

Currently, the Orrhutha were listening to testimony from the School of Ecology and Life Sciences, Hyanchulth-Dzanshu. They were discussing events in Jeaniaurduin and the ecological damage that was taking place there. As Hyanchulth-Dzanshu was a co-ed school, a small group of serious-looking men and women were presenting to the Orrhutha. At the moment, an ecologist whom Orobai knew as Othu Yot, a senior member of the faculty, was addressing the council. As Ashi still only had a rudimentary knowledge of Ulusi, Orobai translated what the ecologist was saying for her.

"From the best of our knowledge this mineral extraction has been taking place for a number of years now," said Othu Yot, a tall and lanky ecologist with graying hair and long fingers. He shuffled through papers on the podium before him. "Possibly several decades have passed since the first mines were created in some locations in the interior, and probably even longer further to the west. Given the source of the mining, I would venture to guess that more local deposits of the mineral have been exhausted some time ago now, and those responsible have been actively seeking new extraction sites."

Othu searched through some more papers, scanning them quickly. A colleague jumped up and handed him an official looking collection of reports. After briefly leafing through them, he continued.

"Overall, the process has recently accelerated," he said. "From what we can determine, those responsible have undertaken larger-scale projects and far more of the mineral is being excavated at an increased rate. The result is a far more dramatic impact on the ecology of Jeaniaurduin than previously recorded. We suspect that there have been recent technological advancements that have precipitated this acceleration. Or there might simply be a greater need for this mineral, or even both. The overall effect has been quite significant."

Othu Yot neatened his pile of papers, as though to accentuate the legitimacy of his conclusion.

"And what effect is that?" asked the ministers.

"Toxic. The effect is toxic," he said, bringing out new reports from a folder that he quickly scanned before continuing. "Plants, animals, birds, fungi, insects, everything is being duly affected by this mineral extraction." With each category, Othu Yot placed a voluminous folder on the podium before him, all accumulated evidence of the destruction. "We have found that less tolerant species are dying off. Others are affected more gradually. The longer they are exposed, the greater the effect, eventually resulting in death. Genetically, we are also seeing a far greater increase in mutations and defects with each subsequent generation.

"We have always known that genetic mutations are a natural and inevitable part of biological development," continued Othu, "but we have never recorded such overly-abundant appearances of mutations of this severity, and so highly concentrated in specific ecological areas. Genes are reconfiguring in ways that are unpredictable, having disastrous effects on species viability. If left unchecked, we can expect to see serious, and possibly irreparable damage to local ecosystems. And over time, perhaps even these effects will not remain local."

"How are the effects promulgated?"

"Largely through wind and rain or water runoff. What we have found is that tailings are left as a result of the extraction procedures. These tailings contain a significantly high amount of the mineral in question itself. It can then be transported through either the air or water. The effects are reduced the further one moves from the extraction sites, though the overall damage in surrounding areas is still significant and of great concern."

"Are humans subject to the same ill effects as plants and animals?" asked another of the ministers.

"Absolutely," said Othu. "Humans are in danger by simply being in the area, breathing the air, drinking the water, or eating any plants and animals that have themselves been exposed. This has made our research difficult as we have had to severely limit our own exposure time and these studies have not been undertaken without significant cost to ourselves, I might add."

"What risk do we have here in Laftandiar-Urya? Are our people in any immediate danger?" asked the ministers, obviously greatly concerned by this news that was causing the gathered public to whisper nervously among themselves.

"At present the risk at this location is minimal," said Othu with a tone that meant to communicate reassurance and calm. "There are a number of factors contributing to this. The first is that the prevailing wind patterns blow from east to west. Secondly, water mostly flows out of Jeaniaurduin to the west as well. Furthermore, the mountains about the city and the ridges to the south could serve to protect us even if the wind patterns shifted, for most of the contamination would fall as precipitation on the western sides of the mountains. This would, of course, affect the ecology of Norgath and surrounding areas, however, though we have not been able to predict what the outcome might be."

"And is Avengath affected?"

"To our knowledge, not significantly, though the possibility remains open to such and we have not been able to conduct direct research there. Nulthali directs most of the contamination along the southwest slope of the plains. It stands to reason that the coastal areas where the plains meet the sea are most likely widely affected. This is not confirmed, however, as we have not ventured so far in our expeditions."

"Thank you for your thorough report, Mr. Yot," said the ministers. Then, looking to the gathered delegates, added, "Could someone speak to the more subtle effects that this is having on Aurduin?"

"I believe that I can help with that," said Nataali-Wantalth, moving to take the podium as the ecologist graciously stepped aside. She looked authoritative and sure of herself, dressed in her formal finery. She moved with a grace and elegance that only the sisters of her school could so aptly express. It was clear by the hushed reaction of the crowd that all eagerly awaited to hear what the celebrated and highly respected Mother of the School of Mystical Arts would have to say about this serious issue.

"As many of you know," Nataali began with a sweeping gaze around the room, "I have just returned from meditative retreat on Norgath. There, in meditation, I focused my intentions on the Khutan-Scyr of Aurduin. What I learned greatly disturbed me. I can claim, without a doubt, that there is a fundamental imbalance present within the living system of subtle energies of Aurduin. It is undeniable that the direct cause is the extraction and use of this mineral that we have been discussing. Given time, Eyar would surely adapt and eventually bring the Khutan-Scyr back into a more balanced equilibrium, but the effects are currently proceeding too quickly for the system to adjust in the present time. The time of Eyar is measured in eons, not human years. It is a magnificent self-healing system, given its own time. However, we are not dealing with such a time scale. These are human years and the results are already here. If this continues unchecked, we will undoubtedly see far greater effects both on the ecological and subtle levels.

"Many of our sisters can confirm this independently," she continued. "Though it is difficult to describe, while in the meditative state, the majority of sisters have perceived a poisonous or disruptive energy-band of space-time. It draws other energies into it and works on a subtle level much as we have heard of from the distinguished representatives from Hyanchulth-Dzanshu on the more material levels. And our greatest fear is that this energy resides at the very heart of Aurduin. All the subtle energies flow in and out of Jeaniaurduin in some way or another, just as in our own psycho-physical bodies it is the heart center that regulates all our energies. Affect the heart, and eventually the rest of the body will feel it. It is inevitable. It is imperative that we understand that this is both a coarse and a subtle problem and that it is only becoming worse."

"Is there anything that the practitioners of Hyanchalth-Murira can do about this?" asked the ministers, hopeful that Nataali could provide some positive reassurance.

"Only locally. The disturbance is far too great to attempt any kind of global realignment in the fields of subtle energies. Through our individual and collective actions of Xhutai-Ku, we have been able to assist the Dzanshu who have gone into the field to do their research, providing them with something of a temporary immunity. And through our Khutan-Scyr practices, we can preserve a kind of spiritual immunity for the local area, or selected places outside of Laftandiar-Urya, but I must emphasize that these are only temporary solutions. The energies of our protective actions wear away over time, if not continually directed by the sisters or other skilled practitioners. The disturbing force of which I have spoken is simply too strong and will, given time, pull all other currents towards it, like a great river carving out the landscape under its own natural force and momentum. Eventually, even other 'rivers' will become as tributaries to this stronger force. We simply do not have the spiritual technology to counteract the entire accumulated effect of this energetic disturbance."

"If you did, what would you propose?"

"I would propose that we work to transmute the mineral at an energetic level, thereby rendering it impotent. Cut it off at the source. It is the most effective and immediate solution."

"Is this possible, even theoretically?"

"It is hard to say, for such an act is currently beyond our knowledge or ability," said Nataali. "Speculatively I would say that yes, it might be possible. Practically, I do not know how we could achieve this. It would be an alchemical act beyond anything I have ever learned of. There would need to be some form of system – some methodology by which to effect the grand transformation."

"Could you speculate, however? In theory, how could this happen?"

"I would say that we would need to find the root of the energy in space-time in the subtle body of Eyar. All things have causes, and often finding the cause or root is sufficient knowledge for counteracting the energy. This we know to hold true for the energies of the mind, for we practice this in meditation when we seek to cleanse and purify the mind of all obstructing thoughts. Even seemingly random events can be found to have subtle causes when larger patterns are observed, for ultimately, all things are interconnected. We can also cut off negative energies by transmuting them into their opposite, or simply counteract them through reestablishing balance within a system of dynamic equilibrium. According to such a theory, it should be possible to transmute the subtle energy through its opposite or cut it off at the root. At the very least, we'd have to understand its patterns of manifestation at a very deep and subtle level on a global scale. Isolated attempts would never achieve total success – only temporary solutions. It would have to be one simultaneous transformation."

"It would seem that you propose some kind of global alchemy," said the Orrhutha.

"I suppose you could call it that," said Nataali. "The teachings of the Khutan-Scyr imply that such is possible, but as I have said, I do not know how we would effect such a profound transformation on a global scale. We'd need a mechanism, a paradigm to work from. None currently exists, that I am aware of."

"Could the girl do it?"

A hush fell through the crowd as all eyes turned to Miraanni who seemed to be aware of the attention, sitting up gracefully in Ashi's arms.

"Perhaps," answered Nataali, looking first at Miraanni and then Ashi and Orobai. "It is too early to tell. She's still too young to judge what her ultimate powers and abilities will be. She has been among the sisters for several weeks now and we learn more about her and from her every day. In time, she will far exceed all of us in ability. You might prefer to speak to the Gem Seeker about such matters as he would know best, however."

"What can you tell us, Grundin?" asked the Orrhutha, turning now to Orobai.

At this summons, Orobai stepped forward, joining Nataali at the podium. He furrowed his brow for a moment and then said, "Primarily what I can tell you that you do not already know is that if you ask me this again in a year's time, I will know far more."

"Explain. This is not a time for riddles."

"Soon I will leave Laftandiar-Urya to travel in pilgrimage to the Goargathr," said Orobai. "Once completed, I will be able to perform a ritual that should reveal far more of the purpose and ability of the child, Miraanni, and all things that are coming to pass in Aurduin. Before that, I can only tell you of what I have seen and experienced since the girl first came to me."

"And you expect to be successful in this quest and ritual?"

"Yes."

"But what of your safety?" asked the ministers, obviously concerned. "We have already heard here today that you and the girl were the target of a flying ship from the west. You were almost killed in your attempt to get here and several of your party died, did they not? Surely you must be concerned for your own wellbeing and fear the danger that awaits you on this quest."

"The circumstances of my traveling will have changed," answered Orobai confidently. "I assure you that I will be much harder to find and track when traveling on my own. Besides, I do not think I was the real target. The ship was after the child, not me."

"You can confirm that this technology killed several people and animals in your company?"

"One person, two horses, and a wolf. We were able to heal another man and my eagle companion, though their wounds were severe. Were it not for the girl, I believe that it would have been hopeless to expect their recovery."

"The Djinari woman can confirm this as well?" the ministers asked, looking to Ashi

"Yes," answered Orobai with a nod to Ashi, who nodded in assent, though she did not understand what they were saying about her.

"And do you know of any more deaths caused at the hands of this technology?"

Orobai paused for a moment, deciding whether to reveal what little he knew. He thought it best to be candid so he answered openly, knowing the reaction it would cause. "According to the Arnyar, two of their own were killed at Avengath by a weapon similar to what we encountered."

Audible gasps escaped from the audience at this revelation. The Orrhutha were undaunted though, and pressed on with their questioning, determined to glean as much information as possible.

"But you have only seen this one flying ship?"

"I have seen others, and more, in my dreams. Being strange to me, I dismissed them as visions at first, but I believe that there are many other such weapons and machines in the west, and some perhaps far more destructive. If I understand the Arnyar correctly," Orobai added, "there is a veritable empire of such machines to the west."

The din of the audience grew louder. Tension could be heard in the rising voices.

"Would you be willing to discuss what you have seen with our technological experts?"

"Of course. They have only to ask."

"Thank you. That will be all for now."

Orobai sat back down. The crowd whispered and shuffled about as people discussed what they had heard. The thought of strange and powerful technology seemed to agitate the general public more than either the ecological or metaphysical issues. Orobai got the feeling that the Orrhutha wanted to discuss this matter more in private so as not to excite the already worried crowd.

Though the Ulusi-Rata had their own machines and technology, they had never used these skills in the practice of war craft or the manufacture of weapons. It was obvious to all that such weapons must be powerful indeed to kill not one, but two of the Arnyar. Nothing that any of them knew of would even come close to being powerful enough to do so. It filled the room with a pervasive sense of dread and unease.

Next to testify were the technological experts who gave various speculations on how the mineral being excavated in Jeaniaurduin was being used as a power source by the west. Much of the talk was beyond Orobai's comprehension as it was conducted in their special vocabularies and terms that only others in the technological fields fully understood. However, certain issues did catch his ear.

"And what of this waste?" asked the ministers in response to the technologists.

"From the best that we can surmise, the waste product of this mineral, once converted, would be itself extremely toxic. Even very small quantities would be sufficient to kill or genetically damage large numbers of beings. If such elements were to find their way into the ecological system, it would be devastating. We surmise that it would have to be buried, and even then there would be significant danger. By our estimates, this by-product of the energetic process would remain in this highly toxic state for at least 10,000 years. This is shocking, we know, but according to our best deductions, it is accurate."

A reaction swept through the people gathered in the great hall like a wave of awe and disbelief. How could something be so deadly for so long? Why would anyone use such a thing? What would be done with it? Was there anything they could do?

These and many other questions echoed through the hall as everyone turned to his or her neighbor to absorb the shock of these revelations. The thought of such destructive and toxic technology was nearly unbelievable for these people who took such great care and pride in their own use of technology. Their guiding principles were moderation and care. With their technology they sought to have the least possible impact on the natural world around them. They produced no toxic by-products and they used their knowledge to create conveniences for everyday living, not weapons and machinery built for terrorizing and killing. What was more, their overarching concern as people was to increase beauty, peace, and harmony within their environment, not to wantonly destroy the world about them for temporary gains.

The thought of leaving a legacy of poison and destruction, of death and mutation, was almost too much for the crowd to bear. How could any people have strayed so far from the guiding principles that they had thought served as the moral and ethical standards of all peoples of Aurduin, regardless of who they were? Though surely all peoples of Aurduin had their own beliefs, teachings, and practices, never before had something so heinous and odious come to the awareness of the Ulusi-Rata. Here was a crime against all people, against all beings, and against Eyar itself.

Testimony continued for several more hours. Many experts and concerned individuals came forward to speak their minds or share what they could of the emerging picture of what was happening in the west. A consistent picture of greed and pain became clear from all that was said. Beyond the environmental disaster, rumors were discussed of forced slavery, destruction of cultures, misuse of other resources, and examples of darkness and ignorance that pointed to a root of selfish desire and attachment of these long forgotten relatives of the Ulusi-Rata in the far west. The knowledge that their distant relatives were perpetrating all this pained the Ulusi-Rata all the more. How could their values have been ripped asunder so completely that their development and history as peoples could become so divergent? How could the westerners have forgotten, or worse, deliberately disregarded, those values that the Ulusi-Rata held so dear?

Though many questions were left unanswered, one thing was clear – they had to take some action.

After private discussion, the Orrhutha addressed the crowd.

"We have heard grave tidings on this day," they said. "We have learned of many things that fill us with dread and unease. It is clear to us all that we cannot stand idly by while such things come to pass anywhere in Aurduin. The question is therefore; what is to be done? Now that we know what is happening in Jeaniaurduin, we must act. There is far too much at stake for us not to. But what form shall this action take? Can our distant relatives be reasoned with? Can we sway them from their chosen course of action in this world? And if we try and fail, what then?"

Nataali was the first to answer.

"It is my suggestion that we send a delegation to the west," she said, standing authoritatively among her colleagues. "We should send representatives of our various schools of learning and study so that we may engage in intelligent discourse with our relatives and learn more of their ways. Only then may we hope to influence them in some positive way. And perhaps there is still much that we do not know about them and their practices. This is no time to rely on rumor or speculation. We must make our decisions based on fact, on evidence that we have gathered ourselves.

"However, we must go with the knowledge that we walk precariously close to great danger. If left unchecked, the powers that they have released will surely affect us all, in time. And we have seen that they are willing to use force to exert their interests, for as we all know, the Gem Seeker and the girl, Miraanni, were driven here by violence and death at their hands. We can reasonably expect that they know where their prey lie and may seek to take them by force, or perhaps punish us for protecting them. We cannot know their minds on this matter. All we do know is that if we do not act, things will not improve on their own. And in time, we may become prey ourselves."

Reactions to Nataali's proposal were swift and clear – a delegation would be sent to the west to learn what they could and try to exert some positive influence on those who were responsible for the crisis. Though urgent, it was decided that the delegation would set out for the west after the celebrations of the Spring Equinox. Each school could choose a representative, along with representatives of the city administration and outlying areas. It would be intended as a mission of goodwill, though they would seek to learn as much as they could in the event that they could not achieve a positive outcome. As all agreed, the meeting was concluded on condition that they would reconvene after the Equinox to confirm the makeup of the delegation.

Many of the delegates began their own private conversations about the matter as they left Kur-Aku and made their way through the city to their destinations. Word spread quickly among the inhabitants of the city of the nature of the meeting held that day and what Nataali had proposed. Soon everyone was talking about the "problem of the west" and what must be done to resolve it. Some were apathetic, others aggressive, but most were simply concerned and hopeful that the planned delegation might come to some good and bring about a happy resolution for all.

Perhaps the hardest to accept, however, was the relation between the Ulusi-Rata and the people of the west. They shared a common past, now seven thousand years distant. After all this time, they were being drawn together again under grim circumstances.

Orobai and his companions were no exception to the ongoing discussion. In the waning light of the early evening, Orobai strolled along the waterfront with Nataali, Ashi, and Miraanni, after having spoken for some time with the technological experts about the machines of the west. Orobai and Nataali walked along ahead with Ashi carrying the girl some distance behind to give them some privacy.

"I would nominate you to go as a member of the delegation, were it possible, Orobai," said Nataali, looking out over the waters of the bay as they glimmered in the light of the low western sun. "If anyone should see what they do, it should be you. You discovered the gem that became the girl, and if it had not been for their digging up the land, you never would have found her. Your fates are all bound together. It can be no accident that she appeared in the time and place that she did. Perhaps this is why they too seek her out. There is so much you could learn, were you to go. Though perhaps sending you to them would be sending you to your doom, seeing what they have already attempted."

"Yes, but I do not know how much I was really the target," said Orobai. "Of course I was *a target*, but they do not truly know me in the west. It has been many of their generations since I have walked among them. I am probably only a legend, a phantom, to them. What they want is the girl. I know this to be so. I would only be an obstacle to overcome for them – something interfering with their goal."

"And what do you think is their ultimate goal?"

"At best, power. At worst, domination."

"You think they would seek to dominate all of Aurduin?"

"Perhaps. Why else create such powerful and deadly technology? What end could it serve other than the domination of others? These rumors of expansion, slavery, destruction of other cultures, all point to this. It is only a matter of time before they seek more. However, there are still limits to their technology. It cannot cross the mountains, or else they would have followed us here directly. These mountains here protect Laftandiar-Urya more than just against the winds and the waters that might bring the poison with them. For now, Laftandiar-Urya is perhaps the safest place in all of Aurduin, but how much longer can that last? And at what cost?"

"In the end, the cost may be too great for all of us." Nataali was grim, almost as though some shadow of darkness within her heart portended what was to come.

"I hope not, Nataali." Orobai could feel it as well. *Will hope be enough?*

"The Yamné, they foresee destruction, do they not?"

"They do."

"And what do you think of their prophecy?" Nataali stopped to look directly in Orobai's dark eyes.

"They are wise and learned," he said. "Their Ul'mult'ah give them deep insights into the subtle workings of time. I had not thought much of their prophecies until late, however . . ."

"Of course, now you see their relevance." Nataali continued to walk slowly down the beach.

"And you, Nataali, what do you see of the future?"

Nataali closed her eyes for a moment, and then answered, glancing behind her.

"Darkness. I see darkness . . ." and then glancing towards Miraanni, "but there may yet be a light among us . . ."

The Call of the Goargathr

O robai arose before the sun. He had to walk a short way through the woods before he found a clearing large enough so that he could see over the trees to the bay down below. It was a clear day with a brilliant sky above. Unlike many days in Laftandiar-Urya, there was no coastal fog this morning, and the sea glistened in the early morning light with a clear and sharp line dividing it from the horizon of the sky and surrounding mountains. Orobai offered his morning prayers to the world before and about him, asking for blessings for all beings as Urya broke the surface of the sea and began its climb into the sky.

Each day that Orobai had watched the sunrise from the hills above the city, the sun had arisen just behind the mountains of the Eastern Gate, and had not passed into the mouth of the bay. On this day, a sliver of the golden orb slipped past the southern edge of the mountains. Urya was undeniably moving north and soon would pass directly between the mountains of the northern and southern shores. It would then be the Spring Equinox and the changing of the seasons. The people of Laftandiar-Urya and the sisters at Hyanchalth-Murira would have much to do over the coming days. There would be festivals, ceremonies, songs, dances, initiations and rituals. But Orobai would see none of it. Not this year. It was nearly time for him to go. He would have to leave Miraanni behind as the Goargathr, the Great Mountains, called him ever onward to his fate.

From the west Sto'orn flew down from the mountains towards the dark shape that was Orobai. He came with a message from the Arnyar. The day before, when Orobai had attended the council at Kur-Aku, Sto'orn had answered a summons by the Arnyar at Norgath. He came now to where he expected to find Orobai and the cubs on their daily outings in the woods.

"Good morning our feathered friend!" said Orobai, greeting the weary eagle. "You have been busy already today, I see."

"I have traveled far through the night to find you this morning," said Sto'orn as he ruffled his feathers and tucked his wings beside him.

"And where have you been?"

"On Norgath. I answered the summons of the Arnyar. They say that it is time for you to begin. The Equinox will soon be upon us and there is much for you to do. They are confident that the girl will be safe here. They say that you have done well, but the time has come to continue onwards."

"Yes," said Orobai, nodding knowingly. "I watched the rising of Urya this morning and knew the time had come. It would seem that our companionship has come to an end, Sto'orn," said Orobai. "I hereby give you your leave. Fly to the mountains, or where you will. You need not accompany me and I would not keep you here, far from your own home."

"Thank you, but I would stay," said the golden eagle. "I have grown to care for these two here, and after the death of their mother . . . they still need someone to watch over them."

"And you would do this? You would care for Elkil and Fenruk?" Orobai smiled at the thought of an eagle worrying about two wolves.

"Yes, I would. I will also keep watch on the girl. I owe her my life."

"Then so it shall be. You have been a good companion and a trustworthy friend. I know that you will be welcome here in Laftandiar-Urya. It will be good to keep your eyes on the cubs and continue to help them learn and grow. I would stay with them myself if I could."

"I know, and that is why I choose to do so."

It was difficult for Orobai to explain to Elkil and Fenruk that he had to leave them, perhaps as long as a year. They had grown very fond of Orobai and looked upon him as a mentor, provider, and protector. He had become a surrogate parent for them in the absence of their mother just as Faen had been a surrogate mother for Miraanni. First, violence took their mother from them, and now the only "father" they had ever known was to leave them out of necessity. The cubs whimpered as Orobai explained the reality of the situation. If it had been possible, they would have gone with him, but Orobai would no longer be traveling in a manner in which they could accompany him, for he would fly from mountain to mountain. The time of traveling by foot, water, and horse was now over.

As Orobai explained all of this to the cubs he suddenly felt the presence of someone near by. Turning around, Orobai realized that Nataali was standing directly behind him, as though she had stepped out of thin air and simply materialized. Neither he, the cubs, nor Sto'orn had been aware of her approach. Had she been there long or just arrived, Orobai wondered.

"Nataali, you have surprised us," said Orobai, greeting her.

"I apologize if I have startled you," said Nataali. "I sensed that you would be leaving us and did not want to miss you. I had to come unannounced."

"Ah, well, you have not missed me, and I would not have gone without saying farewell," said Orobai.

"I thought as much, but I know of your urgency."

Fenruk and Elkil whimpered, almost as a reminder to Orobai. "I would ask you about the cubs . . ." he said.

"They are welcome here," Nataali assured him, reaching out her hand to the cubs so that they could familiarize themselves with her scent, and then gave them gentle pats on their heads. "No harm will come to them, but they should stay within the bounds of the forest here by the school. It would frighten the people were they to go to the city proper. Here they can roam the forested hills in peace where they can find prey and live as they are meant to. And of course the one who watches above them is welcome as well, as are all of his kind," Nataali added as she glanced up at Sto'orn.

"And Miraanni, I would have Ashi care for her, if she is willing," said Orobai.

Saying this now Orobai suddenly realized that the thought of leaving Miraanni truly pained him. He was happy to be leaving her with Ashi, in whom he trusted and had complete faith, but that could not ease the pain of separation. He knew that he would miss her and that a part of his life would be absent as long as they were apart.

"Ashi is more than happy to care for the child," assured Nataali sympathetically, seeing the conflict of emotions in Orobai's dark eyes. "I have already spoken with her. Though it is unusual for new students, I have granted her permission to live in the home that was provided for you and the girl. There she will live with Miraanni and take care of her when she is free from her duties as a student. I can assure you that Miraanni will receive only the best treatment and that you will find her healthy and happy when you return to us at the end of your pilgrimage. She is as one of us now and we will do all that we can for her. They both await you now at the home to bid you farewell."

"So all has been made ready," mused Orobai, suddenly aware that there was really nothing left for him to do here. "Then I should linger no longer and set out upon the quest that the Arnyar have set before me. Though I am tired and would like to stay here in comfort and ease, my fate draws me on and I must obey."

Orobai sighed a long and heavy sigh, the weight of what he must do pressing down upon him. "I am an old being, Nataali," he said. "Would that this had happened when I was more rested . . ."

Nataali looked into Orobai's eyes. There she saw his age and his weariness. The old Grundin had been through much just to arrive there at the City of the Rising Sun, and now he had to move on to yet another difficult challenge.

"Your weariness is deep, old friend," said Nataali, taking Orobai by the shoulders in her slender hands. "No amount of rest will cure that. But I can help you a little before you go."

"What would you do?"

"I would use the art of Xhutai-Ku. Surely you know that I myself am not as young as I seem. Through these same techniques I can revitalize the energies of your body, for a time. Granted, it will not last forever, probably not even a year, but you will feel a profound difference. Do I have your permission?"

"Of course, Nataali," said Orobai, glad for any assistance.

"Good. Let us first meditate and clear our minds and bodies of obstructing thoughts, emotions, and energies."

The two friends sat down together in the green grass in the shade of the trees facing downhill towards the east as they drew their minds inward. Each concentrated on the flow of breath, in and out, in and out. Orobai sat in silence, but as Nataali sank deeper into the meditation, she began to vocalize the chants of the Xhutai-Ku, sacred syllables that drew upon the living power of the universe. The sisters used such chants and sounds to free the mind and body of all limitations and attachments. When done with the proper state of rarified meditation, one could dispel all illusions of separateness. In such a state, one could experience the direct Suchness of existence. It was an ancient and profound philosophy that the sisterhood had practiced and perfected for millennia.

Deep as he was in his own meditation, Orobai did not at first notice that Nataali stood before him now. Seeing her, he was not sure if there was one of her, or four, all standing in the four directions about him. It was a perplexing sensation, for he could not really focus on her and time had taken on a peculiar quality. Was he seeing Nataali in four places simultaneously or was he seeing her in four different times simultaneously? He did not know.

Nataali continued the chants she had begun in her meditation, but now she added rhythmic and stylized movement, carefully posturing and manipulating her hands, arms, legs, and body. She moved about Orobai in a graceful dance where there was no distinction between thought, body, music, and action. As she did so, Orobai's perception became fluid and clear. He could distinctly see every blade of grass, every leaf, and every crevice and crack in the bark of the ancient trees about him. Through everything moved an energy that was a living life force, a great organic flow of being. Every ripple of the grass in the wind, every sway of the branches of the trees, the glide of an insect or bird – all responded to this living flow. Even the clouds above and the waters below danced to the same subtle rhythm that was now being articulated through the aesthetics of Nataali's body. Orobai felt his own breathing and the rhythms of his body join in unison to the vast undulation of the world in his sensory field. It gave him the impression that Nataali was drawing the power through him and bringing him into deep harmony with it.

At first it felt as though he were being drained. He was so drained that he struggled to maintain his awareness as consciousness slipped down into darkness. It was emptiness. It was not a full emptiness, not the boundless, chaotic energy of the Abyss, but just empty, as though he had been sucked dry and remained as only a withered bag of flesh. But just as quickly as the sensation of this emptiness had come upon him, it changed. Now Orobai felt as though he were being filled up. The energy and power rushed in through his abdomen. From there it spread out to his limbs, climbing up his spine and spiraling to the very top of his head and to the tips of his finger and toes. It was as though he himself were part of some great lung that breathed the fullness of pure and rarified air. The wind blew through his body, inflating him with new life. He could almost hear it, he thought, and almost feel it as it spiraled out the whorls on his fingertips. From his lower abdomen and feet the great wind joined his body to the breath of the earth itself. From his head and shoulders the great wind joined him to the breath of the infinite sky above. And there was no longer his breath, or Nataali's breath, or the breath of anything else. There was only the One Breath, the great Xhutai-Ku, and he knew the Shaping of the Wind.

Slowly the four images of Nataali resolved back into one cohesive form before Orobai's eyes. Once more he could see the distinct shape and form of her body. Looking at her now, however, she seemed more alive than she had before. It was as though a great sleep had fallen from Orobai's eyes and he could now see the course and pulse of life through her. He could see the centers of energy in her body and how the physical limits of her being could not bind them, but rather the energy radiated outward in all directions. It was beautiful to look upon, seeing one so healthy in mind, body, heart, and spirit. It reminded Orobai of seeing T'inshar sick with the spider eating at his heart, but free from all disease. Here the life flowed like a strong river that filled the space granted it, and in it he saw the delicate interconnection and balance between all things.

It was almost enough to make Orobai weep. The sheer beauty was incomparable. And looking at himself he could see that he too looked much like Nataali. There was a new vitality in him and it filled all the space of his being. He saw that his own heart energy was bound to the heart energy of Nataali, and that they themselves were bound to the heart energy of the other beings around them. And this binding extended on infinitely to encompass all living beings. And not just conventionally living beings, but clouds, rocks, streams, mountains, oceans, the sky . . . there seemed to be no limit. It was just beauty. Orobai could think of no other words. Just beauty . . .

Nataali stood smiling at Orobai, extending her hand to help him up. "You have now felt the Shaping of the Wind, the Xhutai-Ku. You will find both your body and your perception altered for quite some time to come, for I completely emptied you before filling you back up. Gradually, this will wear away as your old energy patterns begin to reassert themselves. But what you have now will carry you far."

Orobai knew intuitively that what she said was true. He also knew intuitively why Nataali had given the testimony at Kur-Aku that she had. This was truly powerful and profound, but such a technique would not be enough. It could restore the dynamic balance to an old being such as himself, but the body of Eyar was too old, too vast, and too complex. The Khutan-Scyr could not be fully restored by the sisterhood's Xhutai-Ku. He knew with certainty that only the Altfein could, but how?

"It is time," said Nataali. "You must go now. I too can hear the Mountains calling for you. Come, let us walk together back to the house so you may say good-bye to Miraanni and Ashi."

Orobai walked next to Nataali through the forest in knowing silence, enjoying his new sense of energy and lightness. He had not felt so good in many years. He felt new again, almost as though he had been remade from the body of Eyar. Orobai reached out and took Nataali's hand and they exchanged a knowing look as they walked together, side by side. He did not need to say anything to

Nataali, for she knew what he felt, and she too knew that Orobai had seen the limitations of the practice as well. It was strong, but it was far from enough.

When the two arrived at the house, Nataali said her good-byes to Orobai so that he might part with Miraanni privately. "May you walk with the blessing of the Four Mountains, Orobai," she said, embracing him. "I wish that our time here together had been longer. There is so much more I would like to speak with you about. But time presses onwards. And even if you were to stay, I would be busy now with my duties at the school. You know as well as I what an important time the Spring Equinox is for us. So go now and seek your vision. Find that path that is hidden from the rest of us. Find the key to remove the obstacles and walk in beauty and blessedness."

"Thank you, Nataali," Orobai said, returning her warm embrace.

They lingered for a moment longer, looking at each other knowingly. Orobai could still feel the energetic bond between them as a warmth and light passed between their clasped hands. Slowly Nataali withdrew her arms and stepped back from Orobai. Hearing the door of the house open he turned around to see Ashi standing in the doorframe with Miraanni in her arms. When he turned back around to see Nataali off he found that she was already gone, having mysteriously slipped away in silence in the peculiar way that the sisters tended to do.

Turning back to Ashi and Miraanni, Orobai looked upon them as with new eyes. He knew that it was the lingering effects of the Xhutai-Ku that Nataali had performed for him. Looking at them now he could see the flow of Xhutai through their bodies. Though Ashi was herself strong, Miraanni was like a blazing star, exploding in the darkness of the black void of space. It was both like the light he had seen her produce among the Yamné and also unlike it. It was simultaneously more brilliant and subtler. It burst forth from her heart center and seemed to fill all the space about her, reaching out infinitely. If he concentrated on it, Orobai found that it obscured all else in his vision. Was this what Nataali saw when she looked upon the girl? Did all the sisters see this? It was beautiful and compelling. Orobai felt that he could stand there for an eternity and bask in the light of life that shone from within her deepest being.

Orobai's trance was broken by the sound of a kind voice.

"Nori, you are back. I thought I heard the Mother with you," said Ashi, looking about.

"Yes, she's gone now."

"She came here a little while ago. She told me that I am to live here in this house and care for Ali. That makes me very happy, but I do not want to impose upon you, Ohuantun," said Ashi with a tone of deference in her voice.

"There is no imposition, Ashi, for I must leave you now. The house is for you and Ali. The sisters will provide for you both while you care for her and continue your schooling at Hyanchalth-Murira. You will not want for anything."

"Will you come back?"

"Of course, but it will be some time before I am able to return. For us it will not seem that long, but for Ali it will seem much longer, given her rapid rate of development. You will serve as her guardian until my return, and even then we will see what fate has in store for us all."

"As you wish, Nori," said Ashi, bowing her head and torso in the characteristic manner of the sisterhood.

She is already one of them.

"And you, Ashi, is this what you want? Are you happy at Hyanchalth-Murira and being part of their sisterhood?" Orobai asked, already knowing the answer.

"Yes, I am very happy. I have already learned so much and they treat me very well," Ashi answered enthusiastically with a bright light behind her eyes. "Though I miss my people, my sisters especially, I am thankful to have the opportunity to learn from such wise and powerful women. I love my people, but women do not have the same opportunity to learn of such things as men do. Perhaps some day I will return to my people and teach the women what I have learned."

"I think you will, Lalntush, but take your time. You have much to learn."

"Yes, Ohuantun."

"And tell me, Ashi, are you managing the difference in language? It must be difficult having to rely on translators and having only a few people who know your tongue."

"It is difficult, but Shintan-Vur-Lalntalth, the one who came to us that day in the meadow, has taught me much of Ulusi, and she is well skilled in Djinari as well. She will continue to help me. She tells me that when I have proven myself ready she will perform the Than-Azarn, the direct mind-to-mind empowerment of language. She says that then I will have an intuitive understanding of Ulusi, or any other language I choose to learn."

"It would seem that she has taken to you as a mentor."

"Yes, sister Shintan-Vur is very kind. She says that we two are very alike, for she also left her people to come to Hyanchalth-Murira. She tells me that I too will learn the ways of Ulm-Lanish, the empathy of animals. She will begin to teach me after I have my empowerment during the Equinox celebrations, the Ran-Khuxaita-Ur."

"Yes, I can see that this would be good for you, Ashi. When all others showed fear and wariness of the wolves, you accepted them. It is your natural talent. I am happy that the right teacher has found you. I think that you will go far here at the School of Mystical Arts. I will look forward to seeing how you have grown upon my return."

Sensing that they had said their peace to one another, Ashi handed Miraanni to Orobai and walked back into the house to leave them in private. Miraanni eagerly went to Orobai and held onto his clothing as she gazed up into his eyes, smiling broadly across her beautiful face.

"You are so beautiful, my Sulsar-urn, my little sister," said Orobai softly to the girl. "You have grown so much in such a short time. It pains me to leave you now and to not be able to watch you grow. There is so much that you will learn, so much that you will be capable of. You have no equal in this world, Mysterious Child."

Embracing her now, Orobai felt the pains of separation. He had grown so accustomed to her presence, her beauty, her sheer joy in all that she experienced and encountered. How could he go on without her? How could he go back to being alone in the world? Such thoughts had never been a problem for him before, but now he could not bear to imagine himself without his small companion. Even when they were physically apart, she was still there in his mind, in his spirit. There was a place in his heart that had become Miraanni. Would it remain when they were apart? Would the connection last over time and distance? Or would it slowly dissolve and fade away, leaving Orobai alone, all by himself once more?

Orobai did not even realize that he was weeping until the child in his arms reached up and touched the water that fell down his face. With her touch came the healing knowledge that he should not feel fear, or pain, or loneliness. "Elder Brother, keep your faith and go with a strong heart," came the voice of the child in Orobai's mind.

"Yes, you are right, Little One," said Orobai out-loud to the girl. "I will keep my faith. In time I will return to you in greater wisdom. A fate rests upon us both and I must go and seek it out before it finds us. We are bound together, you and I. The Goargathr, the Great Mountains will show us the way."

Still speaking aloud, Orobai continued, "I must go now. I will travel far. Your new sisters will watch over you. Ashi will give you the love and care you need. Learn from them. Learn their ways and their teachings. These are wise people and they want only what is best for all beings in Aurduin. Perhaps in time, you will teach them, but first you must learn. I will keep you in my thoughts, always, and I will never forget the place you have in my heart."

The brother and sister embraced for one last time. Orobai knew that Miraanni understood all that he had intended, and more. He took her back into the house where he found Ashi awaiting them. He handed the girl back to her guardian in silence and held them both in his arms and sight for a moment. Then, without hesitation, Orobai quickly gathered his things and walked confidently out the door. Ashi followed with Miraanni in her arms but found no one there, failing to see the flash of black feathers as a raven took to the sky and began its flight to the first of the Four Sacred Mountains, Norgath, the Black Mountain of the east, where all things have their beginning.

Norgath, the Black Mountain

Orobai rested on the edge of the Goarnaltrai, the Great Abyss, the dark crescent lake that separated the mountains of Laftandiar-Urya from the first of the Four Mountains, Norgath, the Black Mountain. None of the long geological processes that continually shaped and reshaped the surface of Aurduin had formed the Goarnaltrai, and neither had water nor ice. The Goarnaltrai was a remnant of the very formation of the Black Mountain from the time of the Illan. With the raising of the Mountain, the body of Eyar had been rent asunder and the mountains had cracked open to give birth to the largest of the Orgathen. The process had left a great gap between Norgath and the other mountains about it where the Temple of the East, Northirn, the Black Temple, once had been. Now, the Great Abyss contained the black waters of the deepest lake in all of Aurduin and none had ever measured its unfathomable depths.

These very waters were the Waters of Life, Rushalyaavai. The great mountains surrounding Laftandiar-Urya prevented most of the moist clouds that blew in from the east from reaching Jeaniaurduin, particularly in the southern reaches. In the north of Jeaniaurduin, moisture could pass through the gap of Northrun, though even here the Morianithanlim-Gathr caught most of the clouds. Thus rainfall was often scarce in the Heart of Aurduin. Yet Jeaniaurduin was not a dry or desolate place, such as was the western desert. It was because of the Waters of Life of the Goarnaltrai that Jeaniaurduin was the lush and life-giving place that it was. The waters that cascaded out of the mountains into the crescent lake of the Great Abyss sank deep within the body of Eyar and traveled countless miles beneath the surface, only to rise in the innumerable springs that nourished the Heart of the Sacred Land. As with all things, it was the currents that flowed beneath the surface of the visible world that were the most vital to life.

It had been a long flight for Orobai to reach this point. He had crossed over the mountains and climbed their heights through the cold, wet clouds. At last

Orobai had passed over the Labyrinth, the intricate passageways of stones and natural rock formations that the sisters had carefully manipulated long ago in ancient Ulusi-Rata history. The sisters called this labyrinth Leti-Aurtai, the Path of Unknowing. The Sisters of Hyanchalth-Murira had altered the original geological layout of the large and peculiar stones to render the area a true labyrinth. Not until an initiate had passed successfully all the way through the Leti-Aurtai would she be able to look upon Norgath. It was no ordinary labyrinth, however, and only the most gifted of the students of the School of Mystical Arts could succeed in passing through it; those who were intended for the highest initiation. They were sent through the maze without a map or guide and would have to rely upon their inner sight and ability to perceive the subtle paths of energy that showed the way out. Initiates who succeeded would look upon Norgath for the first time from the same spot where Orobai stood now above the Great Abyss.

Orobai knew why the sisters had selected the Leti-Aurtai as their chosen path for initiates to navigate on their way to Norgath. The view was incomparable. The mountains of Laftandiar-Urya plummeted down into the Great Abyss, up from whose unfathomable depths Norgath towered as an enormous black pillar to the sky, bridging Heaven and Earth. One could hardly tell where the crescent-shaped lake of jet-black waters of the Goarnaltrai ended and the base of the Mountain began, save for the wind blowing across the lake, rippling its surface and refracting the light, providing evidence that it was not stone but liquid.

The Mountain itself was encircled in a ring of cloud and mist, yet still the peak rose higher, emerging from the clouds and towering over all else in Aurduin. Not even the other three mountains could match the sheer height and grandeur of Norgath, First and Greatest of all the Four. The view was enough to inspire any being with awe and humility before the power of the Mountain and the Illan who had collectively sung it into being those many eons ago. It was the greatest singular testament to their ability.

Looking at the mountain now, Orobai saw it in a new way. He knew that the Xhutai-Ku Nataali had performed for him had altered his perception. If he did not center his concentration on the perceptual effects they would fade into the background of his awareness and thus were not ever-present in his vision. But when concentrated upon, Orobai had found in his flight that he could easily see the continual flow of Xhutai, the life force, and that when looking upon the vast landscape, he had a direct perception of the Khutan-Scyr of Aurduin. When he flew over the labyrinth he could instantly see the path through the complex maze. When looking at the mountains, he saw the flow of life in the air, the trees, the rocks, the canyons, the peaks, and all things in between.

But all this paled in comparison to what Orobai saw before him now. As he looked upon Norgath and the Goarnaltrai, he saw the signs of the great flux of the Naltrai, the Void, the Empty Vessel, the Abyss from which all things took their source. How could one see the Void? How could one stand before the great gaping maw of the Abyss and not be consumed by it? It was a paradox, a riddle with no answer, a song of silence and a silence of infinite music. It was both Being and Non-Being, yet neither. It was Form and Formlessness intertwined in their continual dance. It was both beautiful and terrifying to behold. It was beyond all definitions and boundaries.

Yet all the while the Mountain was there, the lake was there, the clouds and sky and sun and air were there. It was both extraordinary and mundane. The Mountain was both a mountain, and yet it was not, for it was a living symbol of the matrix of creation, the very foundation of the teachings of the Illan and the philosophy of the Altfein-Aryat. It contained all the teachings and mysteries of the Black Temple that once rested there. It was the indefinable beginning of all things in Aurduin.

Maintaining awareness, when presented with such a perceptual and experiential paradox, was almost maddening the longer Orobai gazed upon the Mountain. He could neither look upon it, nor find the will to look away. Where was his mind? Where was that "self" he could call his own, if any such thing even existed? Where in the chaos was the past, the present, the future? Was time even a reality or only a perception, one more manifestation of the multitude of the Abyss?

The tension of the experience continued to mount. Orobai felt overwhelmed, consumed, as though a great force from the inside of his mind were eating away at his sense of self and being. It was maddening. Would he lose consciousness? Could he withdraw his perception? Could he regain a sense of perspective, or had the ground of his being been permanently removed, leaving him in an existential free fall?

Pushing off from the cliff before the Goarnaltrai with the Leti-Aurtai at his back and Norgath before him, Orobai leapt into the air. Was it an act of desperation, of faith, or a desire for death itself? For any other it surely would have been the latter. The drop into the Abyss below was several thousand feet. Yet Orobai did not change his form. He did not sprout feathers and soar upon the updraft of wind or open his wings to the sky. He simply leapt, and he fell.

The cold air whipped about him as he plummeted downward, the sound of his black cloak snapping violently in the wind. Slowly, deliberately, he stretched out his arms, still holding his staff, and embraced the wind. Doing so the air became quiet and soft, almost a caress, and was silent. Orobai heard the beat of his heart and the rush of blood through his body, a steady pulse, a coursing of music, of life. He saw himself speeding past the rocks and cliffs of the mountains as the crescent of the lake below loomed ever larger in his perceptual field. It was an eternity, yet only a moment. Orobai embraced it all, and accepted whatever was to come.

He cut through the surface of the icy waters in a violent rush of a thousand knives piercing his body, stealing his breath and seeming to draw every ounce of life from him. But he did not fight it, he did not struggle. He gave himself completely to the waters and was enveloped in their cold dark silence, slowly sinking further beneath their smoothing surface as all sign of his penetration washed away.

There was no light. There was no sound. There was only the blackness of the Abyss. The Deep swallowed him whole and consumed him. Was he near the surface or near the bottom? Was he lost in the underground rivers that fed into the springs of Jeaniaurduin? Orobai did not know. There was only nothingness. Silence. Darkness. The impenetrable Void.

A sound. A sound so simple, yet so complete. It pulled on Orobai, drawing him toward it. How could something be so simple and so infinitely complex at the same time? It was beautiful and terrifying, like the Mountain itself. The sound moved upward, pulling, dragging Orobai's limp body through the cold, black waters. In the sound there was light, and the light broke through the surface of the waters and streamed down on Orobai like bright daggers in the darkness.

Slowly, Orobai began to move his arms and his legs. He desired the light and began to struggle towards it. Strength came into his body once more and despite the cold, his limbs became warm. Life flowed through him. He was remade. The closer he came to the light the clearer his mind became. The madness that had driven him over the edge began to wash away and sink deep into the waters below him.

The Void would not swallow him. Not today. Not yet.

The Mountain had called him back.

Suddenly, Orobai broke the surface of the water and found that he was standing at the very edge of the lake with the Black Mountain, Norgath, before him, a dark and impenetrable monolith reaching to the Heavens above. With staff still in hand, Orobai stood confidently before the Mountain. His mind was smooth, his body was strong. He was ready. He felt the swirl of Chaos within him. He felt the raw potential of the power of pure becoming.

It could begin.

Orobai called out to the Mountain in a strong and resonant voice, lifting up his arms before him and throwing back his hood. "Atluin, Norgath, first and greatest of the Sacred Four!" the Ancient One called out. "I have come to tread upon you, to search deep within your body, and to pass about you in a Sacred and Holy way. May we be strong together. May we walk in wisdom together. May we bask in the power of life together.

"From here all life begins. All things start anew with the yearly round of Urya and Ranya and all power that moves through the Sacred Land, Aurduin, begins here, in your sacred presence. You are the symbol of beginnings. You are the origin of all things in this land.

"You, Black Mountain, were brought forth from the body of Eyar by the Urkir, the Illan, as was I. We are brothers. We are of the same spirit, you and I. In walking upon you I walk upon myself. In seeking your gems and jewels I seek my own treasure. In breathing in your wind I breathe my own spirit. We are as one. One mind, one body, one heart, one spirit. Through the Power of the East, the Black Mountain, I walk in Beauty.

"What I do here, I do for Aurduin. These gems, these sacred stones, these granular manifestations of your very power, are the seeds of hope for this land. Thus I take not for myself, but for all. I ask that you offer up your secret treasures to me in this time of need. With your blessings I seek the knowledge of the Illan, the knowledge of what is to be, and of my own fate. Through your power I walk with great purpose.

"Atluin, Norgath!"

His prayer and benediction having been said with all the force of his spirit, Orobai began his circumambulation of the first of the Four Great Mountains, Norgath. For four days, without rest, without stopping, without sleeping, or eating, he walked in a sunwise circle about the base of the Great Mountain. The path was long and arduous but Orobai kept on.

All the while he sustained the prayers in his mind and heart, ever focused on his task. The farther he walked, the deeper he sank into his meditative trance. By the time he returned to his starting place in the east at the foot of the Mountain, he was an empty vessel. There was no Orobai. There was no one at all. There was merely the task that had been set before him and the actions that must be undertaken. Orobai was now fully immersed in the ritual and all distracting thoughts and concerns had been washed from his mind. He was as the Arnyar said he must be. Every aspect of his being was focused, full of intent, and centered on what he had come to accomplish.

His actions and his identity were one in the same. He could not speak, or laugh, or smile, or even cry. All his words and deeds were now focused on the one thing that he must do. If he spoke, it would be in prayer. If he sang, it would be in spirit. If he saw, it was what he must see. If he acted, it was what he must do. The Seeker of Gems, the first name and identity that the Illan had given Orobai, was now the Seeking of Gems, the pure action, the being in the moment of doing.

Orobai began his ascent of Norgath in the darkness of the pre-dawn morning. He needed no light to guide his way. No rock would cause him to stumble. No obstacle would stand in his way. He was the Mountain walking upon Itself. If he had been blind it would have made no difference for he still would have found his way. He and the mountain were one and there would be no misstep and no faltering.

Higher Orobai climbed, never looking away, never looking back. Upward went his gaze and his body followed, through the fog and mist, clouds and wind, one step at a time, higher and higher upon the body of the Black Mountain.

When Orobai reached the place he needed to be, he stopped. He had found his place of power and purpose, and there he awaited the coming of the new day, the day for which he had come to Norgath. The day of his purpose.

As the Morning Star, Sarnrhobi, climbed the sky, Orobai turned to face the coming of Urya on the sacred morning of Jitanyaavai, the Spring Equinox. On this day, light and dark would share equal time in the world. It was the time of new beginnings and the rebirth of life in Aurduin. From here, the new cycle of life and death would be set in motion in the ever-flowing movement of time. For the Altfein, this was the most powerful moment in the year, when all the powers were in balance. Today, at the rising and setting of Urya and Ranya, Orobai would find the most precious gems in all of Aurduin.

Urya crested the eastern mountains and a radiance of yellow light, like pollen blowing from the trees and flowers, flooded the world below. Standing firmly in the light with the brilliant yellow of the sun before him and the deep darkness of the mountain behind him, Orobai let the warmth and beauty of the sun's rays wash over him. It was a holy moment, a sacred eternity. It was the light of life.

With his staff in one hand and the other raised to let the sacred pollen of the sun fall upon his open palm, Orobai began to sing, standing before a pool of crystal clear water high upon the dark mountain. He sang the pure harmonics of the Omur tones, the tones of the rising sun and the new day. The soaring tones took shape deep within his heart and pulled up on his being, lifting into the deep blue of the sky, rising ever higher, transcendent and beautiful beyond compare. The light of the sun swirled around the ancient one, filling him, lifting him up, pouring into his heart and being. He focused the light in his heart and let it shine down upon the crystal waters. There, the sacred stones heeded Orobai's call, and the Sarnfein showed themselves, taking the light into themselves and reflecting it back to Orobai. They were ready for Orobai to choose that one which was meant for him at this moment.

Up from the depths of the clear waters rose the sacred stones, breaking free of their watery home and standing suspended in the sky before Orobai, filling the space around the old Gem Seeker with the spiritual light of a thousand suns. They came to Orobai in the air and circled round him like stars spinning through the vastness of space about the dark center of their galaxy. Round and round they went, letting Orobai carefully examine each one for its strength, its quality, its spirit.

Orobai was intimate with each one and loved them all, but he had to choose. From all that came to him, he reached out to take only one, the one that was right, the one that was meant for this time. He took it into his hand and felt its power and purpose move through him. He knew; this was the one. This one Sarnfein was the one he was to take from Norgath and none other.

Slowly, Orobai let the sacred tones drift away on the wind and his song was no more. Those Sarnfein that he had not chosen faded and sank back into the waters of the Mountain and gently disappeared from view. There they would wait, until it was their time to fulfill their purpose. For now, Orobai would take no more of these stones.

Orobai sat right where he was. Urya continued its ascent, traveled south, passed around the mountain, and sank down into the western horizon. All the while Orobai did not stir. He did not move. There was little difference between him and the black stones and boulders of the Mountain itself. He scarcely even breathed, so still was he.

The light of Urya faded in the sky. Yellow, orange, crimson, magenta, and then a soft band of purple set against the deep indigo of the dome of the sky played before Orobai, but he showed no reaction. The stars swung overhead and the night wind blew.

Then, as Ranya crested the eastern mountains in all its fullness, Orobai once more stood before the waters and began to sing out the Lumran tones, just as he had with the Omur tones that morning. The light of the moon was drawn to Orobai and swirled about him in a silvery dance, flowing over his long matted hair and catching in whorls about his fingers and cascading before his eyes. He pulled the light into his heart and focused it with his intention, sending it, with his spirit, out over the crystal waters of the mountain pool.

As with the Sarnfein, the Alkeinfein rose to the surface of the small lake like stars in the night sky. They lifted into the air and swirled about Orobai as he stood with arms wide open. Each passed before him in turn, rotating slowly in space, letting Orobai know each one in its fullness. Once more he chose only one from all those that presented themselves to him. It was the one that was meant to be and he took no other. Having chosen, the remainder sank back into the dark waters and were gone as his second song drifted off into the silence of the night.

Now, taking the Sarnfein in one hand and the Alkeinfein in the other, Orobai slowly and deliberately brought the two sacred stones together. The one was angular, the other round. They were fundamentally different, yet fundamentally the same. They were as two parts to an inseparable whole. As Orobai brought them close they touched and instantly began to blend and join together. There were no longer two stones in his hands, but one living jewel that radiated the power of life itself, emanating from deep within its core. It was complete. It was whole. It was beautiful.

Orobai gazed for a moment into the newly formed unity. He turned it over in his hands, inspecting it, sensing it, knowing it. Never before had Orobai done such a thing with the Altfein, yet he did not stop to ponder or contemplate what had happened. He simply gently slipped the precious gem into a seamless water pouch, which he then dipped into the mountain pool, adding just enough water to submerge the stone, and carefully sealed it away. He would need no other Altfein from Norgath.

With these Altfein found, the rest of his task at Norgath still lay before Orobai. While he needed only these two of the sacred stones, there were many other kinds of gems that he needed for the sacred diagram that he would make for his vision. Over the following weeks of the spring season Orobai scoured Norgath for the remaining gems and jewels that he needed from the first of the four Great Mountains. He climbed from bottom to top, always circling in a sunwise manner. He crawled deep within the hidden caves and crevices and dug deep within the body of the Mountain to find his treasures. All kinds of gems he found of different shapes, different sizes, different colors and textures. Many he discarded and took only those that were right, those that were meant for him for this ultimate purpose, letting those he should choose call out to him, each in their own unique way. With each one that he took, he could clearly see in his mind how it fit into the sacred image he would make. He knew each stone's place and purpose. And the more he gathered, the more he understood the meaning of the image and how it would create the sacred space for his vision.

All these stones Orobai sang back to his home by Golgath. There they would wait for him to return from his pilgrimage. There they would await their ultimate purpose. When the time was right, these stones, together with the Altfein and the stones Orobai would gather at the three remaining mountains, would form the sacred space of his most important ritual. Orobai would grind them all down into fine sands of different colors and hues. They would be the palette from which he would paint the intricate circular design the Arnyar had implanted directly into Orobai's mind. They would form his mandala, his sacred circle, the circle of his vision.

But first, three other mountains remained. It was not time for Orobai's vision.

Not yet.

Durngath, the Green Mountain

The days lengthened and the nights grew ever shorter. All the while that Orobai was upon the Great Mountain, Norgath, To'wern and Sals'u'un kept watch over him, lest any harm come to the ancient being. Now, with the Summer Solstice drawing near, it was time to urge him on.

The two great eagles found Orobai facing south near the upper reaches of Norgath, perched high above the world below. They circled above four times and landed one on either side of the black being, who sat in meditation like a boulder perched precariously on the edge of a cliff, just waiting for the right push to send it over the edge.

"It is time," said the two Arnyar in unison. "Go to the south. Durngath awaits you."

Orobai would have gone whether they had spurred him on or not. He could feel the time and the pace of days. He knew where he was and where he must go. He could not have stayed in the east longer even if he had so desired. The compulsion to move on was too strong to resist any longer. But it was the role that the Arnyar had to play in this ritual. As the Keepers of the Great Mountains their duty was clear to them. Thus they said the words that they had to say, and Orobai reacted just as he should.

Orobai stood between the two great feathered beings. With their voices echoing through his mind, he called out to the Altfein. Once more he took the form of a raven, having not changed his form since first arriving at Norgath. It felt good to be back in this familiar shape, but even the dramatic physical change did not stir Orobai from his intention and he took to the air with a clear and focused mind. He took no real notice of the two great eagles that took to the air in perfect unison with him, escorting him from the face of the Black Mountain. Nor did Orobai notice when they banked away to either side after he passed beyond the base of the first of the Four Mountains, leaving him to pursue his solitary journey and the continuation of the task that was his and his alone.

The flight to the south was long. Orobai flew over mountains, valleys, rivers, and many places he had not visited in years. He passed over the abandoned ruins of the hidden valley of Rangorn-Vuchuli with its crumbling temples of black stone and the visages of ancient spirits carved in the faces of dark cliffs, overlooking the once populated valley. He passed over the trade roads that crossed over the mountains from Jeaniaurduin and journeyed east and south into the great Durndlith Basin of the tropical lands where the southern bands of the Ulusi-Rata lived along the coast and warm shores. He passed high over Mwataan Agdlan, the Temple of the Serpent King of the Alngbwat people of the cloud forest, masters of the visionary plants, where people would come from far and wide to learn from their secretive sorcerer-priests and take part in their initiatory rituals to meet with the mysterious and all-knowing Serpent King. And at last he passed above Durndlith, the Green River, which snaked its way along the eastern edge of the cloud forest through the tropical lowlands. Durngath was at last within reach.

Orobai rested on the edge of the cloud forest, overlooking the tropical jungle below and the second of the Great Mountains that rose from the seemingly endless sea of living green life surrounding it. It was the beginning of the monsoon seasons for this region of Aurduin; the warm and moist tropical air that blew in from the southeastern coast carried thick and abundant clouds that continually dropped their life-giving waters in warm showers on the green life below. Huge masses of clouds drifted slowly over the forest whose gentle and bucolic appearance was countered by the continual exchange of electrical charges between clouds and earth as lightning flashed across the sky and thunder pealed through the air. Orobai could feel the electricity as the hair on his head and neck swayed to the pulse of electric life that coursed about him.

Here in the south was the greatest abundance and diversity of life in all of Aurduin. Here were plants and trees of all kinds, many of which were now blooming in a profusion of colorful flowers, attempting to attract pollinators such as various birds, insects, bats, and other creatures of the tropical forests. Thus the many shades of green of the forest were now dotted with vibrant yellows, reds, purples, oranges. Flying about were wildly feathered birds and giant butterflies with iridescent wings and large, oddly shaped beetles with jewel-like exoskeletons.

Looking out upon all this color, Orobai saw life in all its complexity and diversity. Here before him was both life that was ancient with histories stretching back to earliest times, and life that was new, only now just coming into being, perhaps to flourish far into the future. Orobai saw all of it with his entranced eyes as a pulsing, breathing, flowing entity of life-energy. It was as though it were simultaneously one great living being comprised of countless independent beings. Such a vision of life-energy was almost overwhelming as it pulsed in its cyclical organic flow.

The very heart was the Green Mountain, Durngath. To Orobai's eyes it pulsed and ebbed like some enormous regulatory organ in the body of Eyar, taking life in, sending life out. The power swirled around it, through it, over it, under it. It was the power. It was life. And it was beautiful, for it contained the pulse of all manifest things. It was the living matrix of Being, of Manifestation, of Life. It was the both the symbol and embodiment of all that the Green Temple once had been in the time of the Illan.

Adding to this complex vision was the rich symphony of the forest. Insects, birds, and animals all gave their voices to the air, some shrill, some sweet, some like liquid falling over the rocks of a stream, and others like clashing and scraping metal. The sounds never ceased here. The fall of water, the gurgle of creeks, the melodious sounds of the birds and the odd sounds of insects, the growls and grunts of the hunters, the cries of anguish and fear of the hunted – it was all life and it was all beautiful to Orobai and it came to him as a rich music of infinite complexity.

After a meditative rest contemplating these vast riches of life surrounding the Green Mountain, Orobai left his perch and glided through the warm, moist air to Durngath. The mountain was not as large as Norgath, though it struck the eye as more imposing; it stood out from its surroundings in a way that Norgath did not. Whereas other high mountains and rocky peaks mostly surrounded Norgath, Durngath stood alone as a solitary sentinel in the sea of green forest below it. It rose up from the forest floor, towering into the sky. Often the mountain itself was enshrouded in mist and fog that tended to cling to it and kept it in a near constant blanket of life-giving moisture, sending countless waterfalls cascading down the sides of the mountain, feeding the intricate network of waterways within the forested lowlands below.

Vegetation grew heavily upon the mountain. The growth was so thick and the waterways so complex that a walking circumambulation of the mountain was impossible. Thus Orobai did not walk about Durngath as he had at Norgath, but instead flew about the Great Mountain twice in a sunwise circle before eventually landing in the green forest along its southern face. Here Orobai stood before one of the countless waterfalls. There were so many that most were unnamed. Naming them all would be like naming all the leaves on a tree, or all the blades of grass in a field.

Looking up at the water falling down through a wall of fern and moss, lichens and vines, bromeliads and lianas, branches and tangled masses of roots, Orobai saw clearly the life that was contained therein. Moving to the base of the falls he let the water cascade over him, feeling the power of life pass through him in body, heart, mind, and spirit. With the water rushing over him, he listened. He could hear the pulse and rhythm of life all about him. The sound of the water landing on the rocks at his feet, the call of the birds in the trees, the crash of thunder and lightning, the ever-present hum of insects, the sound of small animals secretly moving about the forest floor, the soft slither of a snake making its way up the trunk of a tree. It all coexisted in one great movement, one great manifestation of patterned rhythm, of music. It was the Symphony of Life and each being had its part and its place. No sound was out of tune or unconnected to the whole. Yet even within this orchestration, each sound maintained its unique individual essence and spirit. The parts were not overwhelmed by the whole, but rather were complemented and augmented by it. Each being was able to find its fullest expression in concert with others while not getting lost in the vast complexity of the unity of the experience.

Within that music Orobai regained something of his own individuality, something that had been overwhelmed and overcome at Norgath. Though his mind did not falter from his ritual task and he did not break his meditative trance, he once again found that part of himself that loved music and song. For long now he had been silent. He had sung for the Altfein on Norgath on that one day of the Equinox, but not since. He had passed along in silence and contemplation with a single focus of mind.

Here now at Durngath the joy of music awakened within him once again. Without thought, without purpose, without intention of any kind, Orobai burst into spontaneous song, adding his own unique element to the great symphony of music he heard about him. It was almost as though the mountain were pulling the song out of his deepest being. Orobai gave his voice freely and with joy, letting it pour out of his being like the water falling over him.

Wave after wave of music passed out of Orobai, joining the great collective. At first his own song fit within the larger music, complementing it, adorning it. But the more he sang, the more his own individual voice began to shape and mold the texture of the overall music. With a gentle push here and a pull there, Orobai found that he could direct the music of the mountain and the forest to join his song.

The beings of the forest responded to him like an orchestra before a conductor, awaiting his cues and subtle directions. But he did not try to control the other beings in any way, and rather let them find their own place in his music through invitation. He was not a dominator but a skilled artist who coaxed the spirits about him to enter freely into the work.

The more the other beings joined him, the stronger Orobai's song became. It reached to the sky and brought the thunder and lightning and a great flush of water from the Heavens, cascading down on all things below like a sweeping climax of music. And then he released, and let his song go for the forest to carry it where it would, and he listened.

Orobai had reawakened. He had passed from the chaos of the Void to the great flow of life, and in the passage had rediscovered himself, like one who passes from dreamless sleep to a beautiful and welcoming dream. A dream of life. An awakening to Consciousness, to Self, to Being. This was life. From the vast depth of undivided Consciousness of the Goar Saum, the Great Mystery, individual consciousness was born.

Thus the Green Mountain, the falling water, the teeming mass of green life about him, and the ubiquitous sounds of the forest had brought back this part of Orobai, this sense of self and individual being connected to the endless web of life, the Goartrah, the Great Music of Aurduin. Like a child newly awakened to the world, Orobai looked with new eyes, listened with new ears, thought with a new mind, and sensed with a new spirit. He reached out to embrace the world of his rebirth and found it to be beautiful. In rediscovering this world he had rediscovered himself.

Perhaps it was hours that Orobai stood, listening, letting the water fall over him. Perhaps it was days. He finally stirred when he knew that the time had come. It was the Day of the Highest Sun, Jiurya-Zan, the Summer Solstice. It was the day that Orobai would need to gather the Altfein from Durngath.

Orobai changed to his raven form and took to the air, seeking out one of the many pools of water on the southern face of the Green Mountain. Before long he found a pool of deep, crystal-clear water fed by cascading waterfalls. Circling twice about the pool, he came to rest at the lip of the falls, and there he waited, watching Urya as it passed to the south, awaiting the moment when the sun would reach its peak on this, the longest day of the year.

Though clouds filled the sky Orobai knew with his entire being when the sun had reached its zenith. He stood and began to sing the Jiur tones, the tones of the midday. As he sang, the clouds above him parted and the light of Urya streamed down upon him in a vast curtain of radiant light. Looking up, Orobai saw the sun through the feathers of the Arnyar who circled above him, rejoicing in the light, circling in the warm and moist currents of tropical air.

Unlike at Norgath, Orobai did not now draw forth all the Sarnfein that were in the pool of water before him. Singing the tones of the Jiur, the stones showed themselves while still in the water and did not all rise up together as before. Orobai looked carefully at all that showed themselves beneath the surface, shimmering in the midday light. From the many that he could see he called forth only one of his own choosing. Seeing its light, its pattern, its inner being, he knew that this was the one that he must choose. Its beauty caught his eye in a way that none of the others did. It was special and had an individual, yet somehow indefinable quality, that, to Orobai's eyes, the others lacked.

Modifying the Jiur, tones he focused the energy of his voice on that one Sarnfein. Calling to it in this way, is rose to the surface and emerged from its watery home. Into the sky it ascended until it floated in the air directly between Orobai and Urya above. When it did so a rainbow of light burst forth from the stone and showered Orobai in a scintillating dance. He knew that this was the right one, the one that was meant to be. He reached up and took it and it felt right. This was the Sarnfein that he needed.

Once more Orobai sat back down on the moist forest floor. He did not move, he did not sing, only listened. He listened to the world about him. He listened to the passing of time. He listened to the movement of the sun. He listened, and he waited.

Except for the slow rise and fall of his chest with the rhythm of his breathing, Orobai did not move. Birds came and went about him. Small animals passed through the forest and came to drink from the mountain pool. Rain fell from the sky and thunder shook the ground. But Orobai did not move. Urya sank back into the western horizon and the sky changed through all the colors of the rainbow as the light refracted through the clouds and the moisture in the air. But Orobai did not move.

Through the night the warm, wet storms continued. Lightning filled the sky and lit the clouds from within in brilliant displays of color, but still Orobai did not move from his seat. Predators of the night stirred in the forest about him, yet still he did not move. A large jaguar, nearly matching Orobai in its dark color, even came and curiously sniffed at the Ancient One, but still he did not budge. Only the continual rise and fall of his chest made by his slow rhythmic breathing showed that life was in him.

Though there was no sun above him to tell him the time, Orobai knew that it was now the exact point of midnight and that Urya had now traveled half way back around to the east where it would rise the next morning. It was time to find the Alkeinfein.

Orobai stood once more before the pool of water that now reflected the bursts of lightning in the sky above. Making the Ljiur tones, Orobai repeated the same process as he had done at midday. From the Alkeinfein that revealed themselves in the water, he chose one, which, like the Sarnfein before it, rose to the sky. In it Orobai saw the light and power he sought and knew that it was the correct one.

Taking it in his right hand, he reached for the Sarnfein he had found earlier and held it aloft in his left. As he had done at Norgath, he slowly moved the two stones together. When they touched, they fused together in a brilliant flash of light and became one stone. This one stone, radiant and majestic, Orobai added to the other that had come from Norgath and kept it safe in a secret place, adding now a little of the water of Durngath to that which he had taken from Norgath.

As at Norgath, Orobai had many other stones and gems to find at Durngath, but no more of the Altfein, for he had found what he needed. He wandered about the mountain and in a few weeks had found all that he required. As before, he could see just how he was to use each one. He knew its place in the sacred circle and how its unique color would add to the complex image that he would create. He could feel how its individual power would contribute to the whole. The meaning of the sacred circle became ever clearer to Orobai, its purpose more distinct, but there was still more. Two mountains and two seasons still awaited him, and it was not yet time to move on.

One by one, Orobai sang all the stones of Durngath back to his home. With his task here accomplished, he sat upon the mountain. He sat and he listened and he sang, adding his own voice to the music of the mountain and the forest.

As the days and weeks of the summer passed, Orobai still did not move from his place. He neither ate nor slept. He only sang. Sometimes he sang strongly and boldly and other times he sang softly and subtly, but he took no rest, for the forest itself never rested and its music was constant. All the while the life of the forest continued on. The plants began to grow over him and roots and lianas wrapped themselves around his limbs and body. Soil gathered at his back and around his waist and luminescent mushrooms grew from it that bathed him in an otherworldly green and blue light in the nighttime darkness. Birds landed on his shoulders and took his hair for their nests. Snakes slithered about him and wound about his torso and neck. But Orobai never stirred. He just sat, and he sang.

At long last the fall drew near and Orobai knew that it was time for him to continue onwards to Avengath, the Yellow Mountain. But he had now become a part of the forest, so overgrown was he. He could not move from his place, being trapped by the roots and vines that clung to him and held him there, as if desiring to keep him and claim him as their own.

But not even the forest could keep Orobai. The Arnyar of Durngath had never ceased their vigil over him and they came to him now when their help was needed. Stal'ru'ki and Woten'i'ir'a swooped down out of the sky and landed on either side of the overgrown Gem Seeker. Gently, carefully, they used their enormous beaks to pull back the vines and roots that clung to Orobai. Eventually Orobai was free once more and he stood for the first time in many weeks and ceased his singing.

"It is time. You must move on," said the two great eagles in unison. The three leapt to the air, Orobai as a raven with the two Arnyar at his side. Together they banked to the north and the west as Orobai circled past Durngath one more time as he began the long journey to Avengath, the Yellow Mountain, third of the Four Sacred Mountains in the desert and canyon lands of the far west.

His quest was half over.

Orobai could feel the pull of his vision and the weight of revelation. It was coming. Then, he would know. The mystery of his fate and ultimate purpose would soon be revealed.

But first, the Yellow Mountain of the desert called to him, and he flew on.

Avengath, the Yellow Mountain

The farther Orobai flew to the west the drier and more barren the land became. Forest passed to savanna and then to the great plains of Nulthali, the vast and open grasslands of western Aurduin that emptied out of Jeaniaurduin.

Orobai flew over the grass and mud huts of the Umbwate people who herded cattle on the plains. He passed over the great herds of bison that were slowly making their way south. But the herds did not look as big or as healthy to Orobai as they had in times past. Neither did the cattle of the Umbwate, or even their children. There was a sickness evident in everything. Orobai could see how the sickness that had started in Jeaniaurduin was moving outwards, affecting everything in its path. Orobai could see not only its effects, but he saw the sickness itself as an energy. Just as he had seen the power and energy of Norgath and Durngath and the lands surrounding them, he could see the life force of Nulthali and how the actions of the digging in Jeaniaurduin were affecting all things. It was vivid and palpable. He could trace the flow of the cancerous power with his inner eye, the eye that had been transformed by Nataali's Xhutai-Ku. It was a strong and stark contrast to the overflowing power of life he had seen in the still yet unaffected areas surrounding Durngath. But it was unmistakable that if this were left unchecked, eventually all things in Aurduin would feel the same sickness. The cancer was growing.

There was nothing that Orobai could do about this now and he continued onward. He flew among the great flocks of scavengers, the crows and ravens, vultures and condors, all those birds who circled in the sky looking for carrion below upon which they must feed for their own lives. And there was much for them to choose from. Bison, deer, pronghorn, elk, all the grazing animals seemed affected in one way or another. The old and the young were the hardest hit, leaving few of the wise elders and only sparse new generations. With the elders dying, the young would not fully learn the ways of their kind. So much of their survival depended on the passing on of generations of knowledge. Unique ways of being in the world would be lost. The rich legacy of the animals was in great danger. In this way, entire species might be lost if given enough time, as well as all the knowledge and wisdom that they collectively held.

And where were the people? There had been some Umbwate, perhaps not as many as Orobai had seen in the past, yet they were there. But what of the others? What of the bison hunters and the nomads of the Western Plains, those people who lived like the Djinari and the Tolguin? Orobai should have seen the camps and hunting parties of the Ol-Han and the Chuct'andu, and others besides, but they were nowhere to be seen. There were signs of their camps, but they seemed deserted, as though some years had passed since anyone had been there. The Chuct'andu in particular were a numerous and strong people, not driven easily from their country or their hunting grounds. But the bison they should have been hunting grazed without caution, for there were no hunters to be found.

Farther on, where Nulthali gave way to the dry desert lands of the west along the Avendlith, the Yellow River, where the different Runtai peoples lived in their yellow mud and adobe houses, there were only empty villages and silent homes. These agricultural people who lived by farming along the fertile banks of the Yellow River had abandoned their homes and left their fields fallow. Had the sickness of Jeaniaurduin already driven them away? As Orobai passed over their villages, he saw signs that the people had perhaps left quickly, for many belongings still remained, things that they surely would have taken with them had they had the opportunity. Had they fled? Or were they chased, or even taken by force? *Have they been taken as slaves?* The signs were unclear and the mystery remained.

Despite the ominous signs below, Orobai still found great beauty in the desert. Knowing there was nothing he could do about the missing Runtai now, he directed his course of flight to the isolated and uninhabited regions of the desert were the simple and barren beauty was the most acute. Here he did not need to focus on the complex relations of humans. Here he could bask in raw desert beauty. Particularly in the early morning and the evening, when Urya was low in the sky, the subtle shades, colors, and textures of the desert came alive in a stark and hyper-defined aesthetic. Yellow sands were set off against black and red rocks. Sharp shadows cut across mountain ridges and desert canyons. And each area seemed to have its own blend of colors and textures, making it distinct in its own personal beauty.

Water, that scarce resource in the desert, also helped to shape the beauty and uniqueness of the sparse landscape. Hillsides were carved in deep canyons by the fierce but occasional storms that came through. The sand and earth about huge stones and boulders were washed away while the boulders remained, perched upon their earthen pedestals, only to crash down when the towers became too small and weak, thus starting the long and inevitable process all over again.

Out of the canyons and mountains were large alluvial fans of sand, carrying the color of the place of their origin, covering the land in intricate patterns shaped by where water had once flowed. In yet other places great collections of sands filled basins between mountain ridges in large deposits of uniform colors of white, black, brown, yellow. Vast alkali flats reflected the light of the sun back into the sky with their stark whiteness.

Here the plants and animals that survived best were those with their own natural defenses. Plants and cacti came with thorns and needles, protecting their precious water. Others contained natural poisons to discourage the animals and insects from eating them. Reptiles, spiders, scorpions, and other beings all had poisons of their own.

Most of the animals in this land came out at night. That way they too protected their own water from the harsh sun and hot days. Night was the time for hunter and prey alike. Desert foxes and coyotes sought the smaller mammals, along with the owls. Mountain lions and the large dagger-toothed cats prowled the night and hunted on virtually any animal of their choosing. During the day it was rare to see any animals about the desert, except for the rabbits, lizards, and common desert birds such as ravens and hawks of all kinds and sizes, which drifted upon the wind, seeking small and vulnerable prey below.

The contrast of moving from the lands of Durngath to Avengath was striking. Whereas Orobai was overwhelmed with the abundance of life at Durngath, here in the western reaches in the desert, he was struck with impressions of sparseness, of essentials, of the minimum of existence. Such an environment had a subtle effect on the mind of the one perceiving it, almost forcing Orobai into deeper contemplation and reflection on those things in life that were truly valuable and essential.

There was no room for error or miscalculation in this land, but there was plenty of room for thought and meditation. The flow of light over the harsh landscape was like a mirror for the mind. The way that stark mountains cut a line beneath the expansive sky, or the texture of shadows on a sand dune in the early morning light, or the way water left impressions of its passing in the sand – these were the things of deep meditation. *It is though one walks through a waking dream,* thought Orobai.

Here the mind was forced back on itself. Here there was room for thought, for the imagination. Here the essence of survival and life could be distilled from the busy flux of existence to a careful examination of Being, of Self. Here the rhythms slowed to the contemplative pace of the desert and its long cycles of creation and destruction. Sands drifted across the desert like great waves on the ocean, nearly frozen in time. If one were to sit and watch for years, one might see as many waves of sand pass as waves of water could be seen on the ocean in only a few minutes. Time seemed slowed for even the plants and animals. A desert tortoise might live for several hundreds of years. Plants and cacti grew at a crawl compared to the plants of the tropics, and might bloom only once in a century. Here there was time for reflection.

At times the desert could also take on a surreal appearance, which only added to its already meditative essence. Colors that appeared drab and muted during the day became vivid and deep against the evening and morning sky. Reflections from distant water created mirages and illusions. Sudden sandstorms could conceal all from view, only to blow away as quickly as they had come and reveal that in passing the sand had changed the very shape of the land. In a similar way, the quiet stillness could be broken by the thunderous roar of a flash flood of water, rushing down the canyons, caused by some far-off storm. In only an instant the water could radically transform the land, and just as quickly, the waters could subside and disappear.

The music of the spirit of this place had its own unique rhythms and textures that expressed the essence of the land. The music that Orobai heard here was vast and expansive, with repeating refrains that shaped the tiny rivulets of sand in an arroyo that carried the same shape and pattern as the larger stream, which itself repeated the patterns of the entire wash of sand and water from the mountains. Shapes repeated themselves in endless iterations from large to small. The rocks in the sand mirrored the larger boulders, and even they mirrored the peaks of the mountains. Endless undulations of patterns upon patterns upon patterns. Orobai could look at any scale from the smallest to the largest and find the same patterns, endlessly recreating themselves.

At times the patterns were broken by the wide-open spaces of the desert flats. Here the music turned to silence, to the expansive space between notes, to the pause between the great breaths of the spirit of the land. These silences were just as crucial and significant as the music itself. Such silences could seem to carry on forever through the vast spaces, only to be broken by the reassertion of pattern as sands slowly drifted from the edge of the mountains to the flats where the music was taken up once more as the mountains reached towards the Heavens. Sometimes the music was punctuated by the broken landscape, where a discontinuous stratum of rock had been forced up out of the earth and jutted skyward, or where ancient beds of lava had rolled across the land and suddenly cooled, forever preserving the rhythm and movement that they had expressed at that very moment they froze in time and space, only to be slowly worn down by the rhythms of wind, water, sand, and sun.

Orobai could feel his own internal and external rhythms adjusting to the landscape as he moved farther into the interior of the western desert. Like the other desert ravens, his flight lost its single-minded direct course and instead took on the looping swoops of the warm currents of air that rose into the sky. The patterns of heat and flow took over as Orobai rode one pillar of air as it spiraled upwards, and then glided down to catch another and be taken up again into the desert sky. Orobai knew the lessons of the desert well – those that did not adjust to its rhythms perished.

Thus Orobai's flight across the great landscape of the western desert became a meditation. His movement was slow, deliberate, and executed without thought or exertion of individual will or desire. He simply floated upon the air with the other birds, following the course that the air and land set out for him, ever circling and gliding, circling and gliding. The flight became a metaphor for his own mind, as did the landscape below that he passed over. Sometimes active, sometimes passive, open, expansive, broken by complex and subtle rhythms, ever spiraling along in space and time, seeking further expression. He became a denizen of the desert, one of its own. He was subsumed under its own rhythms, patterns, and subtle music.

His mind was clear. All extraneous thoughts and diversions fell away. He was focused in his meditation. There was no distinction between the flow of his thoughts and flow of the landscape about him. He breathed with the desert mountain air. He moved with its currents. His thoughts mirrored the open landscape below him. His mind was like the clear and vast sky above. All non-essentials had been stripped away. The fullness of Being and Life and endless symphony of music that had expressed itself through his being at Durngath had been forcefully pared away to the central core of Self and Identity in the harsh landscape. And that self and identity had become integrated into the character and rhythm of the land and there he achieved a sense of unity and essential balance in a maturity of understanding and reflection.

At long last Avengath loomed upon the desert horizon in the west. The great Yellow Mountain was like an island in a sea of yellow sand, cresting above the endless flow of waves as the sand swirled about it in its own timeless eddies and currents. Surrounding the large island of the mountain were many smaller islands of yellow rock. These were repeatedly revealed and then swallowed by the ocean of ever-shifting sand. They were like memories from dreams and visions that revealed themselves in the fullness of consciousness and then quietly and inconspicuously slipped back down beneath the surface of awareness, only to reappear later in time, but changed and altered by the subtle currents of the mind. And like memories of visions and dreams, the separateness of the smaller islands of rock from the mountain, the Essential Self, was only an illusion, for beneath the surface they were all part of the same body, the same subterranean unity.

Unique among the Four Mountains, Avengath possessed the illusion of changing size. The drifts of yellow sands could at times reach hundreds of feet high above the rocky surface of the desert floor beneath them. Thus the sands rose and fell like the great tides of the ocean, sometimes revealing more of the Yellow Mountain, sometimes concealing more. Without other fixed points on the horizon, the mountain seemed to shrink and grow with the tides. Like the very notion of the self, the mountain's identity was sometimes more and sometimes less distinct from its surroundings. At times, the rim of mountains surrounding the yellow sea became visible, giving Avengath a clear reference point. At other times, light and heat and desert haze obscured the mountains from view and Avengath stood alone. Only in relationship to the rest of the land could the true nature of Avengath be revealed.

Orobai continued his circling and spiraling path to Avengath across the sea of yellow sand, always moving in a sunwise manner through the warm currents of air. Just as he arrived, Urya was beginning to pass beneath the western horizon. The shadows on the sand were dark and well defined and the mountain cut a sharp profile against the darkening sky. As Urya passed further into the west a band of deep purple ringed the horizon about the Yellow Mountain with a dark blue sky above. Ranya, a thin sliver of a crescent moon, and the Evening Star, shone brilliantly in the western skies and would soon follow Urya out of sight.

A cold wind blew in from the direction of the setting sun. Though hot during the day, the desert nights were cold and the winds tended to blow after the sun had set. Having landed on the western slope of the Mountain and returned to his usual form, Orobai wrapped his cloak about him to protect himself from the cold wind and carefully pulled it in about his face, trying to keep out the sand from his nose, mouth, and eyes. There was no sound except that of Orobai's cloak flapping in the cold wind like a flag.

That night and on into the next several days Orobai walked about the Mountain, eventually arriving back at the western face where he had first landed above the sea of yellow sands. The journey about the Mountain had been difficult in the sweltering sun, bitter wind, and cold nights, but Orobai had persevered. Twice, vicious sandstorms had blown across the desert, blinding and stinging the Ancient One. Orobai would not be deterred, however, and he continued onward, determined in his goal to circumambulate the third of the Four Sacred Mountains.

Orobai found a cave high on the western face of the Mountain. There, out of the wind, sand, sun, and cold, he meditated and awaited the time of the Fall Equinox, Jianigoldruln. From his vantage point Orobai could see the nightly setting of Urya. Each day it passed farther south, shortening the day and lengthening the night. On most days the mountains on the horizon were obscured from view in a thick desert haze so Orobai had no distant feature by which to gauge the progress of the sun. However, ancient mendicants and mystics had used the caves of Avengath for meditation and isolation in ages long past. At the entrance of each cave they had meticulously placed stones to mark the locations of the sun at sunset at the two solstices and the equinoxes. Each night Orobai watched the sun and stones carefully, gauging their visual accuracy against his internal perception of time and the yearly course of the sun. After several days, the time was ripe and Orobai knew that the coming day would be the day he had awaited, Jianigoldruln.

That night Orobai passed directly from meditation to dream, and he dreamt of the Yellow Mountain. It was not a dream of restful sleep, but one of great purpose and intention. Within it Orobai retained full conscious awareness. The continuity of his meditation was unbroken.

In the dream he searched for the Altfein. Unlike the other three mountains, water was extremely scarce on Avengath. To find enough water in which to seek the sacred stones was a challenge for which Orobai did not have an answer, and thus his spirit sought a solution in dream. There were just as many Altfein on Avengath as upon any of the other three mountains, but here they were far more hidden. During the winter, Avengath was high enough to coax snow from the passing clouds. And during the summer, electrical storms would drop rain upon the mountain. But now, in the late fall, it was the driest time of year for Avengath and there was no water upon its the surface.

In the dream Orobai saw the mountain as he had seen on his approach and when he had walked about it. There was no sign of water to be found anywhere. There were no springs, no pools, not even stagnant water left in the depressions of ancient rocks and boulders. Desperately he sought water, fighting the sun and the dry air. In the dream he became parched and thirsted with a profound need for water, yet he could find none. As time passed in the dream, his desperation grew ever more intense, for the knowledge that the Equinox was upon him pressed him onward in his seemingly hopeless search.

Just when Orobai felt he could endure it no longer, the dream changed. Now Orobai was flying about the mountain, but he was no longer seeking water, for the knowledge was clear that it was not there to be found. What was more, he was not in his usual form of a raven, but had taken on the form of one of the Arnyar, yet was all black in color like a raven.

In the dream he flew to the very apex of Avengath. There he stretched his wings heavenwards, spreading his feathers as wide as he could. He stood there, perched like an enormous stone statue in the form of an unmoving Great Eagle, all through the night. His wings and feathers worked as dew-catchers in the cold desert night air. Slowly, drops of water formed on his wings, and when they became heavy enough, they rolled down his feathers, collected into larger drops, and eventually fell to the ground. By the time the morning had come, a small pool of water had collected beneath the shadow of the Great Eagle and the subtle manipulations of light of the Altfein shone therein.

Orobai broke free from the intense grip of the dream with the full recall of what had taken place within it. With haste and determination he quickly roused from his meditative sleep and flew to the place in the dream where he had stood atop the mountain. There, just as he had seen it in the dream, was a small pool of water.

Urya had not yet passed above the eastern horizon, though its light was quickly filling the morning sky and obscuring the view of the stars above. Orobai knew that without protection, the small pool of water would quickly evaporate. He thus took on the shape of a black Arnyar, just as he had in his dream. There, atop the Yellow Mountain, he spread his wings and covered the small pool, sheltering it from the sun in the manner in which the great birds of prey covered a fresh kill with their outstretched wings. All day he stood there, turning with the movement of the sun across the sky, protecting the water, preventing as best he could its inevitable evaporation.

The vigil was excruciating and it took all of Orobai's will and determination to withstand the hot sun and the dry air, there at the very peak of Avengath. But at long last the sun sank down in the sky and reached the western horizon, and a little of the precious water remained.

With the moment upon him Orobai changed from the eagle form into his usual one and stood before the small pool of water as the sun began its descent beyond the horizon. With arms open he made the Lornur tones. There in the muddy water, barely visible to even Orobai's view, was the faint glimmer of a Sarnfein. Whether it was the "right" one or not was irrelevant as it was the only one there. Orobai bent down and picked it up in his hand.

Quickly he shifted to the Thumran tones. Ranya had been following Urya closely in the sky and Orobai did not have much time until it too would sink beneath the horizon, and the water would dry up soon as well. Though the moon was not yet quite full, it was closer to full than not so the tones would do. Once more a light shone softly in the muddy water and Orobai bent down, choosing the one Alkeinfein that was there for him to take. And as before at the other two mountains, Orobai joined these two together into one and then carefully put the one majestic and shimmering jewel safely away with the others, adding what he could of the water as well.

Over the next several weeks Orobai scoured the mountain, mostly at night to keep out of the sun, and searched for the other gemstones that he needed from Avengath. Once he had completely covered the mountain he moved to the islands of stone that surrounded the mountain in the yellow desert sea of sand. For some he had to wait patiently for the sands to move. Others he had to get to before they were swallowed up by the inevitable flow of the ever-shifting yellow sands.

As upon Norgath and Durngath, Orobai could once again see the sacred image of the visionary design before him with each stone he collected. He knew where it was to go and how he was to use it. He saw deeper and deeper meaning to the image and understood now more fully than ever how it would reveal his fate to him.

In time Orobai had all that he needed from the Yellow Mountain and went once more to the caves to continue his meditation and await the call to head north. It came one morning when the two head Arnyar of Avengath, Utra'a'ki and So'math, came to him. At the mouth of the cave they called out together, "It is time! You must come forward and move on to the White Mountain, Golgath. Your final task awaits you!"

At their summons Orobai came to the mouth of the cave, and together, with the two great eagles, took to the sky, turned to the north, and began the long flight to Golgath, the fourth and final mountain on his journey to the Goargathr.

The weight of his destiny grew heavy as the raven crossed the desert to the cold north. His vision would come.

Golgath, the White Mountain

M oving away from Avengath in a northeastward direction, the land slowly became wetter and more heavily vegetated beneath the tireless raven flying to his next destination, the last of the Orgathen. Here water that wound its way out of the high desert mountains cut the land into countless canyons. Many of the more elevated mountains were covered with aspen, pine, spruce, and other trees of the high desert. Now that it was fall moving into winter, the aspens were brilliant gold and the maple trees were turning deep red and orange before dropping their leaves to the earth below. Against this foreground of color were the dry grasses of the hills and the deep greens and blues of the evergreen trees. In the lower elevations were forests of juniper, pinion, and closer to water, cottonwood and willow trees.

Other areas were covered with vast expanses of mesquite, creosote, ocotillo, and other forms of cactus and desert shrubs, all capable of withstanding the hot and dry droughts as well as the torrential flash floods and downpours that were so characteristic of the high desert. With the onset of winter, these areas would all see occasional snow and many of the mountains would retain a white cap throughout the winter in a cold year. The year before had been rather dry, but this year all signs indicated a wet and cold winter ahead.

The cold winter winds were already blowing down from the far reaches of the north where the evergreen and redwood trees grew thick in the northern forest. Beyond the forest was the vast open tundra, and even beyond that was the realm of perpetual snow and ice where only the hardiest of peoples, plants, and animals lived. The southern boundary of the northern forest was the north rim of the Canyon of the Nuerdlith, the Strong River, also called the Goldlith, the White River. The forest had advanced that far south, but had never managed to cross the great gorge of the Nuerdlith and thus came to an abrupt halt along the canyon rim.

Already many of the mountains were dusted with the first snows of the winter season. The stark whiteness of the snow contrasted beautifully with the more muted earth tones of the high desert. The different regions of the high desert all had their own unique palettes of colors. Some areas were more predominantly red and orange, others shades of green from dark to a milky, light color. The many different rivers and watercourses tended to exhibit the colors of their places of origin and the lands that they flowed through. Many of the canyons were still dry as the snows were only beginning to build up and running water had been absent since the summer storms, now several months behind them.

These regions of the high desert were sparsely populated. In earlier times, the Runtai, who now lived along the Avendlith, had resided in the deep canyons here. Ruins from these times could still be found, nestled into the large caves along the riversides at the base of towering cliffs. There was a time when much of this land had experienced a prolonged drought and had caused the Runtai to leave and seek more suitable lands. Most had gone to the south and west, but some had traveled more directly west, closer to the coast and settled there. They still lived there today but now called themselves the Halkin-Jinu. Unlike their ancestors, who lived in the canyon basins and alongside the rivers, the Halkin-Jinu lived high on the mesas and cliffs in their stone houses.

Across the great divide of the Goldlith were the many peoples of the northern forest. The largest populations were along the coasts and rivers, though several lived deep within the heart of the forest amongst the towering redwoods that stretched nearly from coast to coast. Beyond lay the open tundra where the Ooluchnan herded caribou and had even mastered the mighty mastodons and mammoths, which they rode fearlessly across the great open spaces of the wind-swept north.

Many of these northern peoples lived in great buildings made of wood. Some were renowned as master wood-carvers such as the Alguanqui and the Nashar, cousin cultures along the northwest coast. Finest among their works were their elaborately carved and decorated spirit temples where the various divinities of their traditions were carved in relief form, depicting important events from their oral traditions and spiritual histories. They also made large sea-worthy boats and had developed some effective wooden and metal machinery, though these devices remained somewhat crude by the standards of the Ulusi-Rata.

The north was a busy and well-populated place, though one might never realize it. So well integrated into the landscape were the many peoples that one might pass above the forest and never see anyone below. The peoples who lived there all knew each other, however, and trade and visiting was largely common among them, except for the Ooluchnan, whom the other cultures generally feared and therefore avoided. Great ceremonial festivals were also held in the warmer months where the different peoples would come together to share their dances, songs, and ceremonial traditions with one another.

These cultures shared a high regard for the bears of the northern forest, which they considered among the strongest of spirits. The holy people of many of these cultures practiced a form of spiritual shape shifting and could mimetically take on the strength and appearance of bears, appearing nearly indistinguishable from real bears.

For many, the great bears were symbols of the power of the north itself, and the power of Golgath, the White Mountain. Each winter the great bears would dig deep within the earth and enter their trance-like sleep, which many believed to be a profound meditation. Some of the most highly advanced spiritual practitioners would bury themselves in the earth during winter, mimicking the bears' behavior, and in doing so would seek enlightenment through a profound and radical spiritual death and rebirth.

As with the bears, winter was the time when the spiritual powers withdrew to the interior of the earth. Plants withered and died, the leaves fell from the trees, and those who were weak or sick would pass from life. As the powers of the world slept, the great white blanket would cover the earth, preserving the powers below, to be released once more with the coming of the spring and the new cycle of life that began each year from the east.

In this great meditation of life and death, the whiteness of the north was the symbol of the absorption into the All and the passing from Aurduin to Karinduin. It was the mystical extinguishing of the individual, the self, the ego, and all the attachments to the world. It was the end to which all things inevitably flowed. It was the final destination of all that came from the origins of Chaos in the Naltrai and was a symbol of spiritual maturity and realization.

The crowning point of this northern world was Golgath, the White Mountain. Golgath rose rather abruptly at its southern face, but sloped off gradually a great distance to the north and stood as an imposing white ridge, towering over the dark green of the surrounding forest. Though not the tallest of the Great Mountains, it was the most massive in bulk and frame. Entire weather systems could pile up against it and never reach the other side. At other times, weather had to pass far around it for it could create its own climate, such as on a clear day when the white snows and white stone underneath reflected the light back into the sky, pushing away the clouds that might come near. Vast fields of ice also covered the mountain and the remnants of glaciers from colder times slowly flowed down the deeply cut glacier valleys. Once the glaciers had extended far from the mountain and had scoured the landscape. Now the ice was mostly gone this far south and had retreated to the great ice fields of the far north. Upon the Mountain, the ice still rested, however, merely awaiting the day to stretch back out its long fingers and cover the land once more in its icy cold grip.

The high peaks of Golgath broke free of the snow and ice and thrust bare rock high into the northern skies. From a distance, these peaks looked like sharp and jagged ice, given the pure white color of the stone of the mountain. They were not ice, however, but the white crystal of the mountain itself. When the sun hit the mountain just right, or when the mysterious northern lights played in the sky above the mountain at the proper angle, the white crystal of the peaks would refract the light beautifully against the sky and the snow and ice below. At such times the mountain and surrounding area had an otherworldly appearance worthy of the mystical rapture the mountain had come to symbolize, though it was only a reflection of the once great temple that had stood there, the White Temple of the north.

Such was the scene when Orobai reached the Great White Mountain. It was early in the night and Orobai had been flying continuously for most of the day. From afar he had seen the strange colors of the northern lights in the sky, dancing beneath a sea of stars. Now, crossing the Goldlith, Orobai could clearly see Golgath framed against vast shimmering curtains of green, magenta, orange, and blue. The crystal peaks refracted the lights, which exploded in an intricate tapestry of colors and patterns on the snowy slopes of the Great Mountain. After such a long and arduous journey from the dry reaches of Avengath, Orobai thought it was the most beautiful sight he had ever seen. So entranced was he that despite his weariness he continued onward through the night with the mountain drawing him ever forward, calling him to it with its dance of light. He found that it produced an almost overwhelming desire to merge with it, to become one with its radiant beauty and wonder. It seemed to Orobai that there was no other purpose, no other desire – only this beauty, this profound beauty.

By morning Orobai had reached the far northern edge of Golgath. The highest peak of the White Mountain now lay many miles to the south. As his last act of pilgrimage he would climb the ridge from north to south, and if timed correctly, he would reach the highest peak at the exact moment of the Winter Solstice, the Jiurya-Lzan.

Thus Orobai began his final ordeal and started to ascend Golgath. The going was slow. The farther he went the more difficult it became. The snow grew deeper. The ice fields became ever more vast. And every day brought with it ever colder air. At times, the snow fell so heavily that Orobai could not differentiate the mountain from the sky, and all about him was pure white with no visible distinction. The snow froze upon his clothing and coated his hair and face. His own blackness became completely obscured. The wind cut at him and froze him deep to his bones. Icicles clung to him and hung from his nose and chin.

The feeling in his extremities faded away to the point where he could hardly perceive his body anymore. There was no pain, no cold. Just a tired ache, a desire to sleep, a desire to lie down in the soft bed of snow and let it cover him completely, perhaps to awaken in the spring, or perhaps not.

As he climbed ever onwards and upwards, Orobai thought of how the great ice glaciers were retreating. At times he had found people and animals that had been frozen in tombs of ice thousands of years before. If he failed now and gave in to the desire to sleep, this might be his own fate, frozen in time, only to be released from the icy grip of the Mountain far in the distant future. But he knew he could not give in and struggled ever onwards.

So he moved on, higher, colder, and ever more tired, ever more in need of rest and renewal. Yet he did not stop. He did not rest. He pursued his quest and pushed on against the weather, against the snow and ice, and against the very mountain itself. And at long last, after several weeks of climbing, he saw that his goal was within reach.

Towering before Orobai was Goarlilgrun-Zan, the Great Crystal Peak of Golgath. Here the mountain's crystal rock body rose above the snow and ice and cut into the northern sky. The peak itself was utterly insurmountable with its smooth and sheer crystal faces. The crystal glistened in the early morning sunlight as Urya was just beginning its daily ascent into the sky. As Orobai had planned, it was Jiurya-Lzan, the Day of the Sun's Nadir, the Winter Solstice. On this day Urya traveled farthest to the south, being the shortest day of the year. From this point on the days would grow longer, eventually bringing spring and the cycle of new life with it. And now, here at Goarlilgrun-Zan, Orobai could fulfill his task and end his quest for the Altfein of the Four Sacred Mountains.

Orobai seated himself in the cold snow on this clear winter morning, awaiting the proper moment when the sun would reach its nadir. Orobai no longer felt the cold, no longer felt his suffering and weary body. He no longer felt his burning hunger or his frozen lips and extremities. He had completely surrendered to the experience and was no longer bound by concerns of personal comfort, pleasure, pain, or desire. All that had been driven from him in the blinding snow and borne far away on the wind. It was as though Orobai had been emptied of his own desires, thoughts, feelings, emotions, and was left to embrace existence as it was in all its fullness of joy, suffering, life, and death. Such complete surrender was strangely beautiful. How peaceful it was to sit in the snow, awaiting the proper moment, completely indifferent to personal suffering and desire. Orobai simply sat, and waited. He had accepted what was and what would be.

In time the moment came. Urya reached the very midpoint of its daily travel across the southern sky. Though Orobai had his own intuitive inner sense of time, there was no need for him to judge the movement of the sun against his own perceptions, for the moment was clear beyond a doubt. As the sun passed to the precise midpoint the rays of the sun hit the crystal of Goarlilgrun-Zan at just the right angle to produce a dazzling display of refracted light upon the mountain peak. Colors swirled and danced about the nearly frozen figure, giving him inspiration. Orobai began to sing.

Orobai made the Jiur tones, just as he had upon Durngath in the south at Jiurya-Zan, the Summer Solstice. Instinctively he added other tones as well, for there was no pool of water in which he could seek out the Sarnfein. These other tones he worked to shape and direct the brilliant light of the sun that was refracted in the Crystal Peak. Thus concentrated, the light bore down upon the snow in one great beam of intense light, melting the snow. In only a few moments water was running down the face of the peak and collecting in a depression below, which, during the summer months, Orobai knew served as a pool of fresh water at the mountain's summit. The hot and steaming water quickly melted back the ice and snow to reveal a perfectly clear pool of water. And there, glistening and shining beneath the surface, were the Sarnfein.

Orobai intensified his Jiur tones, calling the Sarnfein to life. Together they rose to the sky and made a great arch before Orobai. Intuitively Orobai knew that they were lining up according to their own unique connection to the movement of the sun on this solstice day. Standing directly between the stones and the sun Orobai chose the one that was before him at the precise place of Urya at its nadir.

As Orobai reached up to take the Sarnfein the refracted light of Urya in the Crystal Peak gently faded away. Orobai slowly softened his singing and the remaining Sarnfein sank back into the pool of water and quietly disappeared.

For the remainder of the day Orobai waited. By midnight much of the pool of water had frozen over once more, but not entirely. This night the moon was full and traveled at a matching pace to Urya at the opposite end of its arch through the heavens. Thus when the moment came for Orobai to sing the Ljiran tones, Ranya, as with Urya, was in exact alignment with Goarlilgrun-Zan. The light of the moon gave its own beautiful refraction in the Crystal Peak, which Orobai also directed into the pool of nearly frozen water below as he had done at midday with the light of Urya. The Alkeinfein rose to the sky in a great arch, matching various positions of Ranya's passage through the southern skies. As he had done earlier, Orobai chose the stone that stood directly between him and Ranya, letting the others sink back into the water, which then quickly froze over.

Orobai took both the Sarnfein and the Alkeinfein in his two hands. Holding them to the sky he slowly brought them together. They, like the others before them, joined into one unified jewel. Carefully, he secured them away with the others and added a little water from the cold mountain pool.

The search for the Altfein was now complete. From each of the Four Mountains he had found the stones that were intended for this purpose. Now that they had all joined their companions they sang together in soft and beautiful tones. To any but Orobai and perhaps Miraanni the tones would be too subtle to perceive, but from that moment onward their song never left Orobai's awareness. He knew that he had done what he set out to do with these sacred and mysterious stones. Soon the time would come that he could use them in the ritual as the Arnyar had instructed him at the beginning of his quest. Soon it would be the time of his vision.

But first there was more work to do. Over the next several weeks Orobai searched lower down on Golgath for the other stones and gems he needed from this last of the Four Mountains. So intimate was he with the Mountain of his home that he did not have much difficulty finding what he needed. In time he had found all that he required. The image of the scared diagram was now complete in Orobai's mind. He saw all the jewels he had collected and knew their place. He knew the meanings of the different aspects of the image and how they would play into his vision. It was complete. The search had ended. And for the first time in a year, he went home.

All that was left now was the vision that would reveal Orobai's fate, and the fate of all of Aurduin.

Soon, he would know.

Orobai's Vision

The pilgrimage to the Four Mountains was now complete. From each mountain Orobai had taken precisely what he had needed – nothing more, and nothing less. Each gem, each jewel, each stone would have its place and its purpose. Together, they would create the sacred image that the Arnyar had implanted in Orobai's mind. They would be the key to his vision of his fate and the fate of all of Aurduin.

Since returning from Golgath, Orobai had worked day and night to grind the countless stones he had collected into fine powders of many colors and shades with each kind of gem carefully separated from the rest. With each stone that he ground, he could already see in his mind precisely how he would use it. He saw where it would go in the design, how it would compliment or contrast with other colors, shapes, and images. It was as though Orobai could see the image before him and as he ground each stone his mind would focus in on that particular part of the design it was meant for. He did not need to question or wonder for it was all right there, immediately and intuitively known. And with each stone that was ground, Orobai knew that he was ever closer to his sacred purpose.

It had been nearly a year since Orobai had first set out on his quest. Since leaving Laftandiar-Urya, Orobai had dwelled in a sustained state of meditation and heightened awareness. Though he had rested, in all this time Orobai had never once stopped to truly sleep or renew himself. The effort had required all the stamina and perseverance the Ancient One could muster. Yet despite his weariness and need for long, deep, and sustained sleep, Orobai pressed on, knowing the significance of what he needed to do. His purpose drove him on and he would not rest until his task was done.

At long last Orobai set his pestle and grind stone down. Arrayed about him were all the stones of the Goargathr. Orobai had only a brief moment to survey his work, for it was then that Sem'antu and Rowah't, the Arnyar of Golgath, came to him. The two great eagles called Orobai forth from his home and decreed that the time had come. He now had to finish what he had set out to do and seek his vision. If successful, it was the hope of all that Orobai would discover key insights into his fate, the fate of Miraanni, and ultimately, of all of Aurduin. It would be a defining moment in the history of the world. It was time for Orobai to seek his vision and pull back the veil of mystery that for so long had enshrouded the future in darkness.

* * * *

At the coming of the dawn on a brisk winter day, Orobai set out to a solitary hill that was to the south of his home by Golgath. He brought with him all the powdered stones and precious gems that he had collected on his journey across the land of Aurduin, each wrapped into separate bundles and carried together in a heavy bag that he slung over his shoulder. He also had the Altfein, those four stones of combined Sarnfein and Alkeinfein. With all ready and staff in hand, Orobai walked to the place he had chosen to fulfill his sacred duty, not knowing what secrets would reveal themselves to him upon that hallowed ground, but full of anticipation and pregnant expectation.

All around the Ancient One the world was waking to a new day. Small birds began to chirp in the trees and the forest animals stirred in their dens. To the east were high clouds, just now beginning to show the faint color of the coming of Urya. Above the clouds Orobai could clearly see the Morning Star in the deep blue of the Heavens. The land was covered with dew, reflecting the fading starlight and the coming of the new day. All was auspicious, and Orobai set out with haste.

As Orobai arrived at his chosen hill, Urya was just rising over the ridge of the low mountains to the east and a soft wind came with the warming light. Orobai shook off the cool of the new morning and turned to face Urya and offered a morning prayer. He gave his thoughts to the coming day, to the wisdom and blessings it would bring for all beings, and gave his voice to the Four Directions and the Orgathen, praying that the land and all that dwelt upon it might be blessed. In doing so, Orobai felt the weight of responsibility bear down upon him. The task before him was his alone, but so much depended on what he would learn and what insights he could discover. The knowledge he hoped to learn would shape the future for all. Would he know what to do once the revelation was complete? Would he have the will and strength to carry through with the burden placed upon him? Would Miraanni?

It was no time to give in to doubts. Orobai had to act. He began to construct the sacred diagram as the council of the Arnyar had transmitted to him and firmly implanted in his mind. He could see it all distinctly, each grain of the crushed gems and precious stones of the four colors from the Orgathen. The image was clear in both his mind and his eyes, as though he merely had to replicate before him what he could see internally.

He searched the top of the hill for a large, flat, and open space, free from any obstacle, where he might fully observe the passing of Urya and the revolving sky above. Finding the ideal spot on the south face of the hilltop, Orobai began to clear it of stones and other obstructions, ever mindful of the image caught in his sight. He had to make the space just right; there could be nothing out of place.

In a short time it was ready. The space was cleared and ready to receive the image that Orobai would create there. He opened up his bag and removed all the bundles of crushed gems. Again he clearly pictured the design in his mind and set it firmly in his inner eye so that he could see it before him even as he looked at the empty ground at his feet. Thus he began, purposefully and intricately placing the fine multicolored grains of crushed gems.

He started in the center, making a raised altar where he would place the Altfein. Working in circles, he moved about the center in a sunwise manner, adding more and more outer layers of the image, always moving about the center in a sacred manner. With each falling grain of colored sand from his fingers, the image that presented itself to Orobai's eyes became fuller and more present, more real. And as the image took shape, Orobai could feel the power in it. He knew his vision would be profound.

The process was long and arduous, yet he worked at a furious pace, as though the weight of the future threatened to crush him if he did not complete the design quickly enough. Even though it was cool, Urya was burning strong that day and brought with it a warming wind from the east and south. As he warmed, Orobai removed his cloak and sat exposed to the air and light, perspiration running down his leathery black skin as he laboriously and meticulously worked at the sacred image.

When Urya paused at midday, overhead and to the south, Orobai paused as well and took some water. He did not drink much and did not rest long, however, for he knew that he must finish his work before the rising of Ranya and the coming of the night. He set himself once more to his task.

As he worked Orobai sang to himself. He sang no words, only the pure tones of his refined voice. It gave him strength and pushed him on. At times the passing song birds would join him in his songs, though Orobai hardly noticed, focused as he was on the intricate design taking full shape before him. It was almost as though the fine sands reverberated with his sound and fell more easily into place, as though he were in some sense singing it into being despite the physical actions of his hands. There was no distinction between Orobai's intention, his song, and his actions. And his song seemed to cement each grain in place so that nothing could disturb it from its intended place. Once the grains fell to the earth, they became fixed there and would not be moved or disturbed.

At last Orobai neared the completion of the complex circular design. Each grain was in place. There before him were the many shades of the four colors of the Orgathen, arranged in geometric patterns with symbolic representations of the Orthirnen, the Four Temples of the Illan, and their transformation into the Orgathen in the four cardinal directions of the jeweled design. Emanating from the Temples were countless other esoteric symbols as the Arnyar had instructed. Reflecting concepts and practices of the Altfein-Aryat and the history of the Illan in intricate detail, the images fit together into complex geometric patterns that were dazzling to behold. Each individual part had meaning and significance, yet there were ever-widening circles of symbolism and meaning so that every part was linked to all the others. Patterned ripples of manifestation emanated from each of the Four Temples and reached to the very center, the altar, the heart of the sacred circle, and joined everything in a symbolic symphony.

The work was nearly complete. Urya was just beginning its descent into the west and Orobai stopped to watch the passing of the yellow orb into the western lands. Darkness crept all around and one by one the stars began to show above. Ranya was not far off.

Orobai's last task was before him now. He took from his sack the Altfein that he had prepared specifically for this moment. He hesitated as he held them all in his hand. Slowly he loosened the tie about the tightly sealed bag and looked within. There were the four conjoined Altfein, still immersed in the collective waters of the Orgathen. Time seemed to stand still. Was he truly ready for this? Was he prepared to accept what the sacred stones would show him? Or could this possibly be his final act, the moment when he reintegrated fully into the body of Eyar and rejoined his creators, the Illan, his purpose fulfilled? Could this vision be his end?

Pushing uncertainties aside, Orobai's ancient hand firmly reached in and felt the Altfein against his fingers. The mystical stones sang as he took them from the water, almost as though they were breathing and sighing with relief. Had they too experienced the moment of uncertainty? Orobai placed them onto the altar that stood at a slight rise in the center of the sacred circle of gems. He carefully set the conjoined Sarnfein and Alkeinfein in each of their four respective directions, east, south, west, and north. Over them all he poured the crystal clear waters of the mountain pools. As he did so the waters and stones joined into one body of shimmering and reflective liquid that pulsed and moved with the subtle organic rhythms of life. All was ready. Doubt and fear lingered no longer.

This is the moment.

As Ranya came rising above the low eastern mountains Orobai moved first to the eastern quarter of the circle and stood before the image of the Black Temple and the Black Mountain. As the Arnyar had instructed, he began to sing with a low, droning note that filled all the space around him. With this note his mind centered on the image before him, scintillating with the light of Ranya and the sparkling stars. With this note a pattern illuminated across the face of the sacred image, joining different elements of the design together into a geometric whole that seemed to live and breathe with its own particular character and essence. It was living symbol of the sound of Norgath and Northirn, the Black Mountain and Black Temple.

Next he moved to the south and stood before the image of the Green Mountain and Green Temple and added a second note to the first, producing both simultaneously. Again his mind became more focused and his intention became clear as another distinct pattern emerged out of the whole, scintillating in the light of the moon and stars. Orobai intuitively knew that this was a symbol of the sound of the south, the tone of Durnthirn and Durngath.

From there he moved to the west, standing before the image of Avengath and Aventhirn, the Yellow Mountain and Yellow Temple, adding a third note to the first two and again his mind centered and went deeper into his meditation. Once more another pattern took shape across the face of the image and Orobai knew this to be a symbol of the tone of the Yellow Temple and Yellow Mountain. It was the pure sound of the west and had a life and essence all its own.

Finally Orobai moved to the north and added yet a fourth note to the first three, standing before the image of Golthirn and Golgath. As with the other three directions, one last pattern emerged from the face of the sacred image, illuminating the symbol of the north, the symbol of the White Temple and the White Mountain.

The sound of the four notes together was clear and pure and filled the space between earth and sky, completely enveloping Orobai and all his senses. It was as though the sound was not his own. It moved through him from all the four directions, centering on the image before him, which became radiantly clear and alive with meaning and significance. The four different patterns of the different directions swirled together now, creating a fifth and more encompassing pattern that joined them all into one unified meaning and significance. Orobai saw, and understood. It was the symbol of all of Aurduin and it contained within it a map to the past, present, and future.

The force of the revelation struck hard and Orobai's mind burst into a profound state of realization and heightened awareness as though flood gates of the deepest and widest waters had opened in his mind and being. These jewels before him were not merely images and colors but true living symbols, embodying the sacred powers and the deep meanings of the truths of the Illan. It was not abstraction or representation but pure manifestation of understanding, crystallized and brought to life by the sound of his voice. Though the music was Orobai's own, coming as it was from his body and spirit, it coalesced into a great symphony of sound that no longer belonged to the one producing it. The patterns, vibrations, and textures of the four simultaneous notes resonated with something deeper, something primal, a universal vibration that lay at the most subtle level of all created things in Aurduin. It was the sound of creation and it was pure, radiant, and without equal. It was the True Sound of Life itself. It was the sound of beginnings, of endings, and of all that passed between the two moments of absolute transformation.

The sound of his singing passed through his body and became a light unto itself, emanating from the circle of stones. The more he sang the brighter the light grew, starting first in each direction in turn and moving in geometric patterns to the Altfein in the center. The patterns undulated, grew, and receded, living and breathing his very same breath. The colors of the light combined and entwined with each other, living threads in a great web that was both contained within the image, yet was not, for the image itself was Orobai's world now and filled his vision and sense of being. Orobai, the sound, the light, and the image were one.

As he sang, the light moved ever closer to the Altfein in the center. As the circle of light entered the altar, the Altfein burst forth in a rainbow of undulating color and patterns infinite in their complexity. It was as if the patterns of the universe itself were there made manifest and visible in a form yet unseen by even the greatest of seers. In this light was the past, present, and future, and all was contained within it, from the vast stretches of space and time to the smallest aspects of all creation. And at the center was a pure light, neither colored nor with pattern, just pure, clear and radiant. It was the Light of All, and as Orobai's singing reached its crescendo, it consumed him entirely.

* * * *

It was either a moment, or it was eternity. The Pure Light suffused all of Orobai's sensory awareness in body, heart, mind, and spirit. There was no distinction between the light and the Ancient One. It was a vastness, like the open and cloudless sky, or the smooth surface of the ocean reflecting the pure and unblemished blue of the Heavens above. Time was lost to an immense ocean of bliss. There was no self, no other, just this. And more than light, it was alive with the fullness of life in the infinity of the cosmos. Yet it was simply there, and it was unified, without parts or differentiation.

Just this.

Orobai's personal awareness returned to him once more and he regained a sense of his individual nature. He felt himself at the center of a great nexus of space and time where the three times flowed together and mingled to become one, and yet not one. He was there, yet not there. It was his own time, yet not his own, as the pulsing of life and eternity coursed through his being. More than any dream, more than any vision, he was there, and the rhythm of cosmic creation was made manifest in a pulsating and undulating flow of vision, sound, color, and being.

Swirling through the totality of the experience, Orobai began to see with eyes made clear through the Pure Light. Looking up, Urya, Ranya, the stars, planets, clouds, and all elements of the endless revolving sky swung overhead and power moved through his being. At last he could focus and make some sense of the enormity of the experience as the vision crystallized from cosmic grandeur to meaning and symbols, a flow of sound and pre-language awareness. It was pure meaning, indescribable, yet profound and certain in depth and intention. Orobai could now experience his own individual awareness in its true nature as both observer and endless participant to the flow of creation. Paradoxically, he seemed to stand at the edge between a pure and detached witness and co-creator of all he experienced. He felt the pull of his own will and intention, yet knew these to be only a part of a much greater unified whole. But the tension of the paradox would not break, and within it Orobai learned the true meaning of balance and selfhood. He saw himself as he truly was. He was ready for what the sacred stones now had to show him.

To the east he heard a great cry, which forcibly drew his awareness to the direction from which it emanated. There in the distance he saw a shape begin to take form, coming towards him over oceans of mountains and pulsating rhythms of land, space, light, and sound. As it drew closer and its piercing cry rose to the sky,

Orobai saw that it was unmistakably an eagle, yet this was an eagle such as he had never seen. The tips of its great wings stretched far across the horizon of his vision, and when they beat they touched both earth and sky. The Great Eagle drew lightning and thunder with it as it approached, causing the earth and all creation to tremble. It was both terrible to behold and utterly compelling in its overwhelming beauty and majestic power.

The Great Eagle flew directly towards Orobai. He could see that it was made of radiant blackness, a blackness so full and complete that it seemed the absence of all light, yet it was still distinct. Orobai could see every feather, every quill, and most of all, he could feel the piercing gaze of the eyes of the great bird that penetrated to the center of his very being.

It flew close. Orobai could feel the tremendous rush of wind. In a commanding voice that was not a voice, its communication was clear: "Behold! They come!" Then, at the moment that the eagle was upon him, it melted away into the fabric of the vision and again Orobai could see the rush of celestial bodies spinning above him in the vault of the sky. But now as he looked to the east from where the eagle had come, Orobai could clearly see Norgath, the Black Mountain. It appeared before him and filled his vision, though he knew the Mountain to be far to the east, well beyond the capacity of his limited vision to discern from such a great distance. But the Mountain was there, nonetheless, and he saw it as he had when he first left Laftandiar-Urya, the great matrix of chaos and the fathomless abyss from which all being flows. And in that form, he saw the First Temple, Northirn.

Once more Orobai heard a cry, this time from the south. As before, another Great Eagle approached from the southern horizon, and it too was terrible in its immensity and power yet utterly captivating to behold. Again the earth shook and Orobai was pierced to the center of his being by the sharp and steely gaze of the great bird. This eagle was a majestic green, as pure and deep as an unspoiled ocean, hiding depths unfathomable and unseen. It too came directly upon him and announced: "Behold! They come!" and was gone. And in its place stood Durngath, the Green Mountain, and it too appeared in the fullness of life and living beings as Orobai had experienced in the months before, and with it came the endless symphony of living sound of the southern tropics. And in that form, he saw the Second Temple, Durnthirn.

Now from the west came the third Great Eagle. This eagle was as radiant as the pure yellow sun, like the shining face of Urya, and it too was terrible to behold and came with fire and lightning and the earth shook once more. And again came its cry: "Behold! They come!" and it too passed into the fabric of the vision. As with the two before, the Mountain of the west, Avengath, the Yellow Mountain, stood in the place of the vision of the Great Eagle. Orobai could feel the heat of the desert and sense its barren dryness and the stark contrasts of that distant land, a dreamscape into which he had awakened. And in that form, he saw the Third Temple, Avengath.

Last came the Great Eagle form the north. With great thunder it came as a storm of the northern skies. It was pure and complete whiteness, deeper and more radiant than pure crystal or new-fallen snow. Blinding it came, as light untarnished by any darkness. It too called: "Behold! They come!" and was gone, only to reveal the sparkling and radiant majesty of Golgath, the White Mountain of the north. And in that form, he saw the Fourth Temple, Golthirn.

Orobai now stood alone at the center of his altar, surrounded by the grace and power of the Goargathr, and it seemed as if this very spot was the absolute center of all things. Orobai once more became aware of being caught in the generating matrix of the cosmic flow. It was all so clear, so immediately intuited. There was no question in Orobai's heart. All was as it was intended to be.

Then from the body of Eyar came a great sound. Soft it was at first, yet strong, pure, and ancient. It was a music more beautiful and more complete than Orobai had ever heard or made himself in all his many lifetimes. It was a music of life, of creation itself and it held within it great and fantastic beauty. Louder it grew until it almost overwhelmed Orobai and it too consumed his being like a fire and he was as lost in a sea of pure sound.

Slowly his awareness returned to him, and he now realized that surrounding him were four beings, each a different color: Black, Green, Yellow, and White. They each stood at their respective directions of the sacred circle he had made. Looking closer, Orobai could see that there were not truly four, for each individual being seemed to contain the essence and spirit of two conjoined beings who were one, yet not one. Orobai could simultaneously sense the presence of eight, four, and one being. It was unlike anything Orobai had previously experienced. The more he concentrated on this perception, the more was revealed, for not only were there eight beings, but in truth, they seemed countless and beyond measure. All things took their source here in the great unity that was itself a multiplicity. There was no limit, no end to the great encompassing circle of Absolute Being, but its center was One.

From these beings, from their very core, Orobai felt an emanation of pure love and compassion that knew no limits or boundaries. He knew that they were the source of the music that continued to fill the vision. In great orchestration of unity the beings pronounced, "Grundin Orobai Rundi Eyarlum, We are Urkir, the Illan."

Though Orobai stood in the center of the four conjoined beings, he could see all four perfectly and in greater detail than he had ever seen anything in all the realm of Aurduin. Hidden deep within the center of each being was the fathomless Abyss, the Void and an immeasurable emptiness. Looking into this emptiness Orobai began to see shape and form emerge and he knew he was witnessing a fantastic symphony of creation. In this creation he saw and recognized all the beings and lands of Aurduin be given form and life of their own. Eons of time were there, and despite the complexity and multitude of creations, at the center the Great Void always remained and gave sustenance and life to all. Orobai witnessed the rising of the Orthirnen and all the magnificent works of the Illan. From the work of the Illan of the Four Temples all things came to be.

So many lives. So many creations. All rise and all fall. There is no beginning. There is no end.

After what seemed an eternity, Orobai then saw the passing of the Illan into the body of Eyar and the rising of the Orgathen. The Four Temples were all transformed into the Four Mountains, each in its turn from east, to south, west, and north. It was the end of the time of the Illan and the beginning of the watchful rein of the Arnyar. And it was his time, the time of the Grundin, Orobai's time.

All that he had done and wrought in his many lives was shown before him. All that he had forgotten, all that he had known, and all that had remained with him as but a dream and distant memory was there. It seemed to all pass in but a few instants, though it also seemed to him to be a reliving of all his lives. He saw and experienced himself rising from the sleep of death, returning to the earth, and rising yet again through the many ages of Aurduin since the passing of the Illan. It was all there and he remembered. And he knew, in being granted this vision, his doom was upon him. Though it was not spoken, the knowledge was firm in Orobai's heart that this time would be his last and that upon his next death, he would return to Eyar forever.

It is the end of my time. I am to be no more. I too will pass into Karinduin, just like the Illan before me.

At this realization the vision began to change and Orobai knew that he was being shown the present age of Aurduin. He saw Aurduin before him and he was glad at the sight for all was beautiful. But then a change came into the vision. As he looked at the beautiful land before him, his awareness was drawn to something deep and dark within the earth. It was as though something that had long been sleeping had awakened. It began to take shape and form and it appeared to Orobai as a vast serpent uncoiling itself beneath the body of Eyar. As the snake uncoiled Orobai could see that it carried a poison deep within its being. It came forth from the earth and held wide its gaping jaws. From its fangs, which appeared like glistening swords, dripped a deadly venom that mixed with the waters of Aurduin. Wherever the poisoned water went, it brought with it death and suffering. So much of the beauty of Aurduin that had been was thus destroyed. It was horrible and sickening to behold and Orobai felt his entire being retch and recoil from the terror before him. But he could not pull his sight away for his attention was fixed on the fullness of the vision. Yet it was also not terrible, for the witness in Orobai's consciousness saw it as merely a moment in the great passing of all life.

Endless creation. Endless destruction. Endless birth. Endless life.

Yet there was another power. The venomous serpent was not without a foe. It could not bring its death and destruction to Aurduin unchallenged. There was another, and it came at the serpent in a blur of white feathers and the serpent was gone. Though Orobai did not understand fully, he knew that the power of the serpent and its foe were connected, that somehow they were ultimately one.

There is balance in all things, even in death.

Again, the vision shifted, and now Orobai saw something new, something that had not been before. In the traces of where the serpent had emerged from the earth there was a light that was whole and beautiful. The light took shape first as a precious gem, and Orobai knew it to be the very same gem he had found in Jeaniaurduin. Its light was healing, beauty, and compassion, though it was not at first strong enough to overcome the power and malice of the terrible serpent. As he fixed his vision on the gem it began to change and the light within it took the shape of a young woman, fairer and more beautiful than any that had ever walked the face of Aurduin. From her inner being radiated all that was good and pure in the world and it was healing and utter compassion for all things. There was a sense of utter selflessness, as though she would give everything of herself for Aurduin. There was no doubt – it was Miraanni.

My sister . . . She is the hope of the world.

Once more the vision shifted and Orobai saw before him a vast and bloody war. It seemed to him that all the peoples of Aurduin fought on the fields of the western plains of Nulthali and in the center of the world. A ring of fire surrounded Jeaniaurduin and the Heart of the Sacred Land was covered with ash and ran thick with the blood of countless victims of the terrible violence. Against some enemy the peoples of Aurduin seemed locked in a hopeless and losing struggle, for there were weapons and machines brought against them the likes of which none had ever seen. Against these machines all hope was futile and all battle without victory.

There in the bloody battles Orobai saw many people he counted as friends. He saw their deaths, their pain, and their suffering. And there were many others besides. Countless lives were lost. So much pain and suffering. Orobai wished he could know them all and remove their pain, but there were too many, and he knew that he could not stop the destruction that was upon them all. He could only feel their pain.

So much suffering.

At last the great war seemed to come to a sudden end, for there, in the very center and heart of Aurduin was a blinding flash of death. A lone star fell from the heavens and pierced the Heart of the Sacred Land. Then a terrible dome of white light burst forth from the center of Jeaniaurduin and swept across the face of the world. From the epicenter of the destruction a great fire rose to the sky like a giant mushroom. It bellowed black and evil smoke that blotted out the sun and moon and all the stars of the Heavens. The great serpent rose in the flames and smoke and reached almost to the Heavens with its power of death and its poison entered into all the waters of Aurduin, making them Waters of Death, not Waters of Life, as they had always been.

All was utterly destroyed in the wake of the terrible wave of death and in the heart of Aurduin was left a great crater. All the land was barren and death and sickness filled the air. Never had Orobai imagined destruction on such a vast scale. It was almost inconceivable that so much destructive power could be wrought by the hands of the beings of Aurduin. To Orobai, the destructive power seemed nearly a match to the creative power of the Illan, equal to it in measure, but opposite in ends.

More blinding flashes of destruction followed in a great chain reaction. Fire and death spread across the world. In this there was no victor and no vanquished, for all perished equally. The destruction did not differentiate between friend and foe, combatant and bystander. Nothing could withstand the power. And after the fires ceased a great cold and darkness settled upon the land, for Urya could not pierce the thick clouds of dust and ash that filled the sky. Death became frozen across the surface of Eyar and it seemed as though life itself had been defeated. The great symphony had reached its conclusion.

Yet all was not lost. Quietly at first, there was music still. It was distinct and pure, first of one voice, then of two, then of many. Once more Orobai saw the beautiful young woman in the core of his vision. She came to the center of the great crater where the utter destruction of the land had begun. There she stood with four radiant jewels of the four colors swirling round her. Though all was lost about her and even the Goargathr spit forth fire and flames, through her power all the waters of Aurduin were drawn to her being. And the waters cleansed the world and it was as though all was made new again, and life once more came forth in beauty and in multitudes. And what had been an empty crater became a great lake in the heart of Aurduin and these were the Waters of Life. Through this power the world was redeemed and renewed. What had seemed an end was in fact a new beginning. It was to be the dawn of a new era of Aurduin. The old world would pass away and another would be born to take its place.

All will be made new again . . .

And there, in the center of the crystal Waters of Life stood a great and magnificent temple. It radiated a pure crystal light to the four directions and all things in Aurduin were bound to its power.

The Fifth Temple will stand at the turning point of the world. One age will end, and another will begin.

But Orobai knew that he would not be present to see this great healing and rebirth of the world take place. He would never look upon this temple with his own eyes. He would not be one of the ones fallen in the great war, nor one of those lost in the great destruction, but he would not witness the recreation of the world either. Somewhere between the destruction and the recreation he would return to Eyar for the last time. Somehow, he would join the Illan and would pass from this world of great beauty and inconceivable horror. But Miraanni would be there. She was the final key. Without her, Aurduin would be lost. With her, hope remained, but it would come at a terrible price.

With that final image and knowledge, the vision began to fade. The music of the four conjoined beings grew fainter and they slowly sank back into the earth. The images of the Four Mountains receded into the distance. Orobai once more became aware of his body, of time, and of the space around him. He saw that Urya was once again beginning to rise over the low mountains to the east, and it was a new day. The weight of the future now pressed down upon Orobai harder and heavier than ever. He felt weak and fragile, sapped of all remaining strength.

Orobai's mind could take no more and his body was consumed with complete exhaustion from his prolonged ordeal. He had seen the past, known the present, and pierced the veil of the future. The fate of Aurduin was revealed and his vision had come to him in prophetic signs. Finally, after so many thousands of years of waiting, Orobai now knew what the future held for him and for Aurduin. He knew his own fate, and the fate of Miraanni. But he also knew the future was not set. It was not determined. Many choices lay between this moment and the rising of the Fifth Temple. So much rested on Miraanni. She was the hope of the world, but she was so much more than that. Her choices could change everything. Orobai's path was set, but hers was not. She would have to choose. She would have to find her own way to this terrible and beautiful future. She would have to come to her own understanding of who and what she was.

She does not know. She does not know who she truly is, or why she is here. This will be her challenge. Our fates are joined, but she must find her own way to the Fifth Temple.

With the warming and comforting light of the new sun shining upon him, Orobai let go of his conscious mind. He fell fast asleep just where he was, slumping down into the center of the sacred image he had worked so hard to create. He could take no more revelations nor seek the answers to any more questions. He was spent. He had received his vision, suffused himself in knowledge, and could continue no longer.

For the first time in nearly a year, Orobai gave himself over to the complete oblivion of deep, fathomless, dreamless sleep. Surrounded by the sacred circle, enveloped in his map of what had been, what was, and what was to be, Orobai slept.

The future was now in the hands of others.

The future was now in Miraanni's hands.

Glossary of Djinari:

Ali – kind, generous, compassionate, Djinari name for Miraanni

Danmakadun – dan: possessive prefix, indicating four or more persons, "our," makadun: Grandmother, Djinari religious reference to the earth as "Our Grandmother"

Djun – a special class of spiritual beings said to reside within mountains, "Mountain Spirits"

Gadun – ga: language, spoken words, (dun) tun: ancient, old, (t changes to d after vowels) "the Ancient Tongue," Djinari term for Illanii, known only by seers and holy people

Heya – spirit

Heyadani – heya: spirit, also breath or "life force," dani: power, ability to create change, "Spirit Power," what is activated and manipulated by the Ohuan

Hindjun – hi: four, ndjun: mountain spirits (djun, singular or indefinite number)

Hindjuni – hi: four, ndjuni: mountains (djuni, singular), "Four Mountains," the Orgathen

Kordjuni – kor: black, djuni: mountain, "Black Mountain," Djinari name for Norgath

Makadun – maka: mother, (dun) tun: ancient (t changes to d after vowels), "Grandmother," in Djinari belief the earth is described as an ancient female and is thus referred to as "Grandmother,"

Makadun-Shiodjan – maka: mother, (dun) tun: ancient, (t changes to d after vowels) "grandmother," shi: possessive prefix, "his or her," –odjan, possessed noun, "bones," "Grandmother's Bones," Djinari name for the Morianithanlim-Gathr

Maku – Djinari greeting

Oguantashi – oguan: sorcerer, ta: female child suffix, shi: enclitic indicating extremely young age, used only with children under two years of age, "Baby Girl Sorcerer"

Oguantun – oguan: sorcerer, somewhat negative or indecisive connotation (as contrasted with ohuan: holy person), tun: enclitic indicating advanced age, "Old Sorcerer,"common name for Orobai among the Djinari among whom he is considered spiritually powerful yet somewhat unfamiliar

Ohuan – holy person

Shijusha – shi: possessive prefix, "his" or "her," jusha: vagina, refers to a cave in the Morianithanlim-Gathr. Said by the Djinari to be the origin place of the bison and their ancestors.

Tashu – no translation, Djinari benediction, stated after prayers, ceremonial songs, or general discussion of matters of spiritual or religious significance

Tushanali-Aka – tu: water, -shan: enclitic indicating large size, "big water," ocean, -ali: enclitic Indicating "along side of," aka: city or town, "City by the Sea," Djinari name for Laftandiar-Urya

Uandi – holy or sacred

Uandigu – uandi: holy, sacred, beautiful - gu: enclitic indicating way, path, or system of practice, "Holy Way"

Wakintunlan – wakin: verbal noun, "grazing beast," tun: enclitic indicating advanced age, also marks respect or honor, lan: relative or kin, "Honored Animal Kin," Djinari name for bison

Wakintunlan-Dashikital – wakin: verbal noun, "grazing beast," tun: enclitic indicating advanced age, also marks respect or honor, lan: relative or kin, "Honored Animal Kin," "bison," dashi: third person plural possessive pronoun, "their," – kital: passage, path, road, "Path of the Bison"

Wintado – Djinari bison hide home

Alkeinfein – alkein: spirit/wind, fein: giver, "Spirit-giver"

Altfein – alt: gift, fein: giver, "Gift-givers," general name of the "creation stones" of the Illan, the knowledge of which is preserved in the Altfein-aryat

Altfein-aryat – altfein: gift-givers, aryat: lore/teachings, "lore of the gift-givers"

Andrim – an: prefix indicating "creating", drim: trance, "trance maker," a small melodious stringed instrument

Arnthanlim-Zan – arn: master, thanlim: "elk", zan: mountain peak, summit, highest point, apex, zenith, "Bull Elk Peak," located in the Elk Horn Mountains, the Morianithanlim-Gathr

Arnyar – arn: master, ya: sky, r: indefinite plural marker, "masters of the sky," eagles, also known as the "true Arnyar," as opposed to "lesser eagles" of greatly diminished size

Atluin – blessings, colloquially, "hello" or "greetings"

Aurduin – aur: good, blessed, harmonious, sacred duin: realm, land, "The Good/Blessed Realm" or "The Sacred Land"

Avengath – aven: yellow, gath: mountain, "the Yellow Mountain," third of the Four Mountains in the west

Avenin – aven: yellow, in: order, "the Yellow Order"

Aventhirn – aven: yellow, thirn: temple, "the Yellow Temple"

Dalnae-urn – daln: elder, older, ae: male, urn: sibling, "elder brother"

Durndlith – durn: green, dlith: river, "the Green River"

Durngath – durn: green, gath: mountain, "the Green Mountain," second of the Four Mountains in the South

Durnin – dur: green, in: order, "the Green Order" of the Illan

Durnthirn – durn: green, thirn: temple, "the Green Temple"

Eyar – earth or earth body

Eyarlum – eyar: earth, lum: third person singular past perfect of li, to be born, "Earth Born," one of Orobai's four names

Goar Saum – goar: great, saum: mystery, "Great Mystery," title given to that which is beyond the knowledge of the Illan

Goardrim – goar: great, drim: trance, "the Great Trance," denoting the final ceremonial act of the Illan when the knowledge of Karinduin was known in fullness by the Illan

Goargathr – goar: great, gath: mountain, r: indefinite plural marker, "the Great Mountains," aka "Four Mountains," all of which are located in the four cardinal directions of Aurduin

Goarlilgrun-Zan – goar: great, lil: clear, grun: gem, "clear stone," "crystal," zan: peak, apex, the "Great Crystal Peak," highest peak of Golgath

Goarnaltrai – goar: great, naltrai: abyss, the "Great Abyss," large geological chasm separating Norgath from surrounding mountians

Goartrah – goar: great, trah: music, "the Great Music," refers to the music made by the Illan when the Four Temples were transformed into the Four Mountains and the Illan passed out of phenomenal existence into Karinduin

Goldlith –gol: white, dlith: river, the "White River," so named for its rapids, also called Neurdlith, the "Strong River"

Golgath – gol: white, gath: mountain, "the White Mountain," forth of the Four Mountains located in the North

Golin – gol: white, in: order, "the White Order" of the Illan

Golthirn – gol: white, thirn: temple, "the White Temple"

Grundin – grun: gem, din: seeker, "The Gem-Seeker," one of Orobai's four names

Illan – no definite translation, colloquially, "the Ancient Ones"

Illanii – Illan: ancient ones, ii: tongue, language, "language of the ancient ones," root language of Aurduin

Jeaniaurduin – je: heart, ani: suffix indicating "belonging to," "The Heart of Aurduin," oak forested area with many rolling hills and natural springs in the center of the four mountains

Jianigoldruln – ji: day, ani: suffix, of or belonging to, goldruln, meditation, reflection, contemplation, from the verb goldru, to meditate, the "Day of Contemplation," the Fall Exquinox

Jitanyaavai – ji: day, tan: suffix indicating new or recreated, "reborn," yaavai, of or belonging to life, "The Day of Re-Creation," Spring Equinox

Jiur – ji: day, ur: light, the "midday" tones used to find the Sarnfein at midday, particularly at the summer and winter solstices

Jiurya-Lzan – ji: day, urya: sun, l: negative prefix, zan: apex, zenith, lzan: nadir, the "Day of the Lowest Sun," the Winter Solstice

Jiurya-Zan – ji: day, urya: sun, zan: apex, zenith, "Day of the Highest Sun," the Summer Solstice

Karinduin – karin: other, duin: realm, "the Other Realm," a quality of existence not bound by the perceived constraints of space, time, and being as experienced in Aurduin: the realm to which the Illan passed in the Goardrim

Lilgurinlth – lil: clear, guri: water, nlth: creek or small river, "Clear Water Creek"

Ljiran – l: suffix indicating the opposite of or negative, ji: day, ran: dark, night, the "midnight" tones used to find Alkeinfein at the summer and winter solstices

Lornur – lorn: evening, sunset, ur: light, bright, tonal pattern to find Sarnfein at sunset

Lumran – lum: circular, round, ran: "dark" moon, a particular tonal pattern used to find Alkeinfein during full moons.

Miraanni – mira: strange, mysterious, unusual, anni: female child

Morianithanlim-Gathr – mori: horns, antlers, ani: of or belonging to, than: dweller, lim: forest,"elk" gathr: mountains, "Elk Horn Mountains"

Naltrai – "void," "empty," "abyss," in Illan philosophy, "The Void," philosophically necessitated quality of existence prior to the discernment or postulation of subject and object, form and formlessness: considered to be accessible to direct mystical perception or awareness under proper conditions

Nordlith – nor: black, dlith: river, "Black River"

Nordlithir – nol: black, dlith: river, i: one, r: plural marker, indefinite, "People of the Black River," Illanii name for the Yamné, also Dlithir: "People of the River"

Norgath – nor: black, gath: mountain, "the Black Mountain," first of the Four Mountains located in the east

Nori – nor: black, i: one (who is), "The Black One," common name for Orobai

Norin – nor: black, in: order, priestly caste, "the Black Order" of the Illan

Northirn – nor: black, thirn: temple, "the Black Temple"

Northrun – nor: black, thrun: valley, "the Black Valley"

Northrunnilth – nor: black, thrun: valley, nilth: creek, "Black Valley Creek"

Nuerdlith – nuer: strong, dlith: river, "Strong River," named after its many rapids and turbulent waters also called Goldlith, the "White River"

Nulthali – nul: open, uncovered, thali: grasslands, name of open plains in western Aurduin

Omur – om: morning, sunrise, ur: light, bright, tone to find Sarnfein at sunrise

Orgathen – or: four, gath: mountain, en: definite plural marker, "the Four Mountains," the final creations of the Illan during the Goardrim, located in the four cardinal directions of Aurduin

Orinen – or: four, in: order, en: definite plural marker, "the Four Orders"

Orobai – or: four, oba: to preserve ways, traditions, i: one who, "Preserver of the Four Ways,"

Orthirnen – or: four, thirn: temple, en: definite plural marker, "the Four Temples"

Ranya – ran: dark, ya: sky or "face", "moon"

Rundi – rund: return, i: one who, "the Returner," one of Orobai's four names

Rushalyaavai – rushal: waters, yaavai: of or belonging to life, avai, "The Waters of Life," generally referring to the waters that come from the many springs of Jeaniaurduin

Salusir – salu: to laugh, express joy socially, i: one (who), r: indefinite plural marker, "ravens"

Sarnfein – sarn: sight/light, by extension "form," fein: giver, "Form-giver"

Sarnrhobi – sarn: light, rhob, verbal root, to herald or announce publically, i: one (who), "Harbinger of The Light," name of the morning star

Stayor – stayo: wind or light spirit, r: indefinite plural marker, "Spirits," postulated as the Original sources of the Altfein

Sulsar-urn – sul: younger, sar: female, urn: sibling, "younger sister"

Shashun-Olurn – shash: ocean, un: verbal root, "to go in a liquid," "Ocean Goers," salmon, olurn: lake, "Salmon Lake"

Tashzal – tash: verbal root, to stand upright or errect, zal: high or elevated rocks, "High Standing Rocks," located along the eastern edge of Jeaniaurduin

Thumran – thum: sliver, crescent, ran: "dark" moon, a particular tonal pattern used to find Alkeinfein during crescent moons. Such stones are not as powerful as those found with Lumran

Urkir – urk: awakened, passive, from root, ur: light/bright/day, i: one who (is), r: indefinite plural marker, "The Awakened Ones," self-designation of the Illan

Urya – ur: bright/light, ya: sky or "face", "sun"

Zallur – zal: high rocks, cliffs, lur: falling water, "Cliff falls," name of a waterfall in the Elk Horn Mountains

Illanii Phrases and Sayings:

Dir elan – d: indefinite person/object prefix, i: one, r: indefinite plural marker, "things," elan: to have a cause, "All things have causes," saying of the Golin

Goar Saum edi laur – goar: great, saum: mystery, edi: third person singular of et: to know(through direct experience), laur: only, saying of the Illan, "Only the Great Mystery knows"

Qui ol lqui – qui: musical note, ol: to be held, l: prefix indicating opposite of whatever follows, qui: note, "A note held is no note," saying of the Durnin

Trah ol ltrah – trah: music, ol: to be held, l: opposite prefix, trah: music, "Music held is not music," saying of the Durnin

Glossary of Ulusi:

Ainchalthta – ain: council, chalth: school, ta: plural marker, "Council of the Schools"

Faltuwan – faltu: home or "mansion," generally indicating an opulent residential building, Wan: mother, "Mother's House," on-campus residence of the School Mother

Hyanchalth-Murira – hyan: advanced, experienced, chalth: school (for women and girls, compare with cholth, masculine), murira: of or belonging to the mystical or esoteric, "Women's University of Mystical Arts"

Hyancholth-Murira – hyan: advanced, experienced, cholth: school (for men and boys), murira: of or belonging to the mystical or esoteric, "Men's University of Mystical Arts"

Hyanchulth-Dzanshu – hyan: advanced, experienced, chulth: school (neuter, co-ed school), dzanshu, living systems, "ecology," "School of Living Systems"

Khutan-Scyr – khu: balance, equilibrium, - tan: enclitic indicating sum total of space and time, "totality," scyr: dynamic, subject to constant change and interaction, the central philosophy of "Dynamic Balance" of the School of Mystical Arts. Refers to the state of all of existence as a constant exchange of energy and power; a process predicated on systemic balance and continual transformation.

Kur-Aku – kur: of or belonging to the sun, aku: place of mastery or governance, "Solar Hall," place of council and governance in Laftandiar-Urya

Laftandiar-Urya – laftand: city, iar: indicating rising or upward movement, urya: sun, "City of the Rising Sun," the city of the East, populated by the Ulusi-Rata

Lalntalth – laln: sister, talth: from chalth: school, "School Sister," official title

Lalntalthta – "School Sisters" plural

Lalntush – laln: sister, tush: diminuitive suffix indicating little, inexperienced, or ignorant, designation for new female students in the various schools

Leti-Aurtai – leti: unknowing, from the Illanii, let: "faith," aurtai: path, the "Path of Unknowing," or the "Labyrinth," a maze of stones used in initiation practices of the Sisters of the School of Mystical Arts in the vicinity of Norgath

Orrhutha – or: four, from Illanii, rhutha: official title of city minister, "Four Ministers"

Ran-Khuxaita-Ur – ran: moon, from Illanii, ranya, "night," khuxaita: equal, evenly proportioned, ur: sun, from Illanii, urya, "day," "Balance of Night and Day," The Spring Equinox. Also the name of a community wide ritual celebration held annually at Hyanchalth-Murira and throughout Laftandiar-Urya

Rata – peoples, indicating different ethnic origins (compare with ra: people)

Than-Azarn – than: to transmit, send, connect, or communicate, a: suffix indicating "by the means of," zarn: individual mind, personal intellect, "Mind-to-mind transmission," used by the Sisterhood of the School of Mystical Arts to implant the knowledge of a teacher to a student

Ulm-Lanish – ulm: to feel with, empathy, sympathy, lanish: animals, beasts, "Animal Empathy," one of the mystical arts taught at Huanchalth-Murira

Ulusi – east, derived from the Illani "urya", sun, also used to mean the language of the Ulusi-Rata or an abbreviated form for Ulusi-Rata

Wantalth – wan: mother, talth, from chalth, school, "School Mother," official title

Xhutai-Ku – xhutai: life-force, breath, energy, wind, mind-body, etc., ku: mastery, effortless control, colloquially "Shaping the Wind," a mind-body technique of exercises practiced at the School of Mystical Arts. However, Xhutai is what is known as a "conventional object" in Khutan-Scyr philosophy and should not be taken as a reification of a metaphysical object. Though Xhutai can be perceived and manipulated, it has no independent existence

Glossary of Yamné:

Gu'yel – an island in the Nordlith where the Morinldah formerly held secret ceremonies, known as the "cursed island"

Ghu'n't'il – ghu'n: red earth, t'il: creek or small river, "Red Earth Creek"

Iryuah'eeh'né – Iryuah: earth, -'eeh'né, verbal root: to renew, restore, remake, reanimate, the "World Renewal" ceremony of the Yamné

Kagdah – kag: raven, dah: spirit society

Krin – objects used by Want'é in ceremonial acts such as feathers, shells, etc.

Kughain – ku: marker indicating space, environment, -ghain: verbal root: to go about in an enclosure, "home"

Maugu'in – name of falls

Mo'rinldah – mo'rinl: salmon, dah: spirit society

Mu'shué – mu': images, visions, -shu: verbal root: to sing (with), é: person marker, singular, "The One Who Sings with Images," Yamné name for Orobai

Nur'ual – nur: black, 'ual: water, "black water," an herbal tea

Sará'é – sará': of or belonging to the Heavens, Sar, é: person marker, "One of the Heavens," Yamné name for Miraanni, also alternate name for Yu'rin, the "Morning Star"

Shan'i'ruh – shan: seven, 'i'ruh: stations, places where one stops temporarily in an ongoing movement, "The Seven Stations," name for Yamné ceremonial arbors of the Iryuah'eeh'né

Shandah – shan: seven, dah: spirit society, "The Seven Spirit Societies"

Shun'shu – shun: spirit, breath, energy, will, 'shu: power, force, ability to create or influence

T'anli – t': indicates singular subject, anli: to exist, be, "it is," or "it exists"

T'unmo'rinlgult' – t'un: teeth, mo'rinl: salmon, gul: mountain, -t': plural, "Salmon Teeth Mountains"

Ul'dzas – ul': highest, dzas: peak, summit, or "head," "Highest Peak"

Ul'mult'ah – ul': hightest, most exalted, mu', changes to mul before "t": visions, images, -t'ah, verbal root: to manifest, make apparent, "Manifestor of Exalted Visions," visionary mushroom used by the Yamné in certain ceremonies

Umyu'á – Yamné greeting

Want'é – want': holy, sacred, mysterious, é: person marker, singular, "Holy One" seer of the Yamné

Want'né – want': holy, sacred, mysterious, né: person marker, plural, "Holy People"

Yamné – yam: river, né: person marker, plural, "The People of the River"

Yu'rin – yu': moring, rin: star, "the Moring Star," figure in Yamné mythology, a woman who came to earth as a star and transformed into a bird of prey, a kite

Yu'rindah – yu'rin: the morning star, dah: spirit society

About the Author

Martin W. Ball has a Ph.D. in Religious Studies with an emphasis on Native American religions and comparative mysticism. He has lived and studied with Mescalero Apache medicine people in New Mexico where he learned about the Mescalero Mountain Spirit tradition, sacred mountains, ritual, and traditional medicine. *Orobai's Vision* is his first book and novel and is the first installment of the *Tales of Aurduin Series,* which continues with *The Fate of Miraanni.* In addtion to the four novels of the series, Martin is also the author of numerous books on entheogens and mystical/non-dual experience and consciousness.

For more books, music, and art by Martin W. Ball, visit www.martinball.net

www.ingramcontent.com/pod-product-compliance
Lightning Source LLC
Chambersburg PA
CBHW031104260626
47172CB00001B/220